The Tycoon's
Mistress

Three sisters swept off their feet!

**Three intense, powerful novels from
a bestselling Mills & Boon® Modern™
author – irresistible!**

In July 2008 Mills & Boon bring back
two of their classic collections, each
featuring three favourite romances
by our bestselling authors…

THE TYCOON'S MISTRESS
by Carole Mortimer
His Cinderella Mistress
The Unwilling Mistress
The Deserving Mistress

HER PASSIONATE ITALIAN
The Passion Bargain by Michelle Reid
A Sicilian Husband by Kate Walker
The Italian's Marriage Bargain
by Carol Marinelli

The Tycoon's Mistress

By Carole Mortimer

HIS CINDERELLA MISTRESS

THE UNWILLING MISTRESS

THE DESERVING MISTRESS

MILLS & BOON
Pure reading pleasure

Harlequin Mills & Boon Limited,
Eton House, 18-24 Paradise Road, Richmond, Surrey TW9 1SR

MARRIED TO A MISTRESS
© by Harlequin Enterprises II B.V./S.à.r.l 2008

His Cinderella Mistress, The Unwilling Mistress and The Deserving
Mistress were first published in Great Britain by Harlequin Mills
& Boon Limited in separate, single volumes.

His Cinderella Mistress © Carole Mortimer 2003
The Unwilling Mistress © Carole Mortimer 2004
The Deserving Mistress © Carole Mortimer 2004

ISBN: 978 0 263 86129 7

05-0708

Printed and bound in Spain
by Litografia Rosés S.A., Barcelona

HIS CINDERELLA
MISTRESS

by

Carole Mortimer

100 Reasons to Celebrate

We invite you to join us in celebrating
Mills & Boon's centenary. Gerald Mills and
Charles Boon founded Mills & Boon Limited
in 1908 and opened offices in London's Covent
Garden. Since then, Mills & Boon has become
a hallmark for romantic fiction, recognised
around the world.

We're proud of our 100 years of publishing
excellence, which wouldn't have been achieved
without the loyalty and enthusiasm of our
authors and readers.

Thank you!

Each month throughout the year there will
be something new and exciting to mark the
centenary, so watch for your favourite authors,
captivating new stories, special limited
edition collections…and more!

Carole Mortimer was born in England, the youngest of three children. She began writing in 1978, and has now written over one hundred and forty books for Harlequin Mills and Boon. Carole has four sons, Matthew, Joshua, Timothy and Peter, and a bearded collie called Merlyn. She says, "I'm happily married to Peter senior; we're best friends as well as lovers, which is probably the best recipe for a successful relationship. We live in a lovely part of England."

Don't miss Carole Mortimer's exciting new novel, *The Sicilian's Innocent Mistress*, out in August from Mills & Boon® Modern™.

CHAPTER ONE

'WOULD you allow me to buy you a drink?'

Sitting at the bar, sipping a glass of sparkling water, taking a well-earned rest after an hour of singing, January turned to politely refuse the offer. Only to have that refusal stick in her throat as she saw who it was doing the offering.

It was him!

The man who had been seated at the back of this hotel bar for the last hour as she sat at the piano and sang. The man who had stared at her for all of that time with an intensity that had made it impossible for her not to have noticed him in return.

She should refuse his offer, had learnt to keep a certain polite distance between herself and the guests who stayed at this prestigious hotel, transient people for the most part, here for a few days, never to be seen again.

Remember what happened on the farm last year, her sister May would have told her. January did remember—only too well!

Remember what you told me—afterwards, her sister March would have said; taking people at face value only brings trouble!

'That would be lovely, thank you,' January accepted huskily.

The man gave an inclination of his dark head, ordering a bottle of champagne from John, the barman, before standing back to allow her to precede him to his table in the corner of the luxuriously comfortable room, made even more so at the moment because, although Christmas had come and gone, the decorations wouldn't be taken down for several more days yet.

January was aware of several curious glances coming their way as they walked by the crowded tables, could see their reflection in one of the mirrors along the walls. She, tall and willowy in the long black spangly dress she wore to perform in, her dark hair cascading down over her shoulders, eyes a mysterious dark smoky grey, fringed by sooty black lashes. The man walking so confidently behind her, the epitome of tall, dark and handsome in the black dinner suit and snowy white shirt he wore, his eyes a deep, unfathomable cobalt-blue.

It was those eyes, so intense and compelling, that had drawn her attention to him an hour ago, shortly after she began her first session of the evening. Those same eyes that even now, she could see in the mirror, were watching the gentle sway of her hips as she walked.

He stood to one side as January sank gracefully into one of the four armchairs placed around the low table, waiting until she was seated before lowering his considerable height into the chair opposite hers, that intense gaze having remained on her for the whole of that time.

'Champagne?' January prompted throatily a few minutes later—when it became apparent he wasn't going to make any effort to begin a conversation, seeming quite happy to just stare at her.

He gave a slight inclination of his head. 'It is New Year's Eve, after all,' he came back softly.

End of conversation, January realized a few seconds later when he added nothing further to that brief comment, beginning to wish she had listened to those little voices of her sisters' earlier inside her head.

'So it is,' she answered dismissively, smiling up at John as he arrived with two glasses and the ice-bucket containing the bottle of champagne, deftly opening it before her anonymous companion nodded his thanks—and his obvious dismissal.

John turned to leave, but not before he had given January a speculative raise of his eyebrows.

Well aware that she always kept herself slightly aloof from the guests staying at the hotel, John was obviously curious as to why this man should be so different. Join the club!

'January.' She turned back to the man determinedly.

He gave the semblance of a smile as he leant forward to pour the two glasses of champagne himself, competently, assuredly, not a single drop of the bubbly liquid reaching the top of the glass to spill over. 'That's what usually follows December,' he drawled dismissively.

'No, you misunderstood me.' She shook her head, smiling. 'My name is January.'

'Ah.' The smile deepened, showing even white teeth against his tanned skin. 'Max,' he supplied as economically.

Not exactly a scintillating conversationalist, she decided, studying him over the rim of her champagne glass. The strong, silent type, maybe, the sort of man who only spoke when he had something significant to say.

'Short for Maximillian?' she asked lightly.

His smile faded, leaving his face looking slightly grim. 'Short for Maxim. My mother was a great reader, I believe,' he added scornfully.

Her eyes widened at his tone. 'Don't you know?'

His gaze narrowed. 'No.'

Obviously not a subject to be pursued!

'And are you in the area on business, Max?' she prompted curiously; after all, it was New Year's Eve, a time when most people would be with family or friends.

'Something like that.' He nodded tersely. 'Do you work at the hotel every night, or just New Year's Eve?'

She found herself frowning slightly, unsure whether he had meant the question to sound insulting—as it did!—or whether it was just his usual abruptness of manner.

She shrugged, deciding to give him the benefit of the doubt—for the moment. 'I work here most Thursday, Friday and Saturday evenings,' she added the last pointedly.

'And as this is a Friday—'

'Yes,' she confirmed huskily. 'Look, I'm afraid I have to go back on in a few minutes,' she added with a certain amount of relief; this man was more than a little hard going!

He nodded. 'I'll wait for you at the end of the evening.' He had so far made no effort to drink any of his own champagne, merely continued to look at January with that almost blinkless stare.

Which was just as unnerving close up as it had been from the distance for the last hour while she sang!

She had accepted his invitation on impulse—curiosity?—and now she was regretting it. Okay, so his brooding stillness made Heathcliff and Mr Rochester, two of her favourite romantic heroes, seem almost chatty by comparison, but it was also extremely uncomfortable to be stared at in this single-minded fashion.

She gave a brief shake of her head. 'I don't think so, thank you.' She smiled to take some of the bluntness out of her own words; after all, he was a guest at the hotel, and she just another person employed here. 'Usually I finish about one-thirty, two o'clock, depending on how busy we are, but as tonight is New Year's Eve I'm here until three o'clock.'

And by the time she had driven home it would be almost four o'clock, by which time she would be physically shattered but mentally unable to relax, which meant she would stay up until her sisters woke shortly before six. Not an ideal arrangement by any means, but she knew she was lucky to have found this job so close to home at all, so beggars couldn't be choosers.

'I'll still wait,' Max answered her evenly.

A perplexed frown furrowed her brow; this was exactly the reason she had always kept a polite, if friendly, distance between herself and the male guests staying at the hotel. What had prompted her to make an exception in this man's case...?

She felt a shiver run down the length of her spine— of pleasure or apprehension?—as that deep blue gaze moved slowly down over the bareness of her shoulders in the strapless dress, the gentle swell of her breasts, the slenderness of her waist. Almost as if those long, artistically elegant hands had actually touched and caressed her!

'I'll wait,' he repeated softly. 'After all, what's a few more hours...?' he added enigmatically.

Very reassuring—she didn't think! In fact, there was a decidedly unsettled feeling in the pit of her stomach, accompanied by mental flashes of those recent newspaper articles about lone women being attacked in this area late at night.

Not that this obviously wealthy and assured man gave the impression of being in the category of the Night Striker—as the more lurid tabloids had dubbed him—but then, what did an attacker actually look like? The other man probably appeared perfectly normal during the day, too—it was only at night that he turned into a monster! She didn't—

'Tell me, January—' Max sat forward intently now, that dark blue gaze once again unfathomable as he looked at her face '—do you believe in love at first sight?'

The hand holding her champagne glass shook slightly at the unexpectedness of his question, her movements carefully deliberate as she placed the glass down on the table in front of her.

What had happened to the social pleasantries? The 'hello, how are you?' The 'do you have any family?' The 'when you aren't singing what do you like to do?' How did you go straight from 'how often do you work at the hotel?' to 'do you believe in love at first sight?' The obvious answer to that was—you didn't!

January's features softened into gentle mockery. 'In a word—no,' she dismissed derisively. 'Lust at first sight—maybe. But love? Impossible, don't you think?' she scorned softly.

He didn't so much as blink at her mocking reply. 'I was asking you,' he reminded softly.

'And I said no.' She was beginning to feel slightly rattled by this man's sheer force of will. 'How can you possibly fall in love with someone without even knowing them? What happens when you discover all those annoying little habits that weren't apparent at first sight?' she attempted to lighten the conversation. 'Like not squeezing the toothpaste from the bottom of the tube? Like reading the newspaper first and leaving it in a mess? Like walking around barefoot whenever possible? Like—'

'I get the picture, January,' he cut in dryly, something like warmth lightening the intense blue of his eyes. 'Are you telling me that you do all those things?'

Was she? Well…yes. And the toothpaste thing annoyed March to the point of screaming. And May was always complaining about what a mess she made when she read the newspaper. As for walking about barefoot—that was something she had done since she was a very small child; it was also something that was totally impractical when you lived in a working farmhouse. Once she had stepped on a plank of wood and ended up with a nail stuck in her foot, followed by a trip to the hospital for a tetanus injection, and another time she had stepped on a hot coal that had fallen out of the fire, again followed by a trip to the local hospital.

'I've been assured that love is supposed to nullify things like that,' Max continued dryly at her lack of reply. 'After all, no one is one-hundred-per-cent perfect.'

She had a feeling that this man might be, had a definite intuition that he would never squeeze the toothpaste tube in the middle, or leave the newspaper in a mess, and as for walking about barefoot—! No, this man gave the impression that everything he did was deliberate, carefully thought through, without fault. But perhaps that was a fault in itself…?

Although why she was even giving his question any serious thought she had no idea; it was simply ridiculous to suggest you could fall in love with the way someone looked!

'It may do, Max—but it doesn't stop hundreds of couples arriving in the divorce courts every year claiming incompatibility because of "unreasonable behaviour" by one or other partner,' she derided.

He smiled, his gaze definitely warmer now. 'I don't think they're referring to how you do or do not squeeze a tube of toothpaste,' he drawled.

'Probably not.' She shrugged. 'But I believe I've adequately answered your initial question.' Although why he had asked it at all was beyond her.

Next time she had an impulse like this, she would ignore it—no matter how handsomely intriguing the man was!

'More than adequately,' he confirmed derisively. 'And I have to say, January, it's very unusual to meet a woman with such an honest view to what everyone else chooses to romantically call love.'

January eyed him warily; she didn't think she had actually said that was the way she felt towards falling in love! 'It is?'

'It is,' he confirmed softly. 'But—'

'January, I'm really sorry to interrupt.' John, the barman, appeared beside their table.

'Not at all.' She turned to him with a certain amount of relief. 'Is it time for me to go back on?' she asked hopefully; she really had had enough of this conversation. And Max…

John grimaced. 'I just thought I should let you know Meridew is on the prowl again,' he warned, referring to the over-efficient manager of the hotel who had just strolled into the lounge bar, his gaze sweeping critically over the room.

Strictly speaking January wasn't exactly a member of the hotel staff, but that didn't stop Peter Meridew, the hotel manager, having his say if he was displeased about something. January had never tested him before on having a drink with one of the hotel guests, but perhaps that came under the heading of 'displeasing' him? Whatever, January needed this job too much to risk losing it over a man she would never see again after this evening.

'Thanks, John.' She smiled up at him before turning back to Max. 'I really do have to go.' She managed to keep her voice evenly unemotional as she prepared to leave.

Max's gaze narrowed. 'Would you like me to have a word with him?'

'Who—? Certainly not,' she protested frowningly as she saw he was now looking at the hotel manager. Although no doubt a word in Peter's ear from this assuredly arrogant man would ensure that no word was ever mentioned to her about sitting down to have a drink with him! 'It's time for me to go back on, anyway,' she dismissed lightly.

Max nodded. 'I'll be waiting here when you've finished.'

January opened her mouth to protest for a third time, and then thought better of it; what was the point? Besides, she was quite capable of slipping quietly away at the end of the evening without this man even being aware she had done so...

She stood up. 'Thank you for the champagne.'

'You're welcome.' He nodded.

January was aware of him once again watching her as she crossed the room to the piano, knowing he would see a tall, beautiful brunette in a sexy black dress. But that was all he would see—because he knew nothing else about her but her name.

Max should see her at half-past six tomorrow morning, up to her wellington-booted ankles in mud, as she trekked through the farmyard to the cow shed for early milking!

What on earth did he think he was doing? Max remonstrated with himself with an inward groan.

Was he trying to frighten the woman away before he even had chance to get to know her? Or—more importantly!—her him? If he was, he was certainly succeeding!

He hadn't wanted to come on this particular business trip at all, would have been quite happy to stay where he was until after the New Year, had been enjoying the mild, if unsuccessful, flirtation with the actress April Robine, a woman at least ten years older than his own thirty-seven, but looking at least twenty years younger than her actual age.

But it had been pointed out to him quite strongly, by his friend and employer, that these negotiations needed to be settled as quickly as possible, and it was his job, after all. Never mind the fact that Jude was as interested in April Robine as he was—and probably with more success, if he knew Jude. Which he did. Only too well.

How could Max possibly have known that a chance drink in the piano-bar of the hotel he was staying in would completely erase April, and every other woman he had ever known, from his mind, would result in his seeing the one woman he knew he had to have for his own?

Well…for a time, anyway; if he was honest with

himself there wasn't a woman in the world he wanted permanently in his life. No matter how beautiful. And January was incredibly beautiful.

She was perfect, from the top of her ebony head to the soles of her delicate feet in those ridiculously strappy sandals she was wearing.

So perfect that he hadn't been able to take his eyes off her the whole time he had been sitting here. So perfect that he had been uncharacteristically tongue-tied in her company. Except when he had asked her if she believed in love at first sight…

And been totally stunned—if pleasantly surprised!—by the honesty of the answer she had given him.

But, then, he had been stunned in one way or another since the moment he'd first looked at her, felt as if he had been punched in the stomach then, felt completely poleaxed now that he had actually spoken to her, her voice huskily sexy, her face even more beautiful close to, and as for her body…!

Perhaps he had better not dwell on the wonder of her willowy body just now; after all, it wasn't even midnight yet, which meant there were at least another three hours or so before he could take her out of here.

They were the longest three hours of his life, Max decided as he waited impatiently for January to play her final song. He hadn't even been able to get close to her when the clocks had struck midnight, had been forced to watch from afar as she'd made the countdown and had then been surrounded by well-wishers. Most of them male, he had noted with dark disapproval. All of whom he had wanted to punch on the nose as they'd claimed a New Year kiss from her.

The hotel manager had claimed her attention during her next break, the two of them talking comfortably together until it had been time for January to go back on. While Max had sat frustratedly at his table just willing her to look in his direction. Which she hadn't.

Deliberately so? After the way he had come on so strongly earlier, he wouldn't be in the least surprised!

How Jude, his longtime friend and boss, would have laughed if he could see him now! Or, more likely, having seen her, Jude would have made a play for January himself…

Now there was a thought he would rather not have had!

Ordinarily it wouldn't have bothered him if Jude was interested in the same woman he was, but he already knew January was different; it would certainly test his long-term friendship with Jude if he were to make any sort of move on her!

When at last she had finished January looked extremely tired, he noted frowningly as he stood up to join her. Not that he was in the least tired himself; jet lag had ensured that he slept this afternoon and now felt wide awake.

'Where are you going?' he prompted as she turned away without looking up.

Smoky grey eyes looked up at him guardedly beneath sooty lashes. 'Home?' she suggested ruefully.

She really did look very tired, Max noted with a frown, dark shadows beneath those incredibly beautiful grey eyes, a weariness to her shoulders too now that she was no longer on public display, the hotel guests and New Year's Eve visitors making their way noisily from the bar.

'I said I would wait for you,' he reminded huskily.

She frowned, seeming on the point of protest, one look at his obvious expression of determination making her shrug defeatedly instead. 'I just have to go and collect my coat and bag,' she told him lightly.

'I'll come with you,' Max told her firmly; having found her, he wasn't about to let her escape him now.

Those dark brows rose mockingly. 'To the women's staff room?'

He grimaced. 'I'll wait outside.'

A look of irritation flickered briefly across her creamy brow at his obvious persistence. 'Fine,' she finally acknowledged tersely. 'Give me a few minutes,' she added lightly before going into the room clearly marked 'Staff Only'.

He wasn't quite sure he could wait much longer to be alone with her. Patience had never been one of his virtues, even less so now it seemed.

But as the minutes passed with no sign of her return it appeared he didn't have much choice in the matter. Where the hell was she?

'Can I be of any assistance?' the manager—Peter Meridew?—paused to enquire politely.

Max turned to him scowlingly, the memory of how this man had monopolized January's company during her next—and only—break, still fresh in his mind. 'Is there another way out of this room?' he prompted hardly, more convinced than ever as the minutes passed that she had somehow managed to elude him.

The other man glanced at the door, his brows raised in surprise as he turned back to Max. 'Why, yes, there is,' he answered slowly, obviously perplexed by a guest's interest in what was clearly marked as a staff only room. 'It opens out into the adjacent corridor, but— Is there anything I can do to help?' the manager prompted at Max's fierce scowl.

'Not unless your name is January,' Max muttered

impatiently. 'Which it clearly isn't!' he added frustrat-edly.

Damn it, she had got away, he was sure of it, knew she had deliberately gone out of this staff room through another door.

Why was he so surprised? a little voice taunted in-side his head; he had come onto her so strongly earlier that he must have sounded like a bored businessman just looking for a female to share his bed for the night!

And wasn't that exactly what he was?

No, it wasn't, damn it! He already knew that one night with January simply wouldn't be enough. And given a little more time in her company, he might have been able to convince her of that.

Don't be too sure of that, that little voice taunted again.

'I'm sorry?' The manager looked more confused than ever at Max's mutterings. 'Is January a friend of yours?' the other man prompted tightly.

Max drew in a deep, controlling breath, aware that January had left his table earlier as soon as she had been informed of the manager's presence in the room. After all, what was the saying, 'tomorrow is another day'…? And as, in this case, tomorrow was a Saturday, Max at least knew where she was going to be tomorrow evening…

'Not yet,' he answered the manager enigmatically. 'By the way—' he turned his full attention on the other man now, his smile at its most charming '—I would like to compliment you on the smooth and efficient running of your hotel. I travel all over the world on business, and this is definitely of a world-class stan-dard.'

The other man visibly preened at this effusive

praise—as he was meant to do; the last thing Max wanted to do was make things difficult for January at her place of work. With any luck, Max's words of praise would override any of this man's previous curiosity as to Max's interest in January.

'It's very kind of you to say so.' The other man beamed.

'Not at all,' Max continued lightly. 'It's refreshing to stay at such an obviously well-managed hotel.' Too effusive? Not if the other man's flush of pleasure was anything to go by.

'If you require any assistance during the remainder of your stay, please don't hesitate to call on me personally,' Peter Meridew told him in parting.

Well, there was one happy man, at least, Max acknowledged ruefully as he watched the other man's retreating back.

Wishing that he could feel the same, Max sobered heavily, his earlier annoyance at what he was sure were January's evasive tactics returning with a vengeance.

But if she thought she would succeed in avoiding him for ever, she was in for a surprise.

A big surprise!

CHAPTER TWO

'MAY, what on earth is wrong with you today?' January frowned concernedly at her eldest sister, May having dropped one of the plates as the three of them stood up to clear away after eating their dinner.

May had been banging the pots and pans around serving the meal when January had come downstairs earlier, had been very quiet during dinner, only adding the odd grunt to the conversation between January and March as the three of them had eaten.

The three sisters—May, twenty-seven; March, twenty-six, and January, twenty-five—were very alike to look at, all tall and dark-haired, with a creamy magnolia skin—although that tended to colour to a healthy tan during the summer months. Only their eyes were different, May's green, March's a mixture of green and grey, and January's smoky grey.

But May, being the eldest, had always been the calm, unruffled one, able to deal with any emergency. Something she certainly didn't seem to be doing this evening!

'Still tired from doing the pantomime?' January sympathized.

Completely absorbed in the farm most of the time, May had found an outlet from that several years ago by joining the local drama group. They had put on the pantomime *Aladdin* in the small local theatre over the Christmas period, with May being given the leading role, traditionally played by a female. It had been tiring

20

but fun, but had necessitated May being involved in evening and matinée performances over several days, as well as working on the farm.

'If only it were that...' May looked up now from picking up the pieces of broken plate. 'We had a visitor today,' she stated flatly.

January instantly stiffened, wary of whom that 'visitor' might have been; she might have escaped from the intense Max the night before, but she doubted he was a man who cared to be fobbed off by anyone. Quite how he might have found out where she lived, she had no idea, but she doubted even that was beyond him...

May's green eyes swam with unshed tears as she straightened. 'You remember that letter we had before Christmas? The one from that lawyer on behalf of some big American corporation? About buying the farm,' she prompted as both March and January looked blank.

'Of course we remember it. Damned cheek!' March scorned as she grabbed some kitchen towel to wipe up the mess from the plate that had landed on the stone floor. 'If we were interested in selling then we would have put the farm on the market.' She threw the soiled towel deftly into the bin.

'Yes,' May sighed, sitting down heavily in a kitchen chair. 'Well, the lawyer came in person to see us today. Or rather me, as I was the only one available at the time.' She grimaced.

January, as was her usual routine on the nights she was working, had been in bed most of the day, and March had been out making the most of the New Year's Day public holiday as she had a job she went to from nine till five Monday to Saturdays usually. May was the only sister who worked full-time on their small hillside farm, who also did most of the cooking and cleaning, too. It wasn't the most ideal arrangement, meant that they all effectively had two jobs, but the farm just wasn't big enough to support all three sisters without the additional financial help of January's and March's outside employment.

Their visitor obviously hadn't been the intense Max, but January wasn't sure she liked the sound of this particular visitor, either.

'I thought it was all just some sort of joke.' January frowned now as she could see just how upset her eldest sister was.

May gave a humourless laugh. 'This lawyer didn't seem to think so,' she muttered. 'In fact, he went so far as to offer an absolutely ridiculous price for the farm.' She scowled as she quoted the price.

January gasped, March swallowed hard; all of them knew that the farm wasn't worth anywhere near as much as the offer being made. Which posed the question, why was this lawyer offering so much for what was, after all, only forty acres of land, a few outbuildings, and a far from modern farmhouse?

'What's the catch?' March prompted shrewdly.

'Apart from immediate vacancy, there didn't seem to be one,' May answered slowly.

'Apart from—! But we were all born here,' January protested incredulously.

'This is our home!' March said at the same time.

May gave the semblance of a smile. 'I told him that. He didn't seem impressed.' She shrugged.

'Probably because he lives in some exclusive penthouse apartment somewhere,' March muttered disgruntledly. 'He wouldn't recognize a ''home'' if he were invited into one. You didn't invite him in, I hope?' she said sharply.

May gave a firm shake of her head. 'I was outside loading hay onto the trailer for feeding when he arrived. Once he had introduced himself, and his reason for being here, I made sure we stayed outside in the yard. His tailor-made suit certainly wasn't suitable for visiting a hillside farm in January, and he got his highly polished handmade shoes all muddy, too,' she added dryly.

January laughed at her elder sister's look of satisfaction. 'And you sent him away with a flea in his ear, I hope!'

'Mmm.' May nodded, that frown back between clear green eyes. 'But I have a distinct feeling he'll be back.'

'What's it all about, do you think?' January frowned her own concern.

'Oh, that's easy,' March answered dismissively. 'The same corporation this lawyer represents bought the Hanworth estate a couple of months ago for development of some kind. And with our farm smack in the middle of the Hanworth land...' She shrugged. 'I expect we're rather in the way.'

James Hanworth, the local equivalent of 'squire' the last fifty-five years, had died six months ago, leaving no wife or children to inherit his vast estate, just half a dozen distant relatives who had obviously decided to sell the place and divide the profits.

'Why didn't you tell us that before?' May turned to March impatiently. 'No wonder they're trying to buy us out!' she added disgustedly.

Yes, no wonder, January mentally agreed. But this farm had first belonged to her grandparents, and then her parents, and now the three sisters, and, although it was sometimes a struggle to financially survive, selling it wasn't something any of them had ever considered. It was the only home they had ever known…

She gave a glance at her wrist-watch. 'Look, I have to get ready for work now, but we'll talk about this further over breakfast in the morning, okay?'

'Okay,' May nodded ruefully.

January reached out to give her sister's arm a comforting squeeze. 'No one can make us sell if we don't want to.'

'No,' her eldest sister sighed. 'But, stuck in the middle like this, they could make life very difficult for us if they choose to.'

'Depends what sort of development they're thinking of having,' March put in thoughtfully. 'I'll check into that tomorrow and see what I can find out.'

'Don't get yourself into trouble over it,' May warned in her concerned mother-hen way. As the eldest of the three sisters, having lost their mother when they were all very young, May had taken on the role of matriarch at a very early age, and after the death of their father the previous year she now took that role doubly seriously.

'Don't worry, I won't.' March grinned dismissively, always the more reckless sister of the trio.

'I'll see you both in the morning,' January told them laughingly, well accustomed to the battle of wills that often ensued between her cautious and more impetuous sisters.

She hurried up the stairs to get herself ready for this evening, choosing another black dress this time, knee-length, with a low neckline and long black sleeves ending in a dramatic vee at her slender wrists. Her hair she pulled back with jewelled combs, leaving wispy tendrils against her creamy cheeks.

It was slightly strange to lead these double lives, dressing glamorously for her role as a singer compared to the usual thick baggy jumpers, old denims and wellington boots when she was on the farm. Somehow the two didn't seem compatible...

It was troubling about the farm, though, she considered on her drive to the hotel. As March was only too keen to point out, no one could force them to sell if they didn't want to—which they certainly didn't. But what May had said was also true: life could be made very difficult for them if some sort of development completely surrounded their land and the farm.

There were such things as right of way, and water rights, for one thing; James Hanworth had never troubled about such things, had accepted that the Calendar farm was adjacent to his, and that access and water were a necessary part of its success. Somehow January doubted the new owner—a corporation, no less—would be quite as magnanimous.

It was testament to how troubling she found the situation that she hadn't even given the man Max a second thought until she went into the almost deserted piano-bar and found him sitting there chatting to John, the barman!

For some reason she had assumed Max would only be staying at the hotel the previous night. Erroneously, as it turned out.

'Ah, January.' Max turned to look at her with mocking blue eyes as she went straight over to the piano to arrange her music for the evening. He strolled over to stand only feet away from her. 'I believe there was some sort of confusion last night as to where we were to meet each other at the end of the evening?'

He believed no such thing, knew very well that she had deliberately slipped away through another door in order to avoid meeting him.

'Was there?' January raised her head to look at him, her gaze steady—despite the fact that she felt an inner quiver of awareness at the physical impact of his attractiveness in the lounge suit and blue shirt.

He really was a very attractive man, and January would be deceiving herself if she denied responding to that attraction. It was his sheer intensity of personality that she found a little overwhelming.

'I like to think so.' He smiled, a pulse-jumping, heart-stopping smile.

As if to give lie to her wariness of his previous intensity… 'Maybe we can do better this evening?' he suggested mildly.

He really was trying to lighten up, wasn't he? January accepted with an inner amusement. But not hard enough to conceal the fact that he was still determined to spend time alone with her…

'Perhaps,' she returned noncommittally. 'If you'll excuse me? I have to start my first session,' she added to take the bluntness out of her previous statement.

'Of course,' he accepted lightly, moving back slightly to allow her to seat herself at the piano, before bending forward, his mouth only inches from her ear. 'You're looking even more beautiful this evening than you did last night,' he murmured huskily, the warmth of his breath stirring the tendrils of hair against her cheeks.

January swallowed hard, tilting her head back slightly to look up into his face. A face still only mere inches away from hers... 'Thank you,' she accepted softly.

Max straightened, that smile back on his lips as he looked down at her admiringly. 'Very graciously said,' he told her appreciatively.

January gave a mocking inclination of her head, determined not to let him see that his proximity was unnerving her. Even if it was! 'I like to think so,' she dryly returned his own comment of a few minutes ago.

He chuckled appreciatively. 'I'll have a drink waiting for you at the bar when you have your break. John tells me that you usually prefer a sparkling water.'

She gave an irritated frown at the thought of this man discussing her likes and dislikes with a third person, even someone as innocuous as John. 'The whole point of my having a break is to give me a few minutes to relax.' Something she certainly couldn't do around him!

'Then we won't talk,' he promised lightly.

No one could have accused him of being a chatterbox the previous evening! But this man didn't need to say anything to totally disrupt her equilibrium; just having him sitting there staring at her was enough to make her nervous.

'Fine,' she accepted tautly.

Max looked at her consideringly for several long seconds. 'The last time you agreed with me so readily you made an escape out the back door,' he said slowly.

January felt the guilty colour warm her cheeks; she had said and done exactly that, hadn't she...?

'Well, this time I won't,' she assured him impatiently. 'Okay?'

'Okay,' he acknowledged with a slight inclination of his head. 'By the way...' he paused before leaving

'...you have the most incredibly sexy voice, speaking or singing, that I have ever heard,' he told her softly before walking away.

Oh, very conducive to calming her already frayed nerves—she didn't think!

Better, Max, he congratulated himself as he resumed his seat on a stool at the bar. Much better. Just the right balance of humour and determination. All he had to do now was keep it up for the next few hours!

All! When January had walked into the room a short time ago wearing that figure-hugging black dress, showing a long expanse of shapely legs beneath its knee-length, he had literally stopped breathing for several seconds, the blood singing heatedly in his veins, and as for the rest of his body—! That sort of response just at the sight of a woman hadn't happened to him since he was a raw teenager!

But he had regrouped, he assured himself, had spoken to her confidently and yet not too forcefully, infusing humour into the banter they had exchanged.

And then he had told her how sexy he found the sound of her voice!

Okay, okay, so he had slipped back a little there. But it had been worth it—if only to see the warm colour that had suffused her cheeks, the sparkle in those incredibly beautiful grey eyes!

At thirty-seven, Max had known many beautiful and accomplished women, been involved with several of them, but those women had been far too worldly-wise themselves to blush at something that was said to them; it was refreshing to know that January wasn't such a sophisticate.

How old was she? he wondered. Mid-twenties, probably, he decided. Not too young that he felt guilty over this single-minded interest he had found in her, but not too old that she had forgotten how to blush at a compliment.

'Great girl, isn't she?' The barman spoke admiringly as he stood polishing glasses in preparation for the busy evening ahead, obviously having followed Max's line of vision. 'Not in the least stand-offish like some of the singers we've had in here in the past,' John added with a pointed grimace.

Max sensed that John could be a great source of information about January. If Max chose to pursue it. Which he didn't...

For some reason he felt a great need to get to know January for himself, to unpeal each protective layer, until he knew her totally. Like that parcel in the children's game where you took one wrapper off at a time as the music stopped, until at last you arrived at the treasure within.

Once again he thanked his lucky stars that his good friend Jude wasn't about to witness his interest in January; he had no doubt that the other man would have found it highly amusing to see Max floundering around in the throes of this unexpected attraction!

Amusing? He doubted Jude would be able to stop laughing for a week!

Although Max's total lack of success so far in the main reason for his being here would probably wipe that smile from the other man's face, Max conceded with a frown as he thought of his meeting earlier today. A more stubborn, unyielding—! Not that he had given up, not for a moment—it was just going to take a little longer to accomplish what he had come here to do than he had at first supposed. But now that he had met

January, that delay certainly wasn't a drawback, as far as he was concerned!

He had the distinct impression that January was going to be an even harder conquest than the business deal he had come here to complete on Jude's behalf!

The piano-bar slowly filled up as the sound of January singing drifted through to the other reception rooms, a rather noisy party of young men obviously on a stag-night part of the crowd that now stood at the bar, several of those young men obviously ogling January in her sexy black dress. Giving him the hitherto unknown feelings of jealousy at the thought of any man looking at her but him!

Which was ridiculous, considering her choice of career; the way she looked was as much a part of that career as her sexily attractive voice.

All well and good, Max, he derided his own logic—but that still didn't stop the need he felt to get up and wrap his jacket around her so that she was hidden from any other male eyes but his!

'Whisky,' he turned to order from John grimly. 'Make it a double,' he added harshly as one of the young men strolled over to chat with January as she turned the music over between songs.

John gave him a quizzical look as he set the whisky glass down in front of Max. 'January knows how to take care of herself,' he offered lightly by way of advice.

Little comfort, when Max wanted to take care of her himself. Take care of her! He wanted to pick her up in his arms, carry her up to his hotel suite and make love to her until they were both too weak to do anything else but lay satiated in each other's arms. And then he wanted to start all over again!

She was laughing up at the young man now, completely relaxed in his company. But it was too much for Max, just too much, when the young man bent his head to give January a less-than-brotherly kiss on the lips!

He wasn't even aware of crossing the room, let alone having grabbed hold of the collar of the other man's jacket as he pulled him forcibly away from January, his face only inches away from the young man's as he glared down at him.

'Max…?' January gasped softly from somewhere behind him. 'What do you think you're doing?' she snapped incredulously.

Max narrowed his gaze briefly on the younger man before he turned to look questioningly at January. 'He was bothering you—'

She was standing now, shaking her head frowningly. 'Josh is a friend, Max,' she murmured as she gently released his hand from the other man's jacket. 'He's marrying my cousin Sara next Saturday,' she added pointedly.

That may be so, Max accepted grimly, but the kiss he had given January had looked far from 'cousin-in-lawly' to him!

'You're causing a scene,' January muttered awkwardly.

Several people in the now crowded bar were watching them curiously, the group of young men who had come in with Josh amongst them. Probably getting ready to come to the aid of their friend, Max conceded self-derisively.

'Sorry,' he muttered to Josh as the younger man straightened his jacket, aware that the manager, Peter

Meridew, was also watching the exchange with a narrowed gaze.

January was right, what on earth had he thought he was doing? He might know that he was more interested in January than any other woman he had ever met, but as far as she was concerned he was merely a guest at the hotel who had bought her a drink last night!

He forced himself to relax. 'I really do apologize if I overreacted just now,' he told the other man more amiably.

'No problem,' Josh assured him dismissively. 'It's nice to know that someone is looking out for January,' he added magnanimously.

'I don't—'

'Perhaps I could buy you and your friends a drink?' Max cut in lightly on what he was sure was going to be January's assertion that she didn't need, or want, anyone looking out for her. 'I'm sure January would love to join us once she's finished this session,' he added challengingly.

January was more beautiful than ever when she was angry, Max discovered as he turned to her with raised brows, her eyes a deep sparkling grey, her cheeks flushed against magnolia skin, even her mouth appearing redder. And more kissable than ever, he realized uncomfortably.

'The wedding is next Saturday, you say?' He turned back to the younger man—as much for his own peace of mind as to break his gaze away from January's fierce glare.

'Three o'clock.' Josh grinned happily. 'You're more than welcome to accompany January, if you would care to,' he invited warmly.

'You—'

'Why don't we go back to the bar and talk about that?' Max suggested firmly at what he guessed was going to be January's heated refusal to that suggestion. 'We really shouldn't interrupt you any longer,' he told her dismissively, turning away with Josh to walk back to the bar.

But he was aware of January's glaring gaze every step of the way!

Was equally sure that her next choice of song, something about 'surviving' and being 'able to take care of herself', was in direct response to what she believed to be his heavy-handed interference a few minutes ago.

So much for his keeping the evening light and amusing, he acknowledged self-derisively. He very much doubted that she would consider his almost punching her cousin-in-law-to-be in the mouth as either 'light' or 'amusing'!

Nevertheless, he couldn't resist raising his whisky glass in a toast to her as the song came to an end, receiving a narrow-eyed glare in return.

Max grinned in response. He couldn't help himself. Persuading her into a relationship with him was not going to be easy. But he had never backed down from a challenge in his life before, and he wasn't about to start now.

Besides, he might not have had too successful a day but, all things considered, it hadn't been a bad evening so far. If all else failed where January was concerned, he could always fall back on the definite invitation he had received from Josh to attend the family wedding the following Saturday!

CHAPTER THREE

'YOU can't possibly go to the wedding with me next Saturday,' January told Max firmly as she sat down at the table opposite him, the opportunity to tell him exactly this being the only reason she had agreed to have a drink with him at the end of the evening in the first place.

He eyed her with some amusement, blue eyes dark with suppressed laughter. 'Why can't I?' he returned mildly. 'Josh seemed perfectly sincere about the invitation.'

'I'm sure that he was,' January acknowledged disgruntledly, more than a little annoyed with her cousin-in-law-to-be for offhandedly having made the invitation at all. Kissing her as a stag-night bet was one thing, inviting Max to come to the wedding with her was something else entirely. 'It simply isn't possible,' she insisted determinedly.

'Why isn't it?' he prompted softly. 'I didn't get the impression, based on the fact that Josh made the invitation, that you intended going with anyone else,' he added hardly.

'Well, you were wrong,' January told him stubbornly. 'I'm going with my family,' she enlightened impatiently as she saw the way his gaze narrowed speculatively. 'Taking a complete stranger to the wedding with me would be tantamount to making some sort of announcement to the rest of my family,' she added irritably as he returned her gaze blandly now. 'An inappropriate announcement!' She glared her annoyance at his inability not to have seen that in the first place.

He might have shown a marked interest in her the last two evenings, but she was sure he wouldn't want to give either her or her family that particular impression!

'It's a week away, January.' He shrugged. 'A lot can happen in a week,' he added enigmatically.

A lot always 'happened' in her week, her work on the farm and the singing at the hotel in the evenings keeping her more than busy—but this man, with his powerful good looks, and his rich sophistication, simply did *not* 'happen' in that life!

'I said no, Max,' she reiterated firmly. 'And I meant no.' She took a sip of her sparkling water, feeling in need of something a little stronger, but unable to do so when she still had to drive home.

'Whatever,' he dismissed uninterestedly. 'You were good this evening, January,' he changed the subject abruptly. 'Despite having been very soundly kissed in the middle of it,' he added hardly.

'It was a bet, Max.' January sighed, too tired and irritable to simply tell him to mind his own business. 'A stag-night dare,' she enlarged. 'I was at school with most of that group; they thought it a great laugh to dare Josh to kiss me.'

In fact, Peter Meridew had had cause to speak to Josh and several of his friends before the end of the evening, claiming their rowdiness was disturbing the other guests.

Max gave her a look that told her precisely how unfunny he had found the whole incident, too!

Peter Meridew was one thing, but what did it really matter what Max thought? Or said, for that matter. He was a guest at the hotel—for how long, she had no idea—but pretty soon he was going to move on. And when he did, he was not going to leave a broken-hearted singer/farmer behind him!

Because she would be deceiving herself if she didn't admit—inwardly, at least!—that she had found his earlier behaviour, in jumping to her supposed rescue, highly chivalrous. An old-fashioned description, perhaps, but that was exactly how it had seemed at the time. No wonder those ladies of old had swooned into the arms of their saviour! And she didn't doubt for a moment that Max would have carried out his intention to knock Josh to the floor if she hadn't stepped in and explained the situation.

'It's late.' She gave a weary sigh, pushing her long dark hair back over her shoulder, looking over to give John a sympathetic smile as he cleaned the bar prior to his own shift ending for the night. 'I really should be on my way.' She wasn't as late as last night, obviously, but she definitely felt more tired.

More emotional? Possibly. One thing she did know: she had better get herself as far away from Max as possible—now!—or risk giving in to that emotion.

Max gave an inclination of his head, his gaze once more as intense as it had been the previous evening. 'You do look as if you've had enough for one night, would you allow me to order you a taxi?'

She gave a rueful smile. 'There would be little point in that.' Tempting as the offer was to relinquish the hour-long drive into someone else's more than capable hands. 'I don't work tomorrow evening, so it would simply mean another drive out tomorrow to pick up my car.'

'I wouldn't mind picking you up.' Max shrugged.

'That way, you could introduce me to the rest of your family,' he added pointedly.

And that way he would no longer be the 'complete stranger' to them she had accused him of being earlier! Very clever, she acknowledged admiringly—if totally out of the question.

'I don't think so, thanks.' She smiled as she stood up to put an end to the conversation.

Max stood up, too, easily towering over her. 'It really isn't a problem,' he assured her smoothly. 'Besides, John was telling me earlier that you have some sort of stalker in the area...?' He frowned as the two of them gave the barman a friendly wave before walking out into the reception area.

He did have a point there. So far, the Night Striker had only attacked women in quiet, country areas, and while the hotel car park hardly qualified as that it was pretty deserted this time of night...

'Hmm,' she acknowledged with a grimace. 'Six attacks in the last six months.'

Max's eyes darkened at the knowledge. 'Then, if you really do insist on driving yourself home...? That's what I thought,' he acknowledged dryly as she gave an affirmative nod. 'In that case, there is no way I'm going to let you walk out to the car park alone while I go upstairs to my warm and cosy hotel suite.'

'It's quite well lit,' she assured him.

'I still don't feel happy about letting you walk to your car unescorted,' he insisted firmly.

She could see by his determined expression that it would be no use pointing out that it was something she normally did three nights of the week. Every week. That she would do again once he had left the hotel...

'You're starting to sound like my elder sister May

now!' January teased as Max moved to drape her coat around her shoulders in preparation for going outside in the cold winter air.

He gave a start of surprise. 'I'm not sure I like sounding like someone's elder sister!'

January laughed softly. 'Will it help if I tell you I'm very attached to both my sisters?'

'It might,' he conceded slowly. 'Here, let me help you,' he offered as she struggled to put her arms into the sleeves of her coat as the cold wind outside penetrated the thin material of her dress.

Helping her into her coat was good manners, January acknowledged frowningly; allowing his arm to drape casually across her shoulders as they walked over to her car was something else entirely!

Not that she wasn't grateful for the added warmth of his body so close to hers—it was that closeness that bothered her. Disturbed her. Excited her!

She had never met anyone quite like Max before, finding his air of sophistication, his complete air of confidence, those overpoweringly good looks, enticing to say the least.

Admit it, January, she derided herself; you're intrigued by the man, in spite of yourself!

Intrigued? Her heart was pounding, her pulse racing, the flush that warmed her cheeks owing nothing to the cold and everything to Max's proximity.

'I really wasn't meaning to sound insulting just now when I likened your concern to my elder sister's.' She burst into speech in an effort to hide the confused emotions welling up inside her. 'I—it was rather—endearing,' she added awkwardly, at the same time glancing across to where her car was parked, quickly gauging how much longer it was going to take to reach it. Not long now, thank goodness. 'As the youngest of three, I've always come in for the biggest amount of sisterly advice. Even March sometimes gets in on the act.' She grimaced. 'And she's known as the more impetuous one of us!'

'January. March. And May,' Max repeated slowly. 'Three months of the year,' he added speculatively.

'Oh, that's easily explained.' January came to a grateful halt beside her little car, at the same time searching in her bag for her keys. 'You see—'

'All I can see at the moment, January, is the most beautiful woman I have ever set eyes on,' Max cut in harshly. 'It's all I've been able to see for the last thirty-six hours!'

January looked up at him sharply, becoming suddenly still as she found herself drowning in the fathomless depths of his eyes.

'January!' he groaned throatily even as his head lowered and his lips claimed hers, at the same time as his arms moved about the slenderness of her waist to pull her close to the warm hardness of his body.

Drowning must be something like this, January guessed dreamily a few minutes later; the initial fight against the inevitable, before the complete surrender to a force of such strength it was impossible to fight it any longer.

She knew nothing about this man but the little he had told her—the little he had chosen to tell her. She didn't even know his surname, she realized with a shocked jolt, and yet—

She couldn't think any more, couldn't formulate two words together in her brain, could only breathe and feel Max, her body on fire with the desire his kisses engendered.

Her arms moved up to his shoulders as she held on to him, one of her hands becoming enmeshed in the dark thickness of his hair, that hair silky to the touch.

Max groaned low in his throat, evidence of his own pleasure at her touch, his mouth moving more fiercely against hers now as he deepened the kiss, his tongue moving searchingly over the sensitivity of her inner lip before probing deeper.

January had never felt such oneness with another person before, as if she were a part of Max, and he a part of her, having no idea any more where Max began and she ended.

It was—

Tiny pinpoints of icy cold were falling against the warmth of her face, January's eyes opening wide in puzzlement as the unwanted intrusion persisted, blinking dazedly as she looked up to see the snow gently falling down on them.

Max broke the kiss reluctantly, his arms remaining firmly about her waist as he gave a rueful grimace at the steadily falling snowflakes. 'Almost as good as a cold shower,' he murmured self-derisively, his gaze warm as he turned back to January. 'Probably as well,' he conceded ruefully. 'I would like the first time I make love to you to be somewhere a little more—comfortable than a hotel car park!'

The first time…? That statement implied it would only be the first time of many…!

January pulled gently out of his arms, turned away to hide her confusion, determinedly turning her attention to a renewed search in her handbag for her car keys. Where on earth were they? What—?

'January…?' Max reached out a hand to lift up her

chin, his gaze becoming searching as he saw the paleness of her face.

'I really do have to go now, Max,' she told him awkwardly, sighing her relief as she at last located her keys at the bottom of her bag. 'It's very late—'

'Or early,' he put in lightly. 'Depends on your point of view, doesn't it?' he teased. 'I want to see you again, January,' he told her firmly. 'Tomorrow,' he added determinedly. 'Will you have lunch with me?'

Would she? Could she? *Dared* she?

Because she was in no doubt that if she agreed to see this man again there would be a repeat of the kisses they had just shared, that the next time there might be no pulling back—that even now her body still burned for the touch of his!

But could she not see Max again? Could she just walk away from him, from the totally new emotions she had known just now in his arms, and calmly get on with the rest of her life? Could she do that? Did she want to do that?

'Lunch tomorrow would be nice,' she accepted huskily, not quite able to meet his gaze now, afraid that he might be able to see the hunger still burning in her eyes if she did. A hunger that seemed to consume every part of her...

'Nice isn't quite the way I would have put it.' Max's mouth twisted ruefully. 'But I suppose it will have to do,' he accepted self-derisively. 'Are you going to be okay driving home in this weather?' He frowned up at the snow that was falling more heavily than ever.

What was the alternative? To stay the night with him in his hotel suite? Somehow she didn't think so! She might respond to this man in a way that was totally new—and a little frightening?—to her, but that didn't mean she was about to fall willingly into his arms at the first opportunity.

'I'll be fine,' she dismissed, willing her hand not to shake as she unlocked her car door. 'This is the north of England, Max; it often snows here. If you allowed your life to be dictated by the weather you would never do anything,' she assured him.

'Okay,' he agreed with obvious reluctance. 'Where shall we meet for lunch?' he prompted as January got into her car.

She looked up at him. 'How about here? At twelve-thirty? There's a nice pub a couple of miles away where they serve a great Sunday lunch.' Working at the hotel, she did not want to be seen by Peter Meridew eating lunch here with one of the guests. Especially a guest like Max!

'Okay.' Max nodded slowly, bending down so that he filled the doorway, making it impossible for January to close the car door. 'You won't change your mind?' he prompted huskily.

She already had—several times! But, no…she wouldn't change her mind.

'I'll be here at twelve-thirty,' she promised, giving an involuntary shiver as the piercing wind and snow entered the car. 'Brr.' She grimaced pointedly.

'Sorry,' Max murmured ruefully, stepping back so that she could close the car door.

January wound down the window. 'You should get inside,' she advised lightly, grateful when her car started the first time she turned the key; it was an old car, and prone to letting her down at inconvenient moments. 'You're getting very wet!' As were his tailored suit and expensive-looking leather shoes.

Now where had she—?

'I'll wait here until you've driven off, if you don't mind,' Max told her grimly. 'It's the least I can do!'

He so obviously wasn't accustomed to having his wishes overridden in this way that January couldn't help but smile. 'I'll see you tomorrow,' she told him as she drove off with a wave of her hand.

She passed John on his way to his own car as she drove out of the car park, giving him a friendly wave too before accelerating out onto the deserted road.

She would be lying if she said it was an easy drive home, because it was far from that, the drive on the untarmacked cart-track that led up to the farm the worst part of it. But at last she arrived in the farmyard, relieved to switch off the car engine and get out of the car, flexing the tension from her tired shoulder muscles.

Tension not just caused from the difficult drive home, January conceded ruefully. There was Max, her response to him, to worry about, too.

But the tension left her completely as she stood looking at the surrounding countryside, at the snow-covered hills, slowly becoming filled with an inner peace. The land, as far as her eye could see, belonged to them. It might be a tough life sometimes, a lot of hard work, often with no obvious return, the weather and circumstances unkind to them occasionally, too, but it was all theirs.

Nothing—and no one—was ever going to change that...

She was late for their luncheon appointment, by precisely ten minutes, Max realized, scowling after yet another glance at his gold wrist-watch as he strolled restlessly up and down the reception area of the hotel.

Always a stickler for being on time for appointments

himself, Max found January's tardiness doubly frustrating. Firstly, because of that abhorrence of lateness in others as much as in himself; secondly—the fact that January hadn't arrived at twelve-thirty, as she had said she would, might mean that she wasn't coming at all!

It was that second reason that was the most frustrating.

Maybe he had come on a little strong with her again last night? Maybe he shouldn't have kissed her quite that passionately?

But once he'd held January in his arms, not to have kissed her in the way he had had been totally beyond his control. In truth, he had wanted to do a lot more than just kiss her!

Her body had been warm and fluid, her breasts pressed invitingly against his chest, her thighs moulding perfectly against his; it had taken every ounce of his will-power not to sweep her off her feet and carry her up to his hotel room. Where he had wanted to explore every delectable inch of her body with his hands and lips!

Stop it, Max, he instructed himself firmly. Wasn't it enough that he had spent a sleepless night, initially worrying in case she hadn't got home safely, and wishing that he had asked her to call him when she'd got in, followed by a hunger just for sight or touch of January, without repeating that discomfort now? He couldn't remember the last time he had hungered for a woman in this way—if he ever had!—let alone got up in the middle of the night to take a cold shower in an effort to deal with the problem.

He glanced at his watch again. She was fifteen minutes late now—

'Er—sir? Mr Golding, isn't it?'

He turned to scowl in acknowledgement as the receptionist called hesitantly across to him.

'I believe there's a telephone call for you.' She pointed to the telephone at the end of the desk, the flashing light indicating the call.

Probably Jude, checking up on progress, Max realized frowningly as he moved to take the call. Just what he needed at this precise moment!

'Yes?' he snapped into the receiver.

'Max?' January returned uncertainly.

He willed himself to relax, not to show how angry he was—and failed miserably. 'Where the hell are you?' he rasped; the fact that she was telephoning him at all meant that she wasn't on her way here—or, in fact, intending to be!

'Well, at the moment I'm at home—'

'You should be here!' he snapped, his hand tightly gripping the receiver.

'But until a short time ago I was sitting in my car in a ditch,' January continued, determined. 'Max, I'm sorry,' she added huskily.

'I really am. I set out in plenty of time to get there at twelve-thirty, but the car skidded on some ice, I lost control, and—well, I ended up in the ditch. I telephoned as soon as I could—'

'Are you hurt?' Max cut in sharply, furious with himself now for having lost his temper with her initially. If she were hurt—! That possibility didn't bear thinking about!

'Just a little bump on the head,' January dismissed. 'But the car is probably a write-off—'

'Forget the car,' he cut in. 'It's easily replaceable. You aren't.'

'Well it might be easily replaceable to you.' She

laughed ruefully. 'I'm not in such a healthy financial position, I'm afraid. But never mind that,' she changed the subject. 'There is no way I'm going to make it for lunch now, so could we make it dinner this evening, instead? March says she doesn't need her car this evening, so I can borrow that. As long as I promise not to put that in a ditch, too,' she added dryly.

Max's head was still full of horrifying visions of the first time she had landed in a ditch, at how nearly he had lost her, when he had only just found her!

'Wouldn't it be easier if I were to pick you up?' he suggested tautly. 'That way, if anyone ends up in a ditch, it will be me!'

'No, that won't do at all,' she came back instantly.

'January, could you just forget this idea you have that my meeting your family is tantamount to an engagement announcement,' he interrupted impatiently, 'and just look at the safety aspect instead? I do not want—'

'Max, this has nothing to do with what my family may or may not think—' The embarrassment could be heard in her voice '—and everything to do with the fact that I live in a very remote area, high up in the hills. Trying to direct you there would be a nightmare.'

In that case, the thought of her driving down to him was a nightmare, too—for him. He—

'Maybe we should just forget meeting up at all,' January continued evenly. 'The weather seems to be against us, and—'

'No!' Max cut in tautly. 'No, January, to me not seeing you today is not an option.' He simply couldn't go through another night like last night!

'To me, either,' she came back softly.

So softly, Max wasn't sure he had heard her correctly, or whether it was just wishful thinking on his part. The former, he hoped!

'Okay, dinner,' he accepted huskily. 'Here. At seven-thirty.'

'Fine,' she agreed breathlessly. 'Oh, before you go, Max, there is just one little thing...' she added teasingly.

'Yes?' he prompted warily, feeling his tension rising once again.

'Don't you think it might be helpful if I were to know your surname?' she asked playfully. 'It was a little embarrassing a few minutes ago when I telephoned and had to ask Patty if there could possibly be an irate-looking guest pacing up and down in Reception—because I had no idea how to ask for you by name!'

That thought hadn't even occurred to him. But, now that he thought of it, he didn't know her surname either; it hadn't seemed important at the time.

It still wasn't important; she was January to him, the woman he wanted with a fierceness that was totally consuming his every waking thought. Although he could see her point...

'Golding,' he supplied laughingly. 'Maxim Patrick Golding.'

Complete silence on the other end of the telephone line followed his announcement. A sudden, tense silence.

'January...?' he prompted as the seconds slowly passed with only that silence on the other end of the telephone line.

'Did you say Golding?' she finally asked in a hushed voice.

'Yes, I did,' Max returned warily. 'January—'

'*You're* M. P. Golding?' Her voice rose disbelievingly.

Max's hand tightened about the telephone receiver. Something was wrong. Very, very wrong. 'I just told you I am,' he confirmed slowly, having no idea what the problem was with his name. Only knowing that there obviously was one.

Why had January repeated his name in that formal way, M. P. Golding, as if he were the author of a book, or—? Or…!

'January, what's your own surname?' he prompted with a wince of foreboding.

'With first names like January, March and May? I'm sure, if you try, you can work that one out for yourself, Mr Golding! If there's really any need for you to do so!' she added scathingly. 'Goodbye!'

'January—' Max broke off abruptly, realizing as he heard the clatter of the receiver being slammed down on the other end of the line that he was talking to himself.

Max slowly replaced his own receiver, the colour draining from his cheeks as the truth hit him with the force of a sledgehammer. January, March, and May. All months of the year. All months in the Gregorian calendar.

Calendar…

It was all too much of a coincidence, January having two sisters, their names all months of the year; January's surname *had* to be Calendar!

Damn, damn, damn!

CHAPTER FOUR

'JANUARY, where on earth are you going?' May demanded incredulously as she followed her outside.

January didn't even pause in her long strides across the yard. 'To get my car out of the ditch, of course,' she dismissed impatiently.

'But there's no hurry to do that until the weather improves,' May protested reasoningly as January climbed into the cab of the tractor. 'After all, you said it's probably a write-off, anyway.' Her sister grimaced.

It probably was, the whole of the front wing on the driver's side of the car seeming to have concertinaed into itself as it hit the other side of the ditch.

But it had at least stopped snowing, and January needed something to do, desperately needed to keep herself physically busy in an effort to stop herself from thinking too much. From thinking at all, if possible!

M. P. Golding! She had recognized the name instantly, clearly remembered it as the signature of the lawyer at the bottom of the letter they had received before Christmas—from the Marshall Corporation, offering to buy their farm. The same name of the lawyer who had visited the farm yesterday and spoken to May on the same subject...?

January still couldn't believe it! Couldn't stop thinking of it, no matter how much she tried...

'It can't just stay there, May,' she insisted grimly.

'It can stay there for a couple of days, until the snow clears a little,' her sister insisted.

January gave a firm shake of her head. 'I'm going now.'

'January, what's happened?' May looked at her concernedly. 'You were bright and bubbly this morning, before the accident. Perhaps that bump on the head was more serious than we initially thought. Perhaps we should call Dr. Young—'

'I don't need a doctor, May.' Not that sort of doctor, anyway! She forced herself to relax slightly, turning to smile at her sister. 'It's just a bump,' she insisted lightly—the throbbing pain at her temple was nothing compared to the one in her heart. And a medical doctor could do nothing to cure that! 'Look, I'll just drive down and see if it's possible to tow the car out of the ditch,' she offered as a compromise. 'The fresh air will probably do me good,' she added encouragingly.

May still didn't look convinced, frowning up at her concernedly. 'Aren't you supposed to be going out again later this evening?'

January blinked, no longer able to hold her sister's gaze. 'Change of plan,' she dismissed. 'Look, it's cold out here, why don't you go back inside?' she suggested with an encouraging smile. 'I promise I won't be long.'

'Okay,' May sighed. 'I'll have a mug of hot tea waiting for you when you get back.'

January gave an inner sigh of relief at her sister's belated capitulation, starting the noisy tractor engine before giving her sister a friendly wave and driving out of the farmyard.

She just needed some time to herself. Time to work out exactly what had been happening the last couple of days. Time to consider exactly what Max Golding had been doing the last couple of days!

Because, despite what he had said before she'd

abruptly ended their telephone conversation, she couldn't help thinking that he had to have known all the time that she was one of the Calendar sisters.

Was that the real reason he had shown such a marked interest in her? Had it all been some sort of devious plan on his part, to divide the sisters and, in doing so, perhaps conquer?

That was her worst fear, the dread that held her in partial shock at the realization of exactly who he was. Because last night, as the two of them had kissed, January had known that she was falling in love with Max, that perhaps she already was in love with him.

He was like no other man she had ever known, was possessed of a self-confidence that was totally reassuring, was obviously intelligent, as well as sophisticated, his wealth beyond question.

She had simply been swept off her feet by him!

But was she *meant* to have been? That was the question that plagued her battered and bruised heart.

One thing she knew for certain: once he had had time to think this thing through, it wouldn't take Max too long to make an appearance at the farm. Which was another good reason for her to make herself scarce from the farm as much as possible over the next few days.

Although that didn't appear much of a likelihood as she turned the tractor round a sharp bend in the snow-covered track and found a car creeping slowly along from the other direction, blocking her own way in the process, the person behind the steering wheel visibly Max Golding!

January braked so sharply to avoid actually driving into him that the tractor instantly came to a shuddering halt, Max obviously breaking at the same time, the wheels on his car not having quite the same traction as the vehicle skidded slightly but didn't quite go off the track.

January stared at him in absolute horror; the last thing she had expected was that Max would actually drive out to the farm almost immediately after she had so abruptly terminated their telephone call. She had thought she had some hours to gather her own scattered defences, possibly twenty-four hours if Max needed the same time to think that she did.

But as he climbed out of the car she realized how wrong she had been. He was no longer wearing the 'tailored suit and handmade shoes' that May had taken such glee in watching him get muddy yesterday—and that had struck such a chord with January last night when she'd thought of them. Now he was dressed in a thick blue sweater and denims, heavy hiking boots to protect his feet—obviously he had learnt his lesson about suitable clothing for visiting a working farm the previous day!

Her fingers clenched about the steering wheel as he approached the tractor, his expression grim. What was he going to say to her? What were they going to say to each other?

Attack is better than defence, she remembered her father once telling them, pushing open the cab door to climb down onto the running-board before lowering herself down into the snow, her head back challengingly as she waited for Max to reach her side.

'I didn't know, January,' came his first abrupt comment.

She gave a humourless smile. 'Didn't know what, Mr Golding?' she scorned. 'That my surname is Calendar? That I'm one of the three sisters who owns the farm the corporation you work for is trying to buy out? Forgive me if I find that a little hard to believe!' she derided hardly.

And she did find it hard. It seemed too much of a coincidence that Max should turn out to be the lawyer who had sent that initial letter on behalf of the big American corporation he obviously worked for. That he was the same man who had visited May on the farm yesterday. The same man who was trying to persuade them into selling the farm.

Too much of a coincidence, in those circumstances, that the two of them should have met at all. Even allowing for such a coincidence, it was doubly hard to believe that Max would have made such a beeline for her in the way that he had if it weren't for the fact that he already knew she was one of the sisters who was proving so intractable to the financial offers he was making on behalf of the Marshall Corporation.

Max's expression was grim. 'I can't help what you believe, I can only repeat that until a short time ago I genuinely had no idea what your surname was, or who you are.'

And she could only repeat—inwardly, at least—that she didn't believe him!

She gave him another scathing glance. 'What are you doing here, Mr Golding? I'm sure my sister May has already made it more than plain that we aren't interested—'

'Will you stop calling me by my surname in that contemptuous way?' he protested irritably. 'It was Max before. And I'm still Max.'

Not in the same way, he wasn't. He was the enemy now. The known enemy. Untrustworthy. Worse, he was devious.

'And, yes, your sister May did make it quite clear to me yesterday that you aren't interested in selling the farm,' he continued impatiently. 'Now that I know of the family connection, the likeness between the two of you, apart from the colour of your eyes, is quite remarkable,' he allowed heavily. 'I simply wasn't looking for that likeness when I visited the farm yesterday.'

'No?' January derided disbelievingly. 'Then you're going to get even more of a shock when—or if!—you meet March; "like three peas in a pod", our father used to say about us,' she told him dismissively.

'I said there was a likeness, January; the way you look, the sound of your voice, is utterly unique,' he assured her evenly.

Her mouth twisted humourlessly. 'Of course it is,' she humoured scathingly. 'Well, if you wouldn't mind moving your vehicle out of my way; some of us have work to do.'

Max looked at her closely, a frown between his eyes as his gaze narrowed. 'Is that bump on your head from the accident earlier?'

Her gloved hand moved up instinctively to cover the discolouration at her temple. She would be lying if she claimed that it didn't hurt, because it did; she just had no intention of discussing her injury—or her inner pain—with Max Golding!

'January?' he prompted sharply.

'Yes, it is,' she confirmed dismissively. 'If you turn your car around in the gateway just behind you—'

'January, I am not interested in discussing turning the car around,' he bit out in fiercely measured tones.

Her eyes flashed a warning. 'Well, I'm not interested in discussing anything else with you—which pretty well leaves us with nothing left to say to each other!' She turned back to the tractor.

Only to have her arm clasped between steely fingers as Max swung her back round to face him.

'I have several things I want to say to you,' he told her forcefully, blue eyes glittering dangerously. 'Firstly, I repeat my claim that I had no idea of your connection with the Calendar farm—'

'And I repeat that I don't believe you!' she came back harshly.

Max became suddenly still, his eyes so pale a blue now they looked almost grey. 'I don't tell lies, January,' he bit out coldly. 'Have you seen a doctor about that bump on the head?' he changed the subject frowningly.

Her mouth twisted contemptuously. 'Careful, you're starting to sound like May again!'

His mouth tightened at her deliberate barb. 'If she's as concerned about you as I am then I think I like your elder sister.'

January's cheeks became angrily flushed as she gave a humourless smile. 'I very much doubt the sentiment is reciprocated!'

Max shook his head. 'I'm not out to win popularity contests, I'm only interested in making sure you've suffered no ill effects from the accident—'

'The only "ill effects" I have are from having to look at you any longer than I need to!' January told him insultingly, at last managing to pull her arm out of his grasp as she glared up at him. 'Now, are you going to move your car, or do I have to go round you by taking the tractor into one of the fields?' she challenged hardly.

Move, she pleaded inwardly. Just move. If only so

that she could get away from his overwhelming presence. Because if he didn't soon move, she was very much afraid she was going to cry!

At the moment, her only defence against her feelings for this man was her anger. And she wasn't sure how much longer she would be able to maintain it.

Max stared at her frustratedly. She was, without doubt, the most stubborn, most determined—

More stubborn than he was? More determined than he was? Somehow he didn't think so.

At the moment, January was furiously angry with him for what she thought of as his deception. He could see only too clearly that nothing he said or did just now—or in the immediate future, for that matter—was going to change her feelings for him. Besides, he was in something of a quandary himself, had always made it a rule to keep his private and business life completely separate. That way there was never any question of a conflict of interest.

January Calendar. Of all the women he could have found himself so attracted to, it had to be one of the Calendar sisters!

What were the chances of that happening? Really? Almost nil, he would have said, with the farm being such a distance away from the hotel. That little mischief called Fate, he felt, was playing some sort of game with him.

But he had challenged Fate before, and won; he could win this time, too. If he still wanted to…

That was the real problem here. He had been stunned to learn that January was one of the three Calendar sisters he had been sent here to persuade into selling their farm. More than stunned. In truth, he simply didn't know what to do about it. A most unusual occurrence for him.

'You won't agree to see a doctor about that bump on the head?' He tried one last time to make her see sense about that at least.

'No, I won't,' she came back predictably.

His mouth tightened even as he gave an acknowledging nod of his head; stubborn didn't even begin to describe this particular woman!

'I take it our date for dinner this evening is also cancelled?' he prompted dryly.

Her eyes flashed deeply grey. 'You take it correct!' she snapped.

'I thought so,' he murmured mildly. 'As I obviously no longer have any other plans for today, and as I'm already halfway there already, I may as well drive up the rest of the way to the farm and have another talk to your sisters.'

January's eyes widened incredulously at this suggestion. 'You will be wasting your time!'

He shrugged. 'It's my time to waste.'

Her mouth twisted scathingly. 'I thought your time belonged to the Marshall Corporation?'

It was true that the Marshall Corporation had become the main part of his life for almost fifteen years, that his hours of work weren't the usual nine to five, Monday to Friday of a lawyer in a normal law practice. But with no family ties to speak of, only an apartment in London that he rarely visited to actually call home, that had never particularly bothered Max. In fact, he had welcomed the long hours of work and travel that were often necessary in his job.

In the circumstances, hearing January casting aspersions on that particular aspect of his life was not something he welcomed!

'Even I have weekends and holiday off, January,' he snapped, knowing, even as he made the claim, that it wasn't strictly accurate.

He could probably count the number of holidays he had taken the last fifteen years on the fingers of one hand. But holidays had never seemed important to him, were often an inconvenient interruption to business. Besides, he visited such exotic places during his business travels that holidays weren't really necessary.

'You were still working on New Year's Eve,' January reminded tauntingly.

His mouth tightened at her obvious implication. She still believed he had deliberately singled her out that evening, that it was all a part of some elaborate plan on his part to gain control of the Calendar farm.

But there was no way he would have deliberately planned to meet January in that way, certainly not to have been completely knocked off his feet by her in the way he had been. It was simply an unwritten rule with him never to mix business with pleasure.

Not that he thought there was much chance of him doing that now, either!

Oh, he was still attracted to January, in a way he had probably never been to any other woman, but there were two ways of looking at the fact she had turned out to be one of the Calendar sisters. The first way meant that he now had an uphill struggle ahead of him if he were to continue his personal pursuit of her. The second way was as a timely intervention, Fate not playing games with him at all, but instead stepping in to stop him from making the biggest mistake of his life.

Damn it, he liked his life the way it was: completely

uncomplicated by personal ties! And there was no way, now, that he could have an enjoyable, but brief, relationship with January.

He drew in a deeply controlling breath. 'I'll back my car up and let you past,' he told her evenly.

Her eyes widened at his unexpected capitulation. 'You're still wasting your time going up to the farm,' she assured him hardly. 'My sisters aren't interested in selling any more than I am.'

He gave another shrug. 'If that's the case, it will cease to be my problem and become someone else's.' He hoped!

She gave him a guarded look. 'Are you threatening us?'

'Not in the least!' He gave an exasperated shake of his head. 'January, no one can force any of you into selling if you're really not interested in doing so.'

But even as he said the words he knew that wasn't strictly true; Jude wasn't a man used to hearing the word no, let alone actually taking any notice of it. And he wanted the land the Calendar farm stood on pretty badly...

January didn't look any more convinced of his sincerity than he had actually making the claim, that guarded look having turned to one of wariness now.

'It's cold out here, January,' he added briskly, not quite meeting her searching gaze now. 'I'll back up and let you continue on your way. Your car is a mess, by the way,' he added hardly, having driven past the car in the ditch on his way up here, wincing as he imagined January behind the wheel as she lost control and crashed. Worse, that she had been driving to meet him at the time it had happened...

Not that he thought that would happen again;

January had made it more than obvious the last ten
minutes or so that she would never agree to meet him
again, for dinner or anything else!

Cut your losses and move on, Max, he mentally advised himself determinedly. Goodness knew he had
done it often enough in the past, never in the same
place long enough to allow himself to become too attached to any woman. Or them to him. January
Calendar was no different, he told himself firmly. Only
the force of his attraction to her was different...

All the more reason to get as far away from here as
he could, as quickly as he could!

Except Jude seemed to have other ideas on the subject, Max discovered later that afternoon when he returned to the hotel, after a frustrating hour spent at the
Calendar farm with May and March Calendar, to put a
call through to his boss and friend.

'You can't have put our case strongly enough,' Jude
drawled unsympathetically. 'How difficult can it be to
persuade three old maids that they would be better off
living in a nice bungalow somewhere than working
their fingers to the bone on a hill farm that simply
doesn't, and never will, pay for itself?'

'Three old maids', indeed! Max could easily predict
the reaction of any of the three undoubtedly beautiful
sisters to being called that! It had been interesting to
meet the third sister, March, when he'd got to the farm,
to see the physical similarity between all three sisters.
Although March, he had quickly learnt, was the most
tempestuous of the three, telling him in no uncertain
terms exactly what he, and the Marshall Corporation,
could do with their offer to buy the Calendar property.
May had been a little politer, but her answer had still
been the same as that of her siblings.

But for some reason Max didn't actually want to correct Jude in his mistake concerning the age of the three sisters, didn't want to give the other man the opportunity to perhaps put two and two together and come up with four, to question the reason for Max's own reluctance to pursue this thing any further.

'They were born there, Jude,' he repeated March's indignant remark of earlier. 'The family has lived there for generations—'

'Max, are you going soft on me?' Jude cut in disbelievingly.

As well he might. He and Jude had been at school together, had lost touch for a while when attending different universities, but Jude had sought Max out several years later when his business empire had begun to expand, easily persuading Max to become his personal and company lawyer. It was a decision that Max had never regretted. Until today...

'No, of course not,' he dismissed harshly. 'I just—'

'You just...?' Jude prompted speculatively.

'Leave it with me for a few more days, okay?' he answered impatiently, willing himself to relax as his hand tightly gripped the receiver—so much for his earlier decision to tell Jude to just cut and run over this proposed deal. So that he could cut and run himself! 'How are you doing with the beautiful April?' he prompted tautly.

'Changing the subject, Max?' Jude guessed shrewdly.

That was the problem with Jude: he was too astute. And the last thing Max wanted was for the other man to even begin to guess at the emotional tangle Max now found himself in.

Part of him wanted to just pass the problem of the

Calendar farm over to someone else, and in the process get himself as far away from January as he possibly could—something that he now knew he needed to do. But the professional side of him, the part of him that had been loyal to Jude and the Marshall Corporation for the last fifteen years, decreed that he had to continue trying to talk the Calendar sisters into selling their birthright.

'Not particularly,' he came back easily. 'I merely wondered if you had been any more successful with April than I was,' he added dryly.

'Not in the least,' Jude came back cheerfully. 'She insists on treating me as if I'm nothing more to her than a naughty little brother.'

'Novel.' Max grinned at the thought of the arrogantly successful Jude being cast in such an unflattering role.

The other man chuckled. 'Actually, I'm quite enjoying it. She really is a fascinating woman,' he added appreciatively.

Nowhere near as fascinating, to Max, as January had proved to be! But at least he had veered the other man off the subject of the Calendar sisters, which was, after all, what he had set out to do by introducing the subject of April Robine.

'To get back to the Calendar farm,' Jude continued determinedly—proof that, as usual, he hadn't been veered off the subject at all! 'We really need to get that settled and out of the way in the next few weeks, so that we can get on with drawing up the plans. Offer them more money if nothing else works,' he added hardly.

Dogged. Single-minded. They were qualities in Jude that he had always admired in the past. But where this particular problem was concerned Max found those traits extremely irritating.

'I'm well aware of the time-scale involved, Jude,' he snapped. 'But I don't think, in this case, that the offer of more money is going to make the slightest bit of difference.'

In fact, Max was sure that it wouldn't. The offer already made was far above the market value of the property, and despite the fact that the Calendar sisters obviously weren't exactly wealthy, none of them had been in the least tempted to accept the offer. Money, it seemed, just wasn't important to them.

'I really don't want to have to come over there myself, Max,' Jude said softly.

Max didn't want the other man to come here himself, either. For one thing, it implied failure on his part if Jude had to deal with this himself. For another, he simply didn't want Jude coming here, meeting the three sisters, putting that two and two together, and realizing that Max's real problem was January!

It seemed that, unless he wanted to admit the truth to Jude, that he had unwittingly become personally involved with January, one of the Calendar sisters, something he would rather not do, he really had no choice but to stay here and continue the negotiations on Jude's behalf.

'I asked you to leave it with me a few days longer,' he reminded the other man harshly.

'A few more days is all you have, Max,' Jude conceded warningly before abruptly ending the call.

Max slowly replaced his own receiver before turning to stare frustratedly out of the window of his hotel room, the snow once again falling outside not helping the darkness of his mood. What a damned mess!

There was obviously no way Jude was going to back down from buying the Calendar farm. Which meant that Max couldn't either.

But how to persuade the Calendar sisters into changing their minds was the problem. Having now met all of them, an insurmountable one, as far as he could see.

But nowhere near as insurmountable as the problem January had become to him personally.

Indulging in an affair with her for the time he was in the area had seemed like a pleasant way to spend his free time. The fact that she had turned out to be one of the reasons he was here at all completely changed that. Besides, having got to know January a little better, having met her sisters, he now knew that January was not the type of woman to have an affair. With anyone.

But least of all him.

Whereas he knew he still wanted her with a fierceness that took his breath away, that everything about her fascinated him: the way she moved, the way she talked, everything!

CHAPTER FIVE

'EXACTLY what do you think you're playing at?' January demanded without preamble the moment Max opened the door of his hotel suite to her insistent knock.

To give him his due, he looked momentarily taken aback by her unexpected appearance, although that surprise was quickly masked as he looked down at her with mocking enquiry. 'Changed your mind about our dinner date?' he drawled dryly.

Her eyes flashed a warning. 'I've changed my mind about nothing concerning you, Mr Golding,' she snapped. 'Absolutely nothing!' she repeated as she pushed past him into the sitting-room of the hotel suite, turning to glare at him when she reached the centre of the room.

He slowly closed the door before strolling in to join her. 'You seem a little—agitated?' he prompted lightly.

Agitated? She was blazing! In fact, she was in such a heated temper that she really didn't need the added warmth of her blue anorak, or the gloves and scarf she had earlier pulled on with it.

'Did you have to tell my sisters that the two of us had already met?' she challenged accusingly. 'Yes, of course you did,' she scathingly answered her own question before he even had chance to do so. 'It was all part of the plan, wasn't it?' she said disgustedly. 'All part of that—'

'Stop right there, January,' he cut in softly—although one glance at the grimness of his features was enough to tell January that his tone was deceptive, that he was now actually as angry as she was, he just showed it in a different way! 'You appear to be—upset,' he allowed evenly. 'And I'm sorry for that. But, at the same time, I also think you are becoming slightly paranoid about this situation—'

'Paranoid!' January echoed disbelievingly. 'Is it "paranoid" when my sisters are absolutely stunned that I somehow forgot to mention that I had already met the lawyer Max Golding? That I was actually supposed to be going out on a date with the man this evening!' she added disgustedly.

She didn't add that he was also the man she had allowed to kiss her so passionately yesterday evening. Or that he was also the man she had been falling in love with!

May and March had been far from happy when January had finally arrived home—minus the car; it really was stuck fast in the ditch. Because somewhere, during the course of their conversation with Max this afternoon, he had let drop the fact that he and January had already met!

To say her sisters had demanded an explanation for January's previous oversight would be putting it mildly. The fact that they had both calmed down once she'd told them exactly what had happened, that they were now just as suspicious of Max's motives as she was, didn't alter the fact that Max had deliberately put her in that defensive position in the first place.

Max gave a shake of his head. 'January, so far I'm not having such a good day myself, so do you think we could just sit down and talk about this like two reasonable adults?' he prompted hardly.

'That may be a little difficult—when only one of us is reasonable!' she came back scathingly.

She would never forget the way her sisters had looked at her on her return this afternoon, could still see that uncertainty in their expressions as they'd waited for her explanation. Oh, she didn't doubt for a moment that they had both believed her explanation, that she was completely innocent in the whole matter, it was only when she'd gone up to her room to change out of her damp clothing that she had decided not to waste another minute before telling Max Golding just how underhand and devious she thought him to be.

He shrugged. 'I'm not even going to ask which one of us you consider that to be,' he returned dryly. 'Although,' he continued firmly as she would have snapped a reply, 'I think the fact that you've driven out here, in the middle of yet another snowstorm, rather negates your being eligible for the description!' he added hardly, blue gaze disapproving.

January opened her mouth a second time to give him that sharp reply, and then changed her mind as her gaze drifted past him to the window, where the snow could be seen falling heavier than ever.

To be honest, she hadn't really noticed the snow falling as she'd driven to the hotel, had been so angry, so consumed with all the things she was going to say to Max, going over and over inside her head the conversation that she intended having with him, that she had driven to the hotel on automatic. So much so she hadn't been aware of the snow!

'January, could you come down off your high horse long enough for us to talk?' Max cajoled softly. 'I'll order us a pot of coffee, and you can drink a warming cup of it while we talk. How about that?'

She wanted to say no, to tell him what he could do with his cup of warm coffee, but now that she was no longer as consumed by burning anger she was able to feel the chill that went all the way through to her bones.

That still wasn't a good enough reason to have coffee with the enemy, a little voice chastened inside her head.

No, it wasn't, she accepted heavily. The truth of the matter was, now that she was here with Max, her anger spent for the most part, she was once again becoming aware of the attraction she felt towards him—still felt towards him, in spite of everything!

Fool, she admonished herself disgustedly. Idiot, she added for good measure.

'January?' Max prompted huskily.

She gave a weary sigh. 'Order your pot of coffee, Max,' she conceded. 'But nothing you have to say is going to change my mind about you. Or the Marshall Corporation,' she added hardly.

He gave an abrupt inclination of his head, moving to the telephone to call Room Service and order the coffee.

January was glad of the few moments' respite from his probing blue gaze, moving away to take off her scarf and gloves before shaking her hair loose from the collar of her jacket.

What was she doing here? Really doing here? Because she had already done what she'd come here to do—and now she was staying to have coffee with the man.

She bit her lip, knowing exactly why she was still here. She couldn't believe—part of her didn't want to believe!—Max was actually guilty of the things she had accused him of!

Not that she had any intention of letting Max see that particular weakness; that wouldn't do at all. She just wanted to see—needed to see—some sort of redeeming feature in his character that told her she was justified to feel about him the way that she really did.

'It's on its way.' Max spoke softly behind her.

Too close behind her, she discovered when she spun round sharply, stepping back as she found Max standing only inches away from her.

He looked at her quizzically. 'You were miles away.'

'Wishing myself...' she came back tautly.

He gave a pained wince. 'Then that makes two of us,' he murmured huskily. 'I was wishing the same thing a short time ago,' he explained at her questioning look.

January's breath caught in her throat at the burning intensity of his gaze. 'And now?'

'Now?' he echoed with a self-derisive grimace. 'Now I wish it would just keep snowing. Snowing. And snowing. I wish, January—' he took a step closer to her '—that the rest of the world would just go away, that the two of us could get marooned alone together in here. For a week. A month!' he concluded heavily.

She looked up at him uncertainly, her breath now coming in short, shallow gasps. 'Can you get snowed in in a hotel room?' she breathed huskily.

'Probably not,' he conceded ruefully. 'But—' He broke off as a knock sounded on the door. 'That will be the coffee,' he acknowledged disgustedly.

'So much for being marooned alone together,' January pointed out softly.

He gave a derisive inclination of his head. 'Maybe that wasn't such a good idea, after all,' he rasped before moving abruptly away to open the door and admit the maid with their tray of coffee.

He seemed different this evening, January acknowledgedly frowningly. Apart from that brief lapse just now, he was more distant. More remote. His gaze no longer burning with that intensity, but wary.

Of course he was different, she instantly admonished herself; his cover was blown, which meant he no longer needed to act like a man who was besotted with her.

'Cream and sugar?'

She turned sharply, blinking to clear her head as she saw Max was waiting to pour her coffee, the maid having already quietly departed. 'Black. Thank you,' she added stiffly.

What was she doing here? she asked herself once again. Had she secretly hoped? Had a part of her still thought that perhaps there had been some sort of mistake—

'Thank you.' She moved to take the cup out of his hand, her gaze not quite meeting his as he looked down at her probingly.

January, careful not to let their hands touch as she took the cup from him, moved away from him abruptly to once again look out of the window, blinking back the sudden tears that blurred her vision.

She had been so angry earlier, at the realization of exactly who he was, at what she believed to be his duplicity; now she just felt miserable. Because it was all over? Because for that brief forty-eight hours she had felt wrapped in Max's interest in her? Had known a feeling of being cared for that she hadn't felt since her father had died? Was that why she so desperately wanted to cry?

How stupid she was. She should have known, should

have guessed, that having a man like Max interested in her just couldn't be real. After all, what was she really but a part-time farmer and singer? Hardly the sort of woman Max could ever be serious about. For all she knew about him, he could already be a married man! The very thought of that was enough to stiffen her backbone.

'Max—'

'January—'

They both began talking at once, January giving Max a rueful grimace as she turned to face him. 'You first,' she invited huskily.

His expression was bleak, eyes icy blue, letting her know that whatever he was going to say, she wasn't going to like it.

Whatever he said now, Max knew January wasn't going to like it. If he mentioned Jude and renewed his offer to buy the farm, January wasn't going to like it. If he tried to explain—once again!—that he really hadn't known she was one of the Calendar sisters, he knew she wasn't going to like that, either. Or, indeed, believe him.

Besides, what was the point in even trying to convince her that he was telling the truth about that when he had already decided to back away from that particular situation himself? Back away—he was back-pedalling so fast he was surprised she couldn't hear the pedals going round!

God, she was beautiful, he inwardly acknowledged achingly.

Yes, she was.

But now that he knew who she was, the closeness of her family, he also knew that whatever she might have said about love the night they'd first met, she was actually the sort of woman who wouldn't settle for anything less than marriage—and, no matter how attracted he was to her, the very thought of being married, to anyone, gave him an icy lump of panic in the pit of his stomach.

His mouth thinned grimly. 'I spoke to Jude Marshall earlier,' he bit out forcefully. 'He's willing to increase his offer.'

January recoiled as if he had actually struck her, and it took every ounce of Max's will-power not to take her in his arms, to tell her that everything would be okay, that while he was around no one would ever take the farm away from her, or anything else, if she didn't want them to.

But who was he kidding? He had known Jude most of his life, might be a trusted friend as well as employee, but he also knew the other man well enough to know that what Jude wanted, he got, usually by fair means, but if those means ultimately failed…! Jude had left him in absolutely no doubt earlier that he wanted the Calendar farm, and that he intended getting it.

Max's own inner feelings of a conflict of interest simply wouldn't come into the other man's equation!

Max thrust his hands into the pockets of his denims, his fists tightly clenched. 'My advice to you all is to seriously consider this second offer,' he told January harshly.

Her eyes widened indignantly as she snapped, 'I wasn't aware I had asked for your advice!'

He shrugged with seeming unconcern, hating himself for talking to her in this way, but at the same time knowing that he couldn't back down now from the stance he had taken. Couldn't? More like daredn't, he acknowledged self-disgustedly. Conflict of interest, be damned; he had made his choice in Jude's favour the moment he'd realized just how deeply involved he already was with January. Having her hate him for that choice was the price he had to pay.

'I'm offering it anyway,' he drawled dismissively. 'Jude isn't a man to take no for an answer.'

Her eyes flashed deeply grey. 'Then the two of you must have a lot in common.'

She meant to be insulting, and she succeeded. Although there was no denying, Max accepted hardly, that she unwittingly told the truth. The two men were similar in lots of ways, both successful at what they did, both still bachelors at thirty-seven, and both intending to stay that way.

If not for the same reasons.

Jude made no secret of the fact that although women fascinated him, they as quickly bored him in a one-to-one relationship, claimed that if he ever met the woman who didn't bore him after a few days' acquaintance he would marry her. Whereas Max had no intention of marrying ever, for any reason, least of all love.

He had looked at January on New Year's Eve, and known he wanted her. But it was nothing more than that, he told himself determinedly. He wouldn't allow it to be.

Women, he had learnt at a very young age, were fickle creatures at best, took a man's love and used it as a weapon against him.

His expression was bleak now. 'Resorting to insults isn't going to help resolve this situation,' he rasped.

'Maybe not,' she accepted heavily. 'But it certainly makes me feel better!'

He gave a rueful shrug. 'Then feel free.'

She gave him a searching look. 'Max, can I ask you a question?'

He stiffened warily, not liking the look in her eyes now. 'Go ahead,' he invited tensely.

'How do you sleep at night?' she scorned.

The last two nights—very badly. Usually—very well. But he knew that wasn't what she was really asking!

His mouth twisted derisively. 'January, whatever you may or may not think of me personally, Jude's offer is a fair one—'

'I'm not interested in anything to do with Jude Marshall!' she burst out scathingly. 'Until recently, I had never even heard of the man—and I wish I still hadn't!' she added disgustedly. 'I'm more interested in knowing how you can bear to be used as his—as his—'

'Careful, January,' Max warned softly. 'In view of your obvious anger, there are some insults I'm willing to accept—others I am not,' he added hardly. 'I'm a lawyer. I have never been guilty of committing any sort of unlawful act.'

'Not unlawful, maybe,' she allowed heatedly. 'But there is such a thing as a moral wrong.'

'Granted,' he acknowledged icily. 'But as far as the Calendar family is concerned, I can't see where I have been guilty of that either!'

'You—you can't see—!' January stared at him incredulously. 'You don't consider deliberately setting out to seduce one of us, in order to divide and conquer, to be morally wrong?'

His eyes narrowed coldly. 'You're referring to yourself?'

'Of course I'm referring to myself!' she confirmed

impatiently, becoming suddenly still as she looked at him suspiciously. 'Unless—'

'Don't even suggest it, January,' he warned softly. 'So far I believe I have remained calm and reasonable during your diatribe of accusations—but if you proceed with the present one I may not be answerable for the consequences!'

'*You* may not be—'

'January, I don't believe this conversation is doing anything to calm this situation down,' he cut in impatiently, not sure how much longer he could stand here and take her insults without pulling her into his arms and kissing her into silence!

Which, in the circumstances, wouldn't calm the situation down either!

His mouth twisted. 'Our previous—friendship, may have given you the impression that you had the freedom to come here and throw wild accusations at me.' He scowled darkly. 'But I happen to think otherwise—'

'Friendship?' she echoed furiously. 'Friendship!' she repeated disgustedly, shaking her head. 'We were never friends, Max, and you know it—' She was suddenly silenced as Max's mouth came down forcefully on hers.

He hadn't been able to stop himself. Could no longer stand here and have January look at him with such dislike and loathing. Not that he thought kissing her was going to make her dislike him any less—he really just couldn't help himself!

He might never know a moment's peace again, might never again have complete possession of his soul, either, he realized dazedly. But for the moment, kissing January, holding her close against him, touching the silkiness of her skin, was all that mattered.

CHAPTER SIX

SHE should stop this.

Now.

Yet January couldn't bring herself to do that, inwardly knew that this might never happen again, that she might never again know the taste and feel of Max's lips on hers, the caress of his hands against the warmth of her burning skin.

And she wanted those things.

Wanted them so badly.

Wanted Max.

His hair was like silk against her hands as her fingers became entwined in its darkness, deepening their kiss, heat and moisture, a duel of tongues that spoke of their desire for each other.

January made no demur as her coat fell to the carpeted floor, at the warmth of Max's hands beneath the thickness of her zipped top, flesh catching fire at the caress of his hands against the dampness of her skin.

She was aware once again of that oneness, of not knowing where she ended and Max began, every particle of her seeming joined to him, two halves of a perfect whole.

She groaned low in her throat as he broke the kiss, that groan turning to a throaty ache as his lips moved slowly across her cheek, down the sensitive column of her neck, to the pulsing hollow at its base, lips and tongue probing moistly there, pulses of pleasure shooting down the length of her spine to ignite a hitherto unknown warmth between trembling thighs.

The zip of her top moved slowly down beneath Max's searching fingers, he bending his head as his lips followed the same path, January's back arching instinctively as she felt the moisture of his mouth through the silky material of her bra, his tongue moving in a slow caress over the pouting invitation of her nipple.

His hands encircled the slenderness of her bared waist now, holding her against the hardness of his thighs as his lips paid homage to the warm swell of her breasts. And lower.

January moved against him invitingly, her fingers once again entangled in the darkness of his hair, holding him against her, never wanting this pleasure to stop.

And it didn't, not when Max bent to lift her up in his arms, or when he carried her through to the bedroom to lay her down on top of the bed, or when he lay his long length beside her, his mouth once again taking fierce possession of hers.

Despite the difference in their heights, their bodies seemed to curve perfectly together as they lay turned into each other's arms, January's hands free to touch him in return now, caressing the hardness of his muscled back as they pressed closely together.

She gasped at the unfamiliar touch of hands against the bareness of her thighs, able to feel Max's warmth through the lacy material of her panties, that gasp turning to a groan of pleasure as he easily sought and found the centre of her pleasure, the whole of her body feeling like molten lava now.

'January, if you want me to stop, then you have to say so now—before it's too late!'

She gasped at the sound of Max's voice, felt as if a

bucket of ice cold water had just been thrown over her, as if the roof above them had disappeared to allow the cold snow to fall on her burning skin, awakening her from— From what?

She fell back on the bed, staring up at Max with darkly haunted eyes, his own eyes still dark with desire as he looked at her searchingly.

'Don't look at me like that!' he finally groaned harshly.

She breathed shallowly, her tongue moving to moisten suddenly dry lips. 'Like what?'

Was that husky rasp really her voice? It had sounded completely unlike her usual confident tones, like the voice of a stranger.

And perhaps that was what she had become, even to herself. Because she knew only too well that if Max hadn't spoken and broken the spell it would no longer have just seemed as if they were two halves of a whole—it would have been a reality!

Max continued to look down at her frowningly for several long, searching seconds before flinging himself back on the pillow to stare up at the ceiling. 'As if I'm some sort of monster you need protecting from!' he rasped coldly.

Had she really looked at him in that way? If she had, then it was totally unfair—because the only person she needed protecting from was herself!

'Max—'

He swung away from her as she would have reached out and touched his arm, swinging his legs down to sit up on the side of the bed. 'I think you had better leave, January,' he muttered grimly. 'Before either of us does or says something we're going to regret!'

Hadn't they already done that?

January knew that she certainly had. And one glance at Max's grimly set features told her that he wasn't in the least happy about what had happened, either!

She sat up, fumbling with the zip on her jeans, pulling the sides of her sweater together, her fingers shaking now as she tried to put the zipper together. This was so— Why wouldn't this thing—?

'Here—let me,' Max bit out tautly, at the same time reaching out—with hands that were completely steady, January noticed self-derisively—to put the zipper together and pull up the silver catch.

January looked at him beneath lowered lashes, looking, searching desperately, for some sign of the man from seconds ago, the man who had trembled with the same desire she had. All she could see was Max Golding, his hair slightly ruffled perhaps, a nerve pulsing—with anger or suppressed desire?—in the hardness of his cheek, but otherwise he looked just as self-assured as ever!

'Your look of reproach is a little late in coming, don't you think?' he drawled dryly. 'As well as being misdirected!' he added scathingly.

January flinched as if he had hit her, his words certainly wounding, if not physically then emotionally.

'I have to go.' She pushed back the tangle of her hair as she scrambled over to the side of the bed, wondering when she had ever felt so miserable. Never, came the unequivocal answer!

'Running away, January?' Max murmured tauntingly as she reached the bedroom door.

She turned to give him a sharp reply, the words catching in her throat as she saw herself reflected in the mirror across the room, seeing herself as she never had before.

Her hair was a tangled cloud about her shoulders, her eyes a wild dark grey, her face a white blur, her lips bruised red with passion. She looked exactly what she was—a woman who had recently been roused to a passion she might never recover from!

She swallowed hard, forcing her gaze from that wanton reflection as she looked across at Max contemptuously. 'Not running, Max, walking,' she corrected with hard derision. 'I should never have come here in the first place!' she added bitterly.

'No, you shouldn't,' he acknowledged hardly, moving to sit back on the bed, one arm behind his head as he rested back against the headboard. 'A short time ago, you asked me how I sleep at night,' he reminded tauntingly. 'Well, I can tell you, the answer to that is "very rarely alone",' he drawled mockingly, blue eyes openly laughing at her now.

January stiffened defensively at the pain his words caused, easily able to envisage him in bed with a sea of faceless women—especially with him sprawled out on the bed in that telling way!

Her mouth twisted disgustedly. 'Well, it looks as if you lucked out tonight, doesn't it?' she scorned.

He gave a lazy glance at the gold watch nestling amongst the dark hairs on his wrist. 'There's still time.' He shrugged.

January gasped, glaring at him now as she spat out the words, 'You're despicable!'

He gave another shrug, blue eyes as hard as sapphires now. 'Go home, January,' he scorned dismissively. 'Come back when you've grown up a little.'

Her hands were clenched so tightly at her sides she could feel her fingernails digging into her palms. 'It really was all an act from start to finish, wasn't it?' she burst out emotionally. 'That remark about love at first sight was part of your seduction, too,' she added chokingly.

He grimaced. 'Most women, I've found, respond to the word love rather than lust.' He gave a humourless smile. 'I have to admit, January, you shocked the hell out of me when you called it exactly what it is!' He gave an appreciative inclination of his head.

She felt sick, mostly at herself, she admitted; she had guessed what sort of man Max was from the beginning, had no excuse for what had just happened between them.

'But the feeling of lust, thank goodness, isn't confined to one person,' Max continued dismissively. 'Besides, January—' his gaze was once again mocking '—I have a feeling that if either of us isn't going to sleep tonight it's going to be you!' He looked across at her challengingly.

She had to get out of here. Away from Max. Away from this room, and the memory of how close they had come to making love…!

'My conscience is clear, Max—how about yours?' she scorned, head held high.

He grimaced dismissively. 'The same.'

She gave a disgusted shake of her head. 'Then you must have a very different idea of what I consider acceptable behaviour!'

He shrugged. 'For someone who was leaving at least five minutes ago, you don't seem in any particular hurry to do so?' He quirked mocking brows.

January drew in a sharp breath at his taunt. 'Don't worry, Max—I'm going. And I never want to see you again!' She breathed agitatedly.

He gave a grim smile. 'No chance of that happening,

I'm afraid, January,' he drawled. 'After all, I'm still negotiating on behalf of the Marshall Corporation to buy your family farm.'

'Over my dead body!' she told him with feeling.

'If you insist on driving in snowstorms—that might very well be the case,' he mocked dryly.

She had to go. Now. Before she totally humiliated herself and began to cry!

'Take care, January,' Max murmured softly. 'I hope you sleep well,' he added tauntingly.

She gave a pained frown at this last comment, turning sharply on her heel and almost running from the room, only lingering long enough to grab her coat from the floor where it had fallen before hurrying from the hotel suite as if the devil himself were at her heels.

He was hateful. Horrible. The most horrible man she had ever met in her life!

How could she have been so stupid?

How could she have so totally misjudged a person? How—?

'January…?'

She looked up frowningly as she crossed the reception area of the hotel, her brow clearing slightly as she recognized John, the barman, obviously just coming in for his evening shift.

He looked at her concernedly. 'Hey, are you okay?'

Okay? She might never be 'okay' again!

'Fine,' she assured him huskily, hoping she didn't look as bad as she felt.

She had straightened her hair a little while travelling down in the lift, but she hadn't been able to do anything about the paleness of her face, or that slightly bruised look to her lips.

'You don't look okay.' Obviously John wasn't fooled for a minute, still frowning his concern. 'Come through to the bar and have a brandy,' he encouraged worriedly.

She gave a humourless laugh, shaking her head. 'I won't, if you don't mind. I've already had one accident today,' she explained ruefully. 'My sister will kill me if I prang her car, too!'

His eyes widened. 'You've been involved in an accident?'

'Only with a ditch.' She grimaced. 'I really do have to go, John,' she apologized lightly. 'Is it still snowing?' She really had no idea how long she had been in Max's hotel suite, or what the weather was like, either!

'No, it's stopped,' John told her distractedly. 'You really don't look well, January, are you sure you wouldn't like me to get someone to take over in the bar for me for a couple of hours and drive you home?'

'That's very kind of you.' She touched his arm gratefully. 'But no,' she insisted. 'I drove here, I can drive back.'

'Meridew didn't call you in, did he?' John muttered disgustedly.

'No, nothing like that.' She avoided his concerned gaze. 'I really do have to go, John,' she told him briskly. 'Have a good evening!' She hurried away before he could delay her further.

Or question her further! The fewer people who knew she had been stupid enough to visit Max in his hotel suite, the better!

It was bad enough that she knew. That she was totally aware of what an idiot she had been. Of how totally she had misjudged Max's true nature.

Well, she wouldn't make that mistake again. In fact, she meant it when she said she hoped she never saw him again!

Good, Max. Very good, he congratulated himself as he still lay back on the bed. He had deliberately set out to make January dislike him—and he had succeeded!

Only too well.

The look of loathing she had given him before leaving told him that she didn't just dislike him, she hated him.

Well, it was what he wanted, wasn't it?

Of course it was.

He had deliberately set out to break those tenuous emotional ties with her, to make sure that there was no further conflict of interest. Now that he knew January was one of the Calendar sisters, and Jude refused to give up on buying the Calendar farm, it had been the only thing he could have done.

Then why did he feel so miserable at having succeeded in what he set out to do? Because he did feel miserable. More miserable than he had felt in his life before. Ever. And that included having his mother walk out on his father and him when he was only five years old.

He wasn't naïve, knew that early experience had tempered his future relationships with women, his decision never to fall in love, never to trust any woman enough to lay himself open to that vulnerability.

But in all honesty he couldn't even remember what his mother looked like any more. It was only the devastating loneliness of her desertion that stayed with him. Always.

Well, he certainly had nothing further to worry about in that way where January was concerned; she had really meant it when she said she never wanted to see him again.

Why did that hurt so much?

Because it wasn't lust he felt for January at all, because he—

He had to get out of here, Max decided, standing up compulsively; even he couldn't stand his own company at this particular moment! He needed to do something, go somewhere, anything to distract his thoughts from January and the way he had deliberately hurt her.

It was almost nine o'clock, he discovered when he got downstairs, but even so John was alone in the bar when Max walked into the room. Which suited his mood perfectly; the last thing he felt in the mood for at the moment was a lot of chattering people around him having fun!

'A large whisky,' he requested as he sat down on one of the bar stools.

'Lousy weather, isn't it?' John placed the drink on the bar in front of Max.

'Looks as if you'll have a quiet evening.' Max nodded grimly, taking a large gulp of the fiery alcohol. 'Don't you ever have an evening off?' he prompted abruptly; he might not feel like having chattering people around him, but his own exclusive company wasn't what he wanted at the moment either!

John grinned. 'Mondays and Tuesdays.'

Max grimaced. 'That must play havoc with your social life?'

'What social life?' John dismissed pointedly. 'Still, it's a job, which is more than a lot of people have.' He shrugged. 'You missed January, earlier, by the way,' he added lightly as he moved along the bar filling up the bowls of nuts.

Max stiffened just at the sound of her name. So much for getting out of his hotel room, of doing something to keep thoughts of January at bay!

'She seemed…upset,' John added frowningly.

'Did she?' Max kept his tone bland, not wanting to get into any sort of conversation about January. Certainly not the reason she had seemed upset!

John's brow cleared. 'Perhaps—'

'Mr Golding?'

Max had been so intent on his conversation with the barman, so deliberately trying not to think of January 'upset', that he had been completely unaware of the fact that he and John were no longer alone in the bar.

But there was no mistaking the sound of that voice. No mistaking its likeness to January's. Except he knew, after the way they had parted earlier, that it certainly wasn't January.

He turned slowly to find May Calendar standing behind him, keeping his expression neutral as he stood up. 'Miss Calendar.' He nodded politely.

It was a couple of hours since January had left the hotel, which meant the two sisters could have spoken when she'd returned home. Or not. Until he knew the answer to that, Max intended remaining detached. If wary.

Irritation flickered briefly in those deep green eyes as May looked at their surroundings. 'Could we possibly go somewhere and talk?' she requested abruptly.

'Certainly,' Max acquiesced evenly. 'How about that table over there?' He pointed to the far side of the room. 'Perhaps John could get you a drink—?'

'I would rather go somewhere a little more—private,' May briskly interrupted him. 'No offence.' She gave John an apologetic grimace.

'None taken,' the barman assured her happily. 'I wouldn't be in here either if I didn't work here!'

May gave an obliging laugh before once again making Max the focal point of that steady deep green gaze. 'Mr Golding?' she prompted pointedly.

He still had no idea whether May had spoken to January on her return earlier, or even if January would have confided in her eldest sister what had happened if they had spoken. But perhaps it would be better to err on the side of caution; if May intended hitting him, it would probably be better if it wasn't done in a public place!

'Let's go upstairs to my suite,' he suggested briskly, signing for his drink before escorting the eldest Calendar sister from the bar.

It was uncanny how physically alike the three sisters were, Max ruefully acknowledged, although he already knew from his two visits to the farm that May, as the eldest sister, was a force to be reckoned with, that she didn't suffer fools gladly. More importantly, she wasn't impressed by him in any way, shape or form!

Well, at the moment, after the way he had treated January earlier, he couldn't say he was too impressed by himself either!

'I believe one of the quieter lounges will do as well for my purpose,' May informed him dryly as she paused in the reception area.

Perhaps she wasn't going to hit him, after all...

She obviously had no intention of being alone with him in his hotel suite, either!

'Fine.' He gave an acknowledging inclination of his head. 'There are some small conference rooms down this corridor.' He indicated that May should precede him. 'I'm sure the management won't mind if we use one for a few minutes.'

Almost as beautiful as her sister—in his eyes January was still the most beautiful woman he had ever seen!—May also had a determined tilt to her chin, a way of looking at him with those emerald-coloured eyes, as if she could see straight through him. Which wasn't a very comfortable feeling, Max acknowledged with an inner squirm!

'Fine,' May finally agreed slowly, leading the way down the corridor.

This was the first time Max had seen the eldest Calendar sister out of the bulky sweaters and faded denims she wore to work in on the farm; she was stunning in the black jacket, thin emerald-coloured jumper and pencil-slim skirt, her legs as long and shapely as January's in the heeled shoes.

Why the hell weren't any of these women already married? Max wondered incredulously; it would have solved so much of the problem if they had been! Were all the single men in the area blind? Or was it the sisters who just weren't interested?

May entered the conference room to turn and look at him, her mouth twisting derisively as she saw the way Max was watching her—almost as if she were able to read his thoughts. And found them amusing.

'Many men have tried, and many men have failed!' she drawled mockingly, an imp of mischief leaping now in the beauty of her eyes.

'Why have they failed?' Max didn't even make a pretence of not understanding what she was talking about.

She shrugged. 'Maybe they didn't try hard enough.'

After the way he had deliberately alienated January

earlier, this was not, Max told himself firmly, the sort of conversation he should be having with any of the Calendar sisters! 'What can I do for you, Miss Calendar?' he prompted hardly.

The mischief faded from her eyes, leaving them as cold and hard as the jewels they resembled. 'Stay away from my sister,' she told him flatly. 'And please don't pretend not to know which sister I'm talking about,' she added as he would have spoken.

'I wasn't going to,' he assured her bleakly. 'But, unless I'm mistaken, after this evening January will never come near me, through choice, ever again!' Hadn't she said as much?

May looked at him with narrowed eyes for several long minutes. 'What makes you say that?' she finally murmured slowly.

'That isn't for me to say,' he bit out tautly; was it possible the sisters hadn't already spoken this evening, that May was here on some crusade of her own that had nothing to do with what had happened between January and himself earlier...?

May's mouth twisted humourlessly. 'Isn't it a little late in the day for you to be acting gentlemanly?'

He stiffened at the deliberate insult. 'You know, Miss Calendar, I believe I've already taken quite enough insults from your family for one day!' he rasped.

That impish humour flickered once again in the depths of her green eyes. 'That's good.' She nodded unrepentantly. 'But, unless I'm mistaken, March hasn't even started yet!'

Max gave a heavy sigh. 'Tell her not to bother,' he muttered tautly. 'You know...' he sat on the side of the long conference table '...I came here thinking this was just going to be another routine job, the usual buying and exchanging of contracts—no one warned me I was going to have to deal with the Calendar Mob!' He shook his head self-disgustedly.

May gave a throaty chuckle. 'We try to keep that one quiet!'

'Your secret is out,' Max informed her dryly. 'And for some reason my employer, Jude Marshall, thinks you're three little old ladies who sit and knit bedsocks in front of the fire on cold winter evenings!' He shook his head derisively.

'Really?' May said interestedly. 'Perhaps Mr Marshall should come here and do his own dirty work,' she suggested grimly.

'Perhaps he should.' Max nodded; the same idea had occurred to him during the last few hours!

'In the meantime—' May's gaze had became suddenly intent '—don't hurt my sister, Mr Golding,' she told him softly. 'January has already been hurt enough, without adding you to the list!'

Max looked at her sharply. 'What do you mean?' Had there already been someone in January's life, some man, who had let her down and hurt her? Somehow the thought of that did not please him one little bit!

'Never mind.' May gave an enigmatic shake of her head. 'Unless your intentions are serious— Are they?' She looked at him with narrowed eyes.

His mouth tightened. 'No,' he bit out harshly.

'As I thought.' She gave an acknowledging inclination of her head, picking up her bag in preparation of leaving. 'Then my advice to you is to leave January alone.'

'And if I don't?' he challenged warily.

May shrugged. 'Then the Calendar Mob will have to pay you another visit!'

Max couldn't help it, he smiled. 'I wish I had had a sister like you to look out for me when I was younger!' Instead he had been an only child, brought up alone by his father, a man who had also never trusted in love again.

But who, by that single act, had died alone, too…?

May gave him a rueful grimace. 'Somehow, Max, I doubt you've ever let anyone do that,' she murmured enigmatically. 'Now, if you will excuse me? I've said all I came here to say.' She walked over to the door, quietly letting herself out.

Now exactly what had she meant by that last remark? Max wondered frowningly. Had May guessed at the barrier he kept firmly around his heart? If so, how had she guessed?

Not that it particularly mattered; her message concerning January had come across loud and clear.

Well, May Calendar needn't worry herself on his account; he had no intention of ever putting himself in a position of being close to January again. She was a definite no-no as far as he was concerned.

Except he couldn't stop himself wondering about the implication May had given of some man having hurt January in the recent past…

CHAPTER SEVEN

'WHAT do you want?' January gasped, having opened the farmhouse door to find Max standing on the door-step beside her muddy boots.

It was barely thirty-six hours since she had last seen this man, the memory of Sunday evening not even having begun to fade from her mind—in fact, she doubted it ever would. Although she was certainly going to try to erase it!

She certainly didn't welcome the fact that Max had turned up at the farm when she was alone, March out at work, May having an appointment in town.

'I asked what you want,' she repeated hardly as Max made no effort to answer her, just standing on the door-step staring at her, his face grim, a guarded look in those deep blue eyes.

'Are you okay?' he finally murmured harshly.

January gave him a scathing look. 'Why shouldn't I be okay?' she scorned derisively.

Surely he didn't think she would still be visibly upset about Sunday evening? If he did, he was going to be sadly disappointed! She had made a mistake, had to-tally humiliated herself as far as she was concerned, but there was no way she was going to let anyone see that. Certainly not Max. She had more pride than that.

Max thrust his hands into his denims pockets, the grimness of his expression not having eased in the slightest. 'It was on the television, on the local news, that there was another attack late last night,' he bit out tautly.

Her eyes widened. She hadn't heard anything about that. But then, she didn't have time to watch television in the day, and it was too early for March to have returned from work with any local gossip.

'And?' she prompted hardly.

He swallowed hard, grimacing. 'They are being particularly cagey about this one, not giving out any names, or other details, just that the latest victim had been badly beaten but was recovering in hospital.'

January glared her impatience. 'And?' Really, why didn't he just say what he had come here to say—and then leave? 'I'm really sorry there's been another attack, hope that the woman will be okay, but if you've come here to discuss buying the farm—'

'I haven't come here for that!' he cut in harshly, a nerve pulsing in his tightly clenched jaw.

She gave a puzzled shake of her head. 'Then why are you here?'

'Isn't it obvious?' he snapped frustratedly.

Not to her, no. He had made it clear on Sunday evening—painfully clear, she recalled with an inner wince—that other than wanting to buy the farm he had no personal interest in her than as a possible casual bed-partner. A role she had made clear was completely unacceptable to her.

'I'm afraid not.' She gave a puzzled shake of her head.

Max gave a sigh of impatience. 'Haven't you been listening to a word I said?'

She gave a humourless smile. 'When usually most people hang on your every word?'

He scowled darkly. 'January, I'm more than aware of your opinion of me—'

'I doubt that very much!' she scorned; he couldn't possibly know how angry she still was. With him. But more so with herself.

She had been so careful after the mistake she had made the previous year, been friendly but distant to any man who might have shown an interest in her, hadn't even been out on a date since Ben had let her down so badly—only to end up making a complete idiot of herself over a man who was ten times more dangerous—to her heart!—than Ben had ever been!

Max gave the ghost of a smile. 'Oh, I think I am. But I heard that radio announcement and I— Where are March and May?'

'March is at work and May is at the dentist,' she dismissed.

He nodded grimly at this explanation for her sisters' absence.

'Obviously I made a mistake,' he dismissed hardly, preparing to leave.

January looked at him frowningly as he began to walk back to his car. He was arrogant. Hateful. Had hurt her pretty badly on Sunday evening. But the things he had said just now… Could he possibly—? Had he come here because—?

'Would you like to come in for a cup of coffee?' she heard herself offer abruptly.

Max turned slowly back to look at her, his expression once again wary. 'In the circumstances, that's very kind of you,' he finally murmured slowly.

She gave a shrug. 'Didn't you know—? I'm a kind person!' she attempted to dismiss lightly.

Whereas, in reality, she had no idea why she had

offered him a cup of coffee. It certainly wasn't because she wanted to spend any time in his company; she usually came off worst in any encounter the two of them had, verbal or otherwise!

Then why had she made the offer? Perhaps because she suspected, from the things Max had said, that he had come here because he had thought it was either her, or one of her sisters, who had been attacked the previous night. And if that were the case…

'The offer is only open for another ten seconds, Max,' she told him derisively. 'My toes are starting to freeze standing here!' she added with a rueful glance down at her feet.

Max looked down, too, the frown clearing from his brow. 'You really were serious about the bare feet, weren't you?' he murmured incredulously as he followed her into the kitchen, closing the door—and the extreme cold—behind him.

January glanced back from placing the kettle on the Aga. 'I don't tell lies, either, Max,' she told him huskily.

And then wished she hadn't. Whether her suspicion as to why he had come here was correct or not, she would rather not think of any of their previous conversations. Or anything else!

'If you must know, my feet are bare because I was just on my way to my bedroom for a pair of dry socks when you knocked on the door; I was coming back from the barn when I slipped and fell into a snowdrift. The snow went in my boots,' she explained abruptly.

Max raised dark brows. 'Are you always this accident prone? First a ditch and now a snowdrift,' he added mockingly.

'Hmm.' She grimaced. 'I do seem to have bumped

into more than my fair share of immovable objects just recently, don't I?' she dismissed self-derisively.

Max being the prime one!

Something that he seemed all too aware of as his mouth tightened. 'January—'

'Sit down, Max,' she invited with a general wave in the direction of the kitchen table and chairs. 'Coffee is almost ready.' She turned back to the task in hand, deliberately keeping herself busy for the next few minutes, although she was very aware of Max as he sat at the table watching her every move.

Why had he come here today? Was it really, as she suspected, because he had been concerned that one of the sisters might have been the Night Striker's latest victim? But if that were the reason, wouldn't that have to mean that he actually cared—?

'Did May tell you that she came to see me on Sunday evening?'

'Yes, she told me,' January confirmed lightly, picking up the two mugs of coffee before strolling over to place one of them in front of Max and sitting down opposite him. 'Help yourself to sugar.' She indicated the bowl that stood in the middle of the table. 'Since our mother died, May has been the family champion, I'm afraid.' The lightness of her tone totally belied the fact that she had been furious with May when she'd returned on Sunday evening and admitted where she had been.

Max gave a humourless smile. 'She certainly did a good job of warning me off you!'

'A little too late, obviously.' She nodded, staring down at her steaming mug of coffee.

May had been protecting March and January for as long as the two of them could remember, the two younger sisters, as they'd got older, often finding this fierce protectiveness irksome to say the least. January had been so furious at May's uninvited intervention on her behalf on Sunday evening that the two sisters had only just started speaking to each other again.

Although, to give Max his due, he obviously hadn't told her sister what had happened between the two of them a couple of hours before May's arrival at the hotel.

'When did your mother die?' Max prompted huskily.

January looked up. 'I was three, so…twenty-two years ago now,' she acknowledged with a pained frown.

Max frowned darkly. 'That must have been—' He shook his head. 'I was five when my mother left,' he said abruptly.

And as instantly regretted the admission, January could see by the surprise in his eyes he wasn't quick enough to hide, his expression becoming guarded. Making January wonder if he had ever confided that to anyone before today. Max certainly didn't come across as a man who was comfortable confiding his personal life to other people.

'Shouldn't you go and put something on your feet?' he prompted with unwarranted harshness.

'Yes, I should,' January acknowledged lightly, standing up. 'I won't be long,' she told him as she left the room.

But long enough to give him chance to put his defences back in order; the last thing she needed was to feel any sort of empathy with Max Golding—worse, to actually feel sorry for him!

He wouldn't welcome the emotion anyway. Any

more than he would welcome having her in love with him.

Which, she now realised, despite all those hateful things he had said to her on Sunday evening, she most certainly was.

May, it seemed, had given her warning of caution to the wrong person!

What was he doing here? Max questioned himself impatiently as January left the kitchen. He had known as soon as January had opened the door to his knock that she wasn't the woman who had been attacked last night, so why hadn't he just made his excuses and left?

Because he couldn't! Because he had had one hell of a scare this morning when he'd heard that television announcement about the attacker's latest victim being in hospital! Because just seeing January standing on the doorstep, so obviously alive and well, meant he hadn't been able to drag himself away from just looking at her!

Although why on earth he had compounded that by telling her about his mother, he had no idea!

He never talked about his mother's desertion. Never told anyone of the effect it had had on him. It simply wasn't good enough to claim he had merely been returning January's confidence about her own mother. Her mother had died, for goodness' sake, not walked out on her!

He had to get away from here. Had to go. Now!

But before he could even stand up to leave the outside door opened and May walked in, her eyes widening in surprise as she saw him sitting comfortably ensconced at the kitchen table. Although she recovered well, he thought, that obvious look of surprise turning into a polite smile of enquiry.

'January is upstairs putting on dry socks,' he told her dryly.

Dark brows rose over mocking green eyes. 'What did she do with the last pair?' May drawled, taking off her jacket to hang it on the back of the kitchen door.

'Fell in a snowdrift,' Max supplied wryly.

'Ah,' May nodded, obviously not in the least surprised by the explanation. 'Can I get you another cup of coffee, or are you okay?' she offered as she boiled up some water for her own hot drink.

'I'm fine, thanks,' Max dismissed. 'How did your check-up go?'

May turned to him with a puzzled frown. 'Sorry?'

'January said you were at the dentist,' he explained.

'Ah.' May nodded. 'It was fine,' she added dismissively, busying herself making her cup of coffee.

Max's gaze narrowed shrewdly as he continued to watch her. He hadn't missed May's complete puzzlement at his mention of a check-up, or the fact that her gaze hadn't quite met his when she'd answered him; if May Calendar had been to the dentist then his name wasn't Maxim Patrick Golding!

Which begged the question, where had May really been? And why had she lied to January about it?

Not that it was really any of his business, but—

'May!' January greeted more than a little self-consciously as she came back into the kitchen and found her sister there. 'How did—?'

'We've already done the dentist bit,' Max cut in derisively. 'Your sister's teeth are as healthy as yours,' he added huskily, knowing as he saw January's confused blush that his barb had hit home, that she remembered as well as he did the nip she had given him on the shoulder on Sunday evening with those healthy teeth, as he'd kissed and caressed her breasts.

What January couldn't know was that he still had a bruise on his shoulder as proof of those healthy teeth!

The blush deepened in January's cheeks even as she shot him a warning look.

Ah, so the protective May still didn't know what had happened between January and himself on Sunday evening!

Not that he was exactly proud of himself for the way things had got so out of hand that evening. Or the way he had deliberately made light of it to January afterwards…!

Because, no matter what he might have said to her, he hadn't slept at all on Sunday night. Last night either, for that matter. Instead he had lain awake both those nights arguing with himself. Half of him had wanted to tell January that he hadn't meant any of the hurtful things he had said to her, that it had been pure defence on his part. But the other half of him knew that he would be admitting so much more than that if he were to tell her those things. And that he simply couldn't— wouldn't!—do.

The television announcement this morning about yet another attack had been his undoing, though; the thought that it might be January lying in that hospital bed, battered and bruised, had been enough to throw him into a panic.

Not that coming to the farm had been his first instinct. No, he had telephoned the police first, who had refused to give out any information whatsoever about the attack, least of all the victim's name. The hospital had been no more forthcoming, either. Leaving him no choice—unless he wanted to just sit and go quietly out of his mind with worry!—but to come to the farm.

But now that he was here, could see for himself that January was unharmed, he really had no idea what he was still doing here.

Or how to make a dignified exit!

'I should be going—'

'Don't feel you have to leave on my account,' May drawled as she leant back against the Aga, coffee mug in her hand as she looked across at him with mocking green eyes.

His mouth tightened. 'I'm sure I've kept you both from your work enough for one day,' he insisted hardly.

'It can wait.' May shrugged. 'No matter how hard or how long you work on a farm, Max, there's always more to be done,' she added ruefully.

He frowned. 'In that case—'

'That doesn't mean we're interested in selling it,' January told him harshly.

Max looked across at her calmly. 'I was actually going to say, why don't you get someone in to help you if there's so much to do?'

'Good question,' May derided.

'It isn't good at all!' January corrected snappily. 'There's the little problem of paying someone to help.' She turned on Max sharply. 'Something, it must be obvious even to you, that we aren't in a position to do.'

'January...' May rebuked softly. 'Max was only asking,' she reasoned gently before turning to give Max a rueful smile. 'We did have some help last year after— after our father died,' she explained huskily. 'It didn't work out.' She shrugged.

He couldn't help noticing that January looked rather

pale now, May's gaze once again evasive, making him wonder in what way it hadn't worked out.

He shrugged. 'It was just a thought.'

'A totally impractical one,' January snapped scornfully. 'Although that must be rather good for you to hear,' she continued scathingly. 'After all, it would suit your plans perfectly if we were forced into selling the farm because we simply couldn't manage it any more!'

'January—'

'Don't be fooled by him for a minute, May,' January harshly interrupted her sister's reasoning tone. 'Max—and the Marshall Corporation—would like nothing better than for us to fall flat on our faces! Well, dream on, Max!' she told him forcefully. 'You will never get your mercenary hands on our farm! Now, if you'll excuse me,' she added hardly, grabbing her coat from the back of one of the chairs. 'You can stay and talk to him if you want to, May, but I have work to do!'

The room seemed to reverberate as she slammed the door behind her, May's wince matching Max's as he glanced across at her ruefully.

'What did you do to upset her this time?' May mused with a grimace.

'Do I need to ''do'' anything in order to upset January?' he came back wryly.

'Probably not,' May sighed.

'That's what I thought.' He nodded, his gaze narrowing. 'What was his name?' he rasped.

May looked at him undecidedly for several long seconds, and then she gave a rueful shrug. 'Ben,' she supplied economically.

His admiration for this woman seemed to grow by the minute. She had obviously taken over the role of mother to her two younger sisters while only aged five or six, still a baby herself, in fact, was possessed of a lively intelligence, and her beauty was of the inner as well as outer kind.

'Thank you.' He gave an acknowledging inclination of his head.

May frowned. 'For what?'

'For not insulting my intelligence by denying there was a "he",' Max drawled. 'That "he" was the hired help you had here last summer. I'm also guessing it's the same "he" who hurt January. The same "he" who prompted your warning me off her on Sunday evening,' he added ruefully.

'What would be the point in my denying any of that?' May shrugged. 'I realized on Sunday evening that I had probably said more than I should have done.' She sighed self-disgustedly. 'You're an intelligent man—'

'Thank you again,' he drawled dryly.

'That doesn't mean I like you!' she snapped, green eyes flashing a warning.

'That's a pity...' he smiled ruefully '...because I like you,' he explained at her questioning glance. 'Oh, not in that way,' he assured her as her glance became sceptical. 'One Calendar sister, I've discovered, is one too many!'

'I'm glad about that,' May drawled. 'Max, what are you doing with my little sister?'

He sighed, that sigh quickly becoming a grimace. 'How the hell should I know?' he murmured heavily.

She laughed incredulously. 'Well, if you don't know I certainly don't!'

What *was* he doing? January had made it more than clear when they'd parted on Sunday that she never intended seeing him again through choice, and he knew her well enough to believe she meant it.

So instead the mountain had come to Mohammed. Because he had feared for January's safety after hearing about the latest attack.

But he could have picked up the telephone, called the farm, then any one of the sisters could have given him that information.

Instead he had chosen to drive out here in order to see for himself that January was safe and well.

Why?

'Have you worked it out yet, Max?'

He looked sharply across at May, her too-innocent expression belied by the laughter gleaming in those intelligent green eyes.

'Tell you what,' she continued lightly. 'Go back to your hotel for a few hours, give January chance to calm down,' she added wryly. 'And then come back here this evening and have dinner with us.'

Max's gaze narrowed on her suspiciously. Why was May inviting him to dinner? She had no more reason to trust him than did her sisters...

May laughed softly at his obvious confusion. 'Mark it down as a thank-you for preventing me from telling another lie earlier—when January was about to ask me about my dental appointment,' she told him huskily.

So he had been right about that. He could also see that May wasn't about to confide in him, of all people, exactly where she had been, or who she had really seen this morning.

He grimaced. 'January isn't going to thank you for inviting me to dinner.'

May shrugged. 'If you hadn't noticed, my youngest sister isn't very happy with me at the moment, any-

way.' She sighed. 'My consorting with the enemy isn't
going to make that any worse than it already is!'

Max winced. 'The enemy? Is that really how you all
see me?'

It wasn't a very pleasant feeling, he had to admit.
Oh, not all of the deals he had completed on Jude's
behalf over the years had been easy, or indeed amicable, but he had never actually seen himself as the enemy before!

It wasn't a feeling he liked.

'Come to dinner, Max,' May dismissed laughingly.
'I'm cooking roast chicken,' she told him enticingly.
'I'm sure a home-cooked meal isn't something you
have too often,' she added ruefully.

This woman, Max was slowly realizing, saw altogether too much. God help the man who tried to make
her his own!

CHAPTER EIGHT

'YOU'VE done what?' January stared at her eldest sister incredulously.

'I said you need to lay four places at the table for dinner because I've invited Max to eat with us this evening,' May repeated calmly as she continued to stir the gravy. 'In fact, he should be here any minute.'

That was what January had thought she'd said! 'Have you gone completely mad, May?' she gasped.

May grimaced. 'Not as far as I'm aware, no. Look,' her sister continued firmly as she could see January was about to disagree with her, 'isn't it better to—to, well, get to know Max a little, let him get to know us in return? It's much harder to walk all over someone if you actually know them personally,' she reasoned impatiently as January continued to look furious.

January gave a disgusted snort. 'Max doesn't seem to be having too much trouble with that so far!'

She really couldn't believe May had invited Max to dinner. Or that Max had accepted the invitation...!

He had to know, couldn't fail to appreciate, that he was as welcome here as a rampaging bull! That he actually proposed to be more destructive than that bull!

As for May...!

'I think you're wrong about that, January,' her sister said consideringly. 'In fact, I sense a distinct wavering in his resolve to get us out of here,' she added happily.

January shook her head. 'Then you can see more than I can! March is going to think you've gone completely off your trolley, too,' she assured her with satisfaction.

Her eldest sister shrugged. 'Let's just wait and see, shall we?' she murmured enigmatically.

'You can, if you like,' January snapped, pointedly laying three places at the table. 'I would rather eat out!'

'January—'

'Whew, what a lousy evening!' March complained as she swept into the kitchen, bringing a blast of cold air and falling snow in with her. 'And talking of lousy evenings—look who I met outside!' She stepped aside to reveal Max standing in the doorway behind her.

January stared at him, still unable to believe May seriously expected her to calmly sit down and eat dinner with him. Or that he should dare to sit down to dinner with them!

Was he so insensitive? Could he not see how unwelcome he was here? Could he not see how much she didn't want him here?

'Shut the door, for goodness' sake,' May advised briskly. 'It looks as if it's getting worse out there,' she added frowningly after glancing out of the kitchen window.

'It is,' March confirmed ruefully. 'I wouldn't send a dog out there again tonight,' she added dryly, raising mocking brows in Max's direction. 'Do you intend staying long, Mr Golding?' she prompted pointedly.

Trust March to get straight to the heart of the matter, January acknowledged admiringly, at the same time shooting May a triumphant look.

'Max is my guest, March,' May reproved softly.

'Really?' March looked impressed.

Impressed wasn't exactly the way January felt about this situation! Although March's comment about the worsening weather pretty well put paid to her own idea of going out for the evening!

'In that case, I had better go up and change before dinner,' March taunted.

'Don't bother on my account.' Max spoke for the first time since his arrival. 'May assured me it would be an informal evening,' he added with a glance down at his own casual trousers and what looked like a blue cashmere sweater beneath his thick outer jacket.

The humour increased in March's hazel grey-green eyes. 'I'm going to dress down, Mr Golding, not up,' she told him laughingly before leaving the room.

'Keep an eye on the gravy for me, will you, January?' May asked distractedly as she followed March up the stairs.

Leaving January completely alone in the kitchen with Max. Great! Just what she had wanted!

'Did May tell you I would be here this evening?' he prompted, his sharp gaze passing briefly over the three places set at the table.

January glared at him. 'We were just—discussing it, when you arrived,' she bit out tautly.

His mouth twisted self-derisively. 'What you really mean is that you were making it clear you aren't ex- actly thrilled at my coming here,' he accepted mock- ingly.

'You knew I wouldn't be,' she snapped impatiently, moving to noisily lay the missing fourth place at the table. 'How could you?' She turned to glare at him. 'What do you think you're hoping to achieve? Because May—bless her!—may have been won over by you, for some inexplicable reason, but I can assure you that March and I aren't fooled for a moment!'

He gave an admiring glance upstairs. 'She's something else, isn't she?' he murmured smilingly.

'May or March?' she challenged disgustedly.

'Both of them, actually.' He smiled. 'For different reasons, of course.'

'Oh, of course,' January agreed sarcastically—not having the least idea what he meant! She hardly knew May at the moment, so illogical was her behaviour, although March—thank goodness—was her usual sharp-tongued self.

'I bought a peace-offering.' Max held up the bottle of wine he had been holding the whole time he'd stood beside the closed kitchen door. 'May mentioned we were having chicken, so…' He moved to place the bottle of white wine on the table. 'It's already chilled enough,' he added dryly.

January looked at him frustratedly. 'Why are you here, Max?'

He shrugged. 'May invited me.'

She gave a dazed shake of her head. 'You know, when we were younger, I was always the one who brought home the wounded birds and animals, May was always the one who warned me they wouldn't survive away from their own environment. Their own kind,' she added pointedly.

His gaze was narrowed now, that nerve once again pulsing in his tightly clenched jaw. 'I hope you're not implying that I'm wounded in some way?' he finally bit out harshly.

Her eyes flashed impatiently. 'I was implying that you should stay with your own kind!' Obviously her sarcasm was completely lost on this man! But then, she hadn't had as much practice at it as March had. But that didn't mean she couldn't learn…

Max's brow cleared, his smile rueful now. 'And exactly what is my own kind, January?'

'Predatory!' she answered with satisfaction.

He gave a disarming grin. 'I have a feeling that any man would find himself completely outgunned—as well as outnumbered—by the three Calendar sisters!'

January did her best to maintain her furious expression—and failed miserably as her lips twitched and she began to smile, too. What was it about this man? How could she start off being angry or distant with him—usually angry!—and then end up grinning at him like an idiot? It didn't make any sense!

'January,' he murmured softly, crossing the room to stand in front of her, his hands moving up to gently cradle each side of her face as he looked down at her searchingly. 'I really thought it might have been you who was attacked last night,' he groaned huskily.

Her breath caught in her throat. 'And that would have bothered you?'

A frown darkened his brow. 'Of course it would have bothered me!' he rasped. 'You must have known that…?' He looked down at her frustratedly, fingers lightly caressing her brows.

She gave a shake of her head. 'I'm not sure what I know any more, Max. One minute you're—you're making love to me, and the next—! Well, we both know what happened next,' she remembered hardly, deliberately moving away, his hands falling back to his sides.

Just in time, as it happened, her two sisters coming back into the kitchen at that moment, May's sharp gaze instantly taking in the fact that the two of them stood well apart, the tension between them tangible.

'March was just telling me that there's been another

attack,' May said briskly as she moved to check the food cooking on top of the Aga.

'I meant to tell you earlier,' January groaned. 'But I—it slipped my mind.' She deliberately avoided looking at Max—because they both knew he was the reason she had forgotten to mention this latest attack to her sister.

'I meant to tell you all when I came in,' March muttered self-disgustedly. 'But for some reason it slipped my mind, too.' She gave Max a pointed grimace, having changed into black denims and a bright orange jumper, the latter eye-catching, to say the least.

'There seems to be a lot of it about,' Max murmured appreciatively.

'Yes,' March drawled wryly.

'Tell them the worst part about it, March,' May encouraged impatiently.

'What—? Oh, yes.' March nodded. 'It was Josh,' she announced slightly incredulously.

'What was?' January prompted dazedly, still confused from having Max touch her in that way. Would she ever understand him?

'Josh…?' Max repeated slowly. 'The same Josh who is marrying your cousin—Sara, isn't it?—on Saturday?' He looked accusingly at January, the sharpness of that gaze reminding her that it was the same Josh who had kissed her on Saturday evening!

'That's the one,' March confirmed. 'Although I'm not sure if the wedding will still be going ahead, in the circumstances?' She looked across at May.

'I'll telephone Aunt Lyn in a moment.' May nodded. 'How awful for them all.' She shook her head distractedly.

'Hang on a minute,' January protested, having been

listening to this conversation with increasing incredulity.

She had known Josh most of her life, had, as she'd told Max on Saturday, been at school with him, and while there was no doubting Josh could be a little boisterous at times, liked to have fun, he also didn't have a vicious bone in his body.

'They have to have the wrong man.' She shook her head dismissively. 'Josh isn't capable of attacking anyone, let alone seven women.'

'Oh, no, you misunderstood me,' March apologized with a grimace. 'Josh was the one who was attacked,' she explained disgustedly. 'Beaten up pretty badly, from what I gather.'

What the hell—?

Now Max was as confused as January looked. Although, he had to admit, a few seconds ago he had been angry with her at her defence of the other man...!

'But he's a man!' January burst out incredulously.

As well she might. As far as Max had been able to gather—although, having been out of the country for several months, he was obviously a latecomer to these random attacks—all the other victims had been women.

'Are they sure it was the Night Striker?' He frowned his own puzzlement.

'Positive,' March confirmed, seeming to have forgotten her antagonism towards him—for the moment. 'Same M.O., or whatever they call it.' She grimaced.

'*Modus operandi,*' Max murmured frowningly. 'Latin,' he explained as he glanced up to find all three sisters looking at him.

March nodded, her gaze mocking. 'Being a lawyer, you would know that.'

His mouth twisted. 'I wouldn't be a very good one if I didn't.'

'And we're all sure that you're very good,' March taunted.

'Thank you,' he accepted dryly, easily guessing it wasn't meant as a compliment; March was more sharp-tongued than he was himself. 'I accept that the method may be the same,' he acknowledged slowly. 'But the fact that the victim was a man this time makes it totally different.'

In fact, it didn't make much sense to him. Okay, so the last six victims, all women, had been badly beaten rather than raped, but that still didn't explain why it had been a man who was attacked this time... The good-natured Josh, of all people. No wonder the police were being a little cagey about the information they gave out!

'Sara must be so upset,' January said worriedly.

As Max might have known she would; of the three sisters, January was definitely the most empathetic.

'If none of you mind waiting for dinner, I'll tele-phone Aunt Lyn now and see how Josh is. And Sara, of course,' May murmured distractedly before leaving the room.

'And I'll open the wine,' Max suggested briskly, seeing that a certain amount of shock was starting to set in with all the sisters now; hearing of the attacks the last six months couldn't have been very pleasant, having it arrive on their own doorstep, so to speak, must be even more shocking. 'Could you get me a corkscrew, January?' he said briskly as neither sister moved.

'Oh. Of course.' She moved frowningly to one of

the drawers, taking out the corkscrew to hand it to him distractedly.

'And some glasses, March?' he prompted lightly as he deftly removed the cork.

March blinked, her smile derisive as she seemed to guess what he was doing. 'Certainly, sir,' she drawled, reaching up to take four wineglasses from one of the cabinets.

'Thank you,' Max accepted dryly, starting to pour the wine.

'You're welcome,' March derided. 'Mmm,' she murmured appreciatively after her first sip of the wine. 'Just what we need to cheer us all up.'

'Maybe I should have brought two bottles,' Max teased.

'Maybe you should.' March nodded, grey-green eyes dancing with humour.

'January?' Max prompted as she made no effort to pick up one of the glasses.

In fact, she seemed totally distracted, he acknowledged with a searching frown, her face unnaturally pale, her eyes so deep a grey they looked almost black.

It was awful that their cousin's future husband had been the Night Striker's latest victim, but unless Max was mistaken, January seemed more stunned by it than her sisters…?

'I still can't believe it.' She shook her head before picking up her glass of wine and taking a sip.

For all the notice she took of its delicate taste and fragrance he might as well have brought a bottle of cheap plonk!

'There must have been some sort of mistake,' January said. 'I can't believe anyone could have deliberately set out to hurt Josh. He's just so nice, so un-

assuming; as far as I'm aware, he doesn't have an enemy in the world—' She broke off, a stricken look on
her face now as she slowly turned to look at Max.

It was a look Max didn't like one little bit!

Surely January couldn't think—didn't believe—

'January?' he prompted harshly.

'Yes?' She swallowed hard, looking more bewil-
dered than ever now.

'March, would you leave us for a few minutes?' Max
requested, his gaze still fixed icily on January.

'January?' March prompted softly.

'I—yes. Fine.' January nodded dazedly, her gaze
studiously avoiding Max's now.

'In that case, I think I'll go and see how May is
getting on,' March drawled before leaving.

Max moved to stand in front of January, his hand
under her chin as he tilted her face up to his, forcing
her to look at him. And he didn't like what he saw in
her eyes!

'You don't seriously think *I* had anything to do with
this attack on Josh?' he rasped disbelievingly.

Because he could clearly see that the possibility had
definitely crossed her mind—if only briefly!

Although it was starting to fade now, that bewilderment fading from her eyes, too. To be replaced by self-
derision. 'No, of course I don't.' She gave a firm shake
of her head. 'Of course not,' she added more strongly.

His hands moved to her shoulders as he shook her
slightly. 'I bought the man a drink, for goodness' sake,'
he ground out. 'He bought me one, too!' He tightened his hands painfully on her shoulders, furious that
the thought could have crossed her mind, even for a
minute.

But he knew that it had, no matter what January might claim to the contrary.

And could he really blame her? He had been blowing hot and cold with her from the moment they'd met, his actions appearing completely illogical. One evening he had been prepared to knock Josh to the ground for daring to kiss January, and the next evening, following his discovery of exactly who she was, of how dangerous she was to his own personal equilibrium, he had mocked her for responding to him. Not exactly consistent, was he?

Nevertheless, he found her suspicion of him, even for that brief moment, very unsettling... And hurtful...?

January was smiling now, albeit ruefully. 'No doubt that alone was enough to make the two of you bosom buddies!'

His mouth tightened. 'Not necessarily,' he allowed, realizing how ridiculous his claim must have sounded; the fact that the two had bought each other a drink did not change the fact that seconds earlier Max had been about to hit the other man! His hands dropped away from her shoulders as he stepped back. 'No matter what you may think to the contrary, I am not a violent man. Perhaps I had better leave—'

'Please don't leave on my account,' January cut in awkwardly. 'I—I'm sorry.' She pushed the darkness of her hair back from her face. 'I'm just a little—upset.' She grimaced.

He could see that, and he was sorry for it. But, at the moment, he had to admit to being just a little upset himself! With himself, mainly, for having behaved in such a way as to have given January even the briefest of doubts where he was concerned.

He shook his head. 'I still think it might be better if I left—'

'Who's leaving?' March prompted lightly as she came back into the room.

'I am,' Max told her forcefully. 'I believe I've already outstayed my welcome!' he added hardly.

March grimaced as she gave a shake of her head. 'That may or may not be the case, but I somehow don't think you'll be leaving us just yet,' she informed him ruefully. 'I just listened to the news on television; the snowstorm has turned into a blizzard,' she explained at his questioning look. 'They are advising all drivers in the area to stay at home, if at all possible.'

Home.

It was a long time since he had had one of those. If, indeed, he ever really had. But the Calendar farm was certainly far from being that to him!

'I'm afraid March is right, Max,' May assured him as she came back into the room. 'I asked Aunt Lyn if it was possible for us to visit Josh later this evening. She assured me that it was, but that there had been a warning given out for people not to travel. March turned on the news and—I'm afraid you won't be going anywhere tonight, Max,' she informed him lightly.

His narrowed gaze moved questioningly to January—just in time for him to see the look of dismay on her face she wasn't quick enough to hide!

CHAPTER NINE

'THIS is really very good of you.'

January turned to look at Max as he stood in the doorway watching her make up the bed he was to sleep in.

And it wasn't very good of her at all. She knew it wasn't. And so did he.

She still couldn't believe those brief feelings of suspicion she had had about him earlier. Worse, couldn't believe she had let Max see those suspicions.

Of course he wasn't responsible for the attack on Josh. Yes, Max had been angry at the younger man on Saturday when Josh had dared to kiss her, had looked more than capable of hitting Josh when he'd pulled him away from January. But on Sunday evening, the very next day, Max had made it more than plain that she would never be more than a brief flirtation to him. Rather nullifying any feelings of violence he might have previously felt towards Josh!

She drew in a deep breath before straightening, facing Max across the width of her father's bedroom. 'I really do apologise for—well, for any thoughts I may have had earlier—'

'That I'm the person who attacked Josh?' Max finished scathingly as he strolled further into the room. 'If it makes you feel any better, January, I'm sure the police will have been informed about my—little disagreement, with Josh on Saturday evening, and will be following it up accordingly. They will no doubt be questioning me about the incident,' he explained dryly as she looked puzzled.

January could feel her cheeks paling. She hadn't thought of that.

How awful.

But no more awful, surely, than those brief suspicions she had had concerning Max?

'Was this your father's bedroom?'

She turned back to Max, to see him looking interestedly around the room, her father's brush and comb set still on the dressing table, along with several paperback books, a photograph of the three sisters taking pride of place beside the clock on the bedside cabinet.

Max reached out to pick up the photograph, studying it for several long moments, before putting it carefully back in place. 'Cute,' he murmured.

January turned away. She had been feeling awkward with him all evening. As the four of them had eaten dinner together. As they'd turned the television on later that evening to listen to the weather forecast and heard that the blizzard had now spread over most of the country. The warning had been repeated about not travelling unless it was absolutely necessary, accompanied by several scenes where people hadn't heeded that warning, showing dozens of vehicles that had had to be abandoned.

The least she could do, January had decided, was to offer to make up Max's bed for the night.

'I hope you don't mind?' She indicated the bedroom. 'The only other bed we have available is in the small bedsit we had converted over the garage—and that hasn't been used since the summer.' She grimaced.

Max looked at her with narrowed eyes. 'That would

be the accommodation used by the help you had stay-ing last summer?'

January gave him a sharp look. How did he—? Of course, she and May had discussed that in front of him earlier today. Although she sensed more than casual interest in Max's remark...?

'Yes,' she confirmed slowly, watching him warily now.

His mouth twisted ruefully. 'I wouldn't have thought you would particularly care whether or not I froze to death over there.'

Of course she cared. Too much, as it happened.

She shrugged. 'That may be a little difficult to ex-plain to anyone who comes looking for you,' she re-turned tartly.

He grimaced. 'That's always supposing that some-one did.'

January gave a humourless smile. 'I'm sure Jude Marshall would wonder what had happened to his law-yer!'

Max had once again picked up the photograph of the three sisters, glancing across at her. 'He just might at that,' he conceded dryly. 'You were very young when this photograph was taken.' He frowned down at the image.

'About two and a half.' January nodded, strolling over to look down at the photograph. 'March was three and a half, May a little over four.'

'Three peas in a pod,' Max drawled, referring to what January had said was her father's description of them. 'There seems to be someone standing behind you,' he continued frowningly. 'There, you see.' He pointed to the hand resting on May's left shoulder and another on March's right, January sandwiched between

her two sisters. 'Your father?' he prompted interestedly.

She shook her head. 'My father took the photograph.'

Max looked even more puzzled. 'Then who——?'

'My mother,' she told him abruptly, taking the photograph out of his hand and returning it to its original
place on the bedside cabinet.

Max looked at her frowningly. 'Your mother?
But——'

'Can I get you anything else before I go to bed myself?' January cut in briskly. 'A cup of coffee?
Something else to eat?'

'No, thanks,' he answered slowly, once again looking at the photograph of the three sisters. 'Isn't that a
little strange?' he murmured softly. 'Why would your
mother have been cut from the photograph? Surely it
must have been one of the last pictures your father had
of the four of you together?'

'Probably, yes,' January confirmed sharply, not welcoming his questions.

Because she had asked her father the same question
once. His answer that the photograph wouldn't fit into
the frame if it wasn't cut down had seemed very
strange, even to an eight-year-old. But the look on her
father's face, almost of bewilderment, had been enough
for her never to ask about her mother again.

Max was looking at her searchingly now, his brow
clearing as he answered her previous question, 'I really
don't need anything else, thanks,' he repeated lightly.
'And don't worry, January,' he added dryly. 'I promise
I'll be out of your way as soon as the weather breaks.'

'That's good,' she answered distractedly, her expression instantly becoming stricken as she realized exactly what she had said. 'What I meant—'

'I know what you meant, January.' Max laughed softly, moving to stand in front of her, blue eyes gleaming with laughter. 'You meant exactly what you said!' He shook his head. 'And I can't say I exactly blame you,' he added ruefully. 'If I were in your shoes I would feel exactly the same way!'

This wasn't helping January in her efforts to dislike him! Neither was his close proximity!

But maybe May had been right after all; maybe getting to know them all personally—some more than others, January acknowledged with an inner wince!—was making this as difficult for Max as it was for them? She certainly hoped so!

'I'll see you in the morning,' she told him distantly as she moved away determinedly.

'Aren't you going to tuck me in and give me a good-night kiss?' Max prompted huskily.

'No,' she drawled, turning back to look at him, dark brows raised derisively. 'I'm not going to offer to read you a bedtime story, either!'

'Pity,' he teased, sitting down on the side of the double bed. 'I would like to come with you tomorrow, by the way,' he added seriously.

'Come with me where?' January was having a little trouble keeping up with the jumps in the conversation.

'To see Josh, of course,' he dismissed. 'You will be going in to see him tomorrow, won't you?'

'If the weather breaks,' she confirmed slowly. 'Max, are you sure it's a good idea for you—? What are you doing?' she gasped as he crossed the room in two strides, his fingers biting into her shoulders as he held her in front of him.

'January, I will tell you once more—and once more only!' he warned harshly, shaking her slightly, his eyes glittering darkly. 'I did not—I repeat, not!—have anything to do with the attack on Josh.'

'I don't— Max, you're hurting me!' she gasped at the pressure of his fingers against her shoulders.

He scowled darkly. 'At this moment I would like to very thoroughly beat you,' he told her gratingly. 'But as I've already assured you I am not a violent man—!' His mouth came down fiercely on hers.

His kiss was full of the anger he refused to express in any other way, and January met that anger with the tenderness she longed to give him but daredn't show him in any other way...

It was that tenderness that finally won through, Max groaning low in his throat, his hands cradling each side of her face as he now sipped from the softness of her lips.

Finally he raised his head, his forehead damp against hers as he looked down at her. 'You are the most extraordinary woman I have ever met,' he murmured dazedly.

January moistened her lips before answering, 'I am?'

'Hmm.' He nodded, grimacing slightly, obviously not at all happy with the fact. 'One moment you're thinking I'm some sort of crazed attacker, and the next you're kissing me—'

'Max, you didn't let me finish what I was going to say earlier,' she said huskily, one hand reaching up to briefly touch the hardness of his suddenly clenched jaw. 'I was merely going to ask whether, in the circumstances of your connection to the Marshall Corporation, it was wise for you to come with me to visit Josh. Whether you should become any more involved with my family,' she explained softly as he still frowned.

'I think your warning is probably a little late,' he acknowledged self-derisively. 'And I have every intention of going to see Josh. Maybe he got a look at the person who attacked him. Maybe—'

'Max, I'm sure the police are perfectly capable of dealing with that,' January cut in pointedly. 'After all, you're a lawyer, not a policeman,' she reasoned lightly.

He shook his head. 'There's something wrong with this attack on Josh. Something other than the fact that it was a man this time rather than a woman,' he added wryly at January's knowing look.

'Max—' She broke off as a knock sounded on the bedroom door.

Obviously one of her sisters. Probably wondering why it was taking her so long to make up the bed!

She gave Max a rueful grimace as she moved out of his arms. 'Come in,' she invited dryly, giving her eldest sister a knowing look as she opened the door. 'I was just making sure Max has everything he needs for the night,' she told May teasingly.

May's green gaze flickered reprovingly over Max before moving back to January. 'And does he?'

'As much as an unexpected guest can expect.' Max was the one to answer derisively.

May returned his gaze unblinkingly. 'If you want them, you will find some laundered pyjamas in the top drawer of the dresser.'

'I always sleep in the nude, but thanks anyway,' Max returned tauntingly.

May gave a tight smile. 'You might find the farmhouse a little cooler than you're used to.'

'Not so far,' he came back, dark brows raised challengingly.

'May, I think we'll leave Max to get settled for the night,' January cut in determinedly, having decided this verbal battle of wills had gone on long enough.

'We're usually all up by about six o'clock,' May told Max pointedly.

He nodded, blue eyes dancing with merriment. 'A cup of tea in bed about then will be very welcome!'

May gave a snort of dismissal. 'Guest or not, if we don't have that luxury, then neither do you!'

He shrugged. 'I would be quite happy to bring you all a cup of tea in bed.'

May's gaze narrowed. 'I'll just bet you would—'

'He's winding you up, May,' January cut in once again, shaking her head reprovingly at Max even as she chuckled softly. 'But if you should get the urge to make an early cup of tea, Max, we all take ours without sugar!' she added even as she pushed her sister towards the door. 'You were the one who invited him here in the first place,' she reminded May lightly once they were outside the bedroom, the door safely closed behind them.

'I may have done,' May snapped. 'But I told you why that was. I certainly didn't think he had the nerve to try to seduce my little sister right under my nose!' she added indignantly.

'Your little sister is twenty-five years old,' January reminded her dryly. 'And I'm more than capable of taking care of myself.'

May shook her head. 'Not where Max Golding is concerned, I've just realized,' she said slowly. 'January, are you serious—?'

'Could we leave this for tonight, May?' she cut in

firmly, her earlier humour having completely disappeared. 'I'm really not in the mood to discuss Max any more tonight,' she added heavily.

May looked at her searchingly for several long minutes, before slowly nodding her head. 'Okay,' she agreed huskily. 'But just—never mind.' She shook her head, smiling. 'Everything will look different in the morning,' she added brightly.

January was glad her sister had said different, and not better. Because somehow January doubted it would be that. In the morning she would still be in love with Max. And that couldn't be good. For any of them.

Considering he had doubted that he would sleep at all, with January so close and yet so unattainable, Max found he had slept for almost eight hours, a glance at his wrist-watch telling him it was almost seven o'clock.

Way past time for taking January—or anyone else!—a cup of tea in bed!

He smiled as he imagined May's indignation if he had arrived in the sisters' bedrooms with the suggested morning tea. Whatever had prompted the eldest Calendar sister to invite him to dinner last night, May had definitely changed her mind about the wisdom of that invitation by the time she'd come looking for January in this bedroom later in the evening.

Wisely so, Max acknowledged with a self-derisive grimace.

No matter what he did, how hard he tried to keep a distance between himself and January, to concentrate on the business side of their relationship rather than the personal, he invariably ended up kissing her instead!

Maybe—

He heard a door slam downstairs, followed by muffled noises outside, evidence that the sisters were indeed up and about. And May, at least, was no doubt frowning disapprovingly about his own tardiness in getting up!

She was also right about the coldness of the farmhouse, he discovered a few minutes later as he hurriedly dressed before going to the bathroom across the hall, the tiles in there ultra cold on his sock-covered feet.

And the most he had to compare this cold discomfort with was the times he went skiing, when he spent his evenings and nights in a wonderfully warm ski lodge, his days wrapped up warmly as he skied the slopes. Hardly any comparison at all!

You're getting soft, Golding, he told himself disgustedly, at the same time acknowledging that he was ill-equipped to survive in conditions like these. Which also made him wonder why on earth the Calendar sisters would want to…!

Only May and March were in evidence when he entered the kitchen a few minutes later, this room much warmer than the rest of the house, Max realized thankfully.

'Coffee?' March offered abruptly as she held up the steaming pot invitingly.

'Thanks.' He nodded distractedly, aware of May's brooding silence as she sat at the kitchen table drinking her own warm brew, studiously ignoring him, it seemed.

'Help yourself to milk and sugar,' March told him dismissively as she placed a mug of coffee on the table for him. 'In case you're wondering, January is over in the shed dealing with early milking,' she added dryly.

Was he really that obvious? Max wondered with a

scowl. Probably, he conceded heavily. To January's sisters, at least...

'Now that we've cleared the drifts away from the doors and a path over to the shed,' May put in pointedly.

While he lingered in his bed trying to build up the courage to get out of the warmth of the bedclothes into the cold of the room, May implied, but didn't actually say.

'Is there anything I can do to help?' he offered— and as quickly realized how ridiculous he sounded; what on earth did he know about any of the workings of a farm?

March obviously found the offer just as ridiculous, giving a wry smile. 'Stay out of everyone's way?' she suggested scathingly.

Feeling inadequate did not sit easily on Max's shoulders; having it pointed out to him by the more outspoken of the Calendar sisters only made it worse!

He stood up noisily. 'I think I'll just go over anyway and see if there's anything I can do for January.'

May sat back, looking at him derisively. 'I think you've already done enough for her, don't you?' she murmured enigmatically.

Max's gaze narrowed on her speculatively as he pulled on his heavy jacket. Obviously whatever headway he had made with May yesterday had been completely voided by having January linger in the bedroom with him last night, May definitely back to her old protective self.

Family disapproval was also something Max had never encountered before—mainly because he had never so much as suggested meeting any of the family of the women he had been involved with over the years!

God, he really had to get out of here. And not just the farmhouse, either!

Which may prove a little difficult, he discovered on opening the door; May really hadn't been joking about the snowdrifts! They were as high as four feet along the side of the shed and the hedgerow of the track up here to the house.

'Our uncle—Sara's father—is going to come up from the road and clear it later this morning,' March assured him with a mocking grin—obviously having enjoyed the look of dismay on his face for several minutes first.

Max didn't even bother to reply as he closed the door behind him, pausing in the porch to pull on his walking boots before staggering across to the cow shed. And it really was staggering, the ground extremely slippery underfoot. But at least the snow seemed to have stopped falling.

Quite what he had expected once inside the shed, he really had no idea. But it certainly wasn't to hear the sounds of the electric milking machines—or to see January as he had never seen her before!

Faded denims were tucked into knee-high wellington boots, a coat that looked several sizes too big for her reaching warmly down to her knees, a scarf muffled up about her face, her ebony hair all but hidden beneath a multicoloured woolen hat.

Grey eyes—the only part of her face visible!—were full of laughter as she looked up and saw his astounded expression.

She pulled the scarf down from over her mouth,

grinning ruefully. 'See what I mean about the impracticality of love at first sight!' she derided.

Max recovered quickly, the beautiful grey eyes the same, as was her smile. 'This certainly beats the toothpaste tube and the bare feet,' he acknowledged dryly, moving further into the shed.

It was warmer in here than outside, probably because of the heat given off by the animals themselves. Although there were other disadvantages, the animals giving off a smell that was overwhelming.

He grimaced. 'May still seems a little—annoyed with me, this morning.'

'With you, too?' January shrugged. 'She'll get over it.'

Max was still curious as to where the elder Calendar sister had been when she'd claimed she was going to the dentist. But as neither of her sisters seemed to have the least suspicion, and May herself was completely unforthcoming, he didn't think he stood much chance of finding out.

'I'll be finished in here soon, if you would like to go back to the house,' January offered. 'Unless, of course, it really is a little too frosty over there?' She quirked dark brows teasingly.

'I'm sure I can cope,' Max drawled. 'But I'll wait for you, anyway.'

In actual fact, he quite enjoyed watching January's dexterous movements as she finished milking the first set of cows before moving on to the next.

He also couldn't help smiling as he imagined the faces of the guests staying at the hotel if they could see the glamorous singer from the piano-bar now. January's gorgeous figure was completely hidden in the bulky clothing she wore, and, as far as he could tell, she didn't have on even a dusting of make-up, not even a lip gloss.

And yet she was still beautiful to him, he realized somewhat dazedly. What was happening to him?

It certainly wasn't the right time for his mobile telephone to start ringing. Mainly because he could too easily guess who the caller was going to be!

Despite the time difference between here and America, Max knew from experience that Jude was a man who needed very little sleep—and who didn't appreciate that others might not be quite so fortunate!

'Shouldn't you get that?' January prompted curiously as he made no effort to take the intrusive telephone from his pocket.

He shrugged. 'If it's important, I'm sure they will call back.'

But as the telephone kept ringing Max was more convinced than ever that the caller had to be Jude; the other man really didn't take no for an answer! Besides, when hadn't Max been available to take Jude's calls?

He looked about his surroundings self-derisively. When standing in the middle of a cow shed, with the woman who was slowly driving him insane, that was when!

CHAPTER TEN

JANUARY gave an inner sigh of relief as Max's attention was distracted when he finally decided to answer the call. Despite her earlier self-derision, it had been very unnerving having him standing there watching her as she worked.

For one thing, for all this was her usual garb when she was working on the farm, she looked so unglamorous. For another, she was still so aware of the fact that she couldn't be alone with this man for longer than two minutes without ending up in his arms!

Not that she thought there was much chance of that happening at the moment—Max would need to be blind as well as besotted to find her attractive the way she looked right now. And January knew he was neither of those things...

'Don't you ever sleep, Jude?' she heard him snap into the mobile telephone.

Jude...? Jude Marshall?

'Jude, I believe we had this same conversation yesterday,' he bit out irritably.

About the three of them, no doubt, January acknowledged resentfully, unashamedly listening to Max's side of the conversation now even while she gave every appearance of continuing with the milking.

'They simply do not want to sell, Jude,' Max rasped. 'That is, of course, your prerogative,' he continued coldly. 'No. No, I don't. I—' He broke off as one of the cows gave an extremely loud moo in the back-

132

ground. 'What was that?' he obviously repeated the question that had been put to him, giving January a brief grimace before replying. 'I have the television on, Jude,' he invented. 'The news. Look, Jude, I'm sure you didn't telephone me at this ridiculous hour, wasting your time and money, to talk about what I may or may not be watching on television! But for your information, we've had snowstorms here—Yes, snowstorms! I am freezing cold, and not a little fed up with this whole situation—' He listened for a few seconds. 'So fire me!' he snapped before abruptly ending the call.

January stared at him. Had he really just told the owner of the Marshall Corporation, his friend as well as employer, what he could do with his job? And if so, why had he...?

'Don't look so worried,' Max drawled as he looked up and saw January's stunned expression. 'Jude won't fire me,' he sighed. 'We go too far back for him to ever do that.'

So that challenge had just been bravado on his part? January could hardly contain her disappointment. For a moment there she had really thought—

The mobile telephone began to ring a second time. Obviously Jude Marshall wasn't a man used to taking no for an answer.

Well—obviously, January instantly chided herself, otherwise Max wouldn't be here in the first place. Something she would do well to keep remembering; Max was only here to try and persuade her and her sisters into selling their home.

If only she didn't love him so much!

'January?'

She lowered long lashes over her eyes, determined

that Max wouldn't see her tears. Let him play his stupid power games with Jude Marshall—and leave her alone.

'Shouldn't you answer that?' she said huskily as he came to stand in front of her, the ringing mobile telephone still in his hand.

'I can talk to Jude any time,' Max rasped, the ringing ceasing abruptly as he switched it off. 'January—'

'I'm really very busy, Max.' She moved purposefully away from him as he would have reached out and taken her in his arms—so much for thinking she looked undesirable! 'And you're cold,' she reminded him determinedly. 'My uncle should have cleared the track shortly, so you'll be able to drive back to the hotel,' she added dismissively, her chin rising challengingly. 'Maybe even book yourself a flight back to America, away from this cold weather,' she added scathingly.

A nerve pulsed in his tightly clenched jaw. 'Is that what you want?' he muttered grimly.

'Of course,' she assured him brightly. 'We all just want to get on with our lives. Don't you?' she derided.

His eyes glittered. 'My life isn't in America!' he snapped.

'Well, wherever it is, then,' January shrugged, wishing he would just go—before those threatening tears began to fall.

She simply couldn't bear the thought of Max going completely out of her life, of never seeing him again.

Max stared at her for several long minutes, his expression grim. 'Okay,' he finally muttered forcefully. 'I'll go back to the farmhouse and wait for your uncle. But I'm still coming with you later to see Josh,' he warned hardly.

January gave a weary shrug. 'I doubt I could stop you even if I wanted to.'

His gaze narrowed. 'And do you want to?'

'Max,' she began impatiently, 'as far as you're concerned, what I do or don't want doesn't seem to be particularly important,' she snapped. 'Now, if you wouldn't mind; I'm busy,' she added rudely before turning away, hearing the slam of the shed door seconds later.

Her shoulders slumped wearily after his departure, the tears falling hot on her cheeks. Well, she hadn't ended up in his arms being kissed this time, had she? No, this time she had told him she just wanted him to leave, not just the farm, but the country!

And, with him as Jude Marshall's representative, she most certainly did want that. But as the man she had fallen in love with—!

She had thought herself in love with Ben last year, had been so hurt when she'd found out that the real motive behind his interest in her, with her father now dead, was with an eye to the farm. Not for the redevelopment Jude Marshall had in mind—just as owner by marriage to one of the sisters. That was probably what had hurt January the most when she'd finally got the full story from him: the fact that he had tried it on with her two sisters, and been kindly but firmly rejected, before turning his attention to the youngest sister. And like an idiot she had fallen for it!

Just as she had fallen for Max, she reminded herself derisively.

Yes, and even knowing the full circumstances of his presence here, she still loved Max. He would just never know that she did.

Perhaps, after all, the sooner Max left the area, the better it would be. For everyone. But certainly for January.

Which was the main reason she was so cool towards him that evening when the two of them finally managed to visit Josh.

Not that it was easy to get in to see her cousin-in-law-to-be, a certain amount of police security around him still, but luckily her Aunt Lyn had already left word to expect at least one of the sisters in this evening.

In fact, January was glad in the end that she had Max with her, so shocked was she at Josh's changed appearance. Someone had really beaten him badly, a large discoloured gash on his left temple that had obviously needed several stitches, a huge bruise on his jaw, one of his arms in a sling.

'Hi,' he greeted brightly enough. 'You just missed seeing Sara; I finally managed to persuade her that I wasn't going to die if she went home for a bath and change of clothes,' he explained ruefully. 'Hello again.' He gave Max a smile, although it obviously caused him pain.

January bent to give Josh a kiss on the side of his face that didn't look bruised, more shaken than she cared to admit—that someone had deliberately inflicted these wounds. Fights and scenes of violence were so often depicted on television nowadays that it was easy to become hardened to them, but to actually see Josh in this terrible state because someone had deliberately attacked him...!

'Whoever did this ought to be—'

'Don't worry, January, Sara has already said it all,' Josh assured her with a grimace. 'And to think I never knew she had such a violent streak in her until yesterday!' he added affectionately.

'Whereas I already know what January is capable of,' Max put in dryly.

January gave him a sharp look, the colour entering her cheeks as she remembered the visit she had paid him at the hotel on Sunday evening, when she had quite obviously wanted to hit him for what she considered to be his duplicity.

'And they call them the gentler sex!' Josh joined in teasingly. 'Give me a man to fight any day! Although there wasn't too much chance of that on Monday night,' he sobered frowningly. 'The bast— He hit me on the head with something—' he held a hand up to the bruised gash on his temple '—before kicking hell out of me while I was on the ground!'

'Obviously no one told him about the Queensbury Rules,' Max rasped.

Josh gave the other man a grateful smile for his attempt at humour. 'I wouldn't say it was part of his vocabulary, no.'

January sat down abruptly in the chair next to the bed, still shocked that someone could have hurt Josh deliberately.

A group of them had always gone around together at school, January and her cousin Sara, along with several other girls of the same age, Josh and a group of his friends usually around somewhere, too. That something like this should have happened to one of them…!

It was testament to how shocked January was that she did not demur as Max sat down in the chair next to her and took her hand into his own, his fingers tightening reassuringly against hers. In actual fact, at that particular moment other human contact was very welcome.

'Fortunately, Sara has decided that she doesn't mind

me looking like this in the wedding photographs, so the wedding is still on for Saturday,' Josh said lightly. 'They're letting me out of here tomorrow,' he added with satisfaction.

'Any leads as to who did this to you?' Max prompted grimly.

'Not a one,' Josh answered disappointedly. 'The man was wearing a baclava or something, so I couldn't see his face. The only thing I could tell the police that was of any help was that I thought I recognized his voice.'

January's eyes widened incredulously. Josh actually *knew* the man who had done this to him?

'Did it sound anything like mine?' Max suggested dryly.

Josh looked puzzled by the question. 'What?'

'Never mind,' Max dismissed scathingly.

While at the same time not even glancing at January! Leaving her in no doubt that, despite her apology, Max really hadn't forgiven her for even having had that particular thought. But could she blame him...?

'I have no idea where I know it from,' Josh continued frustratedly. 'I've tried and tried to place it, but it just escapes me. I just know that I had heard it before. Somewhere.' He shook his head disgustedly at his own inability to remember.

'It's time for Mr Williams' rest now, I'm afraid,' a nurse looked briefly into the room to inform them.

Josh grimaced. 'I've done nothing but rest since they brought me in here. I shall be glad to get home tomorrow.'

'And I'm sure Sara will be pleased to have you there.' January bent forward to give him another kiss on the cheek before standing up, Max, to her surprise, retaining that hold on her hand as he too stood up to leave.

'Take care,' he told Josh as the two men shook hands.

'See you both on Saturday,' Josh called after them as they left. 'At the wedding.'

Josh was obviously expecting Max to accompany her. But after seeing the two of them here together today, holding hands no less, was that so surprising…?

'Don't look so worried, January,' Max taunted as he saw her frowning expression. 'I'm sure that Josh won't notice my absence amongst all the other wedding guests.'

Damn it, did she have to make it so obvious that she didn't want him there? As if he were some sort of ogre, for goodness' sake. But, then, perhaps to January he was…?

'I'm making it a new rule,' he continued hardly at her silence, 'never to go anywhere I'm not welcome!'

Which just about ruled out the whole of this part of the *country*, if the Calendar sisters had anything to say about it!

'Max—'

'Don't say anything, January,' he snapped as they got outside the hospital. 'I've really had more than enough for one day! I'll see you around,' he added dismissively.

She frowned her confusion. 'Don't you want me to give you a lift back to the hotel?'

To be honest, he had completely forgotten that January had picked him up from there earlier. But it didn't change the fact that he would rather be alone.

'I'll walk,' he assured her abruptly, turning up the

collar on his heavy jacket in an attempt to ward off the chilling wind.

'But—'

'Just leave it, January,' he rasped, blue eyes glittering warningly.

The fact that she flinched at the harshness of his tone, those incredible grey eyes filling up with tears, was almost his undoing. But, at the same time, he was aware that until he knew exactly what he was going to do next, it was better if he just stayed away from January. He couldn't think straight around her anyway!

'Josh is going to be okay, you know,' he told January huskily. 'A bit battered about the edges,' he acknowledged ruefully. 'But he's young, he'll make a full recovery.'

'Physically, yes.' She nodded slowly. 'But—'

'In other ways, too,' Max cut in firmly. 'I'm sure your cousin Sara is going to make sure of that!'

January smiled for what seemed like the first time today. Much to Max's relief. He didn't like the fact that this had made her so unhappy. In fact, he didn't like anything that made January unhappy...

'I have to go,' he repeated harshly. 'Drive back carefully, won't you?' he couldn't resist adding. The roads had been cleared once they'd got down from the farm, but with evening setting in driving was once again hazardous. And he was still recovering from the shock of the last time January ended up in a ditch!

'Of course,' she acknowledged distantly. 'Take care,' she added abruptly before turning sharply away and walking over to where she had parked her sister's car.

Max stood and watched her leave, aware that this might be the last time he saw her. He had some thinking to do, and the outcome of those thoughts might just mean she would get her wish and he would return to America.

She raised a hand in parting as she drove out of the car park, still pale from her shock at Josh's appearance, but also incredibly beautiful.

Max stood on the pavement until the car had completely disappeared from view, reluctant to give up what might be his last view of her.

He had meant it earlier when he'd assured January that Jude would never fire him, but, in view of his personal difficulty over execution of this latest business venture of Jude's, he did wonder if he ought to resign. To do what, he had no idea, but one thing he knew for certain: he was no longer one-hundred-per-cent committed to the Marshall Corporation.

After the years he had spent with the company as the main focus of his life, coming to terms with that was hard to do!

And he needed time, time on his own, to decide exactly what he was going to do next.

Although maybe walking back to the hotel hadn't been such a good idea, he decided ruefully, after trudging through the snow and ice for half an hour in order to get there and needing to lie in a hot bath for an hour or so in order to thaw out.

The telephone rang in his suite as he lay in the bath, but, guessing it was Jude once again, he chose to ignore it. The walk earlier hadn't done anything to help him with the confused thoughts that were tumbling around inside his head!

'Don't you ever go home?' He smiled at John as he walked into the bar a couple of hours later, having decided that a drink was what he needed to thaw him inside as well as out.

The barman grinned. 'I thought this was home!'

Max laughed softly as he ordered his drink. At least John always gave him a warm welcome—which was more than could be said for anyone else in the area!

Although, on reflection, it was pretty sad that the only person here to show him a friendly face was the hotel barman!

John placed the requested glass of whisky in front of him. 'I'm surprised you're still here?'

Max shrugged. 'My business is taking a little longer than I anticipated,' he understated.

He had still come to no real decision about his own future plans, having left his mobile switched off so that Jude couldn't reach him, knowing he needed to think this through without any outside interference.

John grimaced. 'This snow can't be helping. I—uh—oh,' he murmured ruefully. 'Here comes Meridew on the prowl again,' he explained softly as Max looked up at him questioningly. 'I obviously haven't been in the last couple of evenings, but apparently he's been wandering around all week like a bear with a sore head!'

John moved to begin dusting down the shelves behind him, obviously intent on looking busy while the manager of the hotel was 'prowling' around.

'Mr Golding! I trust you are still enjoying your stay with us?'

Max turned to look at Peter Meridew, his gaze narrowing as he saw the other man's bandaged right hand. 'Of course,' he assured the other man smoothly. 'Been in the wars?' He indicated the bandaged hand.

The other man's face became flushed. 'Just a sprain,'

he dismissed abruptly. 'Well, if there's nothing I can do for you...' He turned to leave.

'I didn't say that,' Max called after him softly, a terrible suspicion starting to form in his mind.

Josh had said earlier that he recognized the voice of his attacker, from somewhere, and hadn't Peter Meridew had cause to have words with Josh and his friends for their rowdiness on Saturday evening, plus there was the fact that the manager seemed to be around a lot whenever January was singing in the bar...? Add that to Peter Meridew's bandaged hand, and what had you got—?

Circumstantial evidence was what you had, Max, old lad!

And as a lawyer he ought to know better.

'Yes?' the manager prompted brightly.

Yes—what? He had called out to the other man instinctively, and now he didn't know what to say to him.

'Er— I'm probably going to book out within the next couple of days,' he improvised. Lame, he knew, but he couldn't think of anything else to say on the spur of the moment.

'No problem, Mr Golding,' the manager assured him. 'Just call down to Reception on the morning of departure and they will have your bill waiting for you when you come down.'

'Thanks.' Max nodded with a dismissive smile.

'Sorry to hear that,' John murmured once the manager had left. 'In this job I very rarely get to meet the same people two nights in a row, let alone for a whole week,' he explained ruefully.

Max grimaced, knowing that his own job wasn't much better. Apart from Jude and a couple of other regular employees, he rarely saw the same person twice either; the Calendar sisters, because of their reluctance to sell, were the exception rather than the rule.

'So what's the real story on Meridew's hand?' he prompted lightly.

'Well—' John gave a knowing grin '—he says he sprained it putting in some cupboards at home, but we all think that Mrs Meridew either hit him or threw something at him!'

Max raised dark brows. 'There's a *Mrs* Meridew?'

'Oh, yes,' the barman confirmed with feeling. 'He wheels her out regularly every year for the staff Christmas party, and a more formidable woman you wouldn't hope to meet. She's twice the size of Meridew, obviously wears the trousers at home— which is probably why he's such a tartar when he's here!' he concluded heavily.

Under any other circumstances, Max would have found the other man's description of Peter Meridew's married life amusing, to say the least. But in this case…

Josh said he had recognized the voice of the man that had attacked him, although he couldn't remember where he remembered it from. Peter Meridew had an obviously soft spot for January. He had been in the room when Josh had kissed her. He had been walking around like a bear with a sore head all week. He also had a suspect injury to his hand. And a formidable wife who probably made his life miserable at home.

Still circumstantial, but surely worth investigating further?

'I have to go and make a telephone call,' he told John before swallowing down the last of his whisky. 'Enjoy the rest of the evening,' he added derisively.

'Not much chance of that!' John grimaced.

Max gave him a sympathetic smile before leaving the bar to go up to his hotel suite. There were still a few bits of information he needed before even attempting to talk to the police, but if his suspicion was correct…!

May was the one to answer the telephone at the Calendar farm, her businesslike tone easily discernible from January's husky voice and the derisive March.

'Hi, May, it's Max,' he told her abruptly. 'Could I speak to January?'

'She isn't here,' May told him with what sounded like a certain amount of satisfaction in her voice.

Max frowned his irritation. 'Where is she?'

'Max—'

'I need to know, May,' he told her determinedly.

'Why?' she prompted suspiciously.

Because he thought January might be at the centre of this latest attack. Because he suspected the manager of the hotel as being the attacker. Because he needed to know where January was now so that he could ensure that she was in no danger!

But he couldn't tell May any of those things without alarming her, possibly unnecessarily!

'I just heard her car outside,' May told him irritably. 'If you'll just hang on a minute…'

Max waited on the end of the line for what seemed much longer than a minute, and as the seconds ticked by he began to wonder if January had refused to speak to him. Not that he could blame her; they hadn't exactly parted on friendly terms earlier!

'Yes?' January finally came on the line to question cautiously.

Max felt a surge of relief just at the sound of her voice. Although, with Peter Meridew still on duty at the hotel, his worries concerning January's safety had probably been groundless.

'Where have you been?' With the suspicions of the last few minutes, his tone was sharper than he intended. 'I thought you were going straight home.' He forced lightness into his tone.

'Not that it's any of your business, but I called in to see Sara,' she explained stiffly.

'How is she?' he prompted huskily.

'As you would expect, very upset,' January came back sharply.

Not half as upset as January was going to be if his fears should turn out to be correct!

'Max, why did you telephone me?' she asked impatiently.

He sighed, knowing from her tone that she was annoyed with him, probably because of his own abruptness earlier this evening. 'I just wanted to ask you a question, January,' he told her briskly.

'Max—'

'Just one question, January,' he insisted firmly at her obvious impatience, 'then I won't bother you again.' Tonight, at least...!

She took a long time answering. 'Okay,' she finally agreed warily. 'One question.'

'How long have you been working at the hotel?'

'How long—? Max!' she murmured frustratedly. 'What on earth does that have to do with anything?'

A great deal, if his suspicions were correct. But he wasn't about to alarm her by telling her any of that.

'I would just like to know,' he came back evasively.

January gave an impatient sigh. 'About seven months, I think,' she told him irritatedly. 'Yes, it would be seven months,' she confirmed. 'I started some time in May. But what—?'

'That's all I wanted to know,' he cut in briskly, his thoughts racing.

Seven months. Seven attacks. What had seemed like an outrageous suspicion on his part now took on a much more sinister turn.

'Max—'

'I promised it would only be the one question, January,' he told her brightly. 'Enjoy what's left of the evening!' He rang off before she could question him any further.

As no doubt she had wanted to do! But there was no way he could confide in January concerning the suspicions he now had about Peter Meridew. That would only alarm and distress her.

Which left him in a position of wondering what to do now!

Of course he could just be overreacting. Could be reading things into situations that simply weren't there. After all, it had been six women who were attacked previously; only Josh was the exception.

Could Max seriously go to the police with his suspicions, or should he just bide his time a bit longer? Even if time wasn't something he had a whole lot of!

One thing he knew for certain, any thoughts he might have had about returning to America in the near future were now put on indefinite hold; he had no intention of going anywhere until this situation was well and truly sorted out!

Until he knew that January was safe...

CHAPTER ELEVEN

'STILL here?' January greeted Max rudely when she arrived at work on Thursday evening and found him once again sitting at the bar. 'Don't you have any little old ladies to throw out of their homes into the snow?' she added challengingly. 'Evening, John,' she greeted more warmly as she walked over to the piano.

Her mood had alternated between annoyance and puzzlement since Max's telephone call yesterday evening, the former usually winning out, her resentment at his wanting to know where she had been far outweighing any puzzlement she might feel concerning the strange unrelatedness of that single question he had asked her.

'And a good evening to you, too, January,' Max drawled as he turned on his bar stool to watch her. 'And, unless I'm mistaken, there isn't any snow left for me to throw the little old ladies onto; it's all melted away!'

'Your boss intends turning Hanworth Manor into a hotel and health club!' she returned scathingly, March at last having come with the information they wanted. 'This is Yorkshire, Max, not the south of France!'

His brows rose over mocking blue eyes. 'You don't think the people of Yorkshire are into health and beauty?'

'On the contrary, I'm sure that they are,' she snapped. 'I just don't think your boss has studied the

148

climate in this area too well. The snow a couple of days ago is typical for this time of year!'

A hotel and health club, with luxury accommodation, as well as a gym and indoor swimming pool, the pièce de résistance an eighteen-hole golf course—of which, according to March's information on the preliminary proposal, their farm stood smack in the middle!

Max shook his head. 'This is all just speculation on your part, January—'

'Actually, it isn't,' she told him with satisfaction; March's information came 'from the horse's mouth', so to speak. Not that she intended telling Max that— he and, from the little she already knew of him, Jude Marshall were not men to let the situation rest there if they were to find out someone was leaking information concerning the plans for Hanworth Manor. 'You're going to meet quite a lot of local opposition to the idea, you know,' she added challengingly.

Although she wasn't too sure that would actually be the case...

Unemployment here was quite high, and the health and country club promised employment for quite a lot of people in the area. Although that was something else she didn't intend telling Max!

'Headed by the Calendar sisters, no doubt,' Max drawled wryly.

'No doubt,' she echoed tauntingly. 'Somehow I don't think our cows and sheep will welcome the idea of having golf balls whistling past their ears as they try to graze!'

Max's gaze narrowed warningly. 'Perhaps we should talk about this some other time—'

'Yes, we could always talk about the strangeness of

your telephone call last night, instead!' she cut in, once again challenging.

His expression became grim as he stood up to walk over to her. 'I would really rather you didn't inform the whole world of our private conversations,' he muttered harshly, glancing around them pointedly.

There were three other people in the bar beside themselves, John behind the bar, and a couple sitting in the corner of the room, obviously having eyes—and ears!—for no one but each other as they talked softly together in between kisses. Hardly the 'whole world'!

January gave a dismissive shrug. 'Well?' she prompted softly, dark brows raised enquiringly. 'Of what possible interest can it be to you when I started working here?'

'I was curious, that's all.' He shrugged.

January's frown turned to one of perplexity. 'You were curious?'

'Yes,' he dismissed abruptly. 'Shouldn't you have started singing by now?' he prompted. 'John tells me that Peter Meridew is in a foul mood this week.'

She had seen that for herself when she'd walked through Reception earlier and the manager had looked pointedly at his watch because she'd been five minutes late in arriving!

She shot Max a dismissive glance. 'Perhaps you should spend a little less time talking to the hotel staff and get on with the business you're paid for!'

His mouth quirked into a smile. 'The Calendar sisters are my business at the moment, and as you're one of them…'

In other words, he wasn't going anywhere, had every intention of staying here for the whole evening.

Great!

But as the bar steadily filled up, most people seeming to welcome getting out for the evening after the recent snow, January was able to ignore Max for the main part. After all, she consoled herself, he couldn't hang around in Yorkshire for ever.

Just long enough to disturb and annoy her!

'I'll walk you out to your car,' he offered as she packed her things away at the end of the evening, the bar having slowly emptied.

Not after what happened last time!

'There's no need,' she refused lightly. 'John has already offered to go with me,' she added triumphantly.

'Unless you would rather go with Mr Golding,' John put in awkwardly, having shut the bar up. 'I just thought, after what happened on Monday evening…' He gave a shrug.

'That's fine,' Max told the other man warmly. 'You see, January, I'm not the only one who thinks you should take more care!'

If he was annoyed at being usurped in this way, then he certainly wasn't showing it, January thought disgruntledly. And then realized how ridiculous she was being. She had deliberately accepted John's offer earlier for the very reason she didn't want to be put in a position of having to accept one from Max—and now she was angry with him for not trying harder!

'I'm sure I would be perfectly all right on my own,' she told Max waspishly.

Max shrugged. 'Better safe than sorry.'

She raised her eyes heavenwards. 'It's too late at night for clichés!'

He chuckled softly before turning to the barman. 'Make sure you actually see her getting into her car and driving away, John; she has a habit of taking diversions!'

She gasped. 'You—'

'Goodnight, January.' Max bent down to kiss her lightly on the lips. 'I'll leave her in your capable hands, then, John,' he told the other man with obvious amusement.

She shot him a furious glare before striding from the bar, John endeavouring to keep up with her. Something he seemed to be having trouble doing as he favoured his left foot slightly.

'I twisted my ankle playing football at the weekend,' he explained with a grimace as January slowed down so that he could catch her up. 'It made me realize I'm getting too old for that lark!' he added disgustedly.

January had no idea how old the barman actually was; with his receding hairline, but boyish looks, he could be anywhere between twenty-five and forty.

'As long as you enjoy it.' She smiled, still completely aware of Max as he walked over to get in one of the lifts. 'I—'

'January...?'

She turned to find Peter Meridew walking purposefully towards her. Just what she needed at the end of an already stressful evening!

'If I could just talk to Miss Calendar alone...?' The manager's words and look gave John a pointed dismissal.

John gave her a rueful grimace. 'I'll see you tomorrow, then, January. Mr Meridew.' He nodded abruptly, leaving with obvious reluctance.

What had she done now? January wondered frustratedly. Okay, so she had been five minutes late arriving, but as the bar had been particularly busy this evening she had also carried on singing fifteen minutes over her usual time...

'Perhaps you would like to come through to my office?' Peter Meridew said firmly.

And perhaps she wouldn't! It was almost one-thirty in the morning, for goodness' sake—and she had a home to go to, even if this man preferred to stay out of his as much as possible; it was common knowledge amongst the hotel staff that Peter Meridew often stayed on working long after his shift should have ended because of the formidable wife waiting for him at home! Normally she felt quite sorry for his obviously unhappy home life, but at one-thirty in the morning she had to admit her sympathy was running a little thin!

'Couldn't this wait until tomorrow evening?' she suggested lightly.

His expression tightened. 'I received a visit from the police today in connection with the attacks being carried out in the area,' he bit out tersely, obviously not at all pleased at having police calling at his hotel, for any reason.

January frowned her confusion. 'What does that have to do with me?'

'On a personal level, nothing,' he accepted. 'However, they are suggesting we change our policy as regards ensuring the safety of certain employees.'

Somehow January didn't like the sound of this...! Besides the fact that it sounded extremely familiar...?

'Yes?' she prompted warily.

Peter Meridew gave a terse inclination of his head. 'I am afraid that, until such time as the attacker is found and incarcerated, we will have to dispense with your services.'

'What?' January gasped, not seeing the connection at all.

The manager's mouth thinned. 'Yes. Of course you may finish off the week,' he added hurriedly.

'That's very big of you,' January muttered, too tired—and angry!—to feel like being overly polite; besides, the man was effectively putting her out of a job at the end of the week!

'I'm really no happier about this than you are.' Peter Meridew sighed. 'We have been more than pleased with your work. But apparently one of the guests has complained that three evenings a week you regularly leave the hotel, alone, at a very late hour—'

'*One* of the guests...?' January cut in forcefully, turning to look at the lifts; as she had suspected Max had already gone up to his suite. But it didn't take her two guesses to know who 'the guest' was who had lodged the complaint.

Or to guess why he had done such a thing! He really was Jude Marshall's man, wasn't he, out to ruin the Calendar sisters if he couldn't get them out of the farm any other way? First put her out of a job, and then he would no doubt start on March. Well, that was what he thought!

She gave Peter Meridew a warm smile. 'I'm sure the police don't actually have the authority to instruct you to sack me?'

'I'm not sacking you, January.' The manager looked slightly flustered at the suggestion. 'But, after giving the situation due consideration, I am of the opinion it is the best way to deal with the problem. For the moment,' he added hastily. 'We don't, of course, want to lose your services indefinitely.'

No, she would just bet they didn't; she never demurred about staying longer than she was supposed to do, or coming in for special occasions if necessary, and the wages really weren't that good. Just necessary in order for them to be able to keep the farm. Which brought her right back to Max Golding…!

She forced herself to remain calm. 'Did they tell you which of the guests made the complaint?' she prompted interestedly.

'I did enquire, but… They were disinclined to tell me,' Peter Meridew snapped abruptly, obviously most displeased with this police reticence. 'However, I do accept that it is in the interest of your safety, and as such—'

'"You have to dispense with my services",' January finished for him tautly. 'And I have no say in the matter whatsoever?' she prompted disgustedly.

His expression softened. 'January—'

'It's okay, Peter,' she cut in impatiently, shaking her head. 'I fully accept the position you have been put in.' And who *had* put him—and her!—there! 'If you don't mind, I would like to leave now…?'

'Not at all,' he accepted, obviously relieved she hadn't made more of a scene about the situation. 'Perhaps I could escort you out to your car?' he offered.

January gave a decisive shake of her head. 'I just have to do something first—but thanks.'

If Max thought he was going to get away with this without protest from her, then he was in for a surprise—because she had every intention of going up to his suite right now and telling him exactly what she thought of him, and his machinations.

Concern for her safety, indeed!

In other circumstances, Max might have felt pleased to find January standing outside his hotel suite at one-thirty in the morning knocking to come in—but one glance at her obviously furious expression, grey eyes blazing, two angry spots of colour on her cheeks in an otherwise white face, was enough to tell him this was not a social call!

'Would you like to come—? Ah, you would,' he murmured derisively as she pushed past him into the suite, closing the door softly behind her before following her back into the room, glad now that he had stopped to check his e-mails rather than going straight to bed; something was obviously seriously wrong. Which meant something must have happened since they'd parted fifteen minutes ago; January hadn't been too enamoured of him then, but she was furiously angry now!

'Drink?' he offered hopefully.

'No,' she refused tautly. 'But you go ahead—with any luck it might choke you!'

'Hmm, in that case, I think I'll pass, too,' he drawled warily.

What could have happened in the fifteen minutes since they'd parted? The last he had seen of January she had been on her way out the door, John at her side.

'Pity!' January snapped, giving him a scathing glance. 'I've just been having a cosy chat with Peter Meridew—'

'What?' Max's wariness turned to shock.

January hadn't left with John, after all?

Damn it, he should have waited until she was safely out to her car, Max remonstrated with himself, should have—

'You heard,' January bit out accusingly. 'You'll be pleased to know, he just sacked me!'

'He what?' To say it was the last thing Max had been expecting to hear would be an understatement!

'Max, as I really don't think there is anything wrong with your hearing,' January began scathingly, 'I have no intention of repeating everything I say! I'm allowed to stay on until the end of the week, but after that my services have been dispensed with. For the moment,' she added harshly. 'And we both know why, don't we?' She glared at him.

Max looked across at her frowningly, totally nonplussed. Peter Meridew had just told January that he didn't want her coming to the hotel after the weekend? In the circumstances, that didn't make any sense to Max whatsoever.

'Do we?' he delayed warily, his thoughts racing.

The anger deepened in those beautiful grey eyes—although Max wisely decided that now wasn't the time to tell January how beautiful she looked when she was angry!

He remembered Jude telling him he had once said that to one of the women in his life—and the next morning he had sported a bruise on his jaw to prove it!

'You won't succeed in getting us out of the farm like this, Max,' January told him scornfully. 'I'll just get myself another job—and then you'll be back where you started!'

She thought he had deliberately—!

His mouth tightened as his own anger started to rise. 'Now, listen here—'

'No—*you* listen,' she cut in forcefully. 'You may have managed to lose me my job, but all that's done is make me all the more determined that you won't succeed.'

'January—'

'Can you deny it was you who made the complaint to the police about my leaving here alone late at night?' she challenged, that small pointed chin raised defiantly. 'A complaint, because of these random attacks late at night, they took straight to Peter Meridew.'

Max winced at the accusation. He hadn't exactly complained to the police, more suggested, in the course of his conversation with them, that it probably wasn't a good idea for a woman to be travelling alone at that time of night. How could he possibly have known that idiot of a manager would turn round and sack January on the basis of that?

Added to which, if his suspicions were correct, the manager's subsequent actions made absolutely no sense to him...!

If they were correct...

And it certainly looked as if they might not be in the light of Peter Meridew's decision concerning January continuing to work here.

Unless it was some sort of attempt at misdirection on the other man's part? Although, for the life of him, Max couldn't think what that could possibly be!

He drew in a sharp breath. 'Look, I admit that during my conversation with the police, concerning that altercation with Josh at the weekend, I may have mentioned your late-night drives—'

'Oh, you "admit" to that, do you?' she flared scathingly. 'Well, I—'

'January, for goodness' sake, listen to me—'

'No!' she snapped forcefully, eyes blazing, her whole body tense with anger. '*You* listen to me!' she snapped even more vehemently. 'Stay out of my life, Max. Stay out of my sisters' lives. In fact, just stay completely away from all of us!' She was breathing hard in her agitation.

She had never looked lovelier to Max!

'January...!' he groaned, his hands moving up instinctively.

'Do not touch me!' She stepped back as if burnt.

Or as if his merest touch might contaminate her in some way!

It was altogether too much for Max, all his own earlier decisions to keep an emotional distance between himself and January evaporating like so much mist. He couldn't bear to have her look at him like that. He just couldn't!

He tried to take her in his arms, only to have his chest pummelled with clenched fists as she fought against him.

'Let-me-go-Max,' she told him through gritted teeth, pushing against his chest now in an effort to dislodge the steel of his arms.

'I can't,' he told her gruffly.

'Let me go, Max, or I'll—I'll—'

'You'll what?' He frowned.

She became suddenly still in his arms, her eyes filled with tears now as she looked up at him. 'I don't want this, Max,' she told him huskily. 'Don't you understand?' she choked, shaking her head.

Only too well! She couldn't wait to be out of his arms, to get away from him!

Max felt pain unlike any he had ever known before, knew that at that moment he would do or say anything to erase that look of loathing—for him!—from her face.

He drew in a harsh breath. 'It's you that doesn't understand,' he rasped. 'I did those things, told the police about your lone drives home late at night, for one reason and one reason only—'

'And we both know what that is, don't we?' she flashed with some of her earlier spirit.

'I did it because I *care*, January!' he bit out tautly, his hands moving to grasp her upper arms as he shook her slightly. 'Because I care!' he repeated harshly.

She shook her head disbelievingly. 'There's only one thing you care about, Max—and that's yourself!' she returned scornfully.

Maybe that had been true once. Maybe it still was, in some ways. But not in the way she meant.

He shook her again. 'You stubborn, pigheaded—'

'Yes, I'm stubborn and pigheaded,' she confirmed self-derisively. 'But I would much rather be that way than cold and heartless—like you!'

Max became suddenly still, his hands falling back to his sides as he stepped away from her, his gaze guarded now as he held his inner emotions firmly in check. 'Is that really what you think of me?' he finally murmured evenly.

January's mouth twisted humourlessly. 'What else?' she sneered. 'But isn't that what you wanted?' she challenged scornfully. 'Of course it is! After all, you're Max Golding, legal henchman of Jude Marshall—and neither of you makes any secret of the fact that you take no prisoners!'

Was that what he had become? Not as far as he was aware. It certainly wasn't what he had set out to be fifteen years ago...

But was that really what he had become? Somehow that wasn't a palatable thought.

'I've said all I came here to say,' January told him dismissively as he made no further comment, picking up her bag from where she had thrown it down on the table earlier. 'But I meant it about staying away from me and my family in the future,' she added warningly.

Max could see that she did, could see the cold anger in her eyes, the scorn for him that she made no effort to hide.

The pain deepened inside him, so much so that it held him immobile as he watched January walk away from him, the door closing softly behind her as she left.

Max knew she hadn't just walked out of the hotel suite, but out of his life.

For ever.

Never before, not once in all of his thirty-seven years, had he told anyone that he cared about them. And he cared more about January than he ever had anyone before.

More than cared, if he was honest. With himself, at least.

And, after the things she had just said, he knew she felt nothing but loathing for him in return…!

CHAPTER TWELVE

SOMEONE was following her!

January wasn't quite sure when she first became aware of the car following some distance behind hers, but she had been sure of it for at least the last three miles, every turn she took down increasingly country roads—deserted roads!—the car behind making the same turn seconds later.

Suddenly Max's scathing comments about the safety of her driving home alone late at night no longer seemed quite so ridiculous!

Unless it was Max himself who was following her…?

Surely not; she knew he was a determined man, but surely not a vindictive one? And it was more than vindictive to scare her in this way!

Then who was it?

She gave another glance in the driving mirror, those two headlights still there, if some distance away, too far back for her to even begin to identify the make of the car, let alone identify the driver. But she certainly didn't intend stopping the car in order to confront the other driver, either!

But she didn't like this, didn't like it one little bit.

Of course, she could be wrong about the other car deliberately following her, it could just be someone else returning home late at night who also happened to live in her area. She could just be overreacting to this because of Max's dire warnings!

There was one way of testing that theory, January realized as she took note of where she had got to in the journey; in about half a mile or so there was a narrow lane that led onto the track that eventually reached the farm. And only their farm. If the person behind her took that same short cut then she was definitely being followed.

January's hands tightened on the steering wheel as the car followed on behind her as she turned down the lane, feeling hot and cold at the same time as she accepted she was definitely being followed.

To say she was alarmed now would be an understatement; she had never been so scared in her life!

The mobile telephone!

They had one mobile telephone between the three of them, May keeping it with her during the day as she worked about the farm, but insisting that January take it with her on the evenings she worked. She had always dismissed the necessity of it in the past, but at this particular moment she was glad of May's over-protectiveness!

But who did she call?

Her sisters at the farm?

Both May and March were heavy sleepers, and with the mobile here with her, the only other telephone was downstairs in the hallway.

Max?

Absolutely not!

The police, to tell them she thought she was being followed?

If she turned out to be wrong about that, she was going to end up looking extremely foolish.

But what if she wasn't wrong…?

The police, then, she decided hurriedly as the car behind followed her doggedly down the narrow lane—

No—wait a minute! The car had stopped, the headlights starting to fade away now as January took the turning up the track that led directly to the farm, able to heave a deep sigh of relief seconds later as she saw the vehicle was being turned around before driving back in the direction they had just come.

How strange. How very, very odd.

Strange and odd it might be, but January was shaking badly with reaction by the time she parked the car in the farmyard ten minutes later and climbed out onto the cobbles!

Perhaps it was as well, after all, that after tomorrow she would no longer have that long drive back from the hotel at night; she had the evening off anyway on Saturday, to attend Sara and Josh's wedding.

Although she had no intention of ever giving Max the satisfaction of knowing he might have been right about these late-night drives, still maintained that he had no right to interfere in her life in the high-handed way that he had.

She had no intention of telling her sisters about the car following her home tonight, either; they had enough worries already. With only one evening left to work, it wasn't worth mentioning.

'I don't understand.' May frowned the following morning as the two of them sat drinking coffee together, March having already left for work. 'What reason did Peter Meridew give for letting you go?'

'Sacking me,' January corrected dryly. 'My own safety, apparently.' She grimaced. 'A likely story!' she added disgustedly, knowing exactly who was responsible for her jobless state after this evening. And why!

'But don't worry, I'll get another job,' she assured optimistically.

Quite where, she wasn't sure. She could always wait for the health and country club to open and apply for a job there—she didn't think!

May still frowned. 'Perhaps, in the circumstances, we really should consider Jude Marshall's offer to buy the farm...'

'What?' January sat up stiffly, staring at her sister incredulously. May couldn't be serious, not after all they had already gone through! 'I will get another job, May,' she assured her determinedly. 'Besides, if we sold the farm, where would we all live?' She frowned.

May shrugged. 'March could get a flat in town, which would save her all the travelling to and fro to work. The two of you could probably get a flat together,' she reasoned.

January couldn't believe she was hearing this! 'And what about you?'

'Me?' Her sister looked a little uncomfortable now. 'Well, the thing is, January— Well, you see— I—'

'What is it?' January prompted warily; May was the least tongue-tied person she had ever known.

May's cheeks coloured. 'I've had this offer, you see—Well, not exactly an offer—more like—'

'May!' January protested impatiently. 'Just spit it out, will you?'

If her sister had a boyfriend, someone May was serious about, then it was the first January had heard of it. But if that were the case... The three of them had always known that they could only continue to run the farm if all three of them were in agreement, if it was what they all three wanted to go on doing. One of them wanting to marry would certainly change that. Even if the man agreed to live on the farm, there was no way he would want the other two sisters living with them, too. As she had learnt only too well from her brief relationship with Ben!

May gave an embarrassed sigh. 'Someone approached me, after I did the pantomime at Christmas, suggested that I go for a screen test, that—well, that—'

'May…!' January said excitedly. 'Really?'

May flushed uncomfortably. 'I wasn't completely honest about going to the dentist the other day, I actually had lunch with this director. He—' She moistened dry lips. 'Apparently he spent Christmas with his sister's family nearby, came to the pantomime with them all, and saw me—January, if I go for the test, and it's successful, he wants me to appear in a film he's going to begin making this summer!' she finished incredulously.

January had known her sister was good, very good in fact, but this—!

It was beyond any of their wildest dreams. Beyond May's, she was sure.

'But don't you see?' May wailed. 'If I have the screen test, and if this director offers me the part, I would no longer be here to work on the farm,' she pointed out emotionally. 'You and March simply wouldn't be able to cope here on your own, job or no job.'

January could see only too well. But, at the same time, this was too good an opportunity for May to turn down.

'But of course you must do it,' she told May decisively. 'May, you didn't say no?' She groaned as her sister still looked unconvinced.

'I said—maybe.' May grimaced. 'I needed time to

think about it,' she defended at January's reproachful look. 'After all, it's a big step.'

'But if you're successful—!'

'I'm not sure I want to be successful. Not in that way,' May added hardly.

'But you have been thinking about it?' January persisted.

'Yes,' her sister sighed. 'And now that you've lost your job, and we have an offer on the farm, anyway… It all seems to be leading to one thing. Maybe this is what we're supposed to do. I don't know, January. I just don't know.' She gave a weary shake of her head.

January knew that she would personally hate having to tell Max that they had changed their mind about accepting Jude Marshall's offer, would hate even more the look of triumph that would be on his face once he had been told. But, at the same time, May deserved her chance at success, didn't she…?

'Let's see what March thinks about it all, hmm?' January prompted, although she was pretty sure March would be of the same mind as herself.

As sisters they had always looked out for each other, but May had always been the mainstay of the family, the one who took the most responsibility; it was only fair that she be given the chance to do something totally for herself.

Having Max arrive at the farm later that afternoon, to inform them that he was returning to America in the morning, along with a recommendation to Jude Marshall that he work his plans for the health and country club around the Calendar farm, was not something either she or May could have envisaged!

But he was intelligent enough to realize that neither January nor May was exactly thrilled by the news, looking at them both with narrowed eyes as the three of them stood in the warm kitchen. 'That was what you wanted, wasn't it?' he rasped.

'It was, yes,' May was the one to answer guardedly.

'January?' Max bit out tautly, blue gaze compelling.

She met that gaze reluctantly, very aware of how disturbingly attractive he looked in the dark business suit and white shirt he was wearing today. Even more aware of the things she had said to him the previous evening—and the huge backdown they were probably about to make.

But it was for May, wasn't it…?

'It was what we wanted, yes,' she confirmed slowly.

His gaze narrowed. 'But you have since changed your mind?' he guessed shrewdly.

January looked pleadingly at May, knowing she couldn't do this. She just couldn't!

'We're—thinking about it, yes,' her sister told Max dismissively.

Max looked at the two of them disbelievingly, shaking his head, obviously completely baffled by this seeming about-face on their part.

As well he might be, January acknowledged with an inward wince.

Women, would he ever understand them? Max wondered dazedly as he looked at January and May.

He hadn't slept at all the previous night, had gone over and over in his mind the things January had said to him, punishing himself for his own determination never to let anyone into his life, never to care about anyone enough for them to be able to hurt him.

Because January had hurt him the night before. Had hurt him more than he had ever been hurt before.

Finally, he had known that the only thing left for him to do was to go back to America, to explain the situation to Jude, and let him take over from there, if he cared to. One thing Max was very sure of: he couldn't do this any more…

And now, it seemed, the Calendar sisters had changed their mind about selling, after all!

Without being invited to do so—he would probably wait all day if he expected any politeness from January!—he sat down abruptly in one of the kitchen chairs. 'Would someone mind telling me what is going on?' he prompted wearily—and not only from lack of sleep.

'Here, have some coffee.' May poured some from the pot into a mug and placed it in front of him.

A double whisky would probably have been more beneficial, Max decided with a grimace, but sipped the hot coffee anyway. 'Well?' he finally prompted when neither sister seemed inclined to add anything.

'I only said we're thinking about it, Max,' May reminded impatiently. 'Circumstances have changed—'

'So January informed me, only too volubly, last night!' He nodded tersely.

May shot January a sharply questioning look, January answering with a warning shake of her head.

'January being temporarily out of a job wasn't the circumstances you were talking about,' Max realized slowly, gaze narrowing speculatively. 'Care to tell me about it?' he prompted lightly.

'No!' January snapped.

'Yes,' May countered firmly, giving January a frown. 'You don't shoot the envoy, January,' she reproved teasingly.

Max's mouth twisted. 'I would like to stick around and watch one of you shoot Jude!'

'Be my guest,' January returned sharply. 'But, of course, you're going back to America, aren't you?' she added scathingly.

What he would most like to do at the moment was put her over his knee and give her a good spanking. A thought May, if the teasing smile she gave him was anything to go by, was all too aware of!

Going back to America was not the ideal thing for him to do with this attacker called the Night Striker still on the loose, but with January hating him in the way that she did, he didn't feel he could stay here, either.

To say he was disappointed in this uncertainty of the sisters about selling the farm after all would be an understatement. He had come to admire all three sisters for their determination this last week, had to admit he had half relished going back to Jude and telling him the answer was a definite no!

No doubt about it, he would never understand women. But this possible change of mind by the Calendar sisters ultimately made no difference to his own plans. Someone else could sort out the details, he really had had enough.

'I am,' he confirmed evenly. 'So what happened?' He turned to May—deciding, of the two, she was probably the one who would give him a straight answer. 'Is one of you getting married or something?' If it was January—!

He felt a jolt in his chest just at the thought of her marrying some faceless man. Just as well he was leaving!

'Or something,' May told him dryly.

Immediately starting Max's heart beating again. Until that moment he hadn't even been aware that it had stopped!

May looked slightly abashed. 'A director has approached me about appearing in a film he's going to make in the summer.' The words came out in a self-conscious rush. 'I'll probably be awful at it, but...' She gave a rueful shrug.

Aha! The answer to May's nonexistent dental appointment earlier in the week? The derisive smile May shot his way told him that his supposition was correct.

Well, well, well. So May might be going off for some time filming. And he already knew that March had a full-time job. So what was January going to do?

As if aware of his curiosity, January snapped, 'I've always wondered what it would be like to be part of the entertainment team on a cruise ship.'

'You have?' May frowned—obviously hearing this for the first time.

'I have,' January confirmed with an awkward shrug, at the same time shooting Max a resentful glare—obviously not at all happy with having him here as part of this family 'baring-of-hearts'.

A sentiment that he wholeheartedly agreed with—although, as January didn't think he had a heart, she probably wouldn't believe that!

He stood up abruptly, once again keeping his gaze firmly fixed on May. 'It all sounds great.' He nodded. 'I hope it works out for you. I just felt I owed it to you all to come and tell you what I plan on doing tomorrow.' He drew in a sharp breath; now that the time had actually come for him to part from January his legs felt like lead, his heart even heavier.

'That was very kind of you, Max,' May told him warmly. 'Wasn't it, January?' she prompted pointedly.

'Very,' she echoed dryly.

He gave a self-derisive smile. 'What she really means, May, is she'll be glad to see me go!' he murmured softly.

January gave him a level stare. 'Is that so surprising? You've done nothing but cause mayhem and confusion since you arrived here!' she accused, her anger obviously starting to rise, two spots of colour in the paleness of her cheeks too now.

'January!' May gasped.

'But he has, May,' she defended impatiently. 'He's harassed us about selling the farm,' she claimed heatedly—a little unfairly, Max thought. 'He's lost me my job, he claims because of concern over my safety,' she continued disgustedly. 'And now he's got me into such a state of paranoia that I've even started *imagining* people are following me home at night!'

Max tensed, his gaze narrowing with sudden alertness. 'Someone followed you home last night?' he echoed slowly.

'Of course not,' she dismissed irritably. 'I just thought they did—'

'Why did you think they did?' he cut in softly, every muscle and sinew of his body tensed now, a nerve pulsing in his cheek.

January gave a dismissive smile. 'Because they obviously live somewhere in the area and were driving home at the same time I was!' she snorted self-derisively.

Max looked at her searchingly. 'Are you sure?'

She nodded. 'I'm still here, aren't I?' she scorned.

Yes, she was—and as verbally resentful as ever. Oh,

well, what had he expected? Nothing had happened to change that since they'd parted last night. In fact, from what she had just said, the opposite!

'So you are,' he conceded dryly. 'But I understand you will be at the hotel this evening?' There was a notice up outside the piano-bar that tonight would be January's last performance for a while.

Max's mouth had thinned disapprovingly as he'd read the notice earlier; Peter Meridew obviously couldn't even do that right! By making such a public announcement the other man was effectively letting anyone who cared to know that January would be driving home alone this evening one last time...!

'Yes, I will,' January confirmed abruptly, her chin raised challengingly. 'Can I expect to see you there?'

His mouth twisted humourlessly. 'I wouldn't be surprised,' he drawled.

Her eyes flashed dark grey. 'Neither would I!'

He gave an acknowledging bow before turning to a frowning May; obviously she wasn't at all happy about her youngest sister's rudeness. 'I wish you every success with your possible acting career,' he told her warmly.

May looked embarrassed again. 'I haven't definitely decided to go ahead with that yet.'

'But she will,' January said determinedly.

'Maybe,' May conceded. 'Have a good flight home tomorrow, Max.'

Once again one of the sisters had assumed that his home was in America. But this time he was too weary to correct the mistake.

'Thanks,' he accepted with a smile. 'I'll see you later, then, January.'

She gave him a look that clearly said, Not if I see you first!

Max chuckled softly. 'Or perhaps not,' he allowed ruefully.

Although that humour faded as soon as he was outside, taking a moment to stand and look at the surrounding countryside with narrowed eyes.

Had someone followed January home last night? Or was it as she said, just another local resident driving home late at night?

He didn't know. And neither did she. Not really. She couldn't.

January wasn't going to like it, he knew, but this was definitely something the police should be made aware of.

He also had one more call to make this afternoon on his way back to the hotel to pack.

To Josh.

January might see all of this as some sort of paranoia on his part, but if it stopped her from getting hurt, paranoid was exactly what he would be!

CHAPTER THIRTEEN

'NO JOHN this evening?'

January turned to find Max just entering the bar, his opening comment drawing attention to the fact that there was someone else working behind the bar this evening.

Before his gaze narrowed on January's own appearance, a shutter coming down over those blue eyes as he took in the scarlet knee-length dress she was wearing this evening.

January's chin rose defensively as Max's gaze swept over her from head to toe; she had decided that if this really was her last evening working here, then she was going out with a flourish! The figure-hugging, scoop-necked scarlet dress was the result of that bravado.

She shrugged, determined to ignore Max's all-seeing gaze. 'He was here earlier, apparently, but has since gone off sick,' she answered Max's earlier comment. 'Probably still having trouble with his ankle,' she dismissed, a little disappointed that she wouldn't see John again before leaving; he had always been very kind to her. 'Football,' she explained at Max's frowning look.

His brow cleared, his smile derisive. 'I've never really understood this fascination with what has become England's national sport.'

'It isn't as boring as cricket?' January returned dryly.

Max chuckled softly. 'You could have a point there!'

Max looked more like a rugby player himself, his physique muscular to say the least, January allowed grudgingly.

175

Not that it was of any of her business, she told herself sharply; there was nothing more she needed to know about Max Golding. It was bad enough that she was in love with him!

'If you'll excuse me,' she said sharply, as usual feeling disturbed just by Max's presence in the same room as her, 'I have to get to work.'

He nodded. 'I have a few things to attend to myself,' he told her enigmatically. 'Perhaps I'll catch up with you later,' he added dismissively.

January watched him leave beneath lowered lashes. Tomorrow he would be gone. From the hotel. From England. From her life. How her heart ached just at the thought of it!

Only a few more hours to get through, she told herself determinedly. And then she could give in to the heartbreak that had been threatening since he'd come to the farm earlier to inform them he was leaving, going back to America.

Perhaps it was as well she would no longer be working here after tonight; she simply wouldn't have been able to come to the hotel without imagining Max here, her loss all the more acute because he really wasn't.

As she was aware of his absence during the early part of the evening. Strange how quickly she had become accustomed to his being here the evenings she worked, how flat the evening seemed because he wasn't there watching her with that intense blue gaze.

She had to stop this, she decided as she stood at the bar sipping sparkling water during her first break. Max had never really been in her life, so how could she feel so devastated now that he was going out of it? She didn't know—she just did!

How could she bear it?

How was she going to survive without his annoy-ing—wonderful!—presence in her life?

'Penny for them?'

She turned sharply at the huskily intimate sound of his voice, hurriedly blinking back the tears that had blurred her vision. 'Shouldn't that be "cent"?' she came back lamely.

Max shook his head, frowning slightly. 'How many more times? I don't actually live in America, January.'

Her eyes widened. 'You don't?'

He gave another shake of his head. 'I have no idea why you thought that I did.'

'Because you said you had flown here from there.' She frowned. 'And Jude Marshall is there. I just as-sumed—' Somehow the thought that Max might actu-ally still be in England somewhere, and not all the way across the Atlantic, made their parting not quite so hard to bear.

'I have an apartment in London, January,' he told her softly, his gaze searching now on the paleness of her face. 'An apartment I have a feeling I will be using a lot more in the near future,' he added dryly.

She looked at him quizzically. 'You will?'

'Yes,' he confirmed with satisfaction. 'January—'

'Mr Golding?'

They both turned at the sound of that enquiring voice, January's gaze widening even further as she took in the police uniform the man was wearing. What on earth—?

'Yes?' Max answered sharply, January actually able to feel his sudden tension.

The policeman glanced at January. 'If you could just step outside for a few minutes, sir,' he prompted qui-etly.

January was feeling tense herself now. What on earth

could the police want with Max? Surely they didn't think—?

'I'm coming with you,' she told Max determinedly as he turned to leave with the other man.

He glanced back at her, blue gaze guarded now. 'I would much rather you didn't,' he said softly.

'Too bad,' she snapped forcefully, moving quickly to his side, her hand moving to rest lightly in his crooked arm.

Max looked down at her questioningly. 'I'm not about to be arrested, January,' he teased huskily.

She wasn't so sure about that! And if that were the case, and it had anything to do with the attacks over the last seven months, she had every intention of telling the police exactly how ridiculous they were being; Max hadn't even been in England when most of those attacks had occurred!

'You would be Miss Calendar?' The policeman frowned as he became aware of her presence. 'Miss January Calendar?'

Her hand tightened on Max's arm. 'I would,' she confirmed warily.

'Don't look so worried, January.' Max bent his head to tell her soothingly. 'They aren't about to arrest you, either!'

'I should think not,' she bristled indignantly.

'However…' Even as Max began to speak the door to Peter Meridew's office opened, several people emerging, obviously also policemen, a couple in plain clothes, two others in uniform restraining another man between the two of them as he struggled and shouted abuse.

'John…!' January gasped, before looking up disbelievingly at Max.

His expression was grim, his hand tight on hers as

it rested on his arm. 'John is the one who has been carrying out the attacks,' he told her gently.

'John is—?' She shook her head dazedly before turning back to look at John.

A John who looked totally unlike the likeable man she had come to know over the last few months, his face twisted into an ugly mask as he continued to shout and struggle as he was taken from the hotel.

John...!

He was the attacker? The man who had attacked six women? Who had beaten Josh so badly on Monday evening? The man who—

The man who had attacked Josh on Monday evening...

She looked up sharply at Max as a terrible truth began to grow inside her, seeing the confirmation of her suspicions in Max's grimly set features—before blackness washed over her and she began to fall.

Max looked down worriedly at January as she lay on the sofa in Peter Meridew's office. Her face was so pale, dark shadows beneath her eyes, her breathing shallow.

He had managed to catch her before she'd actually hit the tiled floor, picking her up to carry her through to the manager's office, dismissing the other man from his own office with an imperious wave of his hand, in one way relieved that January had been spared the next few minutes of dealing with the police, but in another way concerned about what to say to her when she did regain consciousness. Because he had seen the truth in her eyes seconds before she'd collapsed, knew then that she had realized exactly why John had carried out those attacks.

Knew that she was the catalyst...

'It was me, wasn't it?' January murmured beside him, as if the intensity of Max's thoughts had penetrated her unconsciousness.

Max turned to her sharply. 'How do you feel?' he prompted concernedly, taking one of her hands in his, dismayed at how cold she felt despite the warmth in the hotel.

She blinked, tears sparkling against her long lashes. 'John did those things because of some sort of misguided—feelings, for me, didn't he?' she repeated brokenly.

Max's hand tightened on hers. 'It wasn't your fault, January,' he told her firmly. 'You must never think that. The man was obsessed.' He shook his head grimly. 'I never realized before today how normal an insane person can appear!'

She gave the ghost of a smile. 'I'm not sure that remark was exactly complimentary to me...?'

Good, she was getting her sense of humour back; it was a start.

Max gave her a reassuring smile. 'It was meant to be, I can assure you. Are you feeling better?' he asked as she swung her legs to the floor and sat up next to him on the sofa.

She didn't look better, her face still deathly pale, those tears still trembling against her lashes.

'January, you couldn't have known,' he told her intensely. 'Damn it, until I spoke to Josh this afternoon I thought it was Peter Meridew!' he added self-derisively—and instantly wished he hadn't as January's face paled even more. 'It was mentioning that to Josh this afternoon that jogged his memory into realizing it was the *hotel barman's* voice he had recognized. The police have been watching John since this afternoon,' he added grimly.

'You knew?' January gasped. 'You really did know?'

Max gave a pained frown as her voice broke emotionally. 'The attack on Josh set off alarm bells in my head.' He nodded. 'Especially when he told us he had recognized the voice of his attacker. I just came to the wrong conclusion, that's all.' He grimaced. 'Maybe I can be forgiven for that. Peter Meridew was in the room when Josh kissed you on Saturday evening, and he also seemed to be around a lot whenever you were in the piano bar. But then so was John,' he acknowledged hardly.

January still looked totally dazed. 'But if—if John, felt that he had some sort of—of claim on me, why didn't he attack you, too?'

Max gave a rueful smile. 'Good question. I've been wondering that myself.' He grimaced. 'Maybe he just didn't think I was going to be around long enough to be a problem. Whereas Josh and Peter Meridew…' He broke off pointedly.

January shook her head. 'Why did he attack those other women?'

'Because it seems that, at one time or another, he felt they had scorned or rejected him. Who really knows the workings of a disturbed mind?' he rasped harshly.

January swallowed hard. 'Maybe the same thing would have happened to me if I had ever been less than friendly towards him.' She shuddered just at the thought of it.

Max's hand tightened about hers. 'You mustn't think that way, January,' he told her forcefully. 'John has been arrested. He's no longer a danger to anyone— thank goodness. He completely lost it when he came in to work this evening and discovered you were no longer going to be working here, instantly knew who was responsible. The police caught him in the act of attacking Peter Meridew. I don't know if you heard him just now—' Max grimaced '—but he's already said enough for the police to charge him with all the attacks,' he explained softly, all the time watching January concernedly.

She swallowed hard. 'Do you think it was John that followed me home last night?'

'Ah. No.' Max grimaced self-consciously. 'I checked on that earlier. It was actually a police car. Apparently, they had thought they were following at a safe distance, but my constant warnings had obviously put you on a bigger state of alertness than we thought. I'm sorry for alarming you in that way, January,' he added as she looked more pale than ever.

This must all have come as such a shock to her. After all, he had had several hours to come to terms with the idea himself, and he still found the whole thing highly disturbing. January had known John a lot longer than he had, had obviously liked the man. Only to find out he wasn't at all what she had thought he was.

Perhaps he would be able to persuade her that *he* wasn't what she had thought he was either…?

One thing Max knew for certain, whatever his plans might have been before tonight, he no longer intended going back to America.

He couldn't bear the thought of going anywhere if January wouldn't go with him!

CHAPTER FOURTEEN

JANUARY felt ill, had never felt so sick in her life. John. Nice, friendly, *invisible* John. Who ever would have thought of it?

Max had thought of it!

Okay, so he had initially suspected the wrong man, but he had ultimately been perfectly correct in warning her to take care. And all she had done was to give him a hard time over what she had considered his interference!

God, all those times she had talked with John, shared a joke or two with him, accepted his offer to walk her out to her car—!

She repressed a shudder, looked frowningly at Max. 'I owe you an apology—' She broke off as Max stood up abruptly, frowning up at him now.

'I don't want your apology, January,' he rasped, blue gaze blazing, hands clenched at his sides. 'Neither do I want your gratitude,' he added harshly.

She flinched at the force of his emotions. But was it so surprising that Max was angry with her? He had tried to help her, and she had blocked or mocked him at every turn.

She sighed. 'I appreciate you're angry—'

'Too right I'm angry!' he shot back forcefully. 'I should have looked after you better. Should have checked and double-checked on my suspicions, not just told the police about them—before deciding to run away!' he bit out self-disgustedly. 'Well, I'm not running any more, January,' he told her forcefully. 'I'm not going anywhere. Do I make myself clear?' He stood over her gloweringly.

January blinked a little dazedly at this sudden attack. She had meant *he* had a right to be angry with *her*, not himself. 'I don't understand.' She shook her head in puzzlement.

Max came down on his haunches beside her, his gaze intent on her face. 'I'm not going to America or anywhere else, January. In fact, in future I'm going to stick to you like glue,' he added grimly.

'But—but now that John has—now that he's been arrested, I'm not in any danger.' She still felt nauseous at how friendly she had been with a man who attacked seemingly at random. Although she was sure that someone would eventually make sense of John's obsession...

'You may not be,' Max bit out forcefully. 'But I certainly am.' He took both her hands in both of his, his gaze intense on the paleness of her face now. 'January, I intend giving Jude notice that I will no longer be available to work for him.'

She frowned. 'Because of those things I said to you?' she groaned self-reproachfully. 'But I didn't mean them. I was only—'

'No, not because of anything you said to me,' Max assured her firmly. 'I intended telling him all this anyway when I got back to America.'

She blinked. 'You did?'

He nodded. 'January, this is no excuse, I know, but since my mother walked out on my father and me when I was five, I've been pretty determined not to let anyone into my life—particularly a woman—who might hurt me like that again. But you—' He broke off, shaking his head. 'You sneaked in without my even being aware of it. I'm in love with you. I know I'm in love with you,' he assured her with certainty. 'The thought of leaving you, even for a short time, has been driving me crazy! This will tell you exactly how crazy I am,' he added self-derisively. 'I'm even willing to learn how to run a farm if that's what you want to do. Anything, as long as I can spend the rest of my life with you,' he added gruffly.

January looked up at him with dawning wonder in her eyes. Had Max really just said he was in love with her? But Sunday night he had said those awful things to her—

'I'm not expecting you to make any declaration back,' he told her ruefully as he obviously saw the doubt in her face. 'After the way I've behaved I couldn't expect that. I've been so busy trying to protect myself, my own emotions, that I've said and done some terrible things to you. No, I'm not expecting you to love me in return, I'm just telling you how I feel. A declaration of intent on my part, if you like.' He smiled self-derisively. 'In case you're in any doubt, I can be a very determined man when I choose to be. And in your case, I definitely choose to be!' he added with feeling.

January swallowed hard before speaking, but nevertheless her voice was still husky when she spoke. 'Max, having your mother walk out on you when you were five doesn't mean that there won't be someone else to come along who will love you for a lifetime.' She drew in a deep breath. 'I was three when my mother walked out on us, but that doesn't stop me from being able to love you with all my heart.' There, she had said it!

'Your mother walked out on you...?' Max gasped incredulously. 'But—*that's* why your father cut her image from the photograph beside his bed!' he realized with a pained frown.

'Yes.' January nodded. 'May has always tried to protect March and me from knowing, still thinks we believe that our mother is dead, and although we both know the truth we let her go on thinking that. It's the reason May is so protective of us,' she added affectionately.

'How could a mother possibly walk out on three such beautiful little girls who were only aged three, four and five?' Max groaned.

January gave a pained smile. 'I don't know, you would have to ask her that.'

He shook his head. 'I don't understand how any—' He broke off abruptly, suddenly looking at January with widely incredulous eyes.

Ah. The second part of her statement had finally penetrated. How was Max, who had been so wounded at such a young age, going to react to knowing that she was in love with him?

Had January just said—? Had she really just told him—?

She gave what sounded like a huskily nervous laugh. 'Does knowing I love you in return change anything?' she prompted warily.

'Change anything?' he repeated, love for this woman welling up inside him so that he thought he could no longer contain it. 'Change anything!' His voice rose triumphantly. 'It changes everything!' His hands tightened about hers. 'But are you sure you love me?

Enough to marry me?' Still he hesitated, not sure this could be happening to him. 'After all—'

'Why don't you ask me that question again in forty years or so?' January interrupted gently.

'Forty years—? You *will* marry me?' He held his breath as he waited for her answer, his heart beating so loudly he was sure she must be able to hear it.

Her smile was mischievous now. 'I don't think May would let you get away with anything less!'

'I don't want anything less,' he assured her breathlessly. 'In fact, I want more; forty years isn't nearly long enough!'

There were tears of happiness in her eyes now as she reached up to caress the hard curve of his jaw. 'How about fifty years? Sixty?' she added laughingly when he still didn't reply.

He wanted eternity with this woman. Wanted to spend the rest of his life at her side, loving her, being loved in return.

Being loved in return...

'January!' He couldn't wait any longer, sweeping her up into his arms, kissing her with a hunger that would take an eternity to assuage.

Everything else could come later now that he knew January loved him in the way he loved her. Everything. May and March. The farm. Jude. Even poor disturbed John.

January was all that mattered to him now.

She always would be!

THE UNWILLING MISTRESS

by

Carole Mortimer

CHAPTER ONE

'Good morning,' a voice greeted cheerfully, quickly followed by a more tentative, 'er—again…?'

March closed the folder containing the figures she had been frowning over, not at all happy with what she saw there, taking several seconds to automatically assume the polite smile reserved for the clients entering the estate agency where she worked.

Although that polite smile turned back to a frown as she looked up and realized the reason for the man's second tentative query.

It certainly was 'again', wasn't it?

She sat back in her chair, her gaze rueful now as she looked up derisively at the man standing in front of her desk.

Under any other circumstances she would have found this man extremely good-looking.

Very tall, probably aged in his mid-thirties, with a tangible air of self-confidence, he had slightly overlong silver-blond hair, with hard, sculptured features, his eyes the colour of sky on a clear summer's day—which today certainly wasn't!

It was snowing outside—and not half an hour ago this man had neatly slipped into the car-parking space directly outside here that March had been about to parallel-park into!

The politeness of her role as Receptionist in this busy estate agency, and indignation that instead of being able

5

to park outside she had had to park half a mile away and walk back through the snow, warred inside her.

The latter easily won!

'Correct me if I'm wrong,' she bit out caustically, 'but the last time we saw each other I believe you ensured that I would not have a good start to my morning!'

The man gave a pained wince. 'You remember me.'

March eyed him scathingly. She was hardly likely to forget him!

She had been absolutely furious earlier when she'd turned to begin her parallel park and seen this man neatly driving his red sports car into the space instead. If she hadn't already been late for work, due to the bad weather, she would probably have got out of the car and told him exactly what she thought of him. Instead she had driven around for ten minutes trying to find another parking spot, and then had to trudge all the way back in the falling snow. All the time cursing this man for his inconsideration!

The fact that the powerful red sports car had still been parked outside when she'd got back here had only added insult to injury.

Although the reason he had chosen to park in that particular spot was made obvious by the fact that he had now come into the agency. After wasting time by wandering to the newsagent's two doors down, if the newspaper under his arm was anything to go by. Well, it was his own fault if he had had to wait for her to open up for business; she wouldn't have arrived late at all if he hadn't stolen her parking space!

The man gave her a quizzical smile. 'We do seem to have got off to rather a bad start,' he acknowledged ruefully.

Yes, they had, but he was obviously a customer, and

she was the only one to have arrived in the office so far this morning.

March forced herself to once again smile politely. 'How may I help you, Mr...?'

'Davenport,' he supplied lightly. 'Will Davenport. Mind if I sit down—March?' he prompted after a glance at the name tag on the lapel of her suit jacket.

'That's what the chairs are for—Mr Davenport,' she pointed out dryly.

He lowered his long length into the chair opposite hers. 'Tell me, March,' he drawled, 'is everyone here as friendly as you?' A derisive smile curved his own lips now as he eyed her mockingly across the width of the desk.

March felt the colour warm her cheeks at this deliberate rebuke. Probably deserved, she allowed grudgingly. Although that didn't excuse his own high-handedness earlier.

'Only when they've had their parking space usurped!' she returned sharply.

He grinned unabashedly. 'I live in London.' He shrugged broad shoulders beneath the navy-blue sweater and thick overjacket he wore. 'Parking spaces there are up for grabs to the first taker!'

March felt slightly disarmed by that grin. He really was very good-looking, that overlong silver-blond hair falling endearingly over his forehead, laughter lurking in those deep blue eyes, the hardness of his features softened by the grin too.

But the fact that this man was breathtakingly handsome really wasn't the point, was it?

'I was the first taker!' she reminded impatiently.

He gave an irritated frown now. 'Perhaps we could move on?'

Yes, perhaps they had better. Clive, when he finally did put in an appearance, wouldn't be too happy with her for alienating a customer—perhaps their only customer on a day like today!

March drew in a deeply controlling breath, straightening some folders on her desk before forcing herself to resume that polite smile. 'Are you interested in buying a property in the area, Mr Davenport?'

'No.'

Her eyes widened, grey-green eyes surrounded by thick dark lashes, the same colour as her below-shoulder-length hair. If he wasn't interested in buying a property, then why—?

'I'm looking to rent a place for a couple of weeks,' he added mockingly.

Her brow cleared at this explanation. 'For the summer?' She stood up, moving to the filing cabinet behind her. 'We have some rather lovely cottages—'

'No, not for the summer. For now,' Will Davenport corrected even as she pulled open a drawer.

March turned back to him with raised brows before glancing frowningly at the snow still falling outside. It was January, for goodness' sake, none of the people they had on their books rented the cottages out in winter—mainly because very few of the properties actually had any heating in them, apart from an open fire.

'I'm in the area on business for a few weeks.' Will Davenport obviously took pity on her confusion. 'I'm booked into a hotel at the moment, but I hate their impersonality,' he added with a grimace.

March really wouldn't know whether hotels were impersonal or otherwise, never having stayed in one. Living on a farm, the middle one of three sisters, brought up alone by their father since March was four, there had been very little money to spare for things like holidays. And since their father died last year, that situation had only worsened.

She suddenly became aware of the completely male assessment of Will Davenport's gaze as he studied her, from the top of her ebony head to the soles of her heeled shoes.

At twenty-six, she was tall and slender, with long shapely legs, smartly dressed in a navy-blue suit matched with a lighter blue jumper, pale magnolia skin, her make-up light, her lip-gloss peach, only the pointed determination of her chin indicative of the stubbornness of her nature.

Although Will Davenport obviously liked what he saw, his smile warmly appreciative now as he gave a mocking acknowledgement of his head at her questioning look.

Well, really!

He had literally pushed—parked!—his way into her life—and now he was looking at her as if she were the tastiest thing on the menu!

March moved abruptly to resume her seat behind the desk, glaring across at him as she wondered how much longer Clive and Michelle were going to be; quite frankly, she had had enough of trying to deal with Will Davenport for one day.

Clive Carter and Michelle Jones were not only partners in the estate agency of Carter and Jones, but they also lived together on the outskirts of town. The fact that neither of them had arrived yet had to mean that the snow was delaying both of them. More was the pity!

As the receptionist, March usually only answered the telephone and passed clients on to either Clive or Michelle. Something she really wished she could do with this particular client!

'I'm afraid Mr Carter and Miss Jones aren't in the office at the moment,' she began crisply.

'I think I can see that for myself, March,' Will Davenport drawled mockingly.

March flushed irritably at his obvious sarcasm. 'What I'm trying to say is that I think it would be better if you called back later and spoke to one of them,' she snapped, grey-green eyes flashing a warning of her rising temper.

His mouth twisted. 'You aren't qualified to show me details of any properties for rent in the area?'

If he was meaning to be insulting—and he probably was!—then he was succeeding.

March frowned. 'Of course I can show you the properties, Mr Davenport—'

'Then perhaps you had better do so,' he suggested dryly.

March drew in a deeply controlling breath as she desperately tried to resist the urge she had to wipe that confidently mocking smile right off that sculptured mouth!

The man was infuriating! Not only that, he was arrogant, mocking, and he had the cheek to—

Wait a minute... He was looking for somewhere to rent. She might just have the perfect place for him, at that!

Will wasn't sure he altogether liked the cat-who-had-swallowed-the-cream smile now curving March's lips. As if she knew something he didn't...

Not that he could altogether blame her for being initially annoyed with him—he had taken her parking space earlier, something that had obviously infuriated her.

He had felt more than a little guilty about that when he'd entered the estate agent's a short time ago and recognized her as she sat behind the desk, but that guilt had since turned to admiration. March was absolutely beautiful when angry. Those unusual grey-green eyes sparkled with the emotion, her pale skin having a blushing hue, as for her mouth—!

But he wasn't quite so comfortable with that quietly satisfied look on her face now…

'Tell me, Mr Davenport…' she leant across the desk confidingly '…are you particularly looking for somewhere here in town, or would somewhere further out be of any interest to you?'

Will eyed her warily. 'That depends in which direction out it was,' he answered guardedly.

As far as he was concerned, the job he did was completely harmless, moreover he was completely professional, but he had learnt from experience that not everyone looked on it in the same way. The fewer people who knew the reason for his presence in the area, the better it would be. For the moment.

'Over towards the village of Paxton,' March told him lightly. 'If you don't know where that is—'

'I do,' he cut in lightly. 'Towards Paxton would be perfect.'

March looked startled. 'It would…?'

'Perfect,' he repeated mockingly.

She could have no idea how perfect. In fact, it was exactly where he wanted to be. Staying in the area would mean he wouldn't have to keep driving out there, could blend into the scenery more easily, and so not make himself quite so conspicuous to the locals. Certain locals in particular!

March looked a little less certain now. 'The property I have in mind is on a farm in the area, not a cottage but a studio-conversion over a garage.'

'Sounds good.' He nodded. 'When can I see it? I would really like to check out of the hotel and get moved in as quickly as possible,' he added briskly at her surprised look.

She blinked at his decisiveness. 'I'm not completely sure that the owners would be interested in a winter let, so I would have to call them first and check—'

'Go ahead,' he invited smoothly.

March looked totally nonplussed now. Obviously she wasn't used to things moving quite this quickly. Well, she would have to get used to it, because Will didn't have any time to waste, wanted to get the job done, and then get the hell out of Dodge City. Before anyone started baying for his blood!

'Time is money, March,' he prompted dryly.

She blinked, her expression suddenly becoming wistful. 'My father used to say that,' she explained huskily at his questioning look.

'Used to?' Will repeated softly.

March sat up straighter in her chair, that flush returning to her cheeks, as if she had said too much. 'He died,' she bit out abruptly, at the same time picking up the telephone. 'I'll call the farm now,' she told him curtly.

Will watched March rather than listened to her conversation. She really was beautiful. Perhaps his time in Yorkshire wasn't going to be quite as lonely as he had initially thought. If he could get past the prejudice she felt towards him because he had 'usurped her parking spot', that was!

'Will one-thirty suit you for viewing, Mr Davenport?' March looked enquiringly across the desk at him, her hand over the mouthpiece as she spoke. 'Even farmers stop for lunch,' she informed him dryly as he raised blond brows.

'Fine,' he snapped, knowing she was deliberately mocking him.

Was it so obvious that he had been born and lived in cities all his life? Probably. But he liked what he had seen of Yorkshire so far, and this part of the county was particularly beautiful.

Although he still had that niggling feeling that there was something not quite right about the property March was sending him to see. Perhaps the farmer had a particularly fierce bull he liked to set on strangers? Or perhaps a pack of hounds? Or perhaps she just found the idea amusing of placing Will, a man obviously used to the amenities of the city, on a farm?

It might be at that; as far as he was aware, he had never set foot on a farm in his life. But there was a first time for everything, and from the sound of it, the location was perfect...

'That's settled then, Mr Davenport,' March told him briskly as she ended the call, writing an address down on a piece of paper before handing it to him. 'I'm sure that either Mr Carter or Miss Jones would be only too pleased to accompany you—'

'No, thanks,' he cut in briskly. 'I would rather find my own way around.'

She nodded. 'But please feel free to call back and speak to either Mr Carter or Miss Jones if you find this particular rental unsuitable for your needs.'

Giving Will the clear impression that she already knew it wasn't going to be!

Which only incited him into wanting to take that satisfied little smile off her beautiful face! 'March, would you have dinner with me this evening?'

He almost laughed at the sudden stunned look on her face. Almost. Because even as he made the invitation he knew that he really did want her to have dinner with him…!

She was prickly and outspoken, absolutely nothing like a receptionist greeting the general public should be, but at the same time he liked her outspokenness, that sparkle in her eyes, and her beauty was indisputable.

She seemed to gather her scattered wits together with effort, straightening in her chair even as she began to shake her head. 'I don't think so, thank you, Mr Davenport,' she refused tautly, those dark lashed grey-green eyes sparkling with indignation now.

He quirked blond brows. 'No taking pity on a stranger in the area?'

Her mouth twisted derisively. '*Being* a stranger here, you may not have heard, Mr Davenport, but we had a stalker in the area until he was caught quite recently.'

As it happened, Will had heard—although he wasn't quite sure he liked her implication!

'As I recall, the man was a local,' he reminded dryly.

'Yes, he was,' she confirmed abruptly, her cheeks pale now. 'But that's all the more reason to be doubly wary of strangers.'

He gave an acknowledging inclination of his head. 'Maybe I'll come back tomorrow and ask again—I won't be a stranger then!'

March gave the ghost of a smile. 'You can try,' she challenged.

But he would be wasting his time, her words clearly implied. Pity. He would have liked to get to know her better.

'Thanks, anyway, March.' He stood up to leave. 'I'm expected at one-thirty, you said?'

'Lunchtime,' she confirmed dryly.

Good, that would give him time to complete the other

business he had in town. Although, so far, that was proving more difficult than he had imagined.

He turned back to March. 'I don't suppose—no,' he answered his own question, shaking his head ruefully. 'Sorry.' He grimaced at her enquiring look. 'I'm making enquiries about a friend of mine who was staying at the hotel until a few days ago, but as he was another stranger, I don't suppose you would know anything about him, either!'

March eyed him mockingly. 'I don't suppose I would.'

Will grinned. 'Never at a loss for words, are you?' he said admiringly.

'Only when invited out to dinner by a complete stranger,' she mocked her own momentary lack of composure a few minutes ago when he'd made the invitation.

He chuckled softly. 'It isn't too late to change your mind about that…?'

'I'll pass, thanks,' she returned smilingly, her attention distracted behind him at that moment as the bell rang over the door to announce a new arrival.

'Thanks for this, March.' Will held up the piece of paper with the address on it. 'You can have my parking space now, if you want it,' he added goadingly.

March gave him a look from beneath deliberately frowning brows. 'I believe that was *my* parking space, Mr Davenport—and I won't bother now, if you don't mind.' She laughed in spite of herself.

Will nodded politely to the man and woman who had just entered, deciding from their business suits, and general air of ownership, that they were probably the Mr Carter and Miss Jones that March kept referring to.

He glanced back inside before driving away, raising a hand in parting to March as he saw she was looking out of the window at him, too. Still with that self-satisfied smile curving her lips, the little minx.

Pity she had turned down his dinner invitation. Although, perhaps with the controversial circumstances of his being in the area, it was probably better not to involve her.

From what he had already been told, he was going to have enough trouble with certain members of the community, without becoming personally involved with another one of them.

As Max appeared to have done…

CHAPTER TWO

MARCH wasn't in the least surprised to see the powerful red sports car still parked in the yard when she arrived at the farm that afternoon shortly before two. In fact, she had counted on it!

Will Davenport, with his good looks and air of sophistication—his lack of apology for taking her parking spot!—had totally rubbed her up the wrong way this morning. Well, the boot was on the other foot now—as he was shortly going to realize.

Wednesday was half-day at the agency, a fact she had been very aware of when she'd made the appointment for Will Davenport to view this rented accommodation at one-thirty.

'You really didn't have to bother to come all the way out here, you know,' Will Davenport's unmistakable voice drawled from behind March as she turned to get her bag from the back of the car. 'I did tell you I would be able to manage for myself,' he added with confident dismissal.

March slowly straightened before turning to give him a mocking smile. 'And have you?' she taunted.

'Of course.' Will stepped aside so that the person standing behind him was now visible. 'Apart from signing on the dotted line, I believe May and I have settled everything.' He grinned his satisfaction.

March turned to the young woman who now stood beside Will. 'I don't think we have a dotted line for Will to sign on, do we, May?' she prompted lightly.

Her sister smiled. 'Not that I'm aware of, no,' she drawled, at the same time now giving March a quizzical look.

May, as the eldest of the three sisters, had always been the more level-headed one too; it didn't need two guesses to know that she was not going to be pleased with March for the little trick she had played on Will Davenport today.

Never mind; it had been worth it—just to see the puzzled expression as his gaze moved frowningly between the two sisters!

'"We"?' he finally prompted slowly, his expression wary now.

March gave a satisfied grin. 'I didn't come here to check up on you, Mr Davenport—I happen to live here!' she took great delight in telling him.

To say he looked stunned by this disclosure had to be an understatement; he looked as if someone had just punched him between the eyes!

Yes, he looked stunned—and something else, March realized as his expression instantly became guarded. She had thought, from the little she had seen of him, that once Will got over the surprise at learning that it was her family farm she had sent him to, he would laugh about the situation. But obviously she had misjudged his sense of humour, because he certainly didn't look as if he felt much like laughing.

'It was only a joke, Mr Davenport,' she told him ruefully. 'Not a very clever one at that,' she allowed dryly. 'After all, we do have the studio for rent, and you did say you were looking for somewhere in the area...' She trailed off as she could tell that, far from seeing the funny side of the situation, he was now frowning darkly.

'The two of you are sisters,' he realized woodenly.

'I don't think you get any Brownie points for guessing that!' March grinned as she moved to stand next to May, the likeness between the two women more than obvious, both tall and dark-haired, their features similar, only the eyes a different colour, May's a clear emerald-green.

Will Davenport didn't return her smile. In fact, he seemed momentarily at a loss for words.

'Why don't you come into the farmhouse and have a nice cup of tea, Mr Davenport?' May briskly took charge of the situation, shooting March another reproving look as she took hold of Will's arm to urge him towards the house.

March followed slowly behind them. Some people just didn't have a sense of humour, she decided scornfully. It had only been a joke, for goodness' sake. And he had seemed to like the studio well enough before he'd realized she lived here too.

Maybe that was his problem, she realized a little disgruntledly. Perhaps he thought she might try to follow up on his earlier dinner invitation? That she had done this for some hidden reason of her own?

Well, he needn't worry, she had no intention of bothering him even if he did move into the studio for a couple of weeks; she was out at work all day, and busy with chores about the farm the rest of the time. Besides, she had the distinct feeling that Will Davenport was way out of her league...

'Put the kettle on, March,' her sister instructed firmly once they were in the warmth of the kitchen, Will Davenport still not looking any happier as he sat at the kitchen table. 'You obviously had no idea that this was March's home, too?' May prompted as she sat down opposite him.

'None at all.' He seemed to rouse himself out of his

stupor for a few seconds as he looked up at March. 'You would be March Calendar?'

She grinned. 'I certainly would.'

May frowned across at March before turning her attention back to their visitor. 'My sister sometimes has a warped sense of humour—'

'Oh, for goodness' sake!' March cut in impatiently. 'It was only a little joke. What possible difference can it make that I live here too?' she added irritably.

May sighed. 'Well, if I were in Will's shoes—'

'Which you obviously aren't,' March taunted; Will Davenport's shoes, indeed all his clothes, looked much more expensive than anything they could afford!

Her sister glared at her. 'March, when are you going to learn that you just can't do things like this? You're twenty-six years old, for goodness' sake, not six!'

Her cheeks became flushed at her sister's rebuke. 'It was a joke,' she repeated incredulously.

'It may have been—'

'It really is all right, May,' Will Davenport cut in lightly. 'March was just settling a score from this morning. Right?' He looked at her with narrowed blue eyes.

March shrugged. 'Well, I thought it was funny,' she muttered disgustedly.

And, no matter what May might say, it was funny. But March also knew the reason for May's concern; the money they would receive from letting the studio for two weeks would come in very handy. Any extra money always came in handy on a small farm like this one!

Will Davenport seemed to visibly relax. 'It was. It is.' He nodded ruefully. 'You see, May, I rather inconvenienced March this morning by ''usurping'' her parking space,' he explained wryly, at the same time shooting March a derisive look. 'This was obviously pay-back time.' His gaze was mocking on March now. 'Well, I'm afraid the joke is on you, March—because I have every intention of renting the studio for a couple of weeks. If that's okay with you?' He turned back to May.

'Hey, I live here too,' March defended ruefully.

'I think we're now all well aware of that fact!' May bit out impatiently.

Will Davenport began to smile, the smile turning into a chuckle. 'I think I'm going to enjoy my stay here, after all,' he murmured appreciatively.

'How could you have doubted it?' March came back mockingly, more than a little relieved that he had decided to stay after all; May really would never have forgiven her if he had decided not to simply because of the joke she had played on him.

'Only too easily, I would have thought,' May snapped, but she was smiling too now.

'I was thinking of moving in later this afternoon, if that's okay?' their new paying guest prompted lightly.

'He hates staying in hotels,' March put in derisively.

'Of course it's okay for you to move in today,' May confirmed. 'The studio should be thoroughly warm by this evening,' she added apologetically.

Something it obviously wasn't yet. Despite March's prompt call earlier so that May could go over and switch on the heating for their visitor. The studio hadn't been used since last summer, and so there hadn't been any heating on over there, either.

'Although you might prefer to come over and have dinner with us just for this evening?' May continued frowningly.

Now that was just going too far in March's opinion. The man was supposed to be renting the studio, completely independent of them and the farm, not moving in with them!

Will Davenport sat back in his chair to shoot her a knowing smile—as if he were only too well aware of what she was thinking. Which he probably was; she never had been any good at hiding her feelings! And with this man, someone who wouldn't be around long enough to matter, she didn't see why she should bother...

'How about that, March?' he drawled mockingly. 'We can have dinner together, after all!'

Oh, goody—she didn't think!

'Will invited me out to dinner earlier,' she told May bluntly as her sister looked slightly puzzled by the conversation.

May looked speculative now as she glanced first at Will Davenport and then more closely at March. 'Really?' she finally murmured enigmatically.

'Really!' March confirmed with a certain amount of resentment; the last thing she wanted was for her eldest sister to start thinking there was actually anything between Will Davenport and herself—because there wasn't. 'I said no, of course,' she said flatly. 'One can never be too careful, can one?' she added pointedly.

May turned to Will Davenport. 'Our younger sister used to sing at a hotel in town and was recently—involved, in the arrest of a man who was attacking people in this area,' she explained with a grimace.

'I sincerely hope you're not implying that I—'

'No, of course not,' May laughingly dismissed Will Davenport's mocking query. 'It just wasn't very pleasant, for January, or anyone else, for that matter,' she added with a frown. 'In fact, her fiancé has taken her away for a short holiday to get over it.'

'January?' Will Davenport echoed ruefully. 'Your parents certainly liked the names of months for their children, didn't they?'

'Personally, I've always been rather relieved I wasn't born in September,' March put in dryly. 'I can imagine nothing worse than going through life being called Sept! I suppose August wouldn't have been too bad—' She broke off as May spluttered with laughter.

'That wouldn't have suited you at all!' May explained with a grin.

'No, March suits you perfectly,' Will Davenport assured her wryly.

March gave him a narrow-eyed look as she placed the mug of tea on the table in front of him.

He returned her gaze with a look that was just too innocent for her liking. 'I've always looked on the month of March as brisk and crisp, the month that blows all the cobwebs away,' he drawled mockingly.

'That's March to a T!' May confirmed with another laugh.

'Thanks very much!' she muttered disgruntledly.

'You're welcome.' Will gave a derisive inclination of his head before turning back to May. 'Dinner this evening sounds wonderful—if you're sure I'm not intruding?'

Of course he was intruding. But, as March knew only too well, beggars couldn't be choosers, and the money he would pay them in rent over the next two weeks— once they had paid the commission to Carter and Jones, of course—would be very useful. The roof needed fixing on the barn, for one thing, and there were any number of small jobs about the farm that needed doing.

No, all things considered, she didn't mind this man 'intruding' for two weeks.

*   *   *

Will couldn't get over the likeness between the two sisters. He probably should have realized the connection when May Calendar had introduced herself on his arrival, but at the time he had had something much more important to occupy his mind.

As it still occupied his mind!

'You said your sister January is away on holiday with her fiancé at the moment?' he prompted lightly.

'Max.' May nodded with an affectionate smile. 'It's been rather a whirlwind romance, but we like him, don't we, March?' She looked up at her sister for confirmation.

Giving Will a few seconds' reprieve to come to terms with this latest piece of information. Max had got himself *engaged* to one of the Calendar sisters? Well, that certainly explained a lot!

'We do now,' March said with satisfaction.

'Oh?' Will prompted interestedly.

But not too interestedly, he hoped; he might have walked into the lion's den by accident—designed by March Calendar herself, if she did but know it!—but he was staying through choice.

He liked these two women. But especially March, with her quirky sense of humour and her outspokenness. It was refreshing to meet someone who said exactly what she thought. Or, if she didn't exactly say it, looked what she thought.

But he was still stunned by the fact that Max had become so personally involved with this family that he was actually going to marry one of them. Max had been a loner for as long as Will could remember, had always scorned the very idea of love, let alone marriage. Although if January was anything like March and May, perhaps the attraction was understandable…

Yes, he liked these two women, but whether or not they were still going to like him at the end of two weeks was another matter...

'Just a little family problem,' May answered him dismissively.

'Anything I could help with?' Even as he asked the question Will knew he had gone too far, could see the puzzlement in May's expression, March's more openly hostile.

'Not unless you're acquainted with Jude Marshall,' March bit out hardly. 'Max is a lawyer, originally sent here on Jude Marshall's behalf to buy our farm,' she explained at Will's frowning look. 'Which we aren't interested in selling!' she added with a pointedly determined look in May's direction.

A look Will was all too aware of. Dissension in the ranks? It certainly looked like it. May's next words confirmed it.

'We're thinking about it, March,' she told her sister.

'You might be—but I'm certainly not,' March snapped, two spots of angry colour now in the paleness of her cheeks.

May sighed before turning back to Will. 'You'll have to excuse us, I'm afraid, Mr Davenport—'

'Will,' he put in smoothly.

May smiled in acknowledgement. 'I'm afraid that whether or not we should sell the farm is an ongoing problem at the moment.' She gave a rueful shake of her head.

'May thinks we should, and I don't agree with her,' March snapped unnecessarily.

'And what does January think?' Will was intrigued about the younger sister, in spite of himself. Although he had already guessed at the rift between March and May over the situation…

'She'll go along with whatever I decide,' March announced triumphantly.

'Whatever *you* decide?' he prompted mildly; there were three sisters, shouldn't they all decide?

'Yes, you see May is—'

'I think we've bored Mr—Will,' May corrected at Will's gently reproving look. 'We've bored him with our problems long enough for one day, March,' she stated firmly as she stood up. 'The only thing that Will needs to know is that we definitely won't be selling the farm during the two weeks he wants to stay here,' she added lightly.

'That's a relief.' He smiled, preparing to leave as he took May having stood up as his cue to leave. 'I should be back by about five o'clock, if that's okay?'

May nodded. 'The garage beneath the studio is for your use.'

'Yes.' March grinned now. 'One fall of snow and you could lose your little car underneath it!'

What March described as a 'little car' was in fact a Ferrari! It was Will's pride and joy, the culmination of years of hard work. But, he had to admit, March was probably right about the snow! Yorkshire was having a particularly hard winter this year, many people having been snowbound in their homes until the last few days.

He gave a rueful smile. 'I'll try to remember that.' He nodded.

'Dinner is at seven o'clock,' May told him briskly as she walked to the door with him.

'Stew and dumplings tonight, isn't it, May?' March put in with a deliberately mocking smile in Will's direction.

She obviously didn't see him as a man who normally ate such nourishingly basic fare, and in one way she was probably right; he lived alone, had a busy life, and things like home cooking were not a luxury he could afford. Although he didn't think March would understand what he meant by that...

'It sounds wonderful,' he told May warmly.

'Just like your old granny used to make?' March put in tauntingly.

'March!' May winced laughingly.

'Let's hope so,' Will answered March dryly. 'My grandmother is a first-class cook!' he added challengingly, rewarded with the satisfaction of seeing that superior smile wiped off March's beautiful face!

'So was ours, and she taught us all to cook,' May assured him smilingly, lightly touching the sleeve of his coat in apology for March's outspokenness.

Strange that it was their grandmother who had taught the three sisters to cook, and not their mother...?

'There you are, March; something we have in common!' He grinned across at her.

'It's probably the only thing,' she muttered in reply.

Causing Will's grin to widen appreciatively. This woman really did have an answer for everything!

'Any chance of a home-made apple pie to go with the stew and dumplings?' he prompted hopefully. 'My grandmother makes the most mouth-watering pastry too,' he added dryly.

'Would you like us to get out the best silver and white table linen too?' March came back impatiently.

He raised mocking blond brows. 'Not unless it's what you normally do, no.'

'Hardly,' she scorned.

'It was only a suggestion about the pie.' He shrugged,

laughter gleaming in his eyes at March's obvious disgust with the whole conversation. 'Obviously if you can't make mouth-watering pastry—'

'Oh, but she can,' May put in, laughter lurking in her own eyes now as she listened to the exchange with obvious enjoyment. 'The art of making good pastry is having cold hands, I'm told,' she added mischievously.

'"Cold hands warm heart"?' Will returned teasingly.

'Let's leave my heart out of it,' March put in disgustedly.

Hmm, perhaps they had better, Will agreed with an inward frown. It was one thing to have a little fun at March Calendar's expense—as she had done earlier with him!—quite another for him to actually become involved with any of the Calendar sisters.

From all accounts, with Max's recent—surprising!—engagement to January Calendar, his friend had already fallen into that particular trap; he didn't think Jude would appreciate having Will do it too!

CHAPTER THREE

'I CAN'T believe I'm actually doing this,' March muttered as she rolled out the pastry for the apple pie.

May chuckled behind her as she laid the kitchen table for their evening meal.

'Will Davenport had better eat this after I've gone to all this trouble!' March added disgruntledly.

'Why did you send him here if you don't like him?' May sounded puzzled. 'Although, personally, I have to say I found him extremely charming.'

March continued to make the pie. It wasn't that she didn't like Will Davenport—she did, too much if the truth were told—but there was just something about him... Maybe she was imagining it, but she just had a feeling there was something he wasn't telling them.

Which was pretty stupid, when she actually thought about it; considering they really knew very little about Will Davenport, not even the reason he was in the area on business, there was a lot they didn't know about him!

'I hope the studio is warmer now,' May added worriedly, glancing out the kitchen window across to the garage/studio.

Will had arrived back at the farm over an hour ago, the lights on above the garage to show his occupancy, although they had seen nothing of the man himself.

Although that was soon going to change, March realized after a brief glance at the clock; in just over half an hour, Will was going to arrive for dinner.

'Did he say anything to you about why he's in the

area?' March prompted her sister casually as she cleared away her mess.

'Just looking around,' May answered distractedly, obviously still worried about the heating in the studio.

'At what?' March turned to her sister frowningly.

May shrugged. 'He didn't say.'

'Why didn't you ask?' March sighed frustratedly. 'I would have done.'

'I know you would have done.' Her sister gave a frustrated shake of her head. 'You didn't answer my question about why you don't like him?' she reminded shrewdly.

'I don't have to like the man in order to rent the studio to him,' March snapped, totally avoiding meeting her sister's probing gaze.

'Mercenary.' May laughed softly.

Not at all. But if she was going to manage to keep the farm at all then the studio would have to be let as much as possible to help pay the way. Which meant she couldn't be too choosy about whom she let it to!

Until quite recently the three sisters had been unanimous in their determination to keep the farm. But all that had changed in the last few weeks. January had just become engaged to Max, and it was pretty obvious that they weren't going to wait too long before getting married. And May, whose hobby was acting in the local amateur dramatic society, had recently been spotted by a film director who was interested in casting her in the film he was to make in the summer. Which left only March…

Maybe it didn't make much sense, or maybe she was just being her normal stubborn self, but March didn't want to sell the farm to this elusive Jude Marshall just so that he could include it in the neighbouring estate, which he had recently purchased, to make into an extensive health and country club! From the little she had been able to find out, the farm was to become part of the golf club he intended building on the complex. A golf club, for goodness' sake—when her family had lived and worked on this farm for generations.

March turned from putting the pie in the oven, frowning slightly. 'Talking about money—'

'When aren't we?' May put in disgustedly.

March smiled in sympathy. 'For once I wasn't referring to our own lack of it.' She grimaced. 'There's something going on at the agency that just doesn't make sense to me. Well, it does. But—' She broke off as a brief knock sounded on the kitchen door, rapidly followed by Will Davenport's expected appearance. 'Never mind,' March told her sister dismissively. 'I'll talk to you about it some other time.'

'Am I too early?' Will hesitated in the doorway at March's glare.

'Of course not,' May was the one to answer him welcomingly—cutting off March's more blunt reply!—quickly pulling Will inside and shutting the door to keep out the cold.

Something March was grateful for, knowing herself overwhelmed by a sudden feeling of uncharacteristic shyness.

She hadn't really thought that Will Davenport would actually want to rent the studio, had been, as he'd said earlier, just paying him back a little for his ungentlemanly behaviour of this morning. But now that he had decided to rent the studio, after all, she realized just how attracted she was to him.

Which was pretty stupid of her, in the circumstances; Will was only going to be around for a couple of weeks, would then leave to return to heaven knew where. Could even be—that dinner invitation apart!—returning to his wife and children, for all she knew!

But just looking at him beneath lowered lashes was enough to make her heart skip a beat. He was so tall his head almost brushed the beamed ceiling, that silver-blond hair falling endearingly across his forehead, blue eyes gleaming with good humour, lithely attractive in a thick blue sweater and faded blue denims.

Who was Will Davenport? More to the point, what was he doing in the area? Until she at least had the answer to those questions, perhaps she had better err on the side of caution—

Better err on the side of caution! What was wrong with her? Didn't she have enough on her plate, trying to find ways in which she could keep the farm, without adding the complication of being attracted to Will Davenport?

'Is that an apple pie I smell cooking?' He sniffed the air appreciatively, blue eyes gleaming with laughter as he looked across at March challengingly.

Her mouth twisted derisively. 'Somehow I doubt it,' she drawled. 'There is no smell of cooking from an Aga,' she added as she took pity on his look of disappointment.

'Your sister does love her little joke, doesn't she?' He grimaced at May.

'More like a twisted sense of humour,' May murmured affectionately, taking his jacket and hanging it behind the door. 'I hope eating in the kitchen is okay with you,' she added frowningly.

'It happens to be the warmest room in the house,' March put in bluntly; they always ate in the kitchen, so why apologize for it?

'This is great,' Will enthused. 'Once I'm settled in you must let me return the compliment and give the two of you dinner.'

That was an interesting concept—considering the studio was really only a bathroom, and one other large room that had to serve as kitchen, dining-room and bedroom. Very cosy!

'At a restaurant,' Will told March dryly as he was obviously able to read her thoughts.

That was the problem with having a mirror-face—she was completely unable to hide her feelings. But with any luck Will hadn't been looking at her earlier when she'd inwardly acknowledged just how attractive he was. Although she wouldn't count on it!

'Have a glass of wine,' she bit out abruptly, at the same time placing the glass down on the table ready for him to sit down. Maybe if he sat down the kitchen would no longer feel so cramped.

'Thanks.' He moved with fluid grace as he lowered his long length onto one of the kitchen chairs. 'So which one of you is the artist?' he prompted interestedly.

March's hand trembled so much she almost dropped her own glass of wine, looking across at him with widely dilated eyes, the sudden silence in the kitchen seeming oppressive.

Uh oh, looked as if he had put his foot in it again, Will realized with an inward grimace.

Unfortunately, there were so many things he couldn't discuss with the two Calendar sisters that he had decided to opt for what he'd thought was a neutral subject—only to realize by the tense silence that followed his casual enquiry that he had unwittingly walked into what looked like a minefield.

'Or perhaps I'm mistaken in thinking it was ever an artist's studio,' he continued evenly, knowing he wasn't mistaken at all.

His look around the studio at lunchtime had only been cursory, enough to tell him that it would be more than comfortable enough for the couple of weeks he intended staying in the area. A more leisurely mooch around on his return this evening had shown him the huge windows along one wall to allow in the maximum amount of light, pulling down the ladder to go up into the attic, that brief glance enough for him to have seen a paint-daubed easel and the stack of paintings against one wall.

He hadn't actually intruded any further than that brief look—and from the look of consternation now on May's face, the openly accusing one on March's, he was glad that he hadn't!

'I was,' March snapped coldly, her beautiful eyes now the grey-green of a wintry storm-tossed sea.

'Was?' Will echoed softly—dangerously? March certainly didn't look as if she cared to discuss the subject any further!

'She still is,' May briskly broke the awkwardness of the moment.

'No-I-am-not,' March bit out forcefully.

Ouch. He really had put his foot in it this time, hadn't he? It wasn't a feeling he was familiar with. Well educated, known and respected in his own field, he was accustomed to talking comfortably and confidently on any subject that came along. But not, apparently, when it came to the Calendar sisters!

He took a sip of his wine, giving March the time she needed to get past whatever the problem was, at the same time aware of the effort it took her to release the sudden tension she had been under. But why? So she painted in her spare time—what was the big deal?

'More wine, Will?' May offered, holding up the bottle invitingly.

'Thanks,' he accepted gratefully.

'The apple pie, March,' May prompted quietly.

Will waited until the younger Calendar sister had turned to the Aga before looking up at May with raised brows. She gave a barely perceptible shake of her head, enough to confirm that the subject of those paintings in the attic was not one he should pursue.

Not that he had intended doing so, anyway; March was prickly enough already, without adding to the problem.

Although his own curiosity about those paintings had certainly been piqued. What was wrong with them? Were they so amateurish that March simply didn't choose to discuss them?

Would he be violating his role as a temporary lodger if he were to go back up into the attic and take a look at them?

Probably, he acknowledged with an inner grimace. But he knew he wanted to take a look at them, anyway.

'You rented the studio, Mr Davenport,' March snapped as she seemed to read some of his thoughts now. 'At no time were you told that rental included the right to snoop around in the attic above.'

'March!' May muttered in obvious embarrassment at her sister's rudeness.

'It's all right, May,' Will assured her smoothly before turning back to March. 'I wasn't aware of that, March, but now that I am...' He shrugged, reluctant to actually state that he wouldn't intrude on the attic again, his curiosity well and truly roused now.

'Let's eat, hmm.' May seemed more than a little flustered by this sudden awkwardness.

As well she might be. Will had thought March Calendar completely uncomplicated, her emotions totally readable—even that brief moment of complete awareness of him she had felt when he'd arrived earlier!—but now he saw there was much more to her than that. Intriguing…

Was this the way it had been for Max? Had he also arrived here and taken the Calendar sisters at face value: beautiful, friendly, uncomplicated—only to find that they were all so much more than that? January Calendar certainly must be to have captivated Max, to Will's knowledge a confirmed bachelor, into falling in love with her.

Although the fact that Max was now engaged to marry the younger Calendar sister seemed to imply he was more than happy with the arrangement!

Will's smile faded somewhat as he realized he still had to find a way of breaking that little piece of news to Jude…

Although his good humour was somewhat restored by the aroma, and then the taste, of the promised stew and dumplings.

'Just like Granny makes?' March teased after his first mouth-watering taste, obviously not a woman who continued to bear a grudge, this morning's debacle over the parking space excepted.

'Better,' he assured warmly. 'Although don't ever tell her I said that, will you?' He grimaced.

She gave him a derisive glance. 'Somehow, I very much doubt the opportunity will ever arise!'

No, of course it wouldn't. Will had no idea what had even prompted him to say that.

March laughed at his confused expression, her earlier tension well and truly forgotten as she looked at him mockingly. 'Don't look so worried, Will; personally, I've always thought that old adage "the way to a man's heart is through his stomach" was a load of rubbish! If a man's only interested in what you can cook him for his dinner then forget it!'

He couldn't help chuckling at her disgusted expression. 'Maybe he'll be able to cook for you instead?'

'Now that sounds promising!' March said dryly.

'Do you cook, Will?' May put in mischievously.

Not quite the innocent peacemaker he had assumed after all, Will acknowledged with a rueful smile in May's direction.

'Tell me,' he murmured consideringly, 'are all the men in the area blind, deaf, and stupid? I can't believe you weren't all married years ago,' he explained at May's questioning look, a glance at the left hand of both women having shown them to both be unadorned by rings, and January Calendar had only recently—very recently!—become engaged to Max.

March grimaced at the comment. 'Maybe we're the ones who aren't interested,' she challenged.

And maybe three Calendar sisters were two too many? Although Max didn't seem to have had too much trouble getting past that particular problem!

'Good point,' Will dismissed, realizing the conversation was becoming altogether too personal.

He had wondered earlier whether accepting this dinner invitation was a good idea, knowing it would be better for all of them if he maintained a certain distance from the Calendar sisters. But March's obvious reluctance for him to accept the invitation had been enough to prompt him into doing exactly that!

What else might he feel goaded into doing before his time came to leave…?

'So if January is the singer in the family—' that little fact had been confirmed for him at the hotel earlier, and he'd even been able to view one of the publicity photographs of January used by the hotel; January Calendar was as beautiful as her two sisters '—and March works in the estate agent's, that must mean that you're the full-time farmer?' he prompted May curiously.

Farming seemed a very strange choice of career for any of these beautiful women, but Will knew for a fact, from the Calendar sisters themselves, but also from Jude, that they absolutely refused to sell the farm. At least, March did…

'Not exactly,' May laughed dismissively. 'You see—'

'May is an actress,' March put in with a proud smile in her sister's direction. 'She's been offered a part in a film—'

'Not yet, I haven't.' May looked embarrassed. 'Besides, March, I told you I haven't made my mind up yet about even going for the screen test.' She frowned at her sister reprovingly.

Will had a feeling that was something May had probably done a lot of over the years where the outspoken March was concerned!

'An actress?' he prompted interestedly. January was a singer, March was probably—no matter what she might claim to the contrary!—a good artist, and now it seemed that May acted; he couldn't help wondering how three young women obviously brought up on a farm could be so artistically gifted in such different ways.

But if May were to disappear for some time in order to make a film, that probably explained the current rift between the sisters concerning the selling of the farm. It was a start, at least...

'It isn't official yet.' May looked extremely uncomfortable. 'I have to go for a screen test next month—'

'A mere technicality,' March dismissed airily. 'You're going to walk through it,' she added with certainty. 'My sister is an extremely good actress,' she told Will proudly.

Something March, with her see-through face, could never be!

From the derisive smile March now directed at him he wasn't doing too good a job of hiding his own thoughts at the moment, either!

'Sorry.' But even as he made the apology he couldn't hold back his amused chuckle.

'No, you're not,' March acknowledged disgustedly, standing up to clear away the empty plates.

Will stood up too, moving across the kitchen to where March stood filling up the sink with soapy water. 'If I offer to help with the washing-up will I be forgiven?' he prompted huskily.

'Knowing how much March hates washing up—I wouldn't be at all surprised!' May was the one to answer him dryly.

But Will barely heard her reply, his breath suddenly caught in his chest as he found himself held mesmerized by March's luminous grey-green gaze as she turned to look up at him.

Her skin was like alabaster, smooth and creamy white, her mouth wide and sensuous, her neck arched with the delicacy of a swan, the baggy green jumper and fitted black denims she wore doing nothing to hide the allure of her slender body. A body he had been completely aware of from the moment he'd entered the farmhouse half an hour ago...

Once again Will found himself wondering if this was the way it had been for Max. A sudden, driving desire, a numbing of every other sense and sensation except this intense, spine-tingling awareness—

No!

Will wrenched his gaze away from March's, physically stepping away from her too, turning his back on her to further break the spell of sensuality that had briefly held him in its grip.

Will, Max and Jude had been at school together, losing touch briefly as they all went off to university to pursue their chosen careers, but those same careers renewing their friendship ten or so years ago. Now, at thirty-seven, despite having enjoyed numerous relationships, none of them had ever married. Somehow, after all this time, Will had assumed that none of them ever would. But Max, the one Will would have sworn was the least likely of the three friends to succumb, had fallen in love with the youngest Calendar sister.

Will did not intend falling into the same trap where March Calendar was concerned!

He drew in a harsh breath. 'Could I take a rain check on the apple pie?' he bit out tautly, deliberately speaking to May rather than March. 'I've just realized I have an important telephone call to make.'

'So much for helping with the washing-up!' March muttered behind him disgustedly.

It was a little ungrateful of him, he knew, but he needed to get away from here, needed to get some fresh air. Needed to clear his head, and his senses, of March Calendar!

'Take the pie with you,' May offered warmly, moving to pick the pie up off the side and place it in his hands.

'Hey, I like apple pie, too!' March protested.

'Will is our guest, March.' May turned to her sister warningly before giving Will a bright smile. 'I often think I failed miserably where instilling manners into March was concerned!' She gave a sorrowful shake of her head.

Once again Will felt himself being drawn into the warmth that was the Calendar sisters, his good humour returning as he smiled at May. 'March does have a point when she actually made the pie,' he murmured with a derisive grin in her direction.

'Oh, take it,' March dismissed impatiently. 'You probably don't have to worry about the calories, anyway!' she added disgustedly.

Neither did she if the willowy sensuousness of her body was anything to go by—

Not again. Will shook his head self-disgustedly. Okay, so March was beautiful, was quirky and outspoken too, as well as having a curvaceously sensuous body, but was that any reason for him to respond to her with the gaucheness of a callow schoolboy?

No, but it was reason for him to get himself out of here before he did something he would later regret—like kiss that derisive smile right off her pouting lips!

'I'm afraid there's no telephone in the studio,' May pointed out worriedly. 'But you can use the one here if—'

'Why doesn't he just move in here completely? We can charge him bed and breakfast prices then!' March put in scathingly.

Will's lips twitched with repressed humour as he saw

the way May winced at her younger sister's bluntness. March really was irrepressible.

And, despite her obvious despair at March's lack of manners, May was obviously staunchly protective of both her sisters. Making Will wonder how on earth Max, with his reserved haughtiness, had ever got the two older Calendar sisters' approval to marry their younger sister!

'That won't be necessary,' Will answered smilingly. 'I have a mobile in the car.'

'Well, of course you do,' March snapped derisively. 'How silly of us not to have realized that.'

May gave a weary shake of her head, obviously deciding that the best thing to do for the moment was to just give up apologizing for March's lack of manners. 'Enjoy the pie, Will,' she murmured ruefully. 'And if there's anything else you need, more towels, things like that, you have only to ask.'

'We'll send one of the maids over with it immediately,' March muttered disparagingly.

Will could see by the sudden fire that lit May's gaze that she wasn't always the calm, sensible sister, that she could be cutting herself when she felt it necessary. And he had a feeling that she would feel it necessary, where March was concerned, the moment he had gone out the door!

Which was a pity; he really didn't want to be the reason for any dissent between the two sisters. Even if March deserved it!

'This pie looks delicious, March, thanks,' he told her warmly.

She frowned at him suspiciously, but as he calmly returned her gaze that frown eased from between her eyes. 'You're welcome,' she finally murmured lightly.

'Thanks for dinner, May, it was great.' Will lingered

in the doorway, having absolutely no idea why he was having such trouble getting out of the kitchen now that it was time to go—especially as it was his own decision to do so!

'Don't forget to return the compliment,' March was the one to remind him pointedly.

He hadn't forgotten his earlier suggestion, Will acknowledged a little dazedly as he made his way back across the yard to the studio—he was just no longer sure he could cope with taking one Calendar sister out to dinner, let alone two!

He felt slightly disorientated after being with them for less than an hour, slightly dazed, as if he had drunk too much wine in a smoke-filled room—how on earth was he going to feel after spending an evening with them?

One thing he did know, he would have to clear his head before making his telephone call to Jude. A Jude, Will knew with certainty, who was going to be far from happy at Max's obvious defection to the enemy camp...

CHAPTER FOUR

'It's only lunch I'm suggesting, March, not an afternoon in a hotel bedroom!' Clive looked down at her mockingly as he perched on the edge of her desk.

March knew exactly what the male half of her employers was inviting her to—she also knew he wouldn't have made the suggestion about the two of them having lunch together if Michelle weren't out for the day showing a client over several different properties. Besides, she also knew that if Clive thought he could get away with it he would have no hesitation in taking her to a hotel bedroom for the afternoon!

While March was normally blunt to the point of rudeness—as Will Davenport had discovered to his cost the previous evening!—Clive's attentions over the last six months, whenever Michelle had been out of the office, were something March hadn't liked to tell her sisters about. There was nothing anyone could do about it, and they needed the money she earned from this full-time job. Besides, she doubted she was the first employee to suffer this sort of harassment.

It wasn't even that Clive was unattractive, because he wasn't; the epitome of tall, dark and handsome, with an easy charm as an added bonus. He just also happened to have been living with Michelle, the other half of this estate agency, for the last ten years!

'I said no, Clive,' she answered him calmly enough, grey-green gaze glacial as she glared her annoyance at him. For all the good it did. She had been saying no for the last six months, but it didn't stop Clive from repeating the offer whenever the chance arose. 'You know very well we can't just shut up shop for a couple of hours and disappear off to lunch,' she dismissed briskly. 'Besides, I—I already have a date for lunch,' she added with relief, having looked out of the window at that moment and seen a familiar red sports car drive slowly into the square.

Will Davenport's car, with him sitting confidently behind the wheel as he found a parking space directly behind March's more serviceable Metro. He gave her a friendly wave as he got out of the car and saw her watching him out of the window.

'If you'll excuse me.' March stood up hurriedly, moving quickly to open the door and call out to Will before he could lock his car and just walk away. 'I'll be out in a minute, Will,' she called out to him lightly, willing him to wait for her.

He turned, a puzzled frown on that handsome face. 'Sorry?' He looked totally nonplussed.

'I'm just getting my coat,' she told him firmly, aware that Clive had come to stand beside her in the doorway now, a knowing smile curving his lips as he took in the car and the man driving it.

Will turned his cool blue gaze on Clive Carter, that gaze narrowing as he obviously saw the other man's too familiar stance next to March, his arm resting against the door behind her. 'No hurry,' Will answered in measured tones. 'I'll come inside and wait for you,' he added with another speculative glance at Clive.

That wasn't quite what she had wanted, March realized flusteredly as she made a quick grab for her coat and handbag; having these two men size each other up in silent appraisal was more than a little unnerving.

Especially as she could now clearly see the speculation in Clive's mocking grey eyes.

'Nice car,' he murmured softly. 'A Ferrari, isn't it?'

A Ferrari? March did a mental double-take on Will herself now. Okay, so she had realized it was a sporty-looking car, but all she basically required from a car was that it start up in the morning when she needed to get to work. But Ferraris cost tens of thousands of pounds, didn't they? Maybe there was more to Will Davenport than she had realized!

'Let's go,' she said decisively, grabbing hold of Will's arm to almost pull him outside. 'Walk!' she instructed once on the pavement, lips barely moving. 'And try to look happy about the prospect of taking me out to lunch!' she added as he simply stood looking down at her with mocking blue eyes.

'Certainly,' Will gave a derisive inclination of his head. 'As for happy...' He gave March no time to respond to his original comment as he bent his head, his lips taking possession of hers.

Well, there was happy and then there was *happy*...!

At that precise moment March felt so light-headed she didn't know what she felt, Will's mouth making a thorough exploration of her own, his arms firm about the slenderness of her waist.

If he was trying to impress upon Clive the fact that he was the one taking her out to lunch, he was obviously succeeding. If he was trying to render the usually voluble March speechless then he was succeeding in doing that too!

The softness of her body curved into Will's as if it were the other half of the hard contours of his, that silver-blond hair as soft and silky to the touch as she had imagined it would be—

As she had imagined it would be—!

Since when had she imagined touching any part of Will Davenport, let alone entangling her fingers in the thick softness of his hair as his lips sipped and tasted the softness of hers?

March pulled away from him abruptly, her gaze not quite meeting his as she stepped completely away from him. What on earth—

'Too "happy"?' he murmured teasingly.

Her head snapped up defensively, eyes flashing with anger. 'Let's just go, shall we?' she bit out furiously as she took a firm hold of Will's arm, knowing from her peripheral vision that Clive was still watching them as he stood in the doorway of the agency.

'Certainly, madam.' Will gave a mocking inclination of his head. 'Exactly where is it we're going?' he bent down to ask March conspiratorially as she almost frog-marched him along the pavement towards the busier high street of town.

March didn't even bother to answer him until they had turned the corner—and were safely away from Clive's curious gaze. Then she came to an abrupt halt, looking up at Will with glittering grey-green eyes. 'We aren't going anywhere—now,' she assured him firmly. 'You were obviously on your way somewhere else when you arrived, and I—'

'Yes—you?' Will prompted softly, a frown between his eyes now.

She felt the heat in her cheeks. 'I am on my way somewhere else, too,' she told him waspishly, still off balance from the kiss they had just shared. It might have been for Clive's benefit, but that didn't mean she hadn't been affected by it.

Affected by it! Her legs still felt slightly wobbly, her

breathing was erratic, and her lips tingled from the touch of Will's.

Will glanced briefly back in the direction they had just come from. 'Was he bothering you?' he prompted shrewdly.

She forced a derisive smile to her lips. 'Of course not,' she dismissed lightly. 'And even if he was,' she added resentfully as Will raised a sceptical brow, 'I happen to need the job.'

His mouth thinned. 'At the price of sexual harassment?'

'Don't be ridiculous,' she snapped irritably. 'Clive just likes to believe that every woman within a fifty-mile radius thinks he's God's gift to women,' she scorned. 'It doesn't mean anything.'

Will didn't look convinced. 'It looked like something to me,' he rasped.

'Well, it wasn't,' March insisted impatiently. 'Now please don't let me keep you any longer from whatever it was you came here to do.' She placed the strap of her bag very firmly on her shoulder, turning away.

His hand moved, his fingers curling firmly about her upper arm. 'At the moment I intend taking you out to lunch,' he told her determinedly, eyes narrowed as he glanced up the high street for a suitable eating place. 'Where would you recommend?' he prompted tersely.

'The White Swan will serve you an excellent lunch—' she nodded in the direction of the hotel across the road '—but for myself, I intend taking my sandwiches—' she pointedly took a foil-wrapped package from her handbag '—and sitting in the park for half an hour while I eat them,' she told him ruefully.

He grimaced. 'In this weather?'

Granted it was still January, and it had snowed yesterday, but that snow had already melted, and the wind wasn't too icy.

'In any weather,' she answered him dryly. 'Beggars can't be choosers,' she added caustically as she could see Will remained unconvinced.

But what was the point of earning every penny she could working, only to waste some of it on buying lunch, when she could just as easily bring sandwiches from home?

'My treat,' Will told her evenly, his hand tightening on her arm, his gaze narrowed as he negotiated the traffic as they crossed the road to the hotel.

'Will—'

'You don't want to make a liar out of both of us, do you?' He looked steadily down at her as she came to a stubborn halt on the pavement outside the hotel.

March gave a rueful smile as she shook her head. 'We both know you hadn't really arranged to take me out to lunch—'

'I have now,' Will cut in determinedly, easily pulling her along with him as they entered the hotel restaurant from the outside door, the warmth inside inviting, a lot of the tables already occupied.

'Will, this is ridiculous,' March continued to protest as a waitress showed them to a table in the window. 'I only said that earlier about the two of us having lunch because I—because I—'

'Yes?' He raised blond brows speculatively as he waited for her to sit down.

She gave a heavy sigh. 'Okay, so Clive was being a nuisance. But that's still no reason for you to have me foisted on you for lunch,' she added impatiently.

'Sit,' Will instructed firmly as he pulled her chair back for her.

By this time March could see that they were attracting a certain amount of attention; several other diners watching them curiously even as they made a pretence of eating their meal.

March sat—but only as a means of diverting attention away from the obvious difference of opinion between Will and herself.

'Woof,' she muttered pointedly beneath her breath, shooting Will a disgruntled look beneath lowered lashes.

Will grinned as he sat down opposite her. 'Woof, woof,' he came back laughingly.

March found herself returning that boyish smile. 'I really do feel awful for having put you in this position.' She made one last attempt to give him the opportunity to extract himself from feeling pressured into having lunch with her.

Will laughed outright at this comment. 'Tell me, March, have you looked in a mirror lately?'

'Sorry?' She frowned her confusion at what seemed like a complete change of subject.

He shook his head impatiently. 'March Calendar, you are a beautiful and desirable woman—no man in his right mind would accept he had ever had your company "foisted" on him!'

She gave him a mocking glance. 'When did you last see a psychiatrist?'

He grinned. 'Oh, I'm completely sane, I do assure you,' he murmured dryly. 'At least, I'm sure I was before coming here,' he muttered frowningly.

'Sorry?' She eyed him curiously.

'Never mind,' Will dismissed impatiently. 'Let's look at the menu, hmm?' he suggested briskly, promptly putting his own menu up in front of his face.

In truth, March was really quite pleased at this unexpected treat, couldn't remember the last time she had eaten out in a restaurant. Although there was one thing the two of them had better get straight...

'The answer is no,' Will bit out implacably after ordering a bottle of red wine to accompany the steaks they had both ordered.

March's eyes widened. 'I wasn't aware that I had asked a question,' she snapped.

His mouth twisted humorously. 'You weren't going to ask a question—you were about to make a statement. Am I wrong?' He quirked mocking brows, knowing he wasn't by the irritated flush that rose in her cheeks.

She scowled. 'I hate my see-through face!'

Will found himself laughing once again; no one could ever claim that March Calendar wasn't entertaining! 'Then you're in the minority,' he assured her softly.

She shook her head self-disgustedly. 'When I was little, my father always knew when I had done something wrong just from looking at me!'

She would have been adorable as a child, all the Calendar sisters would, Will acknowledged ruefully. But again he noticed that March hadn't mentioned her mother...

'Have the three of you been on your own for very long?' he prompted casually, surprised himself at how interested he was in the answer. At how interested he was becoming in anything that involved March Calendar!

She shrugged. 'Our father died last year. And we were all only babies when our mother—oh, no, you don't,' she rebuked decisively. 'No diverting me from what I was about to say earlier,' she told him firmly. 'If we're to have lunch together, and it appears that we are,' she accepted ruefully, 'then I insist on paying my share of the bill—'

'And I already said no,' Will reminded her calmly, a little disappointed that they had gone off the subject of her childhood and family, but accepting that he couldn't have everything his own way. Especially where March was concerned!

Although he had very much enjoyed kissing her earlier. In fact, he couldn't ever remember enjoying kissing any other woman as much. She had felt so right in his arms, and as for the effect holding and kissing her had had on his senses…!

Although that kiss was probably a subject he shouldn't refer to, either. March might have had little choice but to acquiesce earlier, but no doubt there were a few things she would like to say on the subject if given the chance!

He leant over the table, talking softly. 'March, men who drive Ferraris do not go Dutch with a woman on lunch. Okay?' he said pointedly.

It had come home to him very forcefully the previous evening that the Calendar sisters, while not exactly impoverished, certainly didn't have too much money to throw around; he doubted March, at least, would have agreed to rent the studio to him, or indeed anyone else, for a couple of weeks if she didn't have to. There was no way that he, with his own accumulated wealth, could possibly agree to March paying for half the lunch he had insisted she share with him.

'It really is a Ferrari?' she surprised him by saying.

He smiled. 'It really is.'

'Wow,' she breathed admiringly.

His brows rose. 'You like sports cars?'

'I like Clive believing I'm having lunch with a man who owns one!' Her eyes glowed mischievously.

Will couldn't help chuckling at her obvious glee at feeling she had put one over on her lecherous boss. Although his smile faded somewhat as he remembered the way the other man had stood so close to March earlier, almost as if he were stating some sort of proprietary claim on her...

'March—'

'Just leave it, hmm, Will,' she said firmly, sitting back as the waiter arrived to pour their wine. 'I'm more than capable of dealing with Clive,' she assured him dismissively once they were alone again.

Will didn't like the thought of her having to deal with the other man, had an intense dislike for predatory males who took advantage of the women who worked for them. One predatory male in particular!

'What is it?' he prompted as he saw March was frowning now.

Her smile, when it came, seemed slightly forced. 'Nothing,' she dismissed lightly.

He didn't believe her. 'It doesn't look like nothing to me,' he insisted firmly.

She seemed about to argue the point once again, and then gave a heavy sigh instead. 'You're in business, aren't you?' she prompted slowly.

Will felt himself stiffen defensively. 'I am,' he confirmed warily.

'Hmm.' March seemed not to notice his reticence, her thoughts inwards as she ran a finger around the rim of her wineglass. 'Well, is it illegal to buy something, for less than its value, in order that you can sell that—product on a few weeks later, at a hefty profit?'

'I would say that probably depends on what that—

product, is,' he answered slowly. 'And if you deliberately set out to defraud the original seller by knowing the product was undervalued.'

'That's what I thought.' She sighed heavily, obviously not particularly liking his answer.

'I wouldn't try it if I were you, March—your face would give you away!' he added teasingly.

She looked across at him blankly for several moments, and then her brow cleared, her expression indignant now. 'I wasn't talking about me!' she protested impatiently.

'Somehow I didn't think so.' He chuckled.

'Hmm. Well—' she frowned her irritation '—talking of business—'

'Ah, our lunch,' Will murmured with satisfaction as he sat back to allow the waitress to put the plates down on the table.

His relief at the interruption was due to two things. One, he was hungry. Two, he had no intention of pursuing the subject of his own business with March Calendar, of all people. He might end up with this delicious-looking lunch tipped over his head if he did that!

Although, as they began to eat their meal, he couldn't help feeling intrigued by her previous conversation. Who did March know who was defrauding people out of their money? Because he was pretty certain that she did know someone who was...

CHAPTER FIVE

'YOU had lunch with who?' May prompted speculatively as the two women sat and enjoyed a cup of tea together on March's return home from work that evening.

'You heard,' March muttered into her teacup, having decided it would be better for her to tell her sister about her lunch with Will today rather than have him perhaps drop it casually into the conversation at a later date. 'Very nice it was too,' she added lightly. 'I had almost forgotten what a nice steak tastes like.'

Obviously they never went short of food living and working on the farm, but such luxuries as fillet steak weren't usually on their menu.

Although one thing March had decided not to tell May; she had no intention of confiding in her sister about the kiss she had shared with Will.

She was still slightly shaken by her own response to that kiss. After all, what did any of them know about Will Davenport? Apart from the fact that he was good-looking, charming, and was obviously wealthy enough to drive an expensive sports car!

March still had no idea whether he was married or not. Although somehow she doubted it; he had certainly frowned on Clive's behaviour of trying to take advantage of his position as her employer.

But, despite several attempts on her part to introduce the subject during their lunch today, March had found out nothing further about Will's private life. Or, indeed, what exactly he was doing in the area.

'Well, that was nice of him.' May nodded. 'Uncle Sid said he saw Will's car over near Hanworth Estate this afternoon,' she added thoughtfully. 'I wonder what he was doing there?'

March was about to explain that Will had initially said this was the area he needed to be in, when a sudden thought occurred to her, her eyes widening in horror as the thought took root.

That horror only increased as she saw the same thought had occurred to May, her sister's face suddenly pale, her expression stricken. 'You don't suppose—'

'Do you think—?' Both sisters had begun to talk at once, both breaking off at the same time too, March's thoughts racing as she went back over the conversations she had had with Will since his arrival yesterday.

Yesterday? Was it really only a little over twenty-four hours since Will had entered their lives? It seemed like much longer!

It also seemed to March, as she remembered their conversations with him, that Will had found out a lot more about all of the Calendar sisters during that short time than they had about him…!

March's eyes narrowed as her original thought expanded and grew, to the point where she stood up restlessly to move to the kitchen window, glaring across the yard to where she could see the lights on above the garage to announce Will's presence in the studio.

'He's another one of them,' she bit out with sudden certainty, her hands clenching at her sides. 'Another one of Jude Marshall's henchmen! A wolf in sheep's clothing. Nothing but a snake in the grass!' She was building herself up to a rage now. 'Why, I've a good mind to—'

'We don't know that, March,' May soothed as she also stood up to look out of the window, green gaze narrowed speculatively across the yard. 'Although...' she added slowly.

'Exactly—although!' March snapped furiously. 'Another lawyer, do you think? Or something else?' Somehow she couldn't see Will as a lawyer. Max, yes, with his reserved aloofness, but Will was more outgoing than her younger sister's fiancé.

Max...

He would be sure to know if Will worked for Jude Marshall too; after all, until just recently, he had worked for the man himself.

It had been Max's efforts to buy their farm on Jude Marshall's behalf that had brought him into their lives in the first place. It had been falling in love with their younger sister, January, that had decided him that he was no longer suited to that sort of work.

But Max was in the Caribbean with January for two weeks, and March very much doubted that either of them were going to think of telephoning home during that time!

But if Will wasn't another of Jude Marshall's lawyers, what position did he hold in that corporation? Because March was pretty sure now that he was something!

'Something else,' May confirmed. 'Although we can't really be sure about that.' She hesitated.

'We can if we ask him,' March stated, moving with determined strides towards the kitchen door.

'No, I don't think we should do that,' May said slowly, halting March as she reached for the door-handle. 'Let's wait a while, hmm.' She frowned. 'See what else develops.'

'Like what?' March turned to challenge. 'We've already had Max creeping about trying to buy the farm out from under our noses. It isn't funny, May,' she re-proved as her sister began to chuckle.

'Sorry.' May made an attempt to curtail her humour. 'I was just trying to picture our future brother-in-law "creeping" about anywhere!'

'Hmm.' March gave a rueful smile too at the image her sister created. 'I would love to see Jude Marshall's face when Max gets back from this holiday and tells him what he can do with his job!' she added with glee.

May shook her head. 'The two men are friends, March; I don't think Max will be as blunt as that. But you're right about seeing Jude Marshall's face.' She frowned. 'Personally, I would like nothing more than to meet the man face to face!'

'But, in the meantime, what do we do about our snake-in-the-grass lodger?' March reminded pointedly.

'Well, until we're sure—March, where are you go-ing?' Her sister frowned as March picked up a cup and moved to the door.

She paused. 'To borrow a cup of sugar. Isn't that the usual excuse women use when they want to meet a man?' She raised innocent brows.

'You've been watching too many romantic films,' May admonished dryly. 'Besides, we've already met him,' she reminded.

March had done more than meet the man—she had kissed him, and been kissed by him. And if he really was what they suspected, he was going to regret taking advantage of that particular situation himself!

'So I meet him again.' She shrugged dismissively. 'I won't be long,' she added lightly before letting herself out of the house and moving swiftly through the cold of early evening to ascend the steps up the side of the ga-rage and knock on the studio door.

Will did work for the Marshall Corporation, March was sure of it. And if that were the case, then he had known exactly who the Calendar sisters were before coming into the estate agency yesterday. In fact, she wouldn't put it past him to have engineered the whole thing!

The fact that she had been the one to send him here was irrelevant; if Will hadn't originally intended actually renting a property on their land, he had definitely jumped at the chance when it had been offered to him.

Yes, March now had no doubts that Will worked for Jude Marshall. Or that she was personally going to make him regret the day he had ever tried to deceive them!

Will was going over some figures as he sat at the table when the knock sounded on the door. He deftly rolled the papers up and put them away in a cupboard before answering that knock, knowing his visitor had to be one of the Calendar sisters; after all, apart from Jude, they were the only ones who knew he was here.

He burst out laughing as the light shining out of the open doorway revealed it was March standing on the top step, an empty cup in her hand. 'You look like Oliver, about to ask for some more,' he explained as she glared up at him.

She gave him a scathing glance. 'I've come to ask if we can borrow some sugar,' she told him waspishly. 'We've run out.'

'Certainly.' He smiled, holding the door open wider so that she could come inside. 'You're in luck; I've been food shopping today,' he told her as he rifled through one of the cupboards in search of the required sugar.

'Really? What else have you done today?'

Will gave her a brief glance over his shoulder. There

was a certain brittleness to March's voice that wasn't normally there; caustic, cutting, derisive, yes, but never brittle before. He wondered at the reason for it.

She returned his gaze steadily, one dark brow raised in challenge.

She had changed out of her business suit since returning from work, and now wore hip- and leg-hugging blue denims, with a deep green fitted sweater that brought out the same colour in those beautiful grey-green eyes.

Will felt a tightness across his chest as he looked at her, caught in that same lightning desire that had tautened other parts of his body earlier today when he'd kissed her.

He turned away abruptly. 'Here we are.' He brought down the sugar, the lightness in his voice sounding forced even to his own ears.

'Thanks,' March accepted as he poured some into the cup.

Looking more like the vulnerable Oliver than ever, Will acknowledged self-disgustedly, knowing that no one needed—or wanted!—his protection less than the feisty March Calendar.

'Was that all?' he prompted pointedly as she made no effort to leave.

'Am I keeping you from something?' March enquired lightly—at the same time making herself comfortable on one of the two chairs set either side of the small pine table provided for eating on.

'Not at all,' Will answered slowly, still eyeing her warily.

There was definitely something different about her this evening. Normally she had such a readable face, leading him to the correct assumption that she usually called a spade a spade, and to hell with everything else.

Usually... Because, unless Will was mistaken, she was hiding something tonight with that too-innocent expression.

'Thanks again for lunch, by the way,' she told him in that tightly clipped voice. 'I hope I didn't keep you from anything this afternoon?'

He leant back against one of the two kitchen units, his own gaze guarded now. 'Nothing of any importance,' he assured her dismissively. 'And it's I who should be thanking you for your company over lunch; there's nothing worse than sitting in a restaurant eating on your own.' Something he had done a lot of over the last ten years or so.

She gave a rueful grimace. 'So there was a method in your madness, after all,' she scorned. 'I should have known!'

'Why should you?' he returned easily, still uncertain of her mood.

Which was a little unsettling in March's case; it was unusual to meet anyone who showed their feelings—and spoke them—as clearly she did!

She gave a shrug. 'I knew it couldn't have just been gallantry on your part.'

He raised blond brows. 'You don't believe I can be gallant?'

March gave a derisive smile. 'There are very few men around nowadays that are!'

Will gave her a considering look. She seemed to be angry about something, that much he could tell. But whether or not that anger was directed at him—for whatever reason!—he wasn't sure yet...

'Would you like a cup of coffee, or possibly a glass of wine, now you're here?' he offered lightly, guessing by the way she had sat down so determinedly that she wasn't about to leave just yet.

'No, thanks, I've just had a cup of tea,' she refused stiltedly.

Almost as if drinking his coffee or wine might choke her. Will wasn't sure what was going on, but something certainly was.

He moved to sit in the chair opposite hers. 'What sort of man was your father?' he prompted curiously.

To say she looked startled was an understatement, her eyes widening before narrowing suspiciously. 'What does that have to do with anything?' she said guardedly.

Will shrugged. 'I merely wondered if your father had been one of the gallant men you referred to a few minutes ago.'

'Oh.' She blinked, seeming to straighten defensively. 'In that case—he was a blunt-talking Yorkshireman,' she said with obvious affection.

Will nodded. 'There's no doubting who you take after, then,' he returned teasingly.

There was no doubting her defensive attitude now, either, two bright spots of angry colour burning in the otherwise pale magnolia of her cheeks. 'Is there something wrong with being honest?' she challenged hardly, sitting slightly forward over the table. 'Personally, I abhor any kind of dishonesty.'

Will looked at her consideringly. Her eyes were sparkling with anger, her cheeks flushed, her whole attitude since she had arrived here a combatant one.

'March, what's wrong?' he prompted softly.

'Wrong?' she repeated stiffly. 'Who said there was anything wrong?'

'I did.' He sighed, not at all happy with the way this conversation was going.

One thing he had discovered during his conversations with March over lunch earlier today: he liked and admired her. He liked her blunt, no-nonsense manner, her complete loyalty to those she loved, namely her two sisters, and as for the way she looked... Everything about her was beautiful, her face, her hair, the willowy slenderness of her body, the habit she had of using her hands to illustrate a point as she was talking.

Something she hadn't been doing this evening...

Something was definitely wrong, and the sooner Will knew what it was, the better he would like it.

'March, has something—happened, since we had lunch together today?' he pushed determinedly. 'There's nothing wrong with May, is there?' he continued frowningly. 'Or your younger sister—January, isn't it?' he added with a casualness he was far from feeling.

If January and Max had telephoned from wherever they happened to be on holiday, and either March or May had happened to mention to Max the name of their temporary lodger—!

Will knew he couldn't indefinitely keep his reason for being here from March and May, but the longer he left telling them, the harder it was becoming to do so.

When he'd initially come to look at the studio with a view to renting, he genuinely hadn't known it was the Calendar sisters' farm that March had sent him to. Why should he have known? There were dozens of farms in the area, it just hadn't occurred to him that this could be the one where the Calendar sisters lived. Once he had become aware he obviously could have beaten a hasty retreat, but by that time March had arrived home, and the temptation to neatly turn her trick back on her by renting the studio had been too much of a temptation for him to resist.

At the moment both sisters seemed to like him, but learning of his connection to Jude Marshall, a man they both obviously disliked intensely, was going to change all that. And he already knew that having March hate him wasn't something he relished happening. Far from it!

Because he wanted March Calendar. Holding her in his arms earlier today, kissing the soft sensuality of her mouth, feeling the curves of her body moulding into his, had told him that he wanted her very badly. And, in the circumstances of his being here at all, she was probably a woman he could never have...

But, for this evening at least, she didn't know who he was or why he was here!

He stood up abruptly, moving round the table to take March's hand and pull her unresistingly to her feet. Only because she was too surprised to resist, he was sure, but for the moment that didn't matter.

'You are so beautiful, March,' he told her huskily. 'So absolutely beautiful,' he murmured throatily as his mouth began to lower towards hers.

She blinked, stiffening in his arms. 'What—what are you doing?' she gasped.

He smiled self-derisively, his lips only inches away from hers now. 'Guess,' he teased softly.

'But—but—'

A speechless March was just too irresistible, and as Will slowly bent his head to claim the moist softness of her lips he knew he had no intention of even trying...

CHAPTER SIX

MARCH was so stunned at the suddenness of finding herself in Will's arms that she didn't even try to resist, not when he held her, nor when his lips claimed hers.

And then it was too late to resist anyway. She groaned low in her throat as heated pleasure moved swiftly through her body, her mouth moving instinctively against his as he ran his tongue lightly across her lips, his hands moving caressingly down the length of her spine as he moulded her body against his.

A body that seemed to have turned to liquid fire, totally beyond anything March had ever known or felt before. Making her realize she wanted this man as badly as the arousal of his body seemed to say he wanted her!

His lips were moving heatedly down the length of her arched throat now, her skin seeming on fire where he touched, her own hands entangled in the silky hair at his nape as she clung to him.

Drowning. It must be like drowning, March decided dreamily, knowing there was no point in fighting against the tide of desire that enveloped her, any more than there would be fighting against a whirlpool that had her in its grasp.

Will felt so good against her fingertips, the buttons to his shirt proving no problem as she bared his chest to her searching hands, his skin warm and yet hard to the touch, hearing his own gasp of pleasure as her lips moved moistly against that heated flesh.

March groaned low in her throat as Will's hand cupped

her breast beneath the warmth of her jumper, feeling the nipple harden beneath his touch, the pleasure that coursed through her now making her legs feel weak, at the same time that every nerve-ending in her body responded to that caress.

His lips claimed her parted ones, his thumb moving rhythmically against her pouting breast now, his tongue seeking an answer to his unspoken message.

March answered that call, her response tentative at first, and then becoming more confident as she was the one to deepen the kiss. She couldn't stop this now. She just couldn't!

'Oops!' he gasped softly, his legs having caught the side of the bed, losing his balance slightly to sit down on the edge of the bed looking up at March with cobalt-blue eyes. 'March...?' he groaned uncertainly, his hands lightly clasping her hips.

She moved instinctively towards him, her hands cradling the back of his head as he pushed her jumper aside to kiss her bared breasts.

March really thought she was going to drown now, couldn't believe the heated emotions that swept over her as Will's lips and tongue paid homage to her uptilted breasts.

Where had this man been all her life? Why had it taken so long to find him? How had she existed for twenty-six years without—?

She hadn't been the one to find him—Will had been the one to deliberately find the Calendar sisters! As for where he had been all her life—!

'No!' she gasped, pushing him away from her, hastily straightening her clothing to look down at him with accusing eyes. 'What do you think you're doing?' she rasped accusingly.

Will blinked at the suddenness of her rejection, his eyes still dark with arousal, his cheeks flushed with desire. 'We were *both* doing, March,' he corrected slowly. 'And surely the ''what'' must be obvious,' he added ruefully, at the same time running a hand through the blond thickness of his hair.

The same hand that had touched and caressed her seconds ago! The same hair her own hands had been entangled in seconds ago!

She turned away, her movements jerky and uncoordinated, putting a hand up to her eyes as if to block out what had just happened between them.

But it would take more than that to shut out the memory of the intimacies they had just shared. If she ever could!

'March?'

She swallowed hard, straightening her shoulders defensively before turning to face Will. And just as quickly wished she hadn't; his gaze was still sleepy with desire as he looked at her quizzically, that aroused flush on his cheeks.

March shook her head, denying her own response to that arousal. 'I was referring to your own motivation for—for just now,' she finished hardly.

'Motivation?' he repeated softly, frowning slightly now. 'You're beautiful, March.' He smiled ruefully. 'Beautiful. Desirable. How could I resist you?' He shrugged self-derisively.

Her mouth tightened as she fought her own response to this verbal seduction. 'The fact that I'm also one of the Calendar sisters had nothing to do with it, I suppose?' she scorned harshly.

Oh, she knew she had agreed with May not to challenge Will on this point just yet, could even understand her sister's reticence in wanting to know more about the situation before confronting Will with it; but at the moment, who she was, what she was, was her only defence against what had just happened between them!

She watched as Will's cheeks lost that emotional flush, his gaze seeming wary now as it remained on her even as he slowly reached up to rebutton his shirt before standing up. The same shirt she had so ably unbuttoned only seconds ago!

March had no idea where any of those instincts had come from, had only known a need to be closer to Will than she'd already been, to touch his flesh in the way that he'd been touching hers.

But her response had been instinctive—could Will claim the same?

Will shrugged slightly, grimacing ruefully as he spoke. 'How much do you know?'

Not a lot, if the truth were known. In fact, only a growing certainty that Will worked for Jude Marshall in some capacity, if she were honest. But she didn't intend letting Will know that!

'I'm merely wondering what sort of man Jude Marshall is that he managed to buy the loyalty of both you and Max,' she replied insultingly.

The flush on the hardness of Will's cheeks was due to anger now. 'Jude hasn't bought me—or my loyalty,' he snapped tautly. 'Max's either, for that matter,' he added scathingly. 'You've met Max, he's going to marry your sister, for goodness' sake; does he seem like the sort of man who could be bought? By anybody!'

March met his angry gaze unflinchingly. 'And you?' she challenged scornfully.

His mouth tightened. 'I'm not employed by Jude, March,' he told her hardly. 'I am an architect, however.

A damned good one, if I do say so myself. But I choose who I work for.'

An architect. Which must mean that Will was here in order to draw up the plans for the health and country club Jude Marshall intended building on the Hanworth Estate. On land that the Calendar farm was smack in the middle of!

'You're William Davenport!' she said astoundedly, looking at him with new eyes now. 'You're the man that designed the award-winning building for the new museum in Leeds,' she realized dazedly.

He gave an inclination of his head. 'I am.'

March had visited the museum several times on trips to Leeds, the building a marvel of Victorian-style architecture, totally in keeping with its surroundings and ideally suited for its purpose.

No wonder this man drove around in a Ferrari; he was reputed to be in demand all over the world. Although at the moment he seemed to have settled for a very small part of it. Her part of it!

'And at the moment you choose to work for Jude Marshall,' she came back derisively. 'That only makes it worse!' she assured him disgustedly.

Will's gaze narrowed shrewdly as he gave her a searching glance. 'But until this moment you didn't know that, did you?' he realized slowly. 'Why, you little—' He broke off, giving a shake of his head. 'Minx!' he finished heavily.

March was too angry to feel anything else at the moment, but she knew that later, when she was alone, she was going to feel so much more than that. Which was why she intended clinging to that anger for as long as possible!

'In the circumstances, I think it will be better if you leave,' she told him coldly.

He arched blond brows. 'Now?'

'In the morning will do.' As long as he was gone before she came home from work tomorrow evening!

If she didn't have to see him, to know every day for the next two weeks that he was staying just across the yard in the studio over the garage, maybe she could at least put this evening to the back of her mind!

'No.'

March gave him a sharp look, her eyes widening indignantly as he returned her gaze unblinkingly. 'What do you mean ''no''?' she rasped disbelievingly.

Will shrugged. 'I acknowledge there's no written contract, but there is a verbal agreement between your sister and I. I've already paid over two weeks' rent in advance—'

'We'll return the money to you!' March cut in heatedly. Although quite how they were going to do that, she wasn't completely sure; May had informed her earlier that she had already used the money to order the necessary supplies for mending the barn roof!

Will gave a shake of his head. 'I don't want the money back. I'm comfortable here, I would rather stay.'

'But we don't want you here,' March protested.

'*You* don't want me here,' he acknowledged evenly. 'But does May feel the same way?'

March felt her frustration with this situation rise to an almost unbearable pitch. 'May will agree with whatever I decide,' she told him angrily.

'Will she?' he mused calmly. 'Why don't we stroll across to the farmhouse and ask her?' He made a move towards the door.

'How dare you?' she attacked furiously, not at all

sure, after what May had said earlier, that her sister
would agree with her asking Will to leave. 'You whee-
dled your way in here under false pretences, charming
my older sister along the way—'

'But not you,' he accepted heavily as he turned back
to face her. 'March, I didn't wheedle my way in anywhere,' he rasped. 'Neither did I set out to charm anyone. I told you from the first that I was in the area on
business—'

'Without telling me what that business was!' she reminded him accusingly.

'Because at the time I had no idea it *was* any of your
business!' he came back harshly. 'In fact, I'm still not
sure that it is. Look, March, I know you aren't going to
believe me,' he continued heavily as she got ready to
burst into fresh anger, 'but until you arrived back from
work yesterday and announced yourself as one of the
Calendar sisters, I had no idea that's who you were!
Why should I have known?' he reasoned impatiently at
her sceptical look.

Indeed, why should he? Unless he had found out all
about the Calendar sisters before coming to the area.
Which, in his place, she most certainly would have done!

She didn't believe a word he was saying, Will realized
frustratedly. Not that, in the circumstances, he could altogether blame her. But no matter what she might think
to the contrary, he knew he was telling her the truth.

Of course, in a fair world, he should have told both
sisters, as soon as he'd realized who they were, exactly
who he was, and what he was doing here. But in view
of Max's recent defection—something Jude, when Will
had spoken to the other man on the telephone the previous evening, had been absolutely incredulous about—

and the sisters' obvious fury towards the absent Jude Marshall, there just hadn't been the right opportunity to tell them that he was also in the area on the other man's behalf.

Besides, Will inwardly mocked himself, by the time he had learnt exactly who May and March were—but especially March!—it had been already too late to tell them the truth. Too late for him. Because by that time he'd already known himself to be so attracted to March he hadn't wanted to see the laughter and fun in her eyes replaced by scorn and dislike when told the reason he was in the area.

The same scorn and dislike he could see in those beautiful grey-green eyes at this very moment…!

He gave a heavy sigh. 'I'm sorry, March, but I'm not going anywhere.'

She glared across the room at him. 'You aren't staying here,' she told him just as determinedly.

Who would believe, looking at the two of them now, that minutes ago they had been in each other's arms, with only one obvious conclusion to their roused passions?

March had been like liquid velvet in his arms, arousing a desire in Will so strong that he still ached at the memory of it.

'I'm afraid that I am,' he came back evenly.

She gave him an impatient frown. 'But why? Why do you have to stay here? There are any number of places quite near here that I could recommend—'

'You don't live at any of them,' Will cut in ruefully.

'Me?' She looked startled now, that surprised expression as quickly turning to one of suspicion. 'Why should it matter to you where I live?' She eyed him warily.

Will gave a humourless smile. 'You can ask that, after what just happened between us?'

Her eyes seemed to shoot green sparks at being reminded of what had just happened between them. 'Nothing happened between us!' she scorned dismissively. 'Nothing of any importance, anyway,' she added insultingly.

Deliberately so, Will knew. Even in the short time he had come to know her, Will knew that anger and scorn were March's methods of defence. A defence to hide the warm softness of her nature, the vulnerability of her heart...

'Maybe not to you,' he allowed gently, doubting that it was true—he didn't believe for a moment that March was the sort of woman who went around kissing, and caressing, men she didn't care about—but not wanting to say anything that was going to hurt her. Hurting March Calendar, he was discovering, was something he never wanted to do...

'Or to you, either,' she instantly derided.

March wasn't in the mood to listen to him, Will knew, but he didn't go around kissing and caressing women he didn't care about, either...

He gave a rueful shrug. 'I doubt there is anything I could say to you right now that would convince you otherwise—'

'You're right—there isn't!' she came back scornfully. 'It really would be better, for everyone,' she added firmly, 'if you were to leave.'

Not for him it wouldn't. He liked the Calendar sisters, both of them, although that feeling went a little further where March was concerned. The last thing he wanted to do was hurt either May or March by what he was doing.

'You just don't see it, do you, March?' He gave an impatient shake of his head at her continued mulishness. 'Here you have the ideal opportunity to have some sort of say in the design of Jude's hotel and country club, by having the architect living on your own doorstep, and you want to throw away that opportunity through what I can only describe as prejudice—'

'Prejudice!' she repeated incredulously. 'Don't you understand, Mr Davenport, that we don't *want* the hotel and country club here at all—' She broke off as Will shook his head. 'What?' she prompted tautly.

'That just isn't going to happen, March,' he reasoned lightly. 'Jude is a businessman. A successful one. And he isn't going to back off on this just because of a bit of local opposition—'

'It's more than a bit,' March assured him angrily.

Will gave a grimace of frustration at her continued blinkered opinion.

'The preliminary proposal for the hotel and country club has already been approved by the local planning people. I'm just here—'

'To put the finishing touches to it,' March finished heatedly.

'In a word—yes,' he confirmed ruefully. 'March—'

'You aren't going to convince me,' she cut in determinedly. 'This is farming land. Has been farming land for generations—'

'Successfully so?' he put in softly, knowing by the way the sisters lived, the necessity for at least two of them to have jobs outside of the farm, that it wasn't even enough to support the three of them.

But he regretted his gentle prompting almost as soon as he had made it, March's face paling, eyes suddenly huge, her whole demeanour one of deflation now.

But he knew it was extremely difficult nowadays for small farms like this one to make enough just to subsist, only the larger, more modern farms that had been turned into a commercial concern managing to survive. It wasn't fair. Meant that more and more of these small farms simply went to the wall. No, it wasn't fair, it just happened to be a fact of life. No matter how much March might try to fight against it.

'Jude is offering you a more than fair price for this land, March—'

'Only so that he can make millions out of it once it's been absorbed into the rest of the estate!' she came back scathingly.

Will gave a rueful shrug of his shoulders. Of course Jude was intending to make money out of his latest venture; as Will had already said, Jude was a businessman. And Jude hadn't become as successful as he was by being delicate about it.

'It's very difficult to stop a moving train going at full speed,' he pointed out regretfully; Jude had been moving at high speed ever since Will had known him.

'Really?' March challenged derisively. 'The odd obstruction on the track seems to be effective!'

Will frowned. It was true that Jude couldn't force the Calendar sisters into selling their farm. But Will knew it was also true that Jude could make things very difficult for the sisters if he chose to do so. He knew, because he had checked this afternoon. The Calendar farm was in the middle of the estate the other man had just bought, their utilities were provided across the land Jude now owned, meaning he had the upper hand...

Unless...

'If you're really determined not to sell—'

'We are,' she snapped.

'The why don't you work with me on this rather than against Jude?' he reasoned patiently.

That suspicion was back in her gaze. 'I don't understand what you mean by working with you.'

Neither did he, not really. The idea had only occurred to him as they were talking. Surely there must be a way for this to work out so that no one was hurt in the process, a way for the sisters to keep their farm, but to keep Jude happy at the same time. Most of all, Will knew, he wanted to stop March continuing to look at him in that scornful, suspicious way!

'I'm not sure myself yet,' he admitted self-derisively. 'But there has to be a way.'

Her mouth twisted scornfully. 'Well, when you think of it, let me know. In the meantime—'

'I'm staying put,' he cut in determinedly.

She gave him a disgusted look. 'Please yourself,' she bit out dismissively. 'But don't expect any more invitations to dinner,' she added tartly as she reached for the door-handle.

As a parting shot, it was pretty weak, and they both knew it, Will giving March a rueful smile. 'I still owe the two of you dinner,' he reminded lightly.

'And I'm sure May would enjoy that,' she came back tartly.

'But not you,' he acknowledged dryly.

'As far as I'm concerned, eating with the enemy is as bad as sleeping with them,' March snapped—and as instantly regretted it if the colour that flooded her cheeks was anything to go by. 'I meant—'

'I know what you meant, March,' Will assured her laughingly. 'And let me assure you—I do not want to "sleep" with you.' He moved to open the door for her. 'Nor,' he added huskily, 'do I consider you an enemy.'

They were standing only inches apart now, Will very conscious of the warmth of March's body, the heady perfume she wore, the light dusting of freckles across the bridge of her nose, the pouting perfection of her mouth.

He also knew that if she didn't soon get out of here he was going to kiss her again!

As if aware of the impulse, March moved outside onto the top of the stairs. 'The sentiment isn't reciprocated,' she told him waspishly. 'And next time you speak to Jude Marshall…'

'Yes?' he prompted warily.

She gave a humourless smile. 'Tell him to come and fight his own battles—we're sick of dealing with his minions!' she added insultingly.

An insult Will had no intention of responding to! 'I'll tell him.' He nodded.

Although he doubted the challenge would mean too much to the other man; as far as he could tell, Jude was otherwise occupied at the moment with the attractions of the actress April Robine!

March gave him a sharp look before clattering down the metal steps and moving lightly across the frozen yard to the farmhouse.

Will watched her every step of the way, admiring the coltish grace with which she moved; long-legged, her youthful energy dented by their conversation but not diminished.

He closed the door slowly behind him as he moved back into the warmth of the studio. Apart from that time he had held March in his arms, it hadn't been a very successful encounter.

Apart from—!

He was quickly discovering that the only thing that

did mean anything was holding March, kissing and caressing her!

He closed his eyes, easily conjuring up the feel of March, her warmth, the passion he knew they had shared. He wanted March Calendar, found her mercurial changes of mood fascinating, her seductive beauty affecting him as no other woman ever had.

But, at the same time, his desire for March only made this situation more complicated.

Impossibly so…?

CHAPTER SEVEN

'FLYING a little high with your friend in the Ferrari, aren't you, March?' Clive taunted sarcastically as March placed a mug of coffee down on his desk.

Making the hot drinks throughout the day was apparently also the job of the receptionist, March had learnt shortly after starting work here two years ago. In fact, after only a few weeks' employment March had been amazed at the amount of jobs that came under that title.

If truth were known, Clive and Michelle were just too mean to employ anyone else, preferring to leave all the little incidental jobs to March rather than employ an office junior. After all, it would cut into their profit!

March innocently returned Clive's mocking gaze as she stepped back from his desk. 'I didn't know Ferraris could fly,' she easily returned his sarcasm.

She had never found working for Clive to be easy, and over the last few months, as his flirtatious attitude had increased whenever Michelle hadn't been around, she had found it even harder; obviously Will Davenport's appearance yesterday wasn't going to make that particular situation any easier!

'Very funny,' Clive sneered humourlessly. 'You—'

'Stop teasing her, Clive,' Michelle cut in with light rebuke in the gentle softness of her voice. 'Clive was saying last night that you have a new boyfriend, March.' She turned to her interestedly.

March had never been able to understand how two such different people could not only work together but

79

have lived together for the last ten years too. Where Clive was brash and outspoken, Michelle was quiet and considerate. Where Clive had screen-star good looks, Michelle's were rather mousy, with her light brown hair and brown eyes, her features tending to be a little plain unless animated.

A definite attraction of opposites, March had dismissed uninterestedly after a couple of months of working here; Michelle was probably completely overwhelmed by the fact that a good-looking man like Clive was interested in her, and Clive, as March had come to know only too well, probably thrived as the more attractive of the pair. He certainly liked to feel that every woman in the vicinity found him irresistible, and any woman that didn't quickly became the target of his sharp tongue.

Which included March!

After only two weeks of working in the agency, the needed money aside, March could quite happily have given in her notice. But the gentler Michelle was so much the opposite, so appreciative of everything that March did, that she hadn't liked to let the other woman down by leaving. Luckily it didn't happen too often that she was left alone with Clive in the office, and he usually behaved himself when Michelle was around.

'What's he like?' Michelle prompted interestedly, brown eyes glowing warmly as March gave her a cup of tea.

'Will isn't my boyfriend,' March dismissed, not quite meeting the other woman's gaze. 'I—he—he's a family friend,' she hastily invented—well, he was apparently a friend of Max's, and as Max was almost a member of her family…! 'He's just staying with us for a couple of weeks,' she added dismissively.

Which reminded her, she would have to deal with the paperwork of acquiring a rentee for two weeks through Carter and Jones.

'Yesterday's kiss didn't just look friendly to me,' Clive put in speculatively.

March eyed him coolly. 'Well, I can assure you that it was.' Damn Will for having kissed her in front of Clive in that possessive way!

Admittedly, at the time she had been quite grateful for his proprietary attitude, but not if it was going to make Clive more unbearable to work with than usual.

'Any more news about the Hanworth Estate, March?' Michelle changed the subject with ease.

Although it wasn't really much of a change now that March knew that Will was Jude Marshall's architect!

'Not really.' She grimaced, warming to Michelle for her concern; it had been Michelle who had initially told her what Jude Marshall's intentions were for the neighbouring Hanworth Estate. 'I suppose we will just have to wait and see.'

'Personally, I think you and your sisters are idiots for not selling,' Clive told her disgustedly. 'The man must be offering way over the odds, for a farm that is virtually worthless.'

March felt the rage building within her at this man's complete lack of sensitivity, her eyes sparkling, bright spots of angry colour in her cheeks. 'It isn't worthless to me—'

'I'm sure Clive didn't mean to be unkind,' Michelle put in apologetically. 'It's your home, of course it isn't worthless to you. It's just such a pity that it's in the middle of the Hanworth land,' she added sympathetically.

'A pity' wasn't quite the phrase March would have used! 'I—'

'Good morning!' greeted a cheerful voice that made March stiffen with recognition. 'I wondered if you were free for an early lunch, March?' Will Davenport prompted lightly as he came into the agency.

March slowly turned to face him, unable to hide her amazement at this man's cheek. They hadn't parted on good terms at all last night, and she was sure she had made her feelings completely clear about ever seeing him again. And yet here he was, cheerfully offering to buy her lunch as if the two of them were the best of friends.

And, after what she had said to Clive and Michelle earlier, that was exactly what the other couple thought that they were!

'Go ahead, March,' Michelle invited. 'It's almost twelve o'clock anyway.' She smiled encouragingly after giving Will an appreciative glance.

Michelle obviously had a weakness for good-looking men, March decided disgruntledly, grudgingly acknowledging that Will did look extremely handsome this morning in fitted black denims and a blue jumper the exact colour of his eyes. He was also smiling at March as if last night had never happened!

But what choice did she have but to collect her coat and handbag in preparation for going out to lunch with him? Or, at least, seeming as if she were going out to lunch with him, because once they were outside she intended telling him exactly what he could do with his lunch!

'Make sure you're back by one,' Clive told her hardly. 'I'm taking Michelle out to lunch today to celebrate our tenth anniversary,' he added derisively.

'It won't matter if you're a few minutes late,' Michelle assured March with a definite twinkle in her eye.

March accompanied Will down the street, not having spoken so much as a word to him yet. Probably because she knew that once she started talking she might not be able to stop—and none of it would have been pleasant!

She had hardly slept at all last night, for thinking of that time in Will's arms, alternating between anger that it had happened at all and a wish for it to happen again. Completely illogical, March knew, but nevertheless that was how she had felt.

It hadn't helped that May had been full of questions last night on March's return from the studio. Of course March had told her sister nothing of her time in Will Davenport's arms, only confirming that he was indeed working for Jude Marshall, as his architect. But that hadn't stopped May from speculating, especially as March had returned without the cup of sugar she had supposedly gone over there for!

'As pleasant as this change might be,' Will spoke teasingly at her side, 'are you going to remain silent all through lunch too?'

March turned to glare at him. 'I have nothing to say to you,' she snapped. 'And we aren't having lunch!' she added disgustedly.

'Oh.' He looked disappointed.

She gave an impatient sigh. 'I only left with you just now because to do anything else would have been too awkward to explain.'

'I can deal with awkward,' Will assured her. 'After all, I've been dealing with you for three days now!' he added mockingly.

'Not awkward for you,' she told him irritably, wishing

her heart would resume its normal rhythmic beat, that she wasn't so aware of the intimacies she had shared with this man the previous evening.

Although, to look at Will, that time in his arms might never have happened as he grinned at her in innocent enquiry.

'I had only just finished explaining that you're a family friend when you walked in the door,' she said exasperatedly.

'Well, that's a definite step up from being one of Jude Marshall's minions,' he acknowledged dryly.

March felt her cheeks flush as he repeated the insult she had deliberately thrown at him the previous evening. '"If the cap fits",' she bit out harshly.

'I don't think I've ever worn a cap,' Will remarked consideringly. 'Maybe when I was at junior school—'

'I didn't mean it literally,' March cut in impatiently.

He chuckled at her obvious discomfort. 'Lighten up, March,' he encouraged as she continued to scowl at him. 'May certainly didn't seem to bear any grudge when I had coffee with her this morning,' he added brightly.

'May obviously has a more forgiving nature than I do!' She gave him a glowering look, not in the least surprised that he had called at the farm to see May this morning, or that her sister had given him a cup of coffee; May just didn't seem to see this situation as March did.

May also hadn't spent any time in this man's arms, hadn't completely forgotten the farm—and everything else—as she'd been kissed and caressed by him. As she'd kissed and caressed him back!

It wasn't that she was a complete innocent—she had had boyfriends in the past, had even believed herself a little in love with one or two of them. But never before had she responded in the way she had to Will, knowing even now that she had wanted to make love with him, to lay naked in his arms as they made love to each other. That was just another reason for her to be angry with him!

'Probably,' Will accepted ruefully now. 'She had a phone call from her director while I was there; her screen test has been moved forward to tomorrow. Something to do with the star of the film being in the country next week.'

March frowned at him. 'I'm sure May is perfectly capable of telling me that herself when I get home this evening.'

He shrugged. 'Your big sister has the impression you don't approve of her proposed acting career.'

Her eyes widened. 'That's absolute rubbish!' she gasped indignantly. 'You're making that up,' she accused uncertainly.

Surely May couldn't really believe that…?

Will gave her a searching glance, knowing by her hesitant tone that she wasn't at all sure about her last claim. And with good reason, if his conversation with May this morning was anything to go by.

Max's engagement to the younger Calendar sister had obviously shaken the sisters' resolve to keep the farm, May convinced that Max, once he had completely severed his ties with Jude, would want to go to London to work, and that January would go with him. Which, Will also thought, seemed a pretty astute guess. With May's possible offer of an acting role in a film later this year, that only left March. May, he knew, was seriously considering turning down the film offer in order to support March's stand.

Which was why Will had come into town this morning and done what he had done...

Although perhaps he had better not mention that to March just yet. Wait and see what the reaction was. After all, he could just be wrong...

He had felt restless and unfocused after March had left him yesterday evening, the plans he had been working on before March had arrived offering no incentive whatsoever. Finally he had climbed up into the attic and looked at those paintings that March claimed weren't paintings at all.

They were good.

In fact, they were better than good.

So much so that Will had parcelled six of them up before coming into town to post them off to a friend of his who ran a gallery in London. As far as he could tell March no longer even looked at her own work, so there wasn't much chance of her missing half a dozen of them. And if Will's opinion of them turned out to be the correct one...

Not that he thought March would see his highhandedness that way. Which was why he had no intention of telling her what he had done until he heard back from Graham.

The matriarch of the Calendar family must have been something else, Will had decided after spending some time looking at all of March's paintings, because their father, that bluntly spoken Yorkshireman, certainly hadn't been the one to give them their array of artistic talents.

'Am I?' he gently prompted March now.

'Of course,' she scorned. 'I've done nothing but encourage May to go for this opportunity. You've heard me yourself.'

'At the same time that you're absolutely adamant you aren't going to sell the farm,' Will pointed out ruefully.

'I should have known it would all come back to that again,' March snapped disgustedly. 'Don't you ever think of anything else?' she added scathingly.

He very much doubted she would want to hear about the thoughts that had kept him from sleeping last night!

How could he have possibly slept when his mind and senses were so full of March, of how she had felt in his arms, of how much he wanted to make love with her?

'Oh, I give the odd thought to food now and again,' he answered her dismissively. 'Talking of which...'

'*You* were talking of food—I wasn't,' March came back tartly. 'I haven't eaten my sandwiches from yesterday yet—'

'Ugh, they must be disgusting by now,' Will broke in with a grimace. 'But I'm quite happy to go to a sandwich bar if you insist,' he assured her, at the same time directing her into the sandwich bar they had been about to pass. 'I'll even let you buy me lunch today, if you feel you must,' he added with soft challenge.

Hah! That had her confused, the conflicting emotions easily read on her face: of returning his gesture of yesterday, and as such not feeling beholden to him, warring with her desire to tell him what he could do with this second suggestion of lunch.

As she pushed open the door to the sandwich bar, to precede him inside, he knew the former had won. Luckily for him. Because, for the moment, he had completely run out of options for ways of spending time with March. Something he very much wanted to do.

'You know, the more I see of your boss, the less I like him,' Will told her grimly once they had sat down and ordered their sandwiches and drinks. 'He looks the sort who turns nasty if he doesn't get his own way.'

March looked at him beneath lowered lashes. 'As opposed to...?' she taunted.

He gave a decisive shake of his head at her deliberate barb. 'Nasty isn't in my nature,' he assured her dryly. 'Determination. Arrogance, maybe—'

'Maybe?' she repeated with a derisive snort.

'If warranted,' he acknowledged laughingly. 'But nasty? No, I don't think that's part of my nature at all.' He gave another shake of his head.

March looked at him unblinkingly for several minutes, before slowly relaxing, her smile rueful. 'No, I don't think it is either,' she conceded wryly.

'Thank you.' Will gave a gracious inclination of his head. 'Does Carter have anything to do with the questions you were asking me yesterday concerning undervaluing property?'

The return to his original subject was done so suddenly that March didn't even have time to try to hide her consternation—even if she could have done, which was doubtful!—looking across at him frowningly now.

'Add sneaky to determined and arrogant,' she bit out tersely.

He shrugged unapologetically. 'Does he?'

March's gaze no longer met his; she was obviously perfectly aware of how easily readable her emotions were. 'They were merely abstract questions,' she dismissed huskily. 'Not specifically aimed at anyone,' she added firmly.

'Add evasive to your other list of attractions,' Will returned dryly.

She raised dark brows, a smile now lurking at the

corners of her kissable mouth. 'Do I have a list of "attractions"?' she prompted teasingly.

'Oh, yes,' Will confirmed appreciatively, knowing she was deliberately changing the subject, but at this moment willing to let her do so. 'Would you like me to tell you what they are?' He quirked blond brows at her suggestively.

'Er—no,' she decided hastily, leaning back as their food and drinks arrived, obviously relieved at the interruption.

Not that he could blame her; it could prove highly embarrassing if he were to start talking about all March's wonderful attributes. Besides, this was hardly the time or the place...

Now that he was here with March, having lunch with her, despite her obvious reluctance, he was beginning to feel a slight trepidation about sending those paintings off to London. Last night it had all seemed so simple: send the paintings to Graham and await his artistic criticism. But here and now, with March sitting only inches away from him, he wasn't so sure of his actions.

Of course, it would all be easier if Graham were to agree with March's own opinion of her artistic talent, but if Graham agreed with Will, then he was going to have to talk to March about them, and what he had done. Looking at her now, knowing how hard it was to get past her prickly nature, he knew that wasn't going to be an easy matter!

'Is the sandwich not to your liking? You were frowning,' March explained at his questioning look. 'We can always swap if you want to; I'll be perfectly happy with the tuna if you would like my egg mayonnaise,' she offered lightly.

'"Greater love hath no man—" or woman, and all that?' He grinned.

'It's just a sandwich, Will,' she said dryly.

His grin widened. 'You're fun to be with, do you know that?'

'What does that have to do with exchanging sandwiches?' she came back tartly—although there was a slight flush of pleasure in her cheeks now.

'The tuna is fine,' he dismissed. 'But I'm glad I'm back to being Will; "Mr Davenport" sounds like it should be my father you're talking to.' He grimaced.

'You have parents?' March prompted interestedly.

Will burst out laughing. 'Did you think I was manufactured?' he teased at her puzzled expression.

She gave him a scathing grimace. 'I meant, are your parents still alive?'

'Well, they were the last time I spoke to them.' He nodded. 'Which was only last week. Dad's a retired doctor,' he continued hastily as he sensed March was about to give him another cutting reply. 'My mother was a nurse.'

'A hospital romance,' March mused.

'I don't know—I've never asked them.' Will shrugged ruefully.

'Oh, the disinterest of youth,' she reproved mockingly.

'Unless I'm mistaken, young lady, I'm several years older than you,' he said dryly.

'Almost Methuselah.' She nodded, grey-green eyes glowing with laughter.

'Well, I wouldn't go that far!' He grimaced. 'Do you have anything against older men?'

'Do you have anything against younger women?' she came back tartly, the colour in her cheeks now owing nothing to pleasure as she merely looked embarrassed by the intimate turn the conversation had taken.

'In this particular case—no.' He smiled warmly, perfectly happy with the conversation himself.

March swallowed hard, her gaze once again avoiding his as she took a sip of her coffee. 'Isn't it strange that your parents were both medical people, and yet you became an architect?' she abruptly changed the subject back to his parents.

'Not really—I faint at the first sight of blood!' he admitted with a self-conscious grimace.

March looked astounded for several seconds, and then she burst out laughing, her eyes glowing, two tiny dimples appearing endearingly either side of that smiling mouth.

She continued to chuckle, giving Will chance to enjoy her laughter. Even if it was at his expense! Not that he minded that at all if it meant he could see March smiling.

'Feet of clay?' he finally prompted ruefully.

'Not really.' She shook her head, still smiling. 'I was just thinking how useless you would be on a farm. It's a busy time of year for us. Most of the ewes have already lambed, and we will have the cows calving shortly. But at least I know where not to come for help if there are any complications!' she added teasingly.

'Not unless you want to step over me during the process,' he confirmed lightly.

'I think we'll pass, if you don't mind,' she said dryly, her eyes widening as she glanced down at her wristwatch. 'It's almost one o'clock, I'll have to be getting back.'

Was there a slight note of regret in her voice, or was it just wishful thinking on his part? Probably the latter, he decided, but one could dream, couldn't one?

'One of your bosses at least said you didn't have to hurry back,' he reminded her. 'And you haven't finished your sandwich yet,' he pointed out practically.

'I'm really not that hungry.' March pushed away the plate containing the half-eaten sandwich, taking a last gulp of her coffee before standing up. 'Some of us have work to go to, you know,' she added with a return of her usual tartness, before moving across to the counter to pay for their lunch.

Will let her, knowing it was a pride thing on her part, and having no wish to upset her any more than he already had. Besides, it gave him chance to watch her, to admire the gentle sway of her hips, the silky length of her legs.

Although he wasn't quite so pleased to note that several other men in the room were doing the same thing! But March, to give her her due, seemed completely unaware of the male admiration coming in her direction, looking to neither left nor right as she moved through the room to join Will at the door.

'I may faint at the sight of blood,' Will told her quietly as they moved off down the street together, 'but otherwise I'm pretty good in a crisis. If you should ever need any help,' he added huskily.

March gave him a searching sideways glance. 'I'll bear that in mind,' she finally answered softly.

Will wasn't at all sure what was going on in the estate agency of Carter and Jones, but he was pretty sure that something was. He was equally sure, no matter how evasive she might have been on the subject earlier, that March knew there was too. And Will had meant what he said about Clive Carter; the other man looked as if he might turn nasty if thwarted.

But having offered his help, with March as prickly as

she was, Will knew he couldn't do any more for the moment.

But that didn't mean he didn't intend keeping an eye on the situation, if only from a distance...

CHAPTER EIGHT

MARCH had no intention of telling May of her second lunch with Will, but the two of them had watched the news together, eaten dinner, and still her sister hadn't mentioned the telephone call she had received from the film director earlier that day.

Quite how to approach the subject, without mentioning having lunch with Will, March didn't know. Although she had certainly taken to heart Will's earlier comments about May's reluctance to even go to London for the screen test. And the reason for it!

'Anything interesting happen today?' she attempted casually as the two of them strolled over to the barn where they were keeping the ewes with their more delicate lambs.

May gave her a puzzled glance. 'I told you earlier, I've been at the farm all day.'

March nodded. 'But no visitors? Telephone calls?' A casual glance in the direction of the studio showed it to be in darkness, which meant that Will wasn't home yet. Or he had been home and gone out again. Which was interesting, because she didn't think he knew anyone else in the area...

'I haven't heard from January, if that's what you're wondering,' May assured her lightly as the two of them entered the warmth of the lambing shed. 'But then, I wouldn't expect to. Would you?' she added mischievously as she strolled over to the ewe in the first pen. 'Hello, Ginny, aren't you a clever girl?' she soothed, at the same time running a critical eye over the animal still awaiting the arrival of her offspring.

Their father had always deplored the way the three girls gave each of their animals a name, sure that making pets of the animals would only make it harder for them all when it came time for them to 'go to market', as he delicately put it. That might have been true when they were younger, but as the sisters had grown older, they had come to accept the simplicity of farming life, the cows and sheep going to market for sale, for whatever reason.

Although that wasn't quite the case with Ginny, the ewe having become a firm favourite with all the sisters over the years. She was probably approaching the end of her usefulness now, but all of them were loath to make that decision.

But March really wasn't interested in Ginny, or any other of their livestock, at this particular moment. 'I wasn't actually referring to January,' she prompted tautly.

May gave her a searching glance now. 'Will popped over for a cup of coffee this morning, if that's what you want to know.' She shrugged.

Well, it was a start!

'What did he want?' she bit out abruptly.

'I told you, a cup of coffee. Oh, and he brought back the cup of sugar you went over there to borrow last night,' her sister added teasingly.

March felt the colour in her cheeks as she remembered the reason for her hurried departure from the studio the previous evening. 'Good of him,' she snapped.

May laughed softly. 'You weren't exactly subtle, were you?' She gave an exasperated shake of her head. 'Will didn't say too much about it, but I'm sure you gave him a hard time of it last night once you knew who he was.'

That wasn't quite the way March would have put what had happened between herself and Will the previous evening!

Her gaze was evasive. 'I told you he was a snake in the grass!'

May gave a heavy sigh. 'He's simply doing his job, March, in the best way he knows how. Like all of us,' she added quietly.

'Is that what he told you?' she scorned. 'I happen to think differently.' She gave a dismissive shake of her head, not having missed her sister's second husky remark, and not about to be sidetracked by talk of Will Davenport, either; she had heard far too much from him today already! 'May, how do you really feel about letting all of this go?' She opened her arms expansively, deliberately keeping her own expression neutral.

May had always done what was best for all three sisters, without complaint, without regrets, as far as March knew. But March simply couldn't believe that concerning May's hesitation about the offered screen test, clearly remembering how excited her sister had been after the director had first approached her.

Much as March would hate letting Jude Marshall have his own way where their farm was concerned, she wasn't about to stand in her sister's way, either.

'Well, we aren't going to sell it, are we?' May answered brightly. 'So that possibility doesn't even arise.'

'But—'

'Good evening, ladies,' Will greeted smoothly as he stood in the doorway to the lambing shed. 'None about to give birth, I hope?' He held back cautiously.

'Not right this minute, no,' March answered him dryly

before turning to give her sister a knowing smile. 'Will goes green at the sight of blood,' she informed May derisively.

'I believe that was ''faints at the sight of blood'',' he corrected with a grimace.

May nodded. 'March has the same reaction to spiders.' She shot March a mischievous smile.

'Really?' Will's sky-blue gaze was turned on her mockingly now. 'You didn't tell me that.'

'You didn't ask me!' March came back tartly. He was still wearing the blue jumper and black denims, so perhaps he hadn't been home and then out again, after all...

'So I didn't.' He chuckled in acknowledgement. 'So what are the two of you doing out here if you aren't assisting in a birth?' he prompted interestedly.

'Checking that there isn't one taking place,' March answered him impatiently; she had finally been getting somewhere with her conversation with May, could quite well have done without this interruption. Especially from Will!

He nodded, obviously no more informed about the workings of their farm than he had been a few minutes ago. 'I've just come back from town—anyone feel like joining me in a glass of wine?'

'No, thanks—'

'Lovely—'

Both sisters had answered at once, March in the negative—obviously! May in the positive.

'Two to one against, March,' Will informed her triumphantly. 'The wine wins!'

Her gaze narrowed. He was looking decidedly pleased with himself this evening. Very much as if he knew something they didn't...

'Okay,' she conceded lightly, earning herself a searching glance from Will now as he puzzled over the possible reason for her easy acquiescence.

Oh, well, a puzzled Will Davenport had to be preferable to a knowing one!

'Your place or mine?' he prompted once they were outside in the crisp night air.

March shot him a pitying glance for his facetiousness, receiving a wide-eyed innocent look in return that didn't fool her for a minute. 'Ours,' she answered flatly. 'It's warmer,' she added by way of explanation as he raised questioning brows.

'Really?' He shrugged. 'Obviously I've been out all day, but I've found the heat in the studio in the evenings more than adequate so far.' He gave her a challenging look.

A look March returned with obvious irritation. If he were hoping to embarrass her by covert references to yesterday evening, then he was going to be out of luck; she had more important things on her mind this evening—such as May's screen test tomorrow. Or not...as the case may be.

'You—'

'There's more room in the farmhouse,' May put in briskly. 'We'll go and get out the glasses while you collect the bottle of wine.' She looped her arm firmly through March's in order to pull her towards the kitchen door. 'What's going on?' she hissed softly.

'Going on?' March delayed lightly. 'Why, nothing.' She gave a definite shake of her head.

May gave her a reproving look as the two of them entered the warmth of the kitchen, that look turning to one of narrow-eyed searching as the sudden silence in the kitchen became overwhelming. At least, it seemed so to March!

What could her sister see in her face? What emotion was it giving away now?

'Not another one!' May finally gasped incredulously.

'What?' She frowned, her hands turning into fists at her sides as she tried to withstand that penetrating look from May.

'I don't believe it.' May shook her head dazedly. 'How on earth did that happen? The man's only been here a couple of days!'

March gave an impatient snort as she shook her head. 'I have no idea what you're talking about,' she dismissed impatiently, reaching up into the cupboard to take out the wineglasses. As May obviously wasn't going to!

'You're in love with Will Davenport,' May stated shakily.

March had turned so sharply at her sister's statement that one of the glasses slipped out of her hand and shattered on the tiled floor. Unnoticed by either of them, it seemed.

May simply stared at March disbelievingly, obviously deeply shaken by her own observation.

As for March—shaken didn't even begin to describe how she felt!

In love with Will Davenport?

She couldn't be!

'Here we are—' Will broke off his cheery greeting as he entered the kitchen and saw the two sisters simply staring at each other, both of them pale as magnolias.

A smashed glass lay on the floor between them, and yet it didn't seem as if one of them had thrown it at the other, no anger burning in either of their faces—in fact they both looked more shocked than angry.

Will had no idea what could have taken place between

the two sisters in the short time he had been gone—but something certainly had! May was staring at March in complete disbelief, and March was staring at him in exactly the same manner.

May was the first to recover, seeming to shake herself slightly as she turned to face him. 'Sorry.' She gave the ghost of a smile. 'We were—um—discussing farm business,' she dismissed evasively.

And untruthfully, if Will were any judge of character; March was the more easily readable of the sisters, but May was definitely the more honest. And she wasn't being honest now.

'Someone seems to have had an accident,' he pointed out lightly, glancing down at the broken glass that lay on the floor between the two sisters.

'That was me,' March acknowledged shakily, her face turned away, her hair falling forward to shield her expression as she went down on her haunches to begin picking up the shattered glass.

'Not like that!' Will moved quickly, grabbing her wrist to pull her back to her feet. 'You'll cut yourself—' He broke off as he discovered he was already too late in his warning, March even now pulling a sliver of the glass from one of her fingers, blood instantly welling from the cut it left.

She looked up sharply, her gaze glitteringly hard as she looked at him challengingly. 'Aren't you going to faint?' she bit out harshly.

Strangely enough, no. Perhaps it was only the sight of blood in the abstract, when the person was unknown to him, only the blood seeming real. But he knew he wasn't going to faint at the sight of March's blood, that he only wanted to do something to stop the bleeding, to take away the pain for her if he could.

'Here.' May was the one to hand him a clean cloth.

Will took it, hesitating before wrapping it about her finger. 'Is all the glass out?' he rasped as March winced.

'Don't fuss, Will!' she snapped, at the same time pulling her hand out of his grasp. 'I already have two mother hens in May and January, I don't need a third one!' she added nastily.

'March!' May gasped, obviously scandalized.

'Why don't the two of you just leave me alone?' March cried, eyes blazing angrily, before she turned and ran from the room.

Will looked at May, noting the paleness of her cheeks, the unshed tears swimming in huge green eyes.

May looked back at him concernedly, letting him know that he probably didn't look much better than she did!

'Was it something I said?' he finally murmured ruefully.

May gave a shaky smile. 'No—I think it may have been something *I* said!' She grimaced.

Also the reason for the tension between the two sisters when he'd first entered the kitchen…?

He glanced across to the door that led out to the hallway. 'Should I go up and see if she's okay?'

May actually chuckled. 'Not if you value your life!' She gave a rueful shake of her head. 'Leave it a while; she'll come back down when she's ready,' she advised as she took the wine from him and deftly opened the bottle. 'March is quick to anger, but just as quick to calm down again. Especially when she knows she's the one in the wrong,' she added huskily.

'But—'

'Have some wine, Will,' May told him briskly, pouring it out into the two glasses that had remained intact. 'You'll see, March will come back down soon.'

There didn't seem to be too much chance of that during the next hour as the two of them sat in the kitchen after clearing up the broken glass, talking quietly, slowly emptying the bottle of wine.

They had heard March moving around upstairs once or twice, probably to the bathroom to deal with the cut on her finger, but other than that there was no sign of her.

'I'm sorry about this, Will,' May finally sighed an hour later. 'It's all my fault, and I'm sure it isn't me you want to be sitting here drinking wine with!' she added ruefully.

Will gave her a considering look. 'It isn't?'

'We both know that it isn't.' She laughed, her gaze gently reproving.

His gaze narrowed. 'Do we?'

'Don't you start!' May warned dryly, putting down her wineglass decisively. 'I think I'll just go up and check that she's okay.' She stood up.

'Maybe I should leave—'

'Not on my account, I hope,' March dismissed lightly as she came into the kitchen.

Will looked at her searchingly. Whatever May had said or done earlier to upset March, the latter now had that response very firmly under control. In fact, for once, her expression was totally unreadable!

'I'm just on my way out, anyway,' March continued brightly, reaching for a jacket from behind the kitchen door. 'I told Aunt Lyn that I would go over one evening this week and help her to move all the wedding presents over to Sara and Josh's cottage before they come back from their honeymoon next week,' she added briskly.

'Our cousin Sara was married last weekend,' May took the time to explain to Will. 'And I thought we *both* promised to go over and help.' May looked at her sister frowningly.

March flicked back her long hair. 'Well, as you're obviously busy this evening…'

Will stood up abruptly. 'I was just leaving—'

'No, you weren't—'

'There's absolutely no need for you to do that,' March cut firmly across her sister's protest. 'It doesn't need both of us, May,' she insisted impatiently. 'I won't be long. You stay here and keep Will company.' She gave him a cold glance.

Will couldn't even begin to guess what had caused this rift between the two sisters, but he hoped that it had nothing to do with him. Or his reason for being here.

'No, I really must be going.' He drained his glass with one swallow. 'I have some work to do myself this evening, anyway,' he assured May dismissively.

'That will certainly make a change,' March came back crisply. 'Jude Marshall probably wonders what he's paying you for!'

May simply stared at her sister in embarrassed dismay, obviously having given up, for the moment, on trying to curb March's rudeness.

Will counted to ten before answering her; losing his own temper, something he rarely did anyway, would not help the situation. 'As it happens, he hasn't paid me anything yet.' He kept his voice deliberately even. 'I only get paid when I produce the finished article.'

'Then you had better get on with it, hadn't you?' March bit out scathingly.

He counted to twenty this time, not sure that even that was going to be enough to stop the sharp reply he wanted to give her. He had never met anyone, male or female, who could be as outspokenly rude as March Calendar.

He gave an acknowledging inclination of his head, blue gaze narrowed. 'I intend to.'

Maybe, after all, the best thing for all of them would be for him to remove his presence from the farm as quickly as possible; the last thing he wanted to do was be the cause of a lasting friction between the two sisters.

If, indeed, he was the cause. Which he wasn't sure of. But it was enough that he now felt extremely uncomfortable in their presence. 'Have a good evening,' he told May—more out of hope than a belief that she would, deciding it was best not to try and say anything else to March this evening.

She might be quick to anger, and quick to calm down again, but at the moment that certainly wasn't in evidence!

May walked him to the door, standing outside on the step. 'I'm really sorry about this, Will,' she told him huskily, shaking her head regretfully.

'Don't be,' he assured her. 'It's you I feel sorry for,' he added with feeling.

She chuckled softly. 'Then don't,' she assured him with a smile. 'March is only angry because she knows she's the one in the wrong.'

He raised blond brows. 'You would never know it to look at her!'

'But I know March, you see,' May added softly. 'That's the real problem,' she said enigmatically.

It was just too complex for Will to even begin to work out. If he wanted to. And he wasn't sure that he did. Oh, he still found March the most beautiful and fascinating woman he had ever met, but he hardly knew her in this coldly sarcastic mood, certainly couldn't tell what she was thinking or feeling. And without that, she was merely a beautiful enigma...

'Rather you than me!' he told May with feeling, raising a hand in parting as he walked briskly across to the studio without a backward glance.

What on earth could May have said or done to March to cause her to behave in that uncharacteristic way?

He simply didn't know. From the little May had said on the subject, she wasn't about to tell him, either. And it was a sure fact that March wasn't going to!

CHAPTER NINE

'MARCH—'

'I do not wish to discuss it!' she cut in sharply on May's tentative attempt to breach the strained silence between them once Will had left. 'Other than to say that you're totally wrong,' she added hardly—totally nullifying her previous statement!

'Am I?'

'Yes!' Her eyes flashed, her face pale. 'I am not in love with Will Davenport!'

Yet...

Because she was very much afraid that, until May had made the observation earlier, she had been well on her way to being just that!

She certainly responded to him in a way she never had with any other man. She also quite enjoyed the verbal sparring that went on between them. And there was no denying that her heart gave a jolt every time she saw him.

But that wasn't necessarily love, was it? Sexual attraction. Sexual awareness. But not love.

Because she refused to be in love with a man who was so closely associated with Jude Marshall!

January might have fallen into that trap, and Max, in his wisdom, had decided that it was better for all concerned if he severed his business ties with Jude Marshall. But that didn't mean any relationship March had with Will would turn out the same way. And she refused to even consider anything less.

As such she refused to love Will Davenport!

'You can't choose whether or not to love someone, March.' May's gentle rebuke told March that she must have actually spoken those last words out loud.

She blinked, a little disconcerted at having expressed her feelings so openly. 'Of course you can. I just did,' she dismissed briskly. 'Now are you coming with me to Aunt Lyn's or not?' she prompted abruptly.

'I am,' May conceded dryly. 'But let me have a look at that finger first, hmm?'

March looked across at her sister in exasperation, that exasperation quickly turning to affection as May looked back at her teasingly.

March stepped forward, all the tension going out of her as she gave her sister a hug. 'I do love you, May.' She chuckled ruefully.

'I love you too,' May returned huskily. 'Which is why I don't want you to make yourself unhappy about this situation. It worked out okay for January, why shouldn't it work out for you and—?'

'I'll make a deal with you, May,' she cut in dryly. 'You don't mention Will again this evening, and I'll take care of the farm over the weekend while you go down to London for the screen test.' She gave May a knowing look as her sister gave a surprised gasp. 'I told you he was a snake in the grass!' she added mischievously.

'Will told you?' May frowned. 'But how—when—?'

'Never mind the how or when,' March dismissed briskly. 'Give this director a call before we go out and tell him you'll be there some time tomorrow.'

'But—'

'No buts, May. What's good advice for me also applies to you,' she stated firmly. 'The complication of whether or not we keep or sell the farm can take care of itself for the moment. You have to at least go for the screen test, May,' she reasoned persuasively. 'You'll never forgive yourself if you don't.'

March could see that her last remark had definitely hit home, May heaving a deep sigh.

And she meant it about the farm. She wanted to keep it—certainly didn't want to sell it to someone like Jude Marshall!—but she wasn't about to insist on keeping the farm at the cost of her sister's happiness. May had already sacrificed so much for January and herself, she deserved to have some success of her own.

'January is twenty-five, and engaged to be married,' she encouraged as May still hesitated. 'I'm twenty-six, and more than capable of taking care of myself; when are you going to stop behaving like a mother hen, May?' she teased affectionately.

Her sister gave a rueful shrug. 'Probably when you find someone else to take that place in your life.'

A husband, for instance...

'That isn't going to be for years yet,' she dismissed airily. 'I may even end up that old maid Jude Marshall assumed that we all were before Max put him straight!'

'Not you, March,' May assured her laughingly. 'Underneath that gruff exterior you're the most soft-hearted of all of us. You'll marry one day, and have a houseful of children,' she added with certainty.

But it wouldn't be this house, March began to accept sadly as May cleaned and bandaged her cut finger. If May succeeded in securing the offered film role, then the farm would be sold.

It would be a sad day for all of them if that happened, but maybe that was the way it was meant to be. January would be free to enjoy her happiness as Max's wife, without any feelings of guilt because of leaving her sisters to run the farm alone; May, she was sure, was going to achieve international success an actress. And she—

Well, she had no idea what she was going to do if or when that happened, but she would do something. The job at the estate agency had only ever been a stop-gap situation, a way of bringing money into the household. Without that driving necessity, she could perhaps be a little more choosy about what she did, could maybe even find a job in an art gallery somewhere. Now that was something she would enjoy doing. She might not have sufficient talent to succeed in that field herself, but she would love to be there when other people did.

'Or maybe you'll pick up your paintbrush again,' May probed gently.

March frowned. She hadn't spoken out loud that time, she was sure, and yet the astute May had still managed to discern at least some of her thoughts.

She gave a firm shake of her head. 'I'm not good enough; we both know that.'

'I know nothing of the kind, March Calendar,' May came back impatiently. 'One art exhibition, in what was only a little local gallery anyway—'

'The owner of that "little local gallery" was the only one who would agree to show my work!'

'—does not mean you aren't good enough,' May finished determinedly.

She grimaced. 'I sold a grand total of two paintings, May,' she reminded dryly. 'And I probably only sold those two because they fitted in with the colour-scheme of the sitting-room or the loo!'

That week, two years ago, of the one and only exhibition of her work, had been the most humiliating experience of her life, mooching about the gallery day after day—much to the owner's chagrin—in the hope that someone would actually say something learned about her work!

A couple of those days only one or two people had strolled in—and that, March was convinced, had been only because they'd wanted to be somewhere dry out of the rain! A middle-aged couple on holiday from Somerset had finally bought two of the smaller paintings, but other than that the whole experience had been a waste of time.

It had certainly been humiliating enough for March never to even contemplate doing such a thing again. In fact, she had packed all her things away in the attic of the studio, and never picked up a paintbrush again...

She never would, either!

'As I remember it, May, we weren't actually discussing me,' she reminded pointedly. 'So stop trying to change the subject! Right now you are going to telephone this director. And tomorrow you are going to get on a train to London—'

'We really don't have the money for that, March.' May frowned worriedly.

'We have our emergency fund for a rainy day,' she insisted firmly. 'In my book, this counts as an emergency.'

The three sisters had several hundred pounds, left to them by their father, put away in a bank account for that 'rainy day'. January certainly wasn't going to need it, and if the farm were to be sold...

'Okay?' she prompted May forcefully.

'Okay,' May conceded dryly. 'But do give some thought to—'

'No,' she cut in decisively. 'Now go and make that telephone call so that we can get over to Aunt Lyn's.'

She breathed a sigh of relief when May did exactly

that. She hadn't thought, or talked, about her painting for a very long time, and she had no intention of doing it over the weekend, either.

That time would be spent working on the farm—and putting sight and thought of Will Davenport as far to the back of her mind as she possibly could!

Not that the former turned out to be all that difficult to do over the next two days. Because she didn't have so much as a glimpse of Will during that time!

His car was missing from the garage from early morning until early evening, and even then it was only the lights on in the studio that told of his presence there.

Leading to only one conclusion: Will Davenport was avoiding her as much as she was avoiding him!

Well, it was what she had wanted, wasn't it? Was the reason she had been so rude to him on Friday evening?

If it was what she wanted, then why did she feel so miserable…?

Why did he feel so damned miserable?

Giving March a cooling off period was the best thing to do, Will had decided after Friday evening. Stay out of her way. Give her time to get over whatever had upset her.

Which was exactly what he had done the last two days…

And in the process, he seemed to have made himself thoroughly miserable, he acknowledged ruefully as he stood at the studio window looking wistfully across at the farmhouse, the light on in the kitchen telling him exactly where March was.

May had been noticeably absent about the farm the last two days, hopefully on her trip to London, so wasn't around to invite her lonely lodger in for a cup of tea.

And he had long ago decided that inviting himself over was out of the question—if March was still in the same frame of mind as Friday evening then she was more likely to throw the tea at him than pour it into a cup! Going over and asking to borrow a cup of sugar had already been used—

The dish March had baked the apple pie in!

He had eaten the last of the pie for his lunch, the dish now washed and ready to be returned. He could stroll over and give that back to March without seeming too obvious—

Obvious about what…?

About wanting to see her. About wanting to talk to her. About just being with her.

March Calendar, he had realized this last two days of not seeing her, had very definitely got under his skin. Quite to what degree he wasn't prepared to acknowledge even to himself, he just knew that he hadn't been able to work or sleep since being at the receiving end of the sharpness of her tongue on Friday evening.

But the dish was at least a legitimate reason for him to go and knock on the kitchen door. If she took the dish and then slammed the door in his face, he would at least have tried to breach this puzzling rift that seemed to have developed between them.

Although he wasn't sure for how long…

Graham had telephoned him from London yesterday. Even admitting to March that he had sent her paintings to the other man was sure to bring about her wrath, telling her what Graham had said could prove life-threatening—to him, not Graham!

This was ridiculous, he told himself a few minutes later as he stood nervously on the doorstep after knocking on the kitchen door to the farmhouse. He was behaving like a nervous schoolboy summoned to see the headmistress, but not sure if it was for praise or punishment!

Once again he marvelled at Max for having dared to breach the Calendar bastions. Not only that, for succeeding!

The kitchen door opened with a cautious creak, March peering round the three- or four-inch opening, frowning in recognition as she saw who stood there. 'Yes?' She frowned unwelcomingly.

'You need some oil on those door hinges,' he came back lightly.

Her frown deepened irritably. 'I'll see to it later.'

'I could do it now for you if you have some—'

'Will, I'm rather busy at the moment, so if you could just say what you're doing here...?' she cut in impatiently.

'You are?' he mused; she didn't look very busy to him. In fact, from the towel she had draped about the darkness of her hair, she seemed to have just finished washing her hair.

'I am,' she confirmed shortly. 'So, if you wouldn't mind...'

'I brought your dish back.' He held it up into the thin shaft of light allowed to shine through that small door opening.

March looked at the dish, then up at Will, and then back frustratedly to the dish, as if undecided about what to do next.

Will eyed her quizzically; an uncertain March Calendar was certainly a novelty! 'Is there a problem?' he prompted sharply.

Maybe she wasn't alone? Maybe there was a man in

there with her? There was no strange car parked outside, but that didn't mean March was alone, did it?

His hands tightened about the glass dish, his mouth thinning with displeasure, gaze narrowing warily as he inwardly acknowledged just how much he disliked the idea of any other man being within ten feet of March.

'As I said, I'm busy—'

'What about the dish?' he reminded hurriedly as she would have shut the door.

March glared at him frustratedly. 'Oh, okay,' she finally sighed in capitulation, seeming to have come to some sort of decision as she allowed the door to open fully, at the same time stepping back to allow Will to come inside.

His wariness increased as he stepped inside, quickly looking about the room, some of his tension relaxing as he saw that March was alone, after all. Then why—

His mouth twitched with humour, his eyes gleaming with that suppressed laughter as, having turned to look at March, he saw the obvious reason for her previous discomfort.

She had obviously just had a bath and washed her hair, the latter wrapped in the towel, her only clothing appearing to be a cream bathrobe—something guaranteed to raise his blood pressure!

But at the moment it was definitely humour that was winning out in the emotion stakes; following her bath and washing her hair, March seemed to be in the process of paintings her nails. All of them.

She held her hands out in front of her, obviously allowing the peach lacquer on her medium-length nails to dry. Revealing the reason she had been reluctant to take the dish from him!

But it was the lacquer on her toenails that was the

cause of his amusement, wads of cotton wool between her toes allowing it to dry unsmudged. At least, he presumed that was the reason for it…

'And to think I never knew what I was missing by not having a sister,' he remarked conversationally as he put the glass dish down on one of the worktops, at the same time biting his inner lip to stop himself from laughing openly.

March glared at him, moving awkwardly across the room to sit down on one of the chairs, her heels down, her toes raised off the ground. 'Very funny!' She frowned. 'I was bored, okay,' she added defensively. 'May has been away all weekend and will continue to be away until tomorrow morning. All the work is done on the farm for this evening. As usual, there's nothing on the television—'

'So you decided to paint your toenails,' Will finished appreciatively.

'Yes!' She glared at him challengingly.

'Very sensible.' He nodded, brows raised innocently.

March looked totally unconvinced by his placating attitude. 'I've never painted my toenails before,' she defended irritably. 'It just seemed like a good thing to do at the time.' She grimaced.

Will looked down at the newly painted nails; March even had pretty feet, he realized self-derisively, long and slender, perfectly formed. As for what it was doing to his heartbeat, having March sitting feet away from him dressed only in a bathrobe…!

'Very nice,' he finally murmured gruffly, his gaze returning determinedly to her face.

March looked at him with narrowed eyes, her mouth starting to twitch, those eyes glinting with sudden humour, a humour that obviously won out as she began to chuckle self-derisively. 'I have never felt so ridiculous in my life,' she admitted with a rueful shake of her head.

He grinned. 'You haven't?'

'No,' she sighed. 'Hard as that probably is for you to believe,' she added dryly.

Will felt encouraged enough by her show of humour to sit down at the kitchen table opposite her. 'What's the verdict?' He inclined his head in the direction of her feet.

'Also ridiculous,' she came back disgustedly. 'I look like some sort of pampered princess in a harem!'

Will felt a lurch in the region of his chest at the image that thought created; he wouldn't mind having a harem of one! As long as that one was March…

'I would take it off again—' March hurried into speech as she seemed to realize she had been less than circumspect '—but the varnish remover would just ruin the nails on my hand then so that I would have to start again, and—'

'I could do it for you, if you would like me to,' Will put in lightly, at the same time hoping his eagerness to touch any part of her wasn't too obvious.

March looked across at him uncertainly, colour slowly entering her cheeks. 'No, I—I think I'll just go upstairs and put some clothes and shoes on; that will solve the problem just as well,' she said haltingly.

'Pity,' he murmured under his breath regretfully.

'Sorry?'

'Nothing.' He shook his head, smiling across at her.

She stood up abruptly. 'Er—make yourself some coffee while I'm gone, if you would like,' she told him dismissively. 'I won't be long.'

She hurried from the room.

As if the devil himself were at her heels…!

Will frowned to himself as he stood up to prepare a pot of coffee, knowing from previous visits exactly where everything was kept.

Was it the other evening that had been bothering March the last few days? Had the depth of passion they had both so obviously felt somehow frightened her?

It had frightened him too—although probably not in the way it had March!

He was thirty-seven years old, had been involved in several intimate relationships over the last fifteen or so years, but none of those women had brought out the protective instinct in him in the way that March did.

It was the weirdest emotion he had ever experienced, wanting to look after her, make sure no one hurt her, at the same time that he wanted to make love to her until she cried out for mercy!

If March felt even a tenth of that confusion, perhaps she had been right to be so cool with him on Friday evening!

Although his own confusion hadn't stopped him from coming up with any excuse this evening so that he could come over to the farmhouse to see her...

'Oh, good, you made the coffee.' March bounced cheerfully into the kitchen ten minutes later, seeming to have got over appearing to be disturbed earlier, her hair dry and gleaming darkly down her back, wearing a white tee shirt and fitted denims, her feet—and presumably those painted toenails!—hidden in a pair of green leather ankle boots. 'Not much of an improvement?' she prompted teasingly as she saw Will's gaze linger on the latter.

He gave a shake of his head. 'I've just never seen green boots before.'

'They had a red or blue pair in the shop too, but I

opted for the green,' she told him laughingly, taking over the job of pouring the coffee into two mugs. 'Do you know, you're the first person I've spoken to since May left yesterday morning?' she continued conversationally. 'I've never been here completely on my own before. I had never realized just how remote we are up in the hills here,' she added wistfully. 'In fact, the only comforting fact has been the knowledge that you were over in the studio in the evenings.' She gave him a smile as she brought their mugs of coffee over to the table.

Will grinned. 'Nice to know I'm useful for something!' At least he now knew the reason he had been invited in at all!

She gave a grimace as she sat down. 'I'm trying—not very successfully, I'll admit!—to apologize for my behaviour the last few days.' She shook her head. 'I was very rude to you on Friday evening,' she added huskily, 'and, to be honest, I've been avoiding you ever since,' she admitted quietly, nose suddenly buried in her mug of coffee.

March's honesty was something else that totally threw him, Will acknowledged a little breathlessly, wondering if he ought to own up to the same behaviour. But deciding against it. That would involve an explanation of some sort on his part, and right now he didn't really have one.

'May explained it was something she said,' he dismissed, eager to put that unpleasantness behind them now and move on. Quite where, he still had no idea, but he certainly didn't like feeling at odds with March.

'Did she?' March frowned now. 'Did she say what it was?' she added with a casualness that wasn't fooling anyone.

'No. And I didn't ask,' Will instantly reassured her.

'Have you heard from her? Are things going well for her this weekend?'

March relaxed back in her chair, a smile playing about her lips, obviously happier now that they were talking about her sister and not her own puzzling behaviour on Friday evening. 'Yes, I've heard from her. And she's going out to dinner with the director this evening. But you know May,' she added affectionately. 'She's convinced he's only taking her out in order to let her down gently.'

'That sounds like May,' he acknowledged with a chuckle.

March gave him a quizzical look. 'You like May, don't you?'

'I like all of you,' he corrected firmly. 'Even January—and I've never met her! But Max has been a good friend for over twenty years, so any woman he loves and wants to marry has to be okay with me.' Besides, if January were anything like the other two Calendar sisters, then he couldn't help but envy Max his good fortune!

She nodded. 'How do you think Jude Marshall is going to react to Max's resignation?'

Will gave the matter some thought. Jude was a shrewd businessman, and a very successful one, but the three men had been friends since school-days...

'I don't think Jude will let a little thing like Max's choice of wife influence his complete confidence in him as his lawyer,' he answered truthfully. 'I don't think he will accept Max's resignation,' he explained as March looked puzzled.

'You don't?' She looked astounded now.

'Jude isn't the monster you think him, you know,' Will told her with a smile, knowing even as the words left his mouth that he had once again said the wrong thing, March instantly bristling with resentment, her eyes sparkling challengingly.

'You're bound to say that, aren't you?' she scorned dismissively. 'After all, you're just another friend of his!'

Damn, this was hard work! Like walking through a minefield without any indications of where the explosions might be or when they might occur!

Was it really worth it?

Hell, yes!

If being with March was less than relaxing, it was certainly better than not being with her at all; the last couple of days had been some of the most boring he had ever spent, even his work not having held his interest in the way that it usually did as thoughts of March had gone round and round in his head. All without any conclusions or answers as to why he felt the way he did...

'Maybe it would be better if we didn't discuss Jude,' he began frowningly.

'Have you spoken to him recently?' March came back scathingly.

As a matter of fact, he had spoken to the other man the previous day. But he didn't think telling March now of Jude's intended visit to England was going to please her.

The opposite, he would have thought!

Just as telling her about the paintings he had sent to Graham in London wasn't going to please her!

No, he decided, both those things could wait until May returned tomorrow. May had a soothing influence on March—and if that failed, she could always stand between them when March tried to strangle him!

CHAPTER TEN

MARCH watched Will as a number of emotions flashed across his handsome features, caution finally seeming to win out as a shutter came down over those sky-blue eyes.

What was he keeping from her? she wondered. What *wasn't* he keeping from her? followed quickly on its heels!

She had felt extremely foolish when Will had arrived earlier, but hoped that she had slightly redeemed herself during the last few minutes, apology for her behaviour Friday evening included. Talking of Jude Marshall was guaranteed to put them back where they had begun half an hour ago!

'Sorry.' She held up an apologetic hand. 'I shouldn't have asked you that. It's none of my business whether or not you've spoken to—' 'that man' didn't exactly sound conciliatory, did it? '—to Jude Marshall,' she concluded evenly. 'More coffee?' she offered lightly as she saw his mug was empty, standing to pick up the two mugs.

'No.' Will stood up too.

'No?' she echoed huskily, the atmosphere in the kitchen suddenly so charged—with something!—that she could almost taste it.

'No,' he repeated softly, reaching out to take the two mugs from her unresisting hands to place them back on the table. 'March, you are without doubt the most puzzling woman—'

'You've already told me that,' she put in quickly.

'The fact that I'm repeating it must mean it's true!' He gave an impatient shake of his head. 'March, a few minutes ago you were spoiling for yet another fight, and yet now you're offering me more coffee...' He gave a dazed shake of his head.

She gave the wince of a smile. 'A little too change-able, would you say?' she acknowledged self-derisively.

'I would say, yes,' he confirmed frustratedly.

March gave a heavy sigh. 'I don't want to fight with you, Will. I just want—'

'Yes?' he prompted tautly as she broke off abruptly.

She didn't know what she wanted! All that she did know with any certainty was that the last two days had been completely miserable, partly because May was away and she was on her own, but also because she was very aware of the strain between herself and Will.

Also the reason for it...

Could May possibly be right? Could she already be in love with this man? If the erratic beat of her heart, the dampness of the palms of her hands, the almost weak-kneed feeling she had whenever she looked at him were anything to go by, then the answer was yes!

And if that truly were the case, then what was she going to do about it?

Uncertainty of any kind didn't come naturally to March; she had always been totally decisive, and quick to act on those decisions. But looking at Will, acknowl-edging that breathless, weak-kneed feeling, she had no idea what she was going to do about her love for him!

'I don't know what I want,' she finally answered hus-kily, dark lashes fanning down over her cheeks as she looked down at her feet.

But she heard Will move, felt his hands warm on her

upper arms as he shook her slightly. 'March, look at me,' he instructed softly, his gaze questioning as she raised her lashes. 'Do you want me?'

She gasped her surprise at the question. 'Now who's being excessively blunt?' she came back incredulously.

He gave a self-derisive grimace. 'Maybe I've decided to meet fire with fire!'

Just the mention of that word was enough to bring back memories of her time in his arms on Thursday evening, when the fire of their desire had threatened to totally engulf her.

'At least answer me, March.' He shook her gently.

She moistened suddenly dry lips, swallowing hard, knowing her panic must be evident on her face as she sought to find an answer that wouldn't sweep them both away in that torrent of passion, a passion she simply had no defences against.

Will gave a choked noise in his throat, his hands moving to sweep her into his arms, holding her tightly against his chest as he stroked the silky softness of her hair. 'I didn't mean right this minute, silly,' he soothed huskily.

Her cheek lay against his jumper-covered shoulder, the rapid beat of his heart clearly discernible to her. 'It's just for future reference?' she teased.

'Something like that,' he agreed, the sound of laughter in his voice.

Not laughter at her but with her, March easily read. Just as she knew this situation was fast becoming dangerous. They were completely alone here, would continue to be so until May returned some time tomorrow. And even if she did want him, as he appeared to want her, they didn't know each other well enough to—

'Tell you what, March.' Will moved back with a suddenness that startled her, once again holding her at arm's length as he looked down at her with warm blue eyes. 'Let's go out somewhere and have a drink. Apart from a couple of lunches we haven't actually been out together,' he added persuasively.

It was almost as if he could read her thoughts, as if he knew of her reluctance to admit her attraction to him when they were alone here like this.

And maybe he did know, she acknowledged ruefully; her face was like glass, revealed every emotion that she thought or felt.

'It seems a pity to waste your freshly painted nails,' Will added teasingly as she still hesitated. 'All of them!'

She gave him a rueful smile. 'I'm never going to live that down, am I?'

He grinned. 'Not in this lifetime, no.'

'Okay,' she accepted abruptly, not wanting to dwell on that 'lifetime' comment. 'There's a nice old-fashioned pub a couple of miles from here, we could go there.'

Will nodded, watching her as she collected her coat from the back of the door. 'I think I had lunch there the other day. I don't like to cook, okay,' he defended as she gave him a scornful look.

'Okay,' she acknowledged dryly. 'Your car or mine?' she added mockingly.

'Definitely mine!' He gave a shake of his head. 'I doubt I would fit into yours, anyway.'

March doubted he would either. Quite tall herself, her own head only just missed touching the roof of her little car; Will would simply end up with a crick in his neck.

Besides, it was certainly an experience to be a passenger in the Ferrari, to sink into the leather seat, the array of dials on the dashboard looking too confusing for her to even try to identify what they were all for.

It was also a relief to be away from the intimacy of the farmhouse. Something she was sure Will had been well aware of when he'd suggested they go out...

She studied him surreptitiously as he drove, admiring the assured economy of movement, his hands long and slender on the wheel. Artistically beautiful hands, she realized wonderingly, lean and sensitive.

'Did you always want to be an architect?' she prompted interestedly once they were seated inside the saloon bar of the tiny pub, only one other couple seated on the other side of the room on this quiet Sunday evening.

Will gave her a sharp look. 'Is this a trick question?'

'Sorry?' She frowned her puzzlement.

Will looked decidedly unhappy. 'If I answer this question honestly, are you going to get up and walk out of here?'

March eyed him warily now. Obviously he hadn't always wanted to be an architect, but what could possibly be so controversial about what he had wanted to be that he thought she might actually get up and leave once he had answered her?

Will could see that March was completely perplexed by his reluctance to answer her, knew she had no idea what he was talking about.

Maybe it was his own guilty conscience because of what he had done? Or maybe it was just a reluctance on his part to talk about anything that was going to upset or disturb March. As his truthful answer was sure to do!

Getting March to come out with him in the first place had been a miracle in itself; he didn't want her getting up and walking out on him before they had even taken a sip of the drinks he had just bought them!

'I need your promise first that you won't do that,' he prompted ruefully.

'Okay—I promise.' March shrugged dismissively.

'Too easy.' Will gave a firm shake of his head. 'I'm really serious about this, March.'

'I can see that you are,' she acknowledged slowly, her puzzlement obviously deepening. 'Is it really that bad?' she said wonderingly.

'Depends on your point of view,' he answered evasively.

'And from my point of view...?'

'It just might be.' He nodded consideringly.

'Okay.' She shrugged. 'I promise, no matter what you say your initial career choice was—manager of a nudist colony, astronaut, striptease artist—that I won't walk out of here.'

Will drew in a deep breath. 'The last was close.'

Her eyes widened incredulously. 'Striptease artist!'

He gave her a reproving frown. 'The last word,' he corrected impatiently, only vaguely aware of the interest of the couple seated across the room as their own voices rose in volume.

'The last—ah.' March became suddenly still, frozen in the act of picking up her glass of white wine and taking a sip.

'You promised you wouldn't walk out,' Will reminded evenly, at the same time giving her anxious looks.

'An artist,' she muttered huskily. 'You wanted to be an artist?' Her voice was tight with emotion, her face pale, a nerve pulsing in her tightly clenched jaw.

'I did.' He looked away, deliberately giving her time

to absorb the information. 'As it turned out, I have a little artistic flare, and I'm good at drawing straight lines. Perfect for being an architect. But not good enough to be an artist of any interest to anyone but myself,' he added flatly, his gaze returning to March's face.

She still looked pale, but her other emotions were under control now as she gave a dismissive shrug. 'It seems there are a lot of us about,' she murmured softly.

He was never going to get a more perfect opening than this, he knew that. But he was reluctant to break the guarded friendship that they had only recently built up. But not to tell March now about her paintings that he had sent to London, what Graham had to say about them, would put them back to the very beginning. And he didn't want to go there.

'You haven't tried your wine yet,' he delayed lightly, watching as she obediently took a sip.

Not that he thought her acquiescence was going to last for very long; a submissive March Calendar was totally unimaginable!

'March—'

'Will—'

They both began talking at once, both breaking off at the same time too to look at each other with rueful derision.

Will drew in another deep breath. 'I know it's ungentlemanly of me to go first—' he grimaced, his hand tightening around his glass of beer '—but I really have got to get this off my chest.'

March tilted her head to one side, looking at him quizzically. 'I think I really would have preferred it if you had wanted to be the astronaut!'

He gave the ghost of a smile in response to her obvious effort to try and lighten the conversation. 'It prob-

ably would have been easier,' he agreed ruefully. 'But
"easy" isn't a word I've ever associated with being
around you,' he acknowledged dryly.

March smiled too now. 'Are you complaining?'

Strangely enough, he wasn't. It was the fact that
March was so prickly and outspoken that had piqued his
interest in the first place. What continued to hold his
interest!

He reached out and put his hand over one of hers as
it rested on the table-top. 'Not at all,' he assured her
warmly.

She allowed her hand to remain beneath his. 'Something you had to get off your chest?' she reminded huskily.

He closed his eyes, shutting out the beauty of her face.
Maybe if he didn't look at her...

Damn it, he didn't have this much trouble dealing
with people who wanted impossible things in their ar-
chitectural designs, had seen grown men cry when he'd
told them that their design simply wouldn't work on a
practical basis!

He opened his eyes, looking determinedly into
March's questioning eyes. 'Your paintings are of interest, March,' he stated evenly. 'In fact—'

'How do you know that?' she cut in suspiciously.
'You've been back up in the attic!' she added accusingly, snatching her hand away from his to clasp it together with her other hand in her lap, grey-green eyes
starting to sparkle with anger as she glared at him.

'I was—curious,' he admitted, his grimace apologetic.
'And so I—'

'And so you went back up into the attic,' she finished
tautly, turning on the padded bench-seat to glare at him

now. 'After I expressly told you not to. How dare you—?'

'It's worse than that, I'm afraid, March,' he interrupted determinedly; he had started this, he had to finish it. 'On Friday I parcelled up half a dozen of what I thought were the best ones and sent them to a friend of mine in London who runs a gallery—'

'You did what?' she bit out forcefully, her cheeks white now, her eyes huge in that paleness.

'Graham is something of an expert,' he defended. 'Plus he's always on the lookout for new talent—'

'How dare you?' she burst out furiously. 'How *dare* you?' she repeated incredulously.

'March, just listen to me—'

'No,' she rasped uncompromisingly. 'Absolutely not,' she snapped, standing up to fling her shoulder bag over her arm.

'You promised you wouldn't get up and leave,' he reminded her with a pained wince.

She glared down at him. 'That was over your initial choice of career,' she ground out harshly. 'This is something else entirely.'

He could see that it was. Could see that in March's eyes he really had gone too far.

But what else could he have done? He had looked at the paintings, believed they were good, but at the same time known that if he'd asked March first she would never have agreed to sending any of them off to Graham.

But did that make it right for him to go behind her back and send the paintings to Graham without her knowledge?

Obviously, in March's eyes, the answer to that was a definite no!

'Don't you want to know what Graham had to say about them?' he cajoled reasoningly.

Her eyes flashed sparks of green. 'No, I do not! You are without doubt the most interfering, self-satisfied, arrogant individual it has ever been my misfortune to meet! And, in future, I would suggest you stay well out of my way,' she added forcefully. 'As for the paintings—get them back,' she told him furiously. 'Or risk answering to the police for being in possession of stolen property—'

'But I'm not in possession—Graham is.' He knew was the wrong thing to say as soon as he had said it. This was absolutely no time for levity.

No time at all, he discovered a few seconds later as March poured the contents—the almost-full contents!—of her glass over the top of his head!

She slammed the empty glass down on the table-top with such force it was surprising it didn't shatter from the impact. 'You have twenty-four hours to get those paintings back,' she warned him fiercely. 'After that, I shall put the whole thing in the hands of the police. I mean it, Will,' she added harshly.

Through the wine dripping down from his hair he could see that she did. He could also see that she had never looked more beautiful, her cheeks flushed, her eyes glowing fiercely, every inch of her slender body tense with anger.

But it was because he did have wine dripping down his face that he knew it wasn't a good time for him to make such an observation—she might pick up his own glass of beer next and throw that over him, too!

'Do you believe me?' she prompted tautly.

He nodded. 'In the circumstances, it would be hard

not to believe you.' He sighed, licking the white wine from his lips as it dripped down his face.

'Think yourself lucky it wasn't a whole bottle!' Her eyes glowed triumphantly as she looked at him.

'Oh, I do,' he acknowledged dryly, frowning as she turned away. 'Where are you going?'

'Home,' she answered decisively without even glancing back at him.

'But—'

'I'll enjoy the walk,' she bit out dismissively. 'You stay and finish your beer.' She crossed the room in four strides of those gloriously long legs, the door closing firmly behind her seconds later.

Leaving the room suddenly extremely quiet, only the logs crackling in the fireplace to break that silence as Will became aware of the unmistakable interest of the other couple in the room.

And who could blame them? Will was sure they weren't usually treated to such a display on a quiet Sunday evening out at the pub!

He shrugged across at the elderly couple. 'I guess she would have preferred red wine rather than the white!' he murmured ruefully.

The smiles they gave him were ones of relief rather than anything else; perhaps they had thought there was a possibility of his starting to throw the furniture around now that March had left!

March...

He gave an inward grown. He had really blown it with her this evening. He had known she was going to be displeased about his having taken the paintings without her permission, but he had hoped to be able to sit down and talk to her calmly about the subject. The glass of wine tipped over his head had told him that wasn't going to be possible!

God knew what was going to happen when Graham himself turned up tomorrow!

CHAPTER ELEVEN

MARCH was cold by the time she reached the farmhouse, slightly damp from the rain that had started to fall—and extremely irritated with Will for his high-handed behaviour.

How dared he—

There was someone in the farmhouse!

She had switched off all the lights inside the farmhouse before they'd gone out. She was sure that she had.

And yet a light shone in the kitchen now. Also on the landing upstairs.

She was just in the mood to deal with burglars—not!

Where was Will when she needed him? He was all too eager to stick his nose in where it wasn't wanted, and now that he was needed he was probably still at the pub calmly drinking his beer! He certainly hadn't passed her in the car as she'd walked the couple of miles back home.

She moved stealthily over to the kitchen window, peering inside, careful not to show too much of her face, in case the burglars should be looking her way. The kitchen was empty.

They were upstairs, then. Not that there was anything there to steal. The few pieces of jewellery the sisters had accumulated over the years were worn by them all on a day-to-day basis, and they certainly weren't of the calibre to interest a burglar!

But that didn't alter the fact that there was someone inside the farmhouse who shouldn't be there.

Or the fact that the telephone, her only means of communication, was in the hallway, where she would be heard if she attempted to telephone the police from there! What—

The mobile! They all shared a mobile telephone for when they were out and about on the farm, and she could see it now lying on top of one of the kitchen units. If she could just—

She stiffened as she heard a noise behind her, her hand raised defensively as she turned sharply.

'Why are you looking in the kitchen window in that furtive way?' May prompted frowningly, standing back to look at March consideringly.

March swallowed—her heart, mainly! 'Why aren't *you* still in London?' she returned accusingly, May obviously having just returned from checking on the ewes.

Her sister shrugged, turning away to open the kitchen door. 'I had concluded my business there, I didn't see any reason for me to waste the money for an extra night in a London hotel.' She shrugged dismissively, her voice fading slightly as she entered the kitchen.

March followed her sister a little dazedly; May was the last person she had expected to see this evening.

'I also thought—mistakenly, as it turns out—that you might be feeling in need of a little company after being on your own all weekend,' May added with raised brows as she turned from putting the kettle on the Aga. 'But when I got back an hour ago the farm was deserted...'

March felt the warmth in her cheeks at her sister's speculative look. 'Will took me out for a drink.' There was no point in lying about it.

'Really?' May drawled speculatively. 'He doesn't appear to have brought you back again!'

March gave a pained grimace at the indisputable truth

of that statement. Will obviously hadn't returned with her; May would have heard the powerful engine of his car if that were the case.

She avoided her sister's gaze. 'No. Well—'

'March, have you been upsetting our lodger again?' her sister interrupted laughingly.

She winced, knowing she might as well come clean about what she had done; May was sure to find out eventually anyway! 'Do you think pouring white wine over the top of his head could be classed as that?'

May spluttered with the laughter she could no longer contain. 'I think,' she managed to murmur between chuckles. 'Oh, March, you have no idea how much I've missed you!' She quickly crossed the room to give March a hug. 'What did the poor man do to deserve that?' she prompted, her arm still about March as she leant against her affectionately.

'Don't ask!' she dismissed hardly. 'Just tell me what happened in London. How did the screen test go? Is this David Melton single and gorgeous? When do you—' She broke off abruptly as her sister stiffened before moving away, a shutter seeming to come down over her face, her emotions suddenly unreadable. 'May…?' she prompted uncertainly. 'I thought you were supposed to go out to dinner with the director this evening?' That had certainly been the plan when she had spoken to May earlier this morning…

'Change of plan,' her sister dismissed, her face turned away in profile. 'I'm not going to do the film, March,' she added huskily.

'You aren't?' March was stunned; May had sounded so positive and excited when the two of them had spoken on the telephone this morning. 'But you said everything had gone well. That—'

'I was wrong,' May dismissed hardly.

'But—'

'Just leave it, will you, March?' May's gaze was bleak as she turned to frown at March. 'I was a fool ever to think—' She broke off, shaking her head. 'It was a mistake, okay?' she snapped forcefully. 'A total, disastrous mistake, much worse than I imagined. And I don't ever want the subject mentioned again!' she added fiercely.

'But I don't understand,' March murmured dazedly.

May gave a humourless smile. 'There's nothing to understand. Now could we—' She broke off as the sound of a powerful engine could be heard entering the yard. 'I believe our lodger has returned,' she murmured dryly.

March was well aware of that, could feel the colour leaving her cheeks even as the engine was switched off, followed by the closing of the garage door. If Will came over here—

'Perhaps you should tell me—what did he do to get wine poured over him?' May prompted curiously.

Her mouth tightened as she recalled exactly what Will had done to merit her wrath, his arrogant high-handedness. If he had the temerity to come over here after what he had done—he would learn all over again of her displeasure!

'Never mind,' she muttered in reply, moving silently over to the kitchen window, her gaze narrowing with satisfaction as she saw Will making his way slowly up the metal steps to the studio.

No doubt so that he could have a shower and wash the white wine from his hair!

She was smiling as she turned back to face May, that smile fading to a look of innocence as her sister raised questioning brows. 'He's arrogance personified, okay,' she muttered defensively.

'Will is?' May sounded sceptical. 'He's nowhere near as arrogant as Max,' she pointed out dryly. 'Or Jude Marshall, either, for that matter,' she added hardly. 'In fact, next to the two of them, Will is a perfect pussycat!'

'That's only because you don't know him the way that I do,' March accused, still furiously angry at his having even looked at her paintings after being told not to do so, let alone dared to send them off to a friend of his in London. As for the humiliation of what his friend would have told him about them…!

Admit it, March, she sighed heavily—it was that criticism, relayed through Will, that would have been so impossible to hear. The reason she had so quickly silenced him on the subject. The reason she refused to even discuss it.

'Oh, no, you don't,' she told May firmly, turning determinedly from the window. 'We were discussing you, not Will Davenport,' she dismissed scornfully. 'Now what—'

'March, I may not show it as often as you, or even January for that matter,' May interrupted with quiet finality, 'but I can be as stubborn as the two of you when I choose to be!'

'And on the subject of the screen test and film, you choose to be,' March guessed slowly.

Her sister's mouth was tight. 'I do.'

Which didn't satisfy March one little bit. What had happened in London? Hadn't the screen test gone well? Had this director chap made a pass at May? What had happened?

May gave a rueful laugh as she watched the emotions flickering across March's face. 'Frustrating, isn't it?'

'Very,' she acknowledged heavily.

May shrugged. 'I'm sorry about that, but I really have

said the last word on the subject. Which means, if you
still feel the same way, that we can consider keeping the
farm, after all...' she prompted searchingly. 'But only if
you still feel the same way...?'

When it was put like that, March really had no idea
whether she wanted to keep the farm now or not. She
had spent the last few days reconciling herself to the fact
that it would have to be sold, making tentative plans for
what she would do when it was. Now, it seemed, they
were back to square one.

'I have no idea what I feel on the subject any more,'
she answered truthfully.

'Think about it.' May reached up to give her shoulder
a reassuring squeeze. 'I'm quite happy to fall in with
whatever you want to do. But right now, I just want to
go to bed and have a decent night's sleep.' She shook
her head. 'London is so big and noisy, I haven't slept at
all well since I went away.'

March sat in the kitchen drinking tea long after May
had gone up to bed, totally confused as to what they
should do now. If they agreed to sell the farm, without
the offer of the film role, what would May do instead?

In the circumstances, it no longer seemed to make
sense to sell the farm...

Which left them all precisely back where they had
been several weeks ago—determined not to sell the
farm, with Jude Marshall as the enemy.

And, as his latest envoy, Will Davenport definitely
came under the same heading!

'For goodness' sake, Will, anyone would think you were
terrified of the woman!' Graham derided ruefully.

Will glanced at his old friend from art-school days, hav-

ing just driven to the railway station to pick him up.
Along with March's paintings…

And Graham was wrong; he wasn't so much 'terrified'
of March, as slightly apprehensive as to what she might
say to the poor, unsuspecting Graham. Until the other
man had been at the receiving end of March's caustic
tongue he could have no idea how lethal it could be.

'I'm just warning you that she isn't at all happy about
your having looked at her paintings.' Will shrugged.

'*You* sent them to me!' his friend reminded him
frowningly.

He grimaced. 'Unhappy doesn't even begin to describe how she feels towards me for having done that!'

Graham laughed softly, short and slender, with warm
blue eyes, his blond hair thinning at the crown. Baldness,
he claimed, was like insanity—you inherited it from
your children, of which he had three!

'Finally met your match, have you, Davenport?'
Graham teased now. 'I knew it would happen one day,'
he added with satisfaction. 'I was already looking forward to making the acquaintance of March Calendar, the
artist.' He settled more comfortably into his seat. 'But
now it's doubly intriguing.'

'Graham—'

'I've had to listen to your jokes about domesticity for
years,' Graham continued serenely. 'It looks as if the
tables are about to be turned!' He grinned unabashedly.

'You have that all wrong.' Will shook his head. 'If
anything, March hates me!'

'Even better.' Graham's grin widened.

'With friends like you…' Will gave Graham a last
frowning look before turning his attention back to the
road.

It had been arranged between the two men for Graham

to arrive in Yorkshire around Monday tea time, Will seeing absolutely no point in his arriving during the day when March was out at work. The only problem with that was Will still hadn't told March of the other man's arrival. The *only* problem!

March had been furious enough last night, when he had only mentioned having sent those paintings to Graham, to throw a glass of wine over him; what might she do when he went to the farmhouse door this evening with Graham at his side? Oh, well, Graham couldn't say that he hadn't tried to warn him!

Although that didn't help ease Will's trepidation as he drove into the farmyard to park his car in the garage, March already at home if her little red car parked near the house was anything to go by.

But, with any luck, May would be home too by now, which should help to diffuse the situation somewhat.

'Will you stop grinning in that imbecilic manner?' he snapped at Graham as the two men got out of the car. 'You look almost ghoulish!'

The other man chuckled. 'If you could only see the look on your face—you would be laughing too!' He shook his head incredulously. 'March Calendar must be really something!'

Oh, she was 'something', all right, Will accepted heavily; stubborn, pigheaded, unreasonable, beautiful, *desirable—*

'Let's go,' he told the other man determinedly—the sooner he got this over with, the better. After all, it couldn't really be that bad, could it…?

'With pleasure,' Graham acceded happily, following behind Will's long strides towards the farmhouse.

He couldn't exactly blame Graham for this teasing attitude. Graham had married shortly after leaving art school, his three children arriving in the three years following this, and for years Will had teased him about his obvious enjoyment of his family lifestyle. As far as Graham was concerned, the tables were now turned as regards teasing!

And he was prevaricating, Will acknowledged ruefully as he stood outside the farmhouse door. If May answered his knock, the first few minutes would probably be fine, but if it were March who came to the door…!

'What do you want?' she rasped after jerking the door open, the squeak of the hinges telling Will that she still hadn't put any oil on them.

Although he realized that was the least of his problems as March glared at him with obvious dislike, also aware of Graham's continuing enjoyment of the situation as he stood slightly behind him.

'Er—is May at home?' he prompted, wincing as the sound of Graham's stifled laughter from behind him told him he had sounded like a gawky teenager come round to ask for a date!

'She is.' March nodded, at the same time making no effort to go and find her sister, just continuing to stand there looking at him with those cold grey-green eyes.

His mouth thinned at her deliberate awkwardness. 'Then could I speak to her?' he snapped his impatience.

March gave a slight inclination of her head, her gaze flicking briefly over Graham before returning coldly to Will. 'Perhaps you would care to wait while I go and ask her.' But instead of inviting them inside, March firmly closed the door in their faces.

'Very hospitable,' Graham murmured humorously as he moved to stand beside Will.

He shook his head. 'She isn't usually this— She's

annoyed with me, that's all.' He sighed heavily, knowing from March's attitude that she hadn't softened towards him at all in the intervening twenty-four hours since she had thrown that glass of wine over him.

'She's magnificent!' Graham whistled admiringly.

He turned to glare at his friend. 'I would like to wring her beautiful neck!' he ground out fiercely.

Graham grinned knowingly. 'Amongst other things!'

Was it so obvious how he felt about March? Damn it, he didn't know how he felt about March. She was infuriating, frustrating, just plain awkward most of the time. But the rest of the time he wanted to sweep her up into his arms and kiss her into submission…!

'Cheer up, Will.' Graham reached out and gave his arm a playful punch. 'Perhaps she'll feel more kindly towards you after I've had a little chat with her.'

And perhaps she wouldn't. There was simply no knowing from one minute to the next how March was going to react to something. She could just end up hating him more than ever…

If that were possible!

CHAPTER TWELVE

'YOU'VE left Will standing where—?' May gasped disbelievingly as she hurried down the stairs two at a time. 'And he had someone with him too!' She turned briefly to give March a reproving look before hurrying through to the kitchen.

March followed slowly behind her, in no mood to talk to Will, or his friend, and not too bothered at being polite about it either. After the day she had just had—!

By the time she entered the kitchen quietly a few minutes later Will and the other man had been invited in by May and were seated at the kitchen table while May put the kettle on for a drink.

'Don't be silly, Will, of course you don't have to ask our permission to have a friend stay overnight at the studio,' May dismissed laughingly as she got out the cups.

'Does March feel the same way?'

March bridled resentfully as she suddenly became the focus of attention as she stood back against the door, frowning darkly at Will before her gaze moved to the man sitting next to him. 'You would be the ''friend'' in question?' she prompted speculatively.

The man was short and slight, with thinning blond hair, blue eyes looking huge behind gold-framed glasses.

'Hey, I'm not that sort of ''friend''.' The man laughed dismissively as he held up defensive hands. 'I have a wife and three children at home,' he added for good measure.

March could feel the colour warm her cheeks, deliberately avoiding Will's impatient glare. 'And home is where, Mr—?' she prompted politely.

'London,' the slight man replied evenly. 'And the name is Whitford, Graham Whitford.'

He said the last almost as if—as if—

Graham!

Hadn't Will told her that he had sent her paintings to a friend of his called Graham, a Graham who also lived in London…?

She turned to Will sharply, eyes narrowed suspiciously, knowing by the suddenly too-innocent expression on his face as his gaze steadily met hers that her conclusions had been correct; this was the same Graham that he had sent her paintings to.

But what was the man doing here?

Never mind what he was doing here—today had already been disastrous enough; she simply couldn't deal with anything else this evening.

'If you'll excuse me, I just have to go outside for a while.' She pushed herself away from the door, looking to neither left nor right as she grabbed her coat from the hook and wrenched open the door.

'Could I come with you?' It was Graham Whitford who spoke, standing up as March turned to look at him frowningly. 'Will told me earlier that it's lambing time, and—'

'He did?' March turned to give Will a scathing look.

'He did,' Graham confirmed lightly. 'Having been born and brought up in London, my kids would be thrilled to bits if I can tell them I've seen some newborn lambs,' he added cajolingly.

Because he had sensed she was about to refuse his request, March realized ruefully. She wasn't in the mood to talk to any friend of Will's, but especially the one he had sent her paintings to!

'A lamb is a lamb.' She shrugged dismissively.

Graham grimaced. 'I'm more used to seeing them as the Sunday roast, served with mint sauce!'

March glared at him for his levity. 'You're welcome to tag along if you really want to,' she conceded ungraciously.

'I want to,' Graham assured her determinedly, moving to accompany her outside.

March shot Will a last resentful glare before venturing out into the chilling wind, leaving it up to Graham Whitford to keep up with her if that was what he chose to do.

He did, easily matching his strides to hers, despite being a couple of inches shorter than March.

'He was only trying to be helpful, you know.' Graham spoke quietly at her side.

March had been so deep in thought—angry ones, directed at Will!—that it took her several seconds to take in what the other man had just said. But once she had, her mouth tightened ominously. 'Most interfering people prefer to see their actions in that way, don't you think?' she bit out disgustedly.

She really was not in the mood for this! Today had already been awful, everything such a shambles—to have to stand here and listen to this man's learned opinion of work he should never have seen in the first place was just too much.

And then there was Graham himself, a pleasant-faced man, who really shouldn't have been put in this position, either.

He gave a shake of his head as he followed her inside the lambing shed. 'Will is the least interfering person that I know—wow,' he suddenly breathed in a hushed voice, moving past March to stand next to a pen where a ewe was happily feeding her two newly born lambs. 'Do they always do that?' He watched in fascination as the lambs' stubby tails wagged in ecstasy.

March's expression softened as she moved to stand beside him, arms resting on top of the pen, never having lost her own sense of wonder at this maternal bliss. 'They do,' she confirmed huskily. 'Life is that uncomplicated for them,' she added wistfully, overwhelmed with how complicated her own life suddenly seemed to have become.

'March, I would like to put on an exhibition of your work.' Graham Whitford's gaze didn't leave the ewe and her lambs as he spoke evenly. 'With your agreement, of course,' he added softly.

Once again he spoke with such quiet calmness that it took March several seconds to take in exactly what he had said. But once she had, the angry colour flooded her cheeks as she turned to glare at him. 'Really?' she snapped sarcastically, giving a disgusted shake of her head. 'And whose idea was that?'

He shrugged. 'Well, Will is responsible for sending me some of your work, of course, but I choose who to exhibit in my own gallery.' The last was stated as fact, not arrogance.

March gave another shake of her head. 'Will must really be a good friend of yours. Or perhaps—'

'March, I don't—'

'Or perhaps it was someone else's idea, after all…!' she finished determinedly as her earlier scepticism turned to a deeper suspicion. 'Perhaps it was another "friend" who put the idea in your head?'

Graham gave a perplexed frown. 'I have no idea—'

'I'm referring to Jude Marshall!' she burst in accusingly.

'Jude...?' Graham echoed slowly, obviously familiar with the name.

As she had known he would be! Damn Will Davenport. Damn him!

She nodded abruptly. 'You do know him, don't you?' she stated flatly.

Graham shrugged. 'I've been—acquainted with Jude, for several years, yes,' he confirmed somewhat dazedly. 'But I fail to see what he has to do with my wanting to exhibit your work in my gallery?'

'Oh, please, do stop insulting my intelligence!' March snapped disgustedly, at last knowing exactly what was going on here.

Offer her an exhibition of her work, in London no less, and yet another Calendar sister was neatly out of the way. At least, long enough for Jude Marshall to step in and buy their farm out from under their noses.

'What did he do, offer you money to exhibit my work for the few weeks it would take to distract me?' she continued heatedly, hands clenched into fists at her sides, so angry now that she wanted to hit someone. And it wasn't Graham Whitford!

'Offer me—!' Graham looked astounded at the suggestion. 'March, I can assure you—'

'Oh, don't bother!' she cut in scathingly. 'I sincerely hope that you got one of them to pay your expenses for coming all the way up here—because you have had a completely wasted journey!' She glared at him. 'You see, I know that my work is rubbish,' she scorned. 'Innocently rural rubbish!' she added for good measure, each word cutting into her like a knife.

That much had become obvious to her during that

short local exhibition—she wasn't about to further hu-
miliate herself in the capital of the country!

'But—'

'Oh, I don't blame you,' she assured Graham
Whitford heavily. 'Business is business, and all that.'

No, she knew exactly whom she blamed—and one of
them was sitting across in the farmhouse with May right
this minute!

She marched over to the door. 'Make sure you lock
the shed once you've had your fill of the newborns,' she
told Graham hardly.

'I—but where are you going?' Graham looked completely confused by the way this conversation had turned
out.

'To speak to your accomplice!' Her eyes briefly
glowed with her anger before she wrenched the shed
door open, slamming it shut behind her as she stormed
across to the farmhouse.

How dared he? How dared Will Davenport do this to
her?

To offer to pay some poor little gallery owner to exhibit her work in order to get her out of the way and
leave the coast clear for Jude Marshall to snap up the
Calendar farm!

It was worse than despicable—it was cruel and unkind. To have Graham Whitford come here, to offer her
an exhibition, to give her hope that her work might be
good after all, only for the exhibition to be a flop yet
again, and in London of all places.

This was by far and away the most hurtful thing Will
Davenport had ever done to her!

'March refuses to talk about the reasons behind it,' May
was telling Will frowningly as March burst into the

room, bringing a blast of cold air in with her as she slammed the door behind her.

But that blast of cold air, Will realized as he looked warily at March, was as nothing to the cold fury that her gaze shot across the room at him!

He stood up slowly. 'What have you done with Graham…?' he said slowly, at the same time chastising himself for the heat of desire he felt as he watched her breasts quickly rise and fall in her agitation; this was most definitely not the time to feel desire for March Calendar!

'Figuratively or literally?' March spat back forcefully. 'March—'

'I should stay out of this if I were you, May.' Will spoke gently to the elder sister as she appealed to March, his narrowed gaze remaining fixed on the younger sister. An obviously furious March. 'Both,' he answered March abruptly.

Her mouth twisted into a humourless smile. 'Literally I've left him looking at the lambs. Figuratively I've left him under no illusions as to what I think of him and his offer to exhibit my work. As for you—!' She crossed the room in two angry strides, her arm moving up in an arc as she gave his face a resounding slap. 'You're despicable! Absolutely and utterly beneath contempt!' Her voice shook emotionally.

'March!' May gasped her shock at her behaviour.

Will's gaze remained locked on March's, his left cheek stinging painfully from her slap, his own gaze ice cold now as he met her heated one.

A few seconds ago, as May had explained what had happened to March earlier today, he had been concerned and worried for her, but had hoped that what Graham had to tell her might help alleviate some of her worry. It seemed to have done the opposite!

'I don't think so,' he ground out as she raised her arm a second time, easily capturing her hand in one of his, crushing her fingers as his grip tightened.

'You're hurting me,' she managed to gasp accusingly.

He was hurting *her*! What the hell did she think she was doing to him? And he didn't just mean that slap, either!

His hand remained clenched around hers, feeling the fragility of her bones beneath his, but too angry himself at this moment to care. 'What the hell is wrong with you?' he demanded exasperatedly. 'Didn't Graham explain about wanting to exhibit your work—?'

'Oh, he ''explained'',' she snapped furiously, her eyes flashing with renewed anger. 'And I told him what he could do with his offer!'

The angry tension faded from Will's body as he slowly released her hand, utterly perplexed now. 'You told him—'

'What he could do with it,' March repeated scornfully, her crushed hand now cradled in her other one. 'Do you think I'm completely stupid, Will?' she challenged.

'Not completely, no,' he answered slowly, at a complete loss to know what he thought any more.

He had thought, once March got over her annoyance with him for having sent some of her paintings to Graham in the first place, that she would be over the moon about Graham's proposed exhibition of her work. Far from being over the moon, March was more angry than ever. He didn't understand her response. Any more than he understood March herself, he acknowledged heavily.

'I'm not even a little bit stupid where you're con-

cerned, Will Davenport,' March told him scathingly.
'But you can go back to Jude Marshall and tell him that
none of his schemes to get us out of here have succeeded—'

'Jude…?' Now Will really was puzzled. Puzzled? He
was more confused than he ever had been in his life
before!

'Tell him that the two remaining Calendar sisters are
staying put,' she finished hardly, looking at him challengingly.

Will shook his head, this whole conversation a complete enigma to him. But he felt too emotionally battered
at this moment to try and unravel it.

He turned to May, a May who looked even more be-
wildered by this situation than he felt. 'I'm really sorry
about this, but I think, in the circumstances, that it might
be for the best if I leave,' he told her huskily.

'Yes—go,' March agreed scathingly.

'I meant that I leave altogether.' Will still spoke to
May, too angry himself now to even look at March.
'Move out of the studio. I'm sorry,' he apologized again
as May looked stunned by the way this conversation had
turned out.

And maybe it was a little drastic for him to move out.
But at this moment—and for some time to come, he
felt—the further he was from March, the better it would
be for all of them.

Away from her—well away from her!—he might be
able to think straight, for one thing…

'I'm the one that's sorry, Will,' May assured him
softly, at the same time shooting March searching
glances, glances that obviously yielded her no answers
either. 'But maybe it would be for the best…' she allowed with a rueful shake of her head.

'Yes—go,' March looked at him scornfully. 'Run away!'

Will gave a weary sigh. 'I'm not running away, March, simply removing my obviously unwanted presence.'

She nodded scornfully. 'And take your friend with you.'

Will shrugged. 'After what you said earlier, I doubt he has any more reason to stay here than I do.'

She gave a humourless laugh. 'Well, at last we're all in agreement on something!' she scorned.

But there was something in her voice this time, a catch of emotion that made Will look at her sharply. Was that tears he could see in those beautiful defiant grey-green eyes? And if so, were they tears of anger or distress? As he could see no reason for March to feel the latter, he could only assume—

'I was a fool ever to think you might be different, Will Davenport.' She shook her head as she looked at him, the tears shimmering on her lashes now. 'A stupid, stupid fool,' she added self-disgustedly before turning on her heel and running from the room.

He could hear the sound of her feet moving rapidly up the stairs, followed seconds later by the closing of a bedroom door.

The silence she left behind her in the kitchen was filled with a tension so intense that even the clock could be heard ticking.

May's breath left her in a shaky sigh. 'Whew,' she murmured ruefully. 'I'm so sorry, Will.' She looked across at him appealingly. 'If it's any consolation, I don't think all of that anger was caused by you,' she added with a grimace.

He gave a slow shake of his head. 'It isn't,' he stated flatly.

May looked upset by his answer. 'She's just very upset about losing her job earlier,' she explained pleadingly. 'I was telling you before that I don't even know what really happened there; March just arrived home shortly after lunch to say that Clive Carter had paid her a month's salary and told her to leave.'

Will knew all that, had been as concerned earlier as May obviously was as they'd talked while March and Graham had been checking on the lambs. Especially as Will could probably guess at least some of the reason Clive Carter had dismissed March so arbitrarily—he hadn't forgotten that conversation he had had over lunch with March last week about the buying of property under its market value and then selling it on at a later date for a large profit. Either March had confronted Clive Carter with what she knew, or the man had found out that she knew. But, either way, Carter had decided to remove the problem by dismissing March.

But all of that was really irrelevant now. There was nothing Will could do to help—more to the point, nothing March would want him to do that might help. She had made it more than obvious a few minutes ago that she didn't consider anything he did to be in the least helpful.

He shook his head. 'I'm really sorry about this, May, but I—' He broke off as Graham came into the kitchen. 'How were the lambs?' he prompted his friend ruefully—goodness knew what March had said to him while they'd been outside together!

Graham had initially viewed March's work as a favour to him, although after looking at them it had obviously been Graham's own decision to offer March the showing in his gallery. From the little March had told him, his friend had had his offer very firmly thrown back in his face. Graham must be wondering what on earth he had walked into the middle of!

Graham gave a quizzical smile. 'Puzzling.'

Will nodded, grimacing. 'I thought they might have been!'

'But very interesting,' Graham added lightly as he came further into the room.

'That's one way of putting it,' Will acknowledged heavily, wishing he had never seen March's paintings, let alone involved Graham.

'Hmm.' Graham nodded consideringly. 'Would anyone care to explain to me why it is that March thinks I'm offering to exhibit her paintings because Jude Marshall is paying me to do so?' He looked first at Will, and then at May, obviously hoping that one of them would be able to enlighten him.

Oh, he could enlighten Graham, all right, Will acknowledged with rising fury as all of March's obscure references just now suddenly made complete sense.

That little—!

How dared she?

Did she really think that he had conspired—that he would have been part of some plan to—? No, not *part* of it, the *instigator* of it!

Damn it, March had gone too far this time.

Way too far!

CHAPTER THIRTEEN

'GO AWAY, May, please,' March groaned as her bedroom door opened, lying down on the bed, her face buried in the pillow. 'I really don't want to talk about this just yet,' she added emotionally.

'You may not want to talk about this,' Will Davenport was the one to answer her forcefully, standing by the bed glaring down at her in obvious fury as March spun quickly over to look up at him with wide, disbelieving eyes. 'But I certainly do!' he added grimly, his eyes a pale wintry blue.

March hastily rubbed away the tears from her cheeks, sitting up to look at him. 'And you're used to getting your own way, aren't you?' she said dully. 'You and Jude Marshall.'

His face darkened ominously. 'Let's get one thing straight, March,' he ground out furiously. 'Jude Marshall is not the monster you've built him up to be in your mind. And neither am I,' he added grimly.

Her eyes widened at this last statement. Will wasn't a monster to her, many other things, but never that.

She had looked at him downstairs a few minutes ago, the marks of her fingers still livid on the hardness of his cheek, and known that she loved him. Irrefutably. Irretrievably. Irrevocably!

And to know that she loved him in spite of everything, to know that there was no future for them, was breaking her heart into a thousand pieces.

'I—'

'I haven't finished yet, March,' Will told her harshly, his eyes glittering angrily. 'You're very fond of having your say.' His mouth twisted derisively. 'Now it's my turn.'

She swallowed hard. 'Okay.'

He gave a pained grimace. 'A quiet, acquiescent March Calendar—amazing! I suppose that it's too much to hope that it might last…?'

She gave a shrug. 'Probably,' she conceded heavily.

He gave a humourless smile. '"She was poor but she was honest." That was just one of those meaningless quotes, March,' he added disgustedly as her eyes flashed resentfully. 'Does everything have to be a minefield with you, March?' he added wearily. 'Every word weighed and measured before spoken in case it causes you insult?'

Was that really how it was when talking to her? March wondered frowningly. Had she become so prickly, so defensive, that everyone had to be careful what they said around her? Or was it only Will who felt that way…?

'Never mind.' He gave an impatient shake of his head. 'I'm well aware that nothing I do or say in the next few minutes is going to make the slightest difference to your opinion of me—'

'Then why bother to say it?' she put in softly.

'Because it will make me feel better!' Will answered her forcefully, beginning to pace up and down the bedroom. 'May told me what happened to you at work today—'

'She had no right!' March flared; the fewer people who knew what had happened at the estate agency today, the better!

'She had every right, damn it!' Will turned on her angrily. 'She's your sister; she's worried about you.'

March shook her head. 'There's no need. I'll get another job, and then—'

'Now who's running away, March?' Will challenged grimly. 'You and I both know you can't just leave that situation as it is. From what you told me, Carter is obviously breaking the law. Are you really intending to just walk away and let him get away with that?'

If it was only Clive that was involved, then the answer to that would be a definite no, but there was Michelle to consider too... Quiet, sweet Michelle, who had always been kind to her.

March's chin rose determinedly. 'I have no proof of my suspicions. Clive found the file I had been keeping locked away in my desk drawer. He's probably destroyed it by now,' she added heavily.

For months she had been troubled by the fact that properties had been sold by the agency, to what appeared to be some sort of holding company, only to reappear on the market several months later to be sold for a considerable profit.

Oh, she knew the property market was booming at the moment, but even so it had happened too often, once a month on her estimation, for it to all seem like a coincidence. Clive's response to the file she had started to keep only confirmed that opinion.

'You must have enough information stored inside your head to go to the police with your suspicions,' Will said sceptically.

Yes, she did, probably more than enough. But there was still Michelle to consider...

Will gave a disgusted shake of his head. 'Obviously I can't force you to do anything about that situation,' he rasped. 'Although I never thought of you as a coward before,' he added derisively.

Two spots of angry colour appeared in March's cheeks as she glared at him. He had no idea what he was talking about, none whatsoever.

'Life's full of surprises, isn't it?' she dismissed scathingly.

Will drew in an angry breath. 'Well, here's another one for you! Graham Whitford owns the Graford Gallery in London—mean anything to you?' he challenged impatiently.

Her eyes widened. Of course it meant something to her. The Graford Gallery was one of the most prestigious privately owned galleries in London, was patronized by art collectors from all over the world, was the leading gallery for discovering new and collectable artists—

And Graham Whitford, the owner of that gallery, had just offered her an exhibition of her work…!

'I can see that it does.' Will nodded with satisfaction, his gaze impatient. 'Do you really think a man of that calibre would risk the reputation of his gallery to exhibit an unknown artist with no talent?'

When he put it like that—!

'Worse,' Will grated harshly, 'do you think a man of that calibre would accept *money* as an inducement to risk the reputation of not only his gallery but himself as well by exhibiting that artist with no talent?'

March gave a pained wince as the full import of his words hit her like the slap in the face she had given him earlier.

Graham Whitford had really been serious about that offer of an exhibition of her work!

She swallowed hard, her hand shaking as she pushed the dark swathe of her hair back from the paleness of her cheeks. 'Maybe I was wrong about that—'

'Maybe?' Will ground out harshly.

March moistened dry lips. 'I—I—'

'Maybe you were wrong about a lot of things, March,' Will continued remorselessly over her halting reply. 'Me, in particular. You know, I came to the area knowing I wasn't exactly going to be the flavour of the month. It happens.' He shrugged. 'For different reasons, people resist change—'

'You—'

'For different reasons, they resist change,' he repeated hardly, his expression grim. 'And very often those reasons are perfectly valid—'

'As mine are,' she cut in determinedly.

'Maybe,' he conceded. 'But was that any reason for you to make my life a misery? To be rude and obstructive at every turn? To suspect my every motive?'

'You work for Jude Marshall!' she reminded accusingly.

'At this moment in time, yes, I do.' He nodded tersely. 'But I offered to work with you on this,' he reminded coldly. 'I suggested days ago that there must be some way you and I could work together to come up with a plan that would satisfy all parties. But you're so busy feeling angry, and sorry for yourself, that—not again,' he warned hardly as March rose angrily to her feet, reaching out to firmly grasp her arms and hold her immobile in front of him. 'You're the most beautiful woman I've ever seen in my life, March,' he breathed raggedly. 'But, without doubt, also the most stupid!'

She opened her mouth to protest, but no words came out. Did Will really think she was the most beautiful woman he had ever seen in his life...?

'Oh, to hell with this.' Will sighed disgustedly. 'This is just one more thing to add to the list of reasons to hate me!' he rasped before his mouth came forcefully down on hers.

It was a kiss of anger, of frustration, of sheer impotence of feeling.

But it was a kiss March responded to...

She loved this man, loved him beyond anyone and anything. And very shortly he was going to walk out of her life and she was never going to see him again.

She sobbed low in her throat, her lips answering the passion between them that it was impossible to deny, Will releasing her arms to pull her against the hardness of his body as he deepened the kiss.

March wound her arms about his waist, pressing close against him, wanting only to be part of him, to forget everything else but Will and the overwhelming love she felt for him.

Which was why she was left totally dazed when Will pulled roughly away from her seconds later to move determinedly to the other side of the bedroom, his expression grimmer than ever. March looked at him questioningly.

'Oh, no you don't.' He gave a self-derisive laugh as he shook his head. 'You may feel you have plenty of reason to hate me, March, but I have no intention of giving you reason to regret me too!'

Her face was pale, her eyes dark. 'But I—'

'Graham and I will be leaving as soon as I've got my few belongings together,' Will cut sharply across the protest she was about to make. 'I doubt we shall see each other again, so—well, goodbye,' he concluded abruptly.

Goodbye.

That had to be the saddest word in the whole of the English language.

Especially when March was saying it to the man she knew she loved above all else…!

She had fallen in love with Will in spite of his connection to Jude Marshall. Despite all her own instincts. Or because of them…

'Will—'

'I think you've already said enough, don't you, March?' he rasped scathingly, blue gaze bleak now that his anger had faded somewhat. 'But Graham is probably more forgiving than me—especially when it comes to the discovery of a new and talented artist,' he added derisively. 'So I'm sure he will be only too happy to talk to you if you should change your mind about his offer of an exhibition.'

Despite his own anger towards her, March knew Will was being more than generous in telling her this. Because he didn't have to, didn't have to do anything more for her. Especially when she had shown him nothing more than ingratitude in return.

She so wanted to cry, so wanted to give in to the terrible pain of Will's departure. But that wouldn't be fair to him, not after all she had already put him through.

Besides, she didn't think she could stand to see his pity if he should realize the reason for her pain…

'Thank you,' she breathed shakily. 'I—have a good journey back to London,' she added lamely.

His mouth twisted ruefully. 'Thanks. About the situation at the agency—'

'I'll—think about it.' She nodded quickly, still not sure what to do about that.

Will grimaced. 'If it comes to light anyway, and anyone finds out that you already knew about it, you could—I'm only saying could—be dragged in as an accomplice. At the very least, be accused of perverting the course of justice by keeping quiet about it,' he warned as she would have protested.

March moistened dry lips. She had already thought of that aspect, knew that she didn't really have any choice but to go to the police with what she had discovered. It just wasn't something she wanted to do.

She nodded. 'I'll—sort it out.'

'Fine.' Will nodded abruptly. 'Take care,' he murmured softly.

He was going. Really going. And there wasn't a thing she could say or do to stop him.

'And you,' she breathed huskily.

He closed the bedroom door quietly behind him as he left, the sound of his feet descending the stairs heard seconds later, followed by the murmur of voices in the kitchen, then the closing of the outer door. And Will was gone.

March wanted to run after him, to tell him how sorry she was for her behaviour, how much she wanted him to stay, how much she— What? Loved him? That really would be unfair. Especially when Will couldn't possibly feel the same way about her.

How could he? When she had been 'rude and obstructive' to him. 'Made his life a misery' almost since the moment he'd arrived.

The tears were falling softly down her cheeks when May entered her bedroom a few minutes later, her sister's expression softening as she saw March's tears.

'Oh, March!' May choked even as she gathered her into her arms.

Oh, March, indeed. What a mess she had made of everything. What an unforgivable mess.

'Are you sure this is the right thing for you to do?'

Will turned briefly from throwing his things into his bag

to look at Graham as he sat on one of the kitchen chairs watching him frowningly. 'The right thing to do would have been never to have come here in the first place,' he bit out harshly, at the same time resuming his haphazard packing.

'You know you don't mean that,' Graham rebuked softly.

'Oh, don't I?' He turned sharply, his anger unmistakable. 'This whole situation has been impossible from the beginning. But only because of March. She's the most impossible woman I have ever met in my life!'

Graham grimaced. 'She's—a little fiery,' he allowed.

'A little!' Will scorned. 'She's rude, sarcastic, outspoken—'

'Beautiful,' Graham put in softly.

'Beauty is as beauty does—or something like that,' Will added impatiently as Graham raised mocking brows. 'Why can't she be like May—still beautiful, but charming and reasonable at the same time?'

Graham held back a smile. 'Because you aren't in love with May.'

Will's eyes widened indignantly at this last statement. 'I'm not in love with March either,' he stated firmly.

'Aren't you?' his friend mused softly.

'No, I am not,' Will assured him firmly. 'Damn it, even having a simple conversation with her turns into a confrontation!'

'But it's worth it, I'm sure,' Graham reasoned teasingly.

Will thought of the occasions he had held March in his arms, of kissing her, caressing her, feeling the silky softness of her skin against his...

'Maybe,' he allowed grudgingly, some of his anger starting to fade.

Besides, who was he most angry with: March for being so unreasonable, or himself for feeling about her the way that he did? Not that he accepted Graham's statement that he was in love with her; how could he possibly be in love with someone he felt like strangling half the time?

Because the other half of the time he just wanted to hold her, to take care of her, to ensure that nothing and no one ever harmed her…!

He was not in love with March Calendar!

'No,' he decided firmly. 'The sooner I'm away from here, the better I will like it.' He turned to slam his bag shut and close the zip. 'I honestly wish I had never met March Calendar!'

'Hello, March,' Graham greeted lightly behind him. 'Anything we can do for you?'

'Very funny, Graham,' Will muttered dryly. 'Aren't you a little old for juvenile tricks like that?' he derided as he turned round.

March stood in the open doorway, her face as white as snow, her eyes so darkly enigmatic it was impossible to tell what colour they were. Or whether or not she had heard his telling statement before Graham had announced her presence!

'Who was being juvenile?' Graham murmured under his breath as he watched the two of them curiously.

If the floor could have opened up and swallowed him, Will knew he would have been for ever thankful. But, of course, it did no such thing, leaving him face to face with March after stating quite categorically that he wished he had never met her!

'March—'

'May wanted you to have this.' March moved to put an envelope down on the kitchen table.

So that she didn't have to actually touch him, Will was sure, his anger returning at this obvious display of her aversion to him. 'What is it?' he snapped.

March shrugged. 'A cheque for the second week's rental on the studio. We don't want it,' she added decisively as Will would have protested. 'You aren't staying here, so we aren't entitled to it,' she told him dismissively.

To say he felt as if he had been slapped on the face for a second time this evening was probably putting it a little strongly, but he certainly felt as if May now supported her sister's stand against him.

'Fine,' he rasped, making no effort to pick up the white envelope.

And he wouldn't pick it up, either, would leave it on the table after he had left. But no doubt the Calendar sisters would find some way of twisting even that gesture round so that he once again came out as the bad guy. He just couldn't seem to win with them.

March turned to Graham, some of her stiffness of manner fading as she gave him a rueful smile. 'I believe I also owe you an apology; I shouldn't have said those things to you earlier.' She grimaced. 'It was just—'

'My friend here getting it wrong, as usual,' Graham accepted, standing up, totally ignoring Will's snort of protest. 'I realize now that my being here at all must have been something of a shock to you,' he sympathized with March. 'I'll give you my card.' He took one from his wallet and held it out to her. 'Think it over and give me a call if you decide to go ahead with the exhibition, after all, hmm?' he encouraged.

Will wasn't in the least fooled by Graham's lightly

encouraging attitude, knew his friend well enough to know that he wasn't about to give up on persuading March into the exhibition, that having 'found' her he wasn't going to let her just disappear again.

On the one hand Will was pleased for March, knew that any exhibition of her work that Graham put on for her was sure to be a success. But on the more negative side, if March went ahead with the exhibition it would mean that she would continue to be in Will's life whether he wanted her to be or not. Graham was an old and valued friend, Will godfather to his youngest daughter, and as such it would be impossible for Graham not to talk about March in the future when the two men met.

But the latter was a selfish attitude, he knew, and one best kept to himself...

'Take the card, March,' he advised dryly.

'If you're sure you don't mind...?' She gave him a searching look.

Will gave a humourless laugh. 'I was the one who brought the two of you together in the first place; why should I mind?'

March shrugged. 'Possibly because you wish you had never met me,' she returned with some of her usual spirit, dark brows raised mockingly.

So she had heard his final statement before Graham had announced her presence! He had thought she must have, but March had just bluntly confirmed it.

Not much he could do about that, was there? Especially as it was true! For numerous reasons...

He gave a rueful shake of his head. 'There's never a hole for you to fall down when you want one!'

March gave the ghost of a smile. 'Join the club,' she returned enigmatically before turning back to Graham. 'Thank you for this.' She indicated the card he had given her. 'I'm not sure yet, but—I will call you and let you know one way or the other.'

'Good enough.' Graham nodded.

'No, it isn't,' Will put in forcefully. 'March, you may never have another opportunity like this one,' he told her impatiently as she looked at him questioningly.

'I'm well aware of that,' she acknowledged huskily. 'But there are—other considerations to take into account, before I come to any decision.'

Will wanted to demand to know what those considerations were, but knew that he had forfeited the right to ask by the fact that he had made that blunt statement about wishing he had never met her, and by March overhearing it. Besides, there was always the possibility that having to see him again might be one of those considerations!

His mouth tightened. 'Just don't leave Graham waiting too long, March,' he bit out tersely.

She gave him a dismissive look before turning back to Graham. 'I really am grateful for your interest,' she assured him with much more warmth than she had just shown Will.

And could he really blame her for that, after what she had overheard?

But there was no way he could retract what he had said without making the situation worse than it already was. If that were possible!

He really needed to get away from here, away from March, to sit calmly and collectedly and work out exactly what it was he felt for her. Because he had just realized that leaving her was probably the hardest thing he had ever done in his life!

But leave her he must. For both their sakes.

But March was the one leaving now, raising a hand in farewell before quietly closing the door behind her.

'If I weren't already a married man...' Graham murmured appreciatively.

'But you are,' Will reminded sharply, a shaft of— something, something painful, shooting through him at the other man's obvious admiration of March. 'And likely to remain that way,' he added with satisfaction.

Graham gave an acknowledging inclination of his head. 'But you aren't,' he returned dryly. 'And I would say it's very unlikely that you will remain that way,' he added teasingly.

Will gave a dismissive shake of his head. 'Let's just go, hmm, Graham.' He picked up his bag and briefcase. 'The sooner I'm out of here, the better I'll like it.'

His friend chuckled softly as he joined him by the door. 'You can run but you can't hide,' he rejoined enigmatically.

Will gave him a narrow-eyed glare, not fooled for a moment. 'I'm not even going to qualify that remark with an answer. Just move it,' he grated hardly.

Graham was still chuckling as he clattered down the metal stairs ahead of him.

Whereas Will couldn't see anything funny about this situation, lingering to take one last glance over at the farmhouse before getting into his car.

The light was still on in the kitchen, and Will could easily imagine the two sisters, sitting at the kitchen table, drinking tea or coffee, talking softly together.

Would March do anything about Clive Carter?

Would the sisters sell the farm?

Would May take the film role if it were offered?

Would March take up Graham's offer of an exhibition of her work?

In only a matter of days he had become completely embroiled in the life of the Calendar sisters. And with his abrupt departure he was giving up the right to an answer to any of those questions…

CHAPTER FOURTEEN

'HE HASN'T gone, you know, March.'

March looked up from where she had been pushing the food around on her plate in an effort to look as if she were really eating her dinner, when in actual fact she hadn't been able to eat anything for days. Her throat felt dry all the time from the tears she cried whenever she was alone, and the thought of actually having to swallow anything other than the strong cups of tea or coffee she was constantly making was complete anathema to her.

'March,' May pushed strongly. 'I said—'

'I heard what you said,' March assured her wearily. 'I just didn't understand it,' she admitted ruefully.

May sighed, her frown one of concern rather than censure. 'You really can't go on like this, you know, March. You aren't eating, you aren't sleeping—oh, I've heard you pacing around in your bedroom at night,' she said firmly. 'You've lost weight the last three days, March, and it really doesn't suit you.'

'Thanks!' She smiled ruefully.

May shrugged. 'It's the truth, and you know it. And what I said just now was that Will hasn't gone.'

March frowned uncomprehendingly. 'Gone where?'

'Don't play with your food,' her sister reproved lightly, standing up to move the untouched plate of food from in front of March. 'Uncle Sid saw Will's car over at the Hanworth Estate earlier today; I've been debating all day whether or not I should tell you,' she admitted with a grimace. 'But looking at you this evening—this can't go on, you know, March.' She gave a determined shake of her head.

March sat stunned by the fact that Will was still in the area. On Monday evening he had said—what had he said, exactly? That he had to get away from here, from the farm, from her, not that he was actually going back to London. She was the one who had assumed that.

She swallowed hard, her throat dry. 'So he's still around.' She shrugged. 'What does that have to do with me?'

May frowned. 'March, you're in love with the man—'

'I am not! Well…okay, maybe I am,' she acknowledged gruffly at her sister's reproving look. What was the point of denying it? She had all the symptoms of unrequited love!

'Well?' May prompted impatiently when March added nothing to her original statement.

'Well what?' She stood up, moving restlessly around the kitchen. 'He certainly doesn't feel the same way about me!' To her dismay her voice broke emotionally.

The last three days since Will's abrupt departure had been awful. She was in love with a man who—

'You didn't hear him on Monday evening, May,' she cried painfully. 'He told Graham Whitford that he wished he had never met me!' She buried her face in her hands, the tears starting to fall once again.

May's arms came around March as she patted her back soothingly. 'I'm sure that he does, too,' she acknowledged dryly.

March raised her head sharply. 'Well, then?' she snapped defensively.

'Oh, March.' Her sister shook her head, frustrated affection on her face as she held March at arm's length.

'Of course Will wishes he had never met you—goodness knows you aren't the easiest person in the world to love! Oh, I don't have a problem with it,' she assured hastily at March's woebegone look. 'But I'm your sister. Will hasn't known whether he's on his head or his heels since the moment he met you!'

'Rubbish,' she dismissed hardly, moving away from May to stare sightlessly out of the window.

She loved this place, loved her sisters, and until a few days ago she had been perfectly happy with her life. Now it all felt something like a prison, holding her captive here, with no reprieve in sight.

'After I spoke to Uncle Sid this morning I checked around in town for the likeliest hotel for Will to be staying—'

'You didn't?' March gasped, her eyes wide as she turned to face May.

'Oh, don't worry.' May smiled ruefully. 'I haven't spoken to him or anything like that. I just wanted to know if he had returned to the same hotel. He has,' she added with satisfaction.

'But why did you go to that trouble?' March shook her head dazedly.

'So that I could tell you, of course,' her sister returned impatiently.

'But—'

'March, if you don't go and see Will then I'm afraid I will have to. And I think it might be better if it were you,' May added huskily.

'And just what would I say to him?' she cried frustratedly.

'Well, an apology might not be a bad way to start—'

'I did that on Monday evening—'

'As I understand it, you apologized to Graham

Whitford on Monday evening,' May cut in determinedly. 'Who, incidentally, isn't going to wait for ever for you to call him and accept his offer,' she added frowningly.

'But I—'

'You are going to accept, March,' May told her firmly. 'It's what you've always wanted.' Her voice softened affectionately. 'And you aren't going to let pride stand in your way of accepting. But first you have to apologize to Will, and thank him for going to the trouble of giving you this opportunity.'

She knew that, had known it for the last three days. It was not knowing where Will was, or how to contact him, that had made this time seem so much bleaker.

'What if he won't see me?' She frowned her uncertainty.

May gave a chuckle. 'He'll see you. But if you want an excuse for turning up at his hotel room...' she moved to pick up the envelope that sat on one of the worktops '...he didn't take this cheque with him when he left.' She handed it to March.

He probably wouldn't take it now, either, and it was a pretty feeble excuse for going to see him in the first place. But it was better than nothing...

'Okay.' She took the envelope, turning to leave.

'March, aren't you going to change or—or at least smarten up your appearance before you go?' May frowned concernedly.

She was looking less than her best, March knew, wearing no make-up, had lived in jeans and jumpers the last three days, and her hair could probably do with a wash too. But if she took the time to smarten herself up, as May put it, she might just lose her nerve and not go at all.

'Never mind,' May added hastily, obviously having

read the same thing from March's expression. 'I don't suppose Will will be too interested in the way you look, anyway—I didn't mean it like that, March.' She chuckled ruefully at March's pained grimace. 'If I'm right about the way Will feels about you, then he isn't going to care what you look like, he'll just be glad to see you.'

March had no idea how Will felt about her, only knew that she had to see him, whether he wanted to see her or not.

Although she didn't feel quite so sure about that an hour later when Will opened the door to his hotel suite, his look of polite enquiry turning to a scowl as he saw it was her standing there!

March was the last person he had expected to see this evening. The last person he had ever expected to see at all!

In fact, he was so surprised to see her that it didn't even cross his mind how she had known he was here…!

His gaze ate her up hungrily, noting the dark shadows beneath her eyes, the gaunt paleness of her face—she had never looked more beautiful to him!

'March,' he greeted huskily—inanely—wondering why it was that whenever he was around this woman he ceased to be a confidently articulate man and became a dumbstruck idiot.

She still didn't speak, her eyes—those beautiful grey-green eyes—filling with tears as she looked up at him.

'What is it?' His voice sharpened in concern at her continued silence, a dark frown on his brow. 'Is it May? January or Max?'

She smiled through her tears. 'No. But thank you for your concern,' she added throatily.

Will frowned his confusion. 'Then what—is it Carter?' He scowled. 'Did he turn nasty, after all?'

'No, it isn't Clive, either.' She gave a rueful shake of her head. 'Actually, you're totally wrong about that situation. You see—'

'Come inside and talk,' Will cut in briskly, not at all happy talking to her in a hotel corridor like this, where anyone might stroll along and overhear them.

She hesitated. 'If you're sure I'm not interrupting…?'

His mouth twisted ruefully. 'I'm sure you'll be pleased to know that the only thing you're interrupting is the final adjustments on my plans for the health and country club!' Although, as he saw her frown deepen, he wasn't sure that was an altogether diplomatic subject for him to have mentioned!

But to his relief March merely nodded before accompanying him inside his hotel suite.

She gave him a hesitant, totally un-March smile, deepening his concern that something was seriously wrong.

'You were saying…?' he prompted frowningly.

'Oh, yes.' She nodded, seeming relieved to have a neutral subject she could talk about. 'I'm afraid you totally misunderstood the situation at the estate agency; Michelle was the one who was buying properties under value and then selling them on.'

'Michelle…?' Will couldn't hide his disbelief; to him Michelle Jones most resembled a timid little mouse, didn't seem at all the type to become involved in such subterfuge.

'Yes,' March sighed. 'Apparently she thought Clive was tiring of her, and the estate agency, decided that she needed a little nest egg of her own for that eventuality.' March shrugged ruefully.

Will was stunned. Absolutely stunned. 'You've spoken to her?'

'Oh, yes.' March sighed again. 'She came to see me at the farm yesterday. Apparently she and Clive have discussed the whole thing. Michelle is going to go to the police and tell them exactly what she has done. But first she and Clive are going to be married.'

'She may go to prison for what she's done.' Will frowned.

March grimaced. 'They know that. He has a strange way of showing it, but it seems that Clive loves her and is going to stand by her. I— Would you mind if I sat down? I—I'm really not feeling so good.' She sat down abruptly.

She didn't look so good either, Will realized as he frowned his concern. Her jeans hung loosely on her, those dark shadows beneath her eyes and the gauntness of her face taking on another aspect entirely.

He moved to the mini-bar, taking out a small bottle of whisky and pouring it into one of the glasses before handing it to March. 'Drink it,' he advised gruffly.

She looked up to give him a smile. 'As long as you don't complain when it makes me drunk; I'm afraid I haven't eaten very much the last few days.'

Neither had Will, if the truth were known. He simply didn't have any appetite. And as for sleeping…! Come to think of it, he probably looked as ill as March said she felt!

'The last three days, in fact,' March added huskily.

Three days. Precisely the amount of time that had passed since the last time the two of them had spoken…

'Drink it,' he repeated softly, going down on his haunches beside her chair to look at her concernedly.

'March, what are you doing here?' he prompted gently, at the same time taking one of her hands in his.

Even her fingers were slimmer, just skin covering the delicate bones beneath, a slight tremor to that delicacy as his thumb lightly caressed the back of her hand.

She took a large gulp of the whisky before answering him, the fiery liquid bringing a little colour to the paleness of her cheeks. 'I didn't realize you were still in the area until Uncle Sid saw you earlier today—May was the one who found out you were back at this hotel—Will, I owe you an apology.' Her voice was huskier still from the effects of the whisky. 'I realize you were just trying to be helpful. By sending some of my paintings to Graham,' she explained abruptly. 'I—I've decided to accept his offer.' She looked at him searchingly, as if unsure of what his response was going to be to this decision.

'I'm glad,' Will assured her unhesitantly. 'Really glad,' he added with satisfaction. 'You're good, March. Very good.'

She gave a rueful smile. 'Well, I don't know about that. But Graham seems to think I might be too, so let's hope you're both right.'

'We are,' he told her with certainty. 'Was that—is the apology the only reason you came here?' he prompted carefully.

March gave a self-derisive smile. 'Isn't that enough?'

He grimaced. Not nearly enough, as far as he was concerned.

The last three days had been purgatory for him, with March so close and yet emotionally so far away, and yet he had been loath to leave the area. He hadn't slept much, and food had held no interest for him; the only thing left for him to do had been to concentrate on finishing Jude's plans for the health and country club. And even that irritated him, with its indisputable connection to March and the farm she had lived in all her life.

But now, after those awful three days, March was here with him, and the thought of letting her just get up and walk out the door was completely unacceptable to him.

He straightened abruptly. 'In that case, I have something that needs to be said,' he bit out grimly, thrusting his hands into his denim pockets; if he didn't he might just reach down and pull her into his arms, kiss her until she was senseless, and to hell with any explanations!

March looked up at him warily. 'Yes?'

Will looked down at her frustratedly, wondering where to begin, what to say. And then knowing there was only one thing he really wanted to say. Only one thing that mattered.

He drew in a ragged breath. 'March, will you marry me?'

There.

He had said it.

Said the one thing that had been uppermost in his mind for the last three days without her in his life.

Now it only remained for March to give him another slap in the face, either verbally or physically!

CHAPTER FIFTEEN

PERHAPS she was drunk, after all, because Will couldn't really have just asked her to marry him. Could he...?

She stared up at him disbelievingly, unable to read anything from his guarded expression. Except...

Now that she looked at him more closely, Will didn't look a lot better than she did, dark shadows beneath those gloriously blue eyes, his face thinner too, an unhealthy pallor to the gauntness of his cheeks.

Perhaps he had been as miserable as she had the last three days?

Perhaps for the same reason—because he was also in love with her!

She moistened dry lips before carefully placing the empty whisky glass down on the coffee-table in front of her, standing up to move only inches away from him as she looked up unflinchingly into his face.

His guarded look flickered and died, to be replaced by—by what? Uncertainty? Wariness? Hope?

It was all three of those, giving March the confidence to reach up and gently caress one hard cheek before standing on tiptoe and kissing him gently on the lips.

Will groaned low in his throat, his arms moving to gather her close against him as he deepened the kiss, parting her lips beneath his as he drank in her fullness.

March needed no further encouragement, her arms moving about his shoulders as she pressed close against him, her hands tangled in the blond silkiness of the hair at his nape, wanting this kiss to just go on and on.

But it didn't, of course, Will raising his head with obvious reluctance as he looked down at her quizzically. 'I hope that was a yes to my marriage proposal…?'

He still sounded so unsure, so unlike his usual confident self, that March could only gaze up at him.

'This is not the time for one of your uncharacteristic silences, March,' he told her frustratedly, his hands firm on her upper arms as he shook her slightly. 'I love you. The last three days without you have shown me only too clearly that I don't want to live my life without you in it—'

'Even though I'm rude, and prickly, and outspoken, and far too quick to jump to conclusions—'

'All that!' he confirmed laughingly. 'You're March,' he added simply. 'Every delectable, contrary, stubborn inch of you—and I love every part of you!' he assured her huskily, his gaze intent on the beauty of her face.

'Oh, Will,' she choked emotionally, her hands tightening on the broadness of his shoulders. 'I love you too. I love you so much! This last three days have been—'

'Forget them,' he cut in decisively. 'If you say yes to my marriage proposal we will never be apart again!' His eyes glowed deeply blue as he looked down at her.

March looked up at him, no longer bothering to hide the way she felt about him, the love she felt for him shining in her grey-green eyes. 'Yes,' she breathed forcefully. 'Oh, yes…!'

Will swept her back into his arms, his kiss so poignantly beautiful that March found herself crying once again.

'Hey,' he raised his head to chide gently. 'You aren't supposed to cry at a time like this,' he teased.

She wiped the tears away with the back of her hand. 'I seem to have done nothing *but* cry the last three days.

I thought you had gone, that I would never see you
again, that I—'

'It's over, March,' Will assured her firmly. 'I love
you—'

'And I love you,' she told him fervently.

'Then that's all that matters,' he told her before he
bent his head and kissed her once again, his hands lightly
cradling each side of her face as he looked into her eyes.
'My parents are going to love you,' he said with certainty.

His parents…!

She hadn't given Will's family a thought, been consumed by the fact that Will loved her as she loved him.

She still found that hard to believe, knew that she
hadn't exactly been very welcoming when he'd first arrived, even less so since she had discovered his connection to Jude Marshall.

Jude Marshall…!

What on earth was he going to think? First his lawyer
had defected and intended marrying one of the Calendar
sisters, and now his architect was about to do the same
thing. The man was going to think it was some sort of
Machiavellian plot against him by the Calendar sisters.

'I doubt your current employer is going to be too
pleased.' March grimaced, very much aware that Jude
Marshall was Will's friend as much as anything else.

Will shrugged. 'We'll talk about Jude in a few
minutes. I haven't kissed you nearly enough yet to be
able to talk about such inanities.' He pulled her down
into a chair with him, settling March comfortably on his
knees before kissing her once again.

Heaven.

Sheer heaven.

And she was going to be with Will for the rest of her

life. Nothing, and no one, meant more to her than
he did.

They never would.

It was a long time later, Will having ordered dinner to
be served to them in his hotel suite, that he returned to
those 'inanities'.

'Eat, March,' he encouraged, touching her hand
lightly as she looked at him rather than eating any of the
melon and strawberries on the plate in front of her. 'If
just now was anything to go by, we're both going to
need to build up our strength for our honeymoon!' he
added teasingly, rewarded by the becoming blush that
highlighted her cheeks. 'You are adorable, do you know
that?' He chuckled delightedly.

She shook her head. 'I still can't believe all of this is
true. I was so miserable earlier when I thought you had
completely gone from our lives.' She gave a shudder of
remembered pain.

Will's hand tightened on hers. 'With your agreement,
I would like our engagement to be a short one?'

'As short as you like,' she said instantly. 'Although I
would obviously like my sisters to be present. But as
Max and January will be back at the weekend...'

He couldn't wait to see the look on Max's face when
he was told of Will's engagement to March!

'And May?' he prompted frowningly.

March frowned slightly. 'She says she isn't going to
accept the part in the film. I have no idea why,' she
added as Will was about to ask. 'She just came back
from her weekend away and stated quite categorically
that she wasn't going to do it. Which brings us back to
the same problem concerning whether or not to sell the
farm,' she realized frowningly.

'Hmm.' Will got up from the table, moving to pick up the two envelopes that sat on the desk in front of the window. 'I've drawn up two plans here.' He held up the envelopes. 'One includes your farm. The other one doesn't. Which do you think I should submit to Jude?'

March grimaced as she looked at the two envelopes. 'Perhaps we should let May choose?' she said finally.

'Perhaps we should,' he agreed slowly, putting the envelopes down, knowing there was something else they needed to discuss. 'March, I live in London most of the time—'

'I know that,' she cut in reassuringly. 'May was the one who found out you were still here, and told me about it,' she said softly. 'I'm sure she is well aware that if— if the two of us ever got together that I would move to London to live with you.'

'But if January and Max are moving to London too... May can't run the farm on her own.' Will frowned. He liked May, liked her a lot, was looking forward to having her as his 'sister'.

'Who knows, my exhibition may be a wonderful success,' March told him brightly, 'and then I can still help May out financially if in no other way. Will, I'm sure we'll be able to work something out,' she said determinedly. 'After all,' she added mischievously, 'if you and I have found a happy ending, I'm sure there must be one for May too. After all, having brought the two of us up, she deserves it so much more than January or I do!'

'I'm very fond of May, and I'm sure she deserves to be happy.' Will reached down and pulled March to her feet. 'But no more than you do. And I intend to make sure that in future you are very happy, March Calendar, soon-to-be-Davenport,' he promised huskily.

'I'm already happier than I ever dreamed possible,' she assured him with a glowing smile, standing on tiptoe and kissing him with all the love she had previously kept hidden behind her prickly exterior.

Heaven.

Sheer heaven.

And he was going to spend the rest of his life with March. Nothing, and no one, meant more to him than she did.

They never would.

THE DESERVING MISTRESS

by

Carole Mortimer

For Matthew,
I'm so proud of you.

CHAPTER ONE

'ARE you having a heart attack or just resting?'

May had heard the approach of the car into the farmyard, had even managed to slightly raise one eyelid in order to register the fact that it wasn't a vehicle she recognised. Which meant her visitor was either lost, or a seed or fertilizer salesman, neither of which raised enough enthusiasm to rouse her from her sitting position on the convenient bale of hay outside the milking shed.

She managed a grunt of acknowledgement. 'Which do you think?'

'In all honesty—I'm not sure!' The man sounded slightly surprised by his own uncertainty, as if it weren't an emotion that came naturally to him.

May managed to pry that single eyelid slightly open a second time, just enough to be able to have a look at her unexpected visitor.

Probably aged in his mid to late thirties, the man was tall, very much so, with thick dark hair that looked inclined to curl, dark brows frowning over piercing grey eyes, an arrogant slash of a nose, his mouth grimly set over a squarely determined chin.

Uncertainty about anything certainly wouldn't sit easily on those broad shoulders, either!

'Well, let me know when you've made up your mind.' May sighed wearily, closing her eyelid again.

'Hmm,' he murmured thoughtfully. 'I've never actually seen anyone have a heart attack, but I'm sure they should be in more pain than you appear to be in. On the

5

other hand, falling asleep sitting outside on a bale of hay, in a temperature that can't be much above freezing, doesn't seem too comfortable, either!' he concluded dryly.

May gave a dismissive movement of her shoulders. 'Anywhere is comfortable to fall asleep when you've been up all night.'

'Ah,' the man murmured knowingly.

She opened her eyes just wide enough to glare at him. 'With the vet,' she defended impatiently before closing her eyes again.

'I see,' the man drawled wryly.

May gave a groan as she roused herself to sit up on the bale of hay, every muscle in her body seeming to ache as she rubbed sleep-drowsed eyes before frowning up at her visitor.

When she viewed him more closely, it was possible to see the arrogant lift of his square-cut chin, the complete self-confidence in the way that he stood and the hardness of his handsome features. Just the type of man she felt like dealing with after a sleepless night!

'Can I help you?' she prompted irritably.

'That depends,' the man murmured ruefully.

'On what?' She sighed at this procrastination, really in no mood to deal with a lost out-of-season tourist or indeed a pushy salesman.

He shrugged those broad shoulders. 'On whether or not your name happens to be Calendar.'

Not a lost out-of-season tourist. A seed or fertilizer salesman, then.

'It could be.' She pushed herself up onto her feet with effort, looking up to find the man was still seven or eight inches taller than her own five feet eight in height.

The man gave her a considering look, laughter glinting in those piercing grey eyes now.

Which wasn't so surprising, May acknowledged, easily able to visualise the scarecrow figure she must represent. Her wellington boots were muddy, her jeans likewise; worse, she was still wearing the same clothes she had put on yesterday morning, not having been to bed yet or indeed managed to get inside for a refreshing shower. Her face was probably smeared with dirt from lying on the barn floor most of the night, a woollen hat pulled down low over her ears, mainly to keep out the bitingly cold wind but also to keep her long dark hair from the same muddy fate as the rest of her.

Yes, she had no doubts she did look rather funny. But at the moment, exhausted as she was, she wasn't in the mood to laugh, at herself or anyone else.

'You don't sound too sure,' the man drawled derisively.

'I'm not.' She shrugged, sighing heavily. 'Look, I have no idea what you're selling, and I probably don't want any anyway, but if you could come back tomorrow I might at least be willing to talk about it—'

'Selling?' he repeated frowningly. 'But I'm not the one—I have a better idea,' he stated briskly as May gave a weary yawn, at the same time swaying slightly on her feet. 'Let's go into the farmhouse.' He took a firm hold of her arm. 'I'll make you some coffee. Strong and black,' he decided after another glance at her face, her eyes appearing a deeper green against her paleness. 'And maybe then we can introduce ourselves properly.'

May wasn't sure she wanted to be introduced to this man, properly or otherwise, but the promise of making her coffee was certainly a strong inducement to at least letting him in as far as the kitchen. He probably made good coffee—he looked the sort of man who excelled at most things he did! And he didn't exactly look the type of man who felt the need to pounce on some unsuspecting female—in fact, with those looks, she suspected it was probably usually the other way round!

'Done!' she accepted huskily, allowing herself to be guided across the yard and into the kitchen, sitting down on one of the kitchen chairs as the man moved dexterously about the kitchen preparing a pot of strong coffee.

Lord, that smelt good, she acknowledged a few minutes later as the strong aroma of brewing coffee filled the warmth of the room. A cup or two might even help her to stay awake long enough to complete her chores for the morning.

It had been a long night, if ultimately a successful one, and the thought of all the jobs she still had to do had been the reason she'd sat down wearily on the bale of hay earlier. Only to fall asleep. Which, as this man had already pointed out, was not the most comfortable thing in the world to have done in late January.

'Here you are.' He placed a mug of strong black coffee in front of her before sitting down opposite her with another mug of his own, looking perfectly at ease in the confines of her untidy kitchen. 'I've added two sugars,' he told her frowningly. 'You look as if you need the energy.'

May didn't normally take sugar in her coffee, but she accepted that her visitor was right as she sipped the strong, sweet brew, instantly feeling the surge as the caffeine and sugar hit her bloodstream.

'I've made up my mind,' he murmured softly.

'Sorry?' May glanced across at him, frowning slightly. Obviously the caffeine and sugar hadn't done quite such a good job as she had thought—because she had no idea what he was talking about.

'You were sleeping earlier,' he stated firmly.

She grimaced. 'I already told you that I was.'

He nodded. 'Because you and the vet were up all night.'

When he put it like that…! 'With a ewe that was having a difficult time lambing,' she explained dryly. Not that it was any of this man's business, but still…

Their vet, John Potter, was a man of fifty or so, had been married for twenty years, and had three teenage children; it wouldn't do to have that sort of speculations spread around the neighbourhood. It wouldn't do her own reputation too much good, either!

'Mother and twins are all doing well,' she added dryly as this man continued to look at her with raised brows. 'Look, I'm grateful for the coffee and everything, but I really don't think I'm in any fit condition to—'

'Good Lord!' the man gasped suddenly.

'What…?' May was arrested in the action of removing her woollen hat, long dark hair cascading down over her shoulders and back.

He blinked, frowning darkly. 'You—I—for a moment— You reminded me of someone else.' He gave a dismissive shake of his head, but the dark frown remained on his scowling features. 'Who are you?' he breathed softly.

May gave him a scathing glance. 'Shouldn't I be the one asking you that? After all, I live here!' she reminded him impatiently.

'Yes. Yes, of course.' The man seemed to shake himself slightly, although his frowning gaze remained fixed on her face.

What on earth could he see there to have caused this

reaction? May wondered frowningly. With her long dark hair, deep green eyes, classical features, her looks were nothing exceptional. In fact, she had two younger sisters who looked very much the same as she did! Besides, dressed in her filthy clothing, her face probably covered in mud and goodness knew what else, she was hardly a glamorous figure. And this man, with his arrogant good looks and tailored clothes, did not look as if he usually bothered to look at mud-covered women farmers!

'Well?' she prompted irritatedly as he simply continued to stare.

'Well what...? Ah.' He shifted slightly in his chair as he obviously recalled her previous question, making no effort to answer her as his gaze roamed curiously around the kitchen, but mainly concentrating on the flagstone floor.

'What *are* you doing?' May finally demanded impatiently.

That piercing grey gaze returned to her face, this man seeming to have recovered from whatever had been bothering him about the way she looked. 'Looking for where you might have hidden the bodies, of course,' he drawled dryly.

Was she still asleep? Had her wonderful dream, where a handsome stranger appeared from nowhere and made her delicious coffee, turned into some sort of nightmare? Was she merely dreaming that she was sitting in her own kitchen, drinking coffee with a perfect stranger?

Because she certainly seemed to have lost the plot somewhere, this man's question making absolutely no sense to her!

Perhaps she wasn't dreaming. Perhaps this was all real. Perhaps this man was an escapee from a lunatic asylum!

'What bodies?' she prompted warily.

He was smiling when her gaze returned to his face, as if perfectly able to read her last, disturbing thought. 'Which one are you? May? March? Or January?' he prompted curiously.

Her wariness increased at his knowledge of her own name and those of her two sisters, too. An escapee from a lunatic asylum probably wouldn't know such things, but that didn't mean this man wasn't still dangerous.

'I'm May,' she answered brightly, forcing herself to an alertness she really didn't feel. 'But I'm expecting March and January back at any moment,' she lied.

One of her sisters was still in the Caribbean with her fiancé, and the other one had just gone to London with her fiancé to meet his family. But until she knew who this man was, and what he was doing here, she certainly didn't want him to know how completely alone she was here.

His mouth twisted into a humourless smile. 'Somehow I don't think so,' he murmured softly, that silver-grey gaze intent on the paleness of her face. 'So you're May,' he murmured consideringly.

'I just said so,' she confirmed defensively, shoulders tensed as she faced him across the table. 'And you are...?'

'I am.' He nodded unhelpfully, obviously enjoying her discomfort now.

May stood up forcefully, somehow feeling a little more in control of this situation once she was higher than he was—but at the same time knowing how quickly that would change if he were to stand up, too. 'Look, I didn't ask you here—'

'Ah, but you did,' he cut in softly, his voice almost a purr now, at the same time that his eyes glowed with challenge. 'In fact, I have it from two very reliable sources that you expressly wished to meet me face to face,' he assured her dismissively.

'I did?' May repeated slowly, suddenly becoming very still, looking at him with new eyes now, that mention of 'two very reliable sources' setting off alarm bells inside her head.

Mid to late thirties, very self-assured, obviously wealthy now that she took a good look at his leather jacket and designer-labelled jeans. More to the point, he had obviously already known she was one of the Calendar sisters when he arrived here.

Those alarm bells began to jingle so loudly they threatened to deafen her!

She knew who this man was—

'Jude Marshall,' he introduced confidently even as he stood up and held out his hand, knowing by the shocked look on her face seconds ago that the introduction was unnecessary.

Under other circumstances, that look of horror on her face at exactly who he was might possibly have been amusing. Possibly... Although he doubted it. It wasn't the usual reaction to his identity that he experienced from beautiful women. And May Calendar, despite her tired state, was an exceptionally beautiful woman.

She still stared at him, making no effort to shake the hand he held out to her. 'But—but—you're English!' she burst out accusingly.

Jude's hand dropped back to his side as he once again sat down on one of the chairs. 'Ah, now that is a debatable point,' he drawled, amused now by her stunned expression.

'Either you are or you aren't,' May Calendar snapped

dismissively, at the same time obviously making great efforts to regain her equilibrium after the shock of realising he was the man who had been trying to buy this farm for the last two months.

He shrugged. 'My mother is American, but my father is English,' he explained dryly. 'I was born in America, but educated in England. I visit America a lot, socially as well as on business, but my base is in London. So what do you think?' He quirked dark brows.

She gave him a resentful glare. 'I doubt you would want to hear what I think!'

'Probably not,' he drawled ruefully.

She was taking her coat off now, revealing that the bulky garment had hidden a curvaceous slenderness, her green jumper the exact colour of her eyes, denims fitting snugly over narrow thighs and long legs.

'Tell me,' Jude murmured softly. 'Do your sisters look anything like you?'

'Exac— Why do you want to know?' she amended her initial confirmation to a guarded wariness.

He shrugged. 'Just curious.'

'No, you weren't,' May Calendar said confidently. 'Those bodies you mentioned a few minutes ago, you wouldn't happen to be referring to Max Golding, your lawyer, and Will Davenport, your architect, would you?'

Bright as well as beautiful, Jude mentally conceded. The Calendar sisters—the one he had met so far, at least—were absolutely nothing like the three little old ladies he had assumed them to be several weeks ago when he'd first initiated the buying of their—this!—farm.

'What do you think?' he prompted unhelpfully.

'You're fond of answering a question with a question,

aren't you?' May murmured consideringly as she moved to refill her coffee mug.

It was a defence mechanism he had perfected over the years, meant that he usually obtained more information than he gave—and it wasn't something that most people easily recognised!

He frowned darkly. 'Obviously you share the same trait,' he bit out tersely.

She shrugged narrow shoulders. 'We could carry on like this all morning—except I don't have all morning to waste exchanging verbal arrows with you,' she added hardly.

'Because you and the vet spent a sleepless night together,' he came back with deliberate provocation.

Angry colour darkened her normally magnolia cheeks. 'I have already explained about that once, I don't intend doing so again!' she snapped dismissively. 'What is it you want, Mr Marshall?' she prompted challengingly.

Having now met the elder of the three Calendar sisters, found her to be absolutely nothing like he had presumed her to be, he wasn't absolutely sure. And that wasn't a feeling he was particularly comfortable with.

'Well, you might start off by telling me where Will and Max are?' he prompted cautiously.

'Assuming their bodies aren't hidden under the kitchen flagstones, after all?' she came back scathingly.

'Assuming that, yes,' he conceded with a humourless smile.

May Calendar gave a derisive shake of her head. 'They aren't.'

'Well?' he pushed impatiently a few seconds later when she added nothing to that remark.

She gave him a considering look, green eyes narrowed, her thoughts unreadable even to his experienced eye. 'Will is in London. Max is in the Caribbean,' she finally told him economically.

Jude drew in an impatient breath. 'And your two sisters are where?'

'March is in London. January is in the Caribbean,' she informed him with a challenging lift of her chin.

'How coincidental,' he drawled dryly.

In fact, he had already known exactly where Max and Will were, and who they were with; he had just wanted to see if May Calendar was willing to tell him as much. She obviously was!

'Not really—March and January naturally wanted to be with their fiancés,' she told him with satisfaction.

So Jude had gathered when he had received first a telephone call from Max over a week ago telling him of his engagement to January Calendar, and then a second telephone call from Will a couple of days ago telling him of his engagement to March Calendar!

To say he was surprised by the fact that his two friends were engaged to marry anyone, let alone two of the Calendar sisters, was an understatement.

The three men had been to school together, had worked together for years; despite relationships with numerous women over those years, Jude had always assumed that none of them would ever make the commitment to falling in love, let alone getting married. Obviously he had been wrong.

And that was something else he didn't admit to too freely!

He stood up abruptly. 'You asked me what I wanted a few minutes ago,' he rasped. 'I want exactly what Max was sent here to do before he fell in love with your sister, and that was to buy this farm!'

Her head tilted defensively. 'And I'm sure he's told you that it isn't for sale!'

Jude's eyes narrowed icily. 'Yes, he's told me.'

'And?'

The challenge was evident in her voice, as was the underlying tone of resentment. Both of which were going to get him precisely nowhere, Jude realised.

He forced himself to relax slightly, his smile lightly cajoling. 'May, surely you've realised, after the last few days of managing on your own here, that you just can't do it?'

She stiffened angrily, green eyes flashing with the emotion. 'What I can or cannot do is none of your business, Mr Marshall. And I don't remember giving you permission to call me by my first name, either,' she added churlishly.

He bit back the angry retort that sprang so readily to his lips, at the same time marvelling at the fact that this woman had managed to incite him to such an emotion. Usually he kept his emotions tightly under control, having found that this gave him an advantage over— Over what? His opponent, he had been going to say...

Was May Calendar really that?

Looking at her, tired from hard work and a sleepless night, her face ethereally lovely, much too slender than was healthy for her, it was difficult to think of her in that light. In fact, he was starting to feel guilty for having added to her obvious problems of the day.

Which was a highly dangerous direction for him to have taken!

'Look, maybe this isn't the best time for the two of us to talk,' he dismissed lightly. 'You're obviously busy, and tired, and—'

'And coming back tomorrow, when I might be neither

of those things, isn't going to change my answer one little bit,' she assured him scathingly. 'I'll tell you what I first told Max, your lawyer, and then Will, your architect—this farm is not for sale!'

Jude frowned at her frustratedly. She really was the most stubborn, intransigent—

'Certainly not to someone like you,' she continued insultingly. 'We don't need a health and country club where the Hanworth Estate used to be, Mr Marshall,' she scorned. 'Or the eighteen-hole golf course you intend to make of this farmland!'

She had done her homework, at least, Jude acknowledged admiringly—because that was exactly what he intended doing with this land once it was his. Unless, of course, Max or Will—

No! He didn't believe either man, no matter what his romantic connection with this family, would have betrayed the confidence he had in them. In fact, he knew that they hadn't, had already turned down Max's offer of resignation because of a 'conflict of interest', and viewed the two sets of plans Will had drawn up for this latest business venture, one including the Calendar farm, the other one not doing so.

He shrugged. 'That's only your personal opinion—Miss Calendar,' he added pointedly.

She shook her head. 'I believe, if you cared to ask around in the area, that you would find it's the general consensus of opinion, and not just mine.'

He didn't have time for this, Jude decided as he zipped up his jacket impatiently, better able to appreciate exactly what sort of brick wall Max and Will had come up against in their efforts to secure this farm for development. But May Calendar was going to find that he was made of much sterner stuff than either of his two friends and work colleagues, that he wasn't so easily distracted by a helpless female—or, indeed, three of them!

'We'll talk about this some other time, Miss Calendar,' he dismissed uninterestedly, pausing at the door to add, 'It's enough for now that we have introduced ourselves to each other.' And that she now knew what sort of opposition she was up against.

Because Jude had no intention of giving up on his plans for the property he had already bought in this area, plans that included the Calendar sisters' farm.

No intention whatsoever!

CHAPTER TWO

WELL, that was certainly a turn-up for the book, May acknowledged as she dropped down weakly onto one of the kitchen chairs after Jude Marshall's abrupt departure.

He was the very last person she had expected to see today—or, indeed, at any other time.

Jude Marshall, and the corporation that he headed, had become something of an elusive spectre in the background of the sisters' lives the last couple of months, ever since they had received a letter from that corporation with an offer to buy their farm. A farm that, as far as any of the Calendar sisters was concerned, had never been for sale.

That initial letter had come from America, which was why they had all assumed that Jude Marshall was American, too—and why, when he'd spoken in that precise English accent on his arrival a short time ago, May had made absolutely no connection between her unexpected visitor and the man whose very name the three sisters had all come to loathe the last two months.

Jude Marshall was a surprise in more ways than one, May acknowledged frowningly. She hadn't expected him to be so arrogantly good-looking, for one thing, or have him moving capably about her kitchen making her a much-needed mug of coffee, for that matter!

He was also, she acknowledged less readily, completely right about the strain of running the farm on her own the last few days since her sister March had gone off to London to meet Will's parents, and her younger sister January had telephoned from the Caribbean to say that she and Max had decided to stay on for an extra week. January had sounded so happy and carefree that May hadn't liked to tell her youngest sister that, with March away, too, she was managing here on her own, brightly assuring January that everything was just fine here, and wishing her and Max a wonderful time.

Something she certainly wasn't having herself!

This last few days on her own had been a learning experience, was indicative of how it would be once March and January were married and living away from the farm. Not good, May knew.

But that was still no reason to give in to Jude Marshall's pressure to sell the farm to him, she decided with a determined straightening of her spine. Having now met the man, and seeing firsthand just how arrogantly assured he was, May was even more determined not to do that!

Although she didn't feel quite so confident later that evening when she staggered back into the farmhouse, too tired to even bother to cook herself an evening meal.

The coffee remaining in the pot from this morning was stewed and only lukewarm, but it was better than nothing.

No, it wasn't, she decided after the first mouthful, putting the mug back down on the table with a disgusted grimace.

She was so tired, so utterly exhausted, resting her head down on her folded arms as she sagged tiredly onto the kitchen table. Just a few minutes' rest and she would be all right again, she told herself. Just a few minutes...

'Come on, May, it's time to wake up,' a gently intruding voice cajoled. 'May?' A gentle shaking of her arm accompanied this second intrusion.

She had been having such a nice dream, she frowned resentfully, had been lying on a golden beach, the sun warm and soothing, with a tropical blue sea lapping lightly against the sand at her feet. But the stiffness in her folded arms as she slowly woke to consciousness, aided by the ache in her back, told her only too clearly that it had unfortunately been just a dream!

'May, if you don't wake up in a minute, I'm going to assume that this time you really have had a heart attack—and commence emergency mouth-to-mouth resuscitation!' that intruding voice drawled mockingly.

Jude Marshall's voice!

She recognised those clipped English tones only too easily this time, raising her head to glare at him resentfully, very aware that she probably looked worse now than she had this morning, still in the same clothes, still as dirty—and, to add to her disarray, she probably had crease marks on her face now from having fallen asleep in such an uncomfortable position!

He grinned down at her unconcernedly. 'I thought the mere suggestion of my having to carry out mouth-to-mouth resuscitation might revive you!'

She gave an irritated sigh. 'What do you want, Mr Marshall?'

'You seem very fond of asking me that.' He raised mocking brows. 'A fine way to talk to someone who has brought you dinner,' he admonished derisively, holding up a plastic carrier bag. 'Chinese take-away,' he explained economically. 'Having seen how tired you were this morning, I didn't think you were going to be in any fit state to cook yourself a hot meal this evening.'

May frowned up at him, still not quite awake, but aware enough to view his kindness—and the man himself!—with suspicion. The fact that his surmise had obviously been a correct one wasn't in question—but his response to it certainly was.

'And why should that bother you, Mr Marshall?' she prompted warily, her sleepy state fast disappearing now as she frowned up at him suspiciously.

'Stop dithering, woman, and tell me where the plates are so that I can serve this stuff before it goes cold!' He put the bag down on the table in front of her.

'Second cupboard on the right,' she supplied somewhat dazedly. Plates, he had said. In the plural. Surely this man didn't intend sitting down to dinner with her?

But as he set out two places on the table along with the two big plates, and then commenced to put out the cartons of Chinese food, it appeared that was exactly what he intended doing!

'Er—Mr Marshall—'

'Could we get something clear right now, May?' He straightened, looking down at her with narrowed eyes.

She stiffened warily, wondering exactly what he was going to say. 'Yes?'

He nodded abruptly. 'I'm sure you have your reasons for being deliberately rude to me—I'm sure you *think* you have,' he stressed firmly as she would have protested. 'But I have no intention of sitting down to dinner—a dinner that I actually brought here, remember?—with someone who insists on calling me "Mr Marshall" in that unfriendly tone.' He raised dark brows pointedly.

May's cheeks warmed at the accusation. She was being deliberately rude, there was no denying that. But he was being deliberately friendly, which was just as unacceptable!

'Okay?' he prompted determinedly.

May looked up at him unblinkingly, wanting to tell him to go away, and to take his dinner with him. But the smell of the food was so tempting, her mouth watering at the mixture of aromas that was wafting up from the array of cartons he had put out in the middle of the table. If she told him to go away, he would probably take all this wonderful food with him!

'Okay,' she accepted abruptly. 'Although—'

'Okay will do for just now,' Jude cut in derisively. 'Eat,' he added curtly, sitting down at the place opposite her.

She couldn't remember the last time someone had ordered her about in this way. Probably not since her father had died a year ago, she recognised frowningly. But anyone less like her father—or, indeed, a father-figure—than Jude Marshall, she was less likely to meet!

For one thing she was completely aware of him as the two of them helped themselves to the food, of the slender strength of his ringless hands, the dark hairs that began at his wrist and probably covered his arms and chest, of the way his dark hair fell endearingly across his forehead unless pushed back by an impatient hand, of the piercing intelligence of those silver-grey eyes, of the dark shadow at his jaw that implied he probably had to shave twice a day, but had omitted to spend time on that second shave today.

Because he had chosen to drive out here and bring her dinner instead? Probably, she acknowledged slightly dazedly. In fact, she found it difficult to believe at all that she was sitting here eating a Chinese take-away with Jude Marshall, of all people!

'This is very good, thank you,' she told him huskily, the hot, tasty food more welcome than she had even imagined. And it had been supplied by Jude Marshall, a man she considered to be her enemy...

He looked across at her, eyes gleaming silver with

amusement. 'How hard was that to say?' he mused dryly.

'Very,' she confirmed with a rueful grimace. 'I hope I'm not keeping you from something? Or someone?' she added frowningly.

'Nothing that can't wait.' He shrugged dismissively.

May gave him a quizzical look. Did that mean there wasn't someone waiting for him back at his hotel? Or that the person that was waiting for him wasn't important enough for him to bother rushing back to?

Jude frowned as he saw her looking at him. 'What did I say now?' he prompted impatiently.

'Nothing,' she dismissed abruptly, deliberately turning her attention back to her food.

Although she was completely aware of the fact that he was still looking at her. If she was honest—and she usually was—she had to admit she had never been so aware of another person in her life before.

Just as she felt sorry for whoever—possibly?—might be waiting for him back at his hotel; it would be awful to be so unimportant to this man that his having dinner with a scruffy female farmer took priority. Even with the buying of this farm as the incentive.

'I spoke to Max earlier this evening.'

May looked up at him sharply, but his bland expression was completely unenlightening. She moistened her lips before speaking, choosing her words carefully, deliberately infusing a lightness into her tone. 'Did you tell him the two of us have met—finally?' she couldn't resist adding dryly.

Jude sat back, regarding her derisively. 'Should I have done?' he drawled.

He was doing it again—answering a question with a question.

Because he knew damn well that she would much rather Max, and consequently January, didn't know of his presence in the area, or that he had already introduced himself to her—but especially that she was managing alone here on the farm.

January had had a pretty awful time of things at the beginning of the year, had been caught up in the sick workings of a stalker's mind, May much relieved when her sister had become engaged to Max, even more pleased when he'd suggested taking her away for a few weeks' holiday to get over the experience.

But she had no doubts that, were January to learn of Jude Marshall's presence here, of the fact that May was alone on the farm, her sister would insist on coming back on the next available flight!

'Well?' she prompted impatiently.

Jude gave a rueful shake of his head as she neatly turned the tables back on him. 'You're right—we could go on like this all night, returning a question with a question!'

'Not all night, no,' May assured him scathingly. 'Tonight I intend going to bed early, very early—and alone,' she added so that there should be no more mistakes concerning that particular subject! 'In fact—' She broke off frowningly as a knock sounded on the door, shooting Jude Marshall an accusing look.

'January would hardly knock to come into her own home,' he easily read the accusation in that look—and the reason for it.

Which still didn't tell her whether or not he had mentioned to Max that he had decided to come here himself as he and Will had failed to acquire the Calendar farm for him. But, then, even on this short an acquaintance, May already knew that Jude Marshall was decidedly economical in providing any sort of information about anything.

May stood up as a second knock sounded on the door. 'We'll talk on this subject more once I've dealt with my visitor,' she warned before moving hurriedly to the door, intending to make it very clear to this man before he left this evening that January was not to be worried by the situation here.

And 'situation' it certainly was rapidly becoming, she decided dazedly as she opened the door to find David Melton standing on her doorstep.

Keen on amateur dramatics, May had joined the local society a couple of years ago, only to be spotted by David Melton, a renowned film director, when he'd come to visit his sister's family for Christmas and spotted May as she'd performed in the local pantomime.

To her surprise he had offered her a part in the film he was to shoot in the summer, if the screen test he offered proved to be successful. It had. But, for very personal reasons of her own, May had decided to turn down his offer...

Which was why she had no idea what he was doing standing on her doorstep now.

Jude watched May's face as she obviously recognised her visitor—but obviously wished that she didn't, her expression a puzzling mixture of surprise and dismay.

He turned his narrowed gaze on the other man; probably aged forty or so, tall and slender, with short blond hair and a boyishly handsome face. Which told him precisely nothing, Jude acknowledged ruefully. The man could just be a salesman or something equally innocuous—although, from May's reaction to seeing him, somehow Jude doubted it...

'David,' he heard May greet huskily.

'I was in the area—I had to come, May,' the man returned determinedly.

May shook her head. 'I haven't changed my mind,' she told him firmly.

'But—'

'You'll find someone else,' she assured him, an uncomfortable glance in Jude's direction letting the other man know that she wasn't alone.

David shot Jude an impatient glance of his own before his attention returned determinedly to May. 'I don't want anyone else, May,' he told her forcefully. 'It has to be you. You're perfect—'

'I really don't want to talk about this just now,' May cut in firmly, obviously completely conscious of the listening Jude, even if the other man seemed unconcerned by his presence.

Curiouser and curiouser, Jude acknowledged consideringly. Was this David a spurned lover who simply refused to go away? Or something else? Although quite what that 'something else' could be Jude had no idea. Which brought him back to the spurned lover theory... Although, in the other man's shoes, Jude would have been more than a little concerned at another man's presence here alone with May. Unless the other man considered him to be insignificant in what was going on between him and May? A thought that Jude, who had never thought of himself as in the least 'insignificant' in any situation, found intensely irritating.

He stood up, moving to stand at May's side, deliberately resting his hand on the door behind her. 'Is there a problem, May?' he prompted haughtily.

She shot him a frowning glance. 'Nothing that I can't handle. Thank you,' she added belatedly.

Jude turned his attention on the other man, deliberately looking down the long length of his nose, topping the other man by at least three inches. 'I'm afraid you've caught us right in the middle of eating our dinner...' he said pointedly.

The other man looked displeased at this interruption. 'I just wanted to have a few words with May—'

'And, as I've just told you, we're eating our evening meal,' Jude bit out with hard dismissal, his gaze challenging on the other man now.

May looked up at him frowningly, seeming to sense that the situation was fast moving out of her control, turning back to David smilingly. 'I appreciate your— continued interest,' she told him warmly. 'But, as I told you before, I'm really not interested.'

David shook his head. 'I'm not giving up.'

May looked completely baffled as to what to do or say next to this man, shaking her head dazedly.

'I don't understand what went wrong,' David continued forcefully. 'One minute you were fine with everything that we had talked about, the plans we had made, and the next—'

'How many times does she have to tell you she's not interested?' Jude cut in coldly, stepping forward slightly to drape a proprietorial arm about May's narrow shoulders. Too narrow, he realised frowningly. She really was too thin, too delicate, to live the hard-working life that she so obviously did.

David's gaze became guarded as he looked at that possessive arm about her shoulders. 'And you would be...?' he prompted slowly.

'I would be a friend of May's,' Jude answered harshly.

'I see,' the other man murmured, obviously not seeing at all as he turned to look questioningly at May.

'I would really much rather not talk about this any more, David,' she told him regretfully. 'I-it was a nice dream while it lasted,' she added wistfully. 'But it really isn't for me. I'm sorry.' She grimaced.

Her visitor drew in a ragged breath, hunching his shoulders as he thrust his hands into the pockets of his sheepskin jacket. 'I'm not giving up,' he assured her decisively. 'I'll be back.' He nodded firmly. 'Perhaps we can talk then.'

'I wouldn't count on it,' Jude put in raspingly, his patience wearing very thin where this man was concerned. Couldn't he see, and just accept, that May wasn't interested? That she wanted him to leave and not come back to bother her?

Was this how Max and Will had felt, too? he wondered a little dazedly; protective, but at the same time finding their Calendar woman incredibly attractive?

Except that May Calendar was not his woman. Would never be his woman. Not if he had anything to say about it. And he most certainly did.

'Are you staying with your sister again?' May was talking to the other man again now. 'I'll ring you there some time tomorrow,' she added quickly as she received confirmation of that fact with David's nod.

'I'll be waiting for your call,' he assured her huskily before turning his hard blue gaze on Jude. 'Goodnight,' he added coldly.

'Goodbye,' Jude returned with a challenging lift of his dark brows.

The other man gave a humourless smile of acknowledgement at the obviously male challenge before turning to walk across to his car, a sporty Jaguar, Jude noted with displeasure; obviously this David, whoever he was, was wealthy enough to help May if he wanted to. And, from their conversation, he obviously did.

And yet she seemed uninterested in whatever the other man had to offer, so perhaps—

'And just what the hell did you think you were doing just now?' May's angry challenge was accompanied by the slamming of the door as she turned to face him, her cheeks fiery red with anger, her eyes glittering deeply green.

He raised mocking brows at the unexpected attack. 'Trying to be helpful?' he prompted pointedly. 'The man was obviously bothering you, and so I—'

'Helpful? Helpful?' she repeated incredulously, hands clenched at her sides. 'Can you drive a tractor?'

He blinked frowningly. 'Unfortunately not.'

'Milk a cow?'

He grimaced. 'Definitely not!'

'Nurse a weak lamb?'

He shrugged. 'Probably not.'

'Feed the hens and collect the eggs?'

He drew in an impatient breath, knowing exactly where this conversation was going. 'Look, May—'

'No, of course you can't do any of those things!' she answered her own questions impatiently. 'But I can, and I do. And *those* are the only ways that you could possibly be of any help to me, Mr Marshall,' she told him scathingly. 'I really don't know where you got the impression that I'm some helpless female that needs rescuing—'

'Don't you?' he rasped pointedly.

She had the grace to blush, her exhausted condition earlier having been unmistakable. 'That was an exceptional circumstance,' she dismissed firmly. 'Now, if you wouldn't mind leaving…?' She stood pointedly away from the door, her expression challenging.

Jude gazed at her frustratedly. She really was the most—

Were those tears he could see in those incredible green eyes? And if so, were they tears of sheer frustration with all the work she had to do, or were they for some other reason?

'We haven't finished our meal,' he pointed out softly.

She gave a shake of her head. 'I'm afraid I've completely lost my appetite.'

'May—'

'Will you just go?' she cried emotionally, the tears welling against the darkness of her lashes now.

'No—I won't just go,' he answered impatiently. 'May, I don't think for one minute that you're a helpless female.' How could he, when she had obviously been the female mainstay of this household since she was nothing but a child herself? 'But you are wrecked, anyone can see that from just looking at you—'

'Thanks!' she snapped scathingly.

He sighed heavily. 'There's just no reasoning with you, is there?'

'None at all,' she bit out coldly.

Jude shook his head. He had never met a woman like May Calendar before. Had never felt like shaking and kissing a woman at the same time before, either—

Kissing…?

Damn it, yes, he wanted to kiss May Calendar! Wanted to sweep her up into his arms and kiss her until she was senseless. Until they were both senseless.

Which was why he most certainly wasn't going to do it!

'Fine,' he rasped harshly, picking up his jacket from

the back of the chair before walking determinedly to the door. 'Any message for Max or your sister if he should happen to telephone again?' he challenged hardly, already knowing from her reaction earlier to his casual mention of having spoken to Max that she did not want her youngest sister to know she was coping alone here.

She swallowed hard, her cheeks suddenly pale now. 'No—' she moistened dry lips '—no message. Except—'

'Yes?' He paused at the door.

She gave the ghost of a smile. 'You could tell January that Ginny and the twins are all doing well. The ewe from last night, and her two lambs,' she explained ruefully at his puzzled frown.

Jude gave an acknowledging inclination of his head, not having particularly enjoyed scoring that point, where Max and January were concerned, over a woman who was so exhausted she could hardly see straight. 'I would get that early night if I were you, May—before you fall over!' he rasped.

She gave a shake of her head. 'I still have things to do.'

He gave an impatient shrug at her stubbornness. 'Your choice,' he bit out harshly. 'But, from the look of things, they will still be there for you to do all over again tomorrow.'

She gave the hint of a smile. 'My father used to say that.'

Used to. Because, as Jude now knew only too well, having checked up on the Calendar sisters a little more thoroughly after Max had got himself engaged to one of them, neither of the Calendar parents were still alive, the mother having died while the three girls were still very young, the father only a year ago.

Which really made him feel good about trying to buy the farm out from under them!

'Then you should have listened to him!' he rasped, no longer sure whether it was May or himself that he was angry with.

One thing he did know, he needed to get this whole thing back into perspective, to concentrate on his objective, which was to buy this land and then leave.

And, to do that, he had to get away from May Calendar.

Besides, April would be waiting for him back at the hotel. Charming, entertaining, thoroughly agreeable April.

May Calendar looked at him unblinkingly. 'I did listen to him, Mr Marshall, but I don't have to listen to you—'

'That's it!' His patience, what there was of it, had been blown completely at her determined continuation of the formal 'Mr Marshall'. Damn it, he had tried to be kind to her—even though she would so obviously have preferred that he wasn't—to be reasonable; he had even bought her dinner.

With no ulterior motive? a little voice taunted inside his head.

And what if there had been? She could still have been a little more grateful than she had.

May eyed him mockingly now. 'That's what, Mr Marshall?' She smiled tauntingly.

'This,' he bit out forcefully—seconds before he swept her up into his arms and kissed that mocking smile right off her lips.

Mistake, Jude, he admitted with an inward groan. Mistake!

She tasted of honey. Her lips were soft and responsive—probably because she was too surprised to do anything else, he acknowledged ruefully, even as he moulded her body against his, the warmth of her breasts crushed against his chest, the dark swathe of her silky hair falling down over his arm as he tilted her head back to deepen the kiss.

Nectar.

Sweet, sweet, nectar.

So intent was he on tasting that nectar that he didn't at first notice the tiny fists pummelling against his chest, only coming to a full awareness of her resistance as she wrenched her lips away from his to glare up at him.

'Let go of me,' she ordered furiously, pushing ineffectually at his chest now. 'You—you—'

'Yes?' he derided challengingly even as his arms dropped back to his sides and he stepped away from her.

It had taken several seconds to get his own raging emotions back under control, but now that he had…

Exactly what had he thought he was doing? Okay, so May was beautiful, immensely desirable, challenging— but she was also, in this particular situation, the opposition!

She put up a hand to her slightly swollen lips, her eyes wide and accusing as she looked up at him. 'I have no idea where you thought such behaviour was going to get you, but… Get out,' she told him quietly, shaking her head dazedly. 'Just get out.'

Oh, he was going, intended putting as much distance between himself and this woman as possible.

She was dangerous. To his self-control. To his self-preservation. To his self-possessed existence!

He gave her a deliberately mocking smile. 'Don't feel too bad about responding, May,' he said tauntingly. 'You won't be the first woman to do so—or the last,' he added derisively.

If anything her face paled even more, those glittering green eyes the only colour in her face now. 'Get out!' she repeated between clenched teeth.

Jude calmly bent to pick up the jacket he had dropped seconds ago to take her into his arms, easily holding her accusing gaze as he put the jacket on, deliberately taking his time, much to her obvious impatience.

'Have something else to eat, May,' he drawled as he walked to the door. 'It would be a pity to waste all that food just because you don't like the person who bought it for you,' he added dryly.

'Goodbye, Mr Marshall,' she said as pointedly as he had to the man called David a few minutes ago.

Jude paused in the open doorway. 'Oh, not goodbye, May,' he assured her grimly. 'Unlike my—associates, I don't intend leaving until I've done what I came here to do.'

She gave a scornful laugh. 'Then I would suggest you start looking to buy a house in the area—because I'm not interested in selling the farm, to you or anyone else.'

'No, you're obviously not,' he accepted lightly. 'But your sisters may feel differently now that they are both engaged to be married.'

Jude regretted having made this last challenge even as he made it. He saw the way her cheeks paled once again, that slightly haunted look in those deep green eyes telling him that she was no longer as sure of her sisters' feelings in the matter as she wanted him to think she was.

Making him feel like a complete heel.

Oh, he was determined, forceful, had never let a business challenge get the better of him, but he had never considered himself to be deliberately cruel before.

What the hell was wrong with him?

May Calendar, with her big green eyes, her magnolia skin, her air of fragility, that was what was wrong with him.

And it stopped right now!

'Have a nice day,' he told her glibly, closing the door softly behind him before strolling over to get back into his hire car.

Damn, damn, *damn*!

CHAPTER THREE

'THIS is very kind of you, David.' May smiled shyly across at him as they sat in the bar of the hotel restaurant while waiting to go to their table. 'But I'm afraid it's just a waste of your time, that it isn't going to change anything,' she added with a rueful shake of her head.

'I don't consider having dinner with a beautiful woman as time wasted,' David Melton assured her huskily, blue gaze warm in the rugged handsomeness of his face.

He was so nice; that was what made all of this so difficult. That, and the fact that May really would have loved to accept the part in his forthcoming film he had repeatedly offered her. But, for reasons she had no intention of telling him—or, indeed, anyone else—the whole thing was simply impossible.

But she had kept her promise to telephone David at his sister's earlier today, had repeated what she had told him in London a couple of weeks ago, and again yesterday evening, only to have him ask her to come out to dinner with him this evening. No pressure, he had assured her as she'd hesitated, just a friendly dinner together, when he wouldn't even mention the film role if she would rather he didn't.

It had been too tempting an offer for her to refuse, David extremely handsome as well as being a charmingly interesting man. And with the added incentive not to mention the film role...

And now she had been the one to introduce the subject...!

Primarily because she felt so guilty about the time David had taken to give her the screen test a couple of weeks ago—only to have her turn down his offer after that test had proved successful.

To be offered a film role, on the basis of one performance in a local pantomime, was the stuff that actresses' dreams were made of, and May knew that David must wonder at her sanity for having turned down such an offer.

'Does your reluctance concerning playing the role of Stella have anything to do with the man I met last night?' David prompted lightly, looking at her over the top of his glass as he took a sip of the white wine he had ordered for them both as a pre-dinner drink.

'The man you— Oh.' May grimaced as she realised exactly whom he was talking about. 'No,' she assured him with a firm shake of her head. 'Jude is a total irrelevance to this situation— What's so funny?' she prompted with a puzzled frown as he gave a husky chuckle.

He gave a rueful shake of his head. 'I doubt that particular man has ever considered himself an irrelevance in any situation!' he explained dryly.

May smiled at what she was sure was an accurate observation where Jude Marshall was concerned. 'No, I'm sure that he hasn't,' she agreed. 'But in this case, he is,' she insisted firmly.

David gave her a puzzled glance. 'Who is he, exactly?'

She knew what he was—exactly! Jude Marshall was a sneaky opportunist, a man who had taken advantage of her extreme tiredness the evening before; more importantly—he was trying to buy their farm out from under them.

'No one of any importance,' she dismissed hardly, remembering all too clearly that Jude had kissed her yesterday evening. Worse—she remembered that she had kissed him back.

She had been too surprised initially to do anything but stand in shocked immobility in Jude's arms, but, once the shock had worn off, instead of pushing him away, as she should have done, she had responded. That was something she wasn't about to forgive him for in a hurry!

'I'm glad to hear it.' But David still didn't look totally convinced by her dismissal of Jude.

Time to change the subject, May decided—in fact, it was past time! 'Are you staying in the area long?'

David shrugged. 'Another couple of days or so, I think. May—' he sat forward, his gaze suddenly intense '—there's someone I would like you to meet while I'm here.'

Her eyes widened. 'There is?' As far as she was aware, the only people that David knew in the area were her and his sister's family, and surely he didn't want to introduce her to them?

She found him good company, had enjoyed the time they'd spent together when she'd gone to London for her screen test a couple of weeks ago, but this was the first time the two of them had gone out on anything resembling a social basis...

'Yes.' He was still watching her intently. 'You see—'

'Well, well, well, so you don't spend *all* your time milking cows and feeding hens, after all,' an all-too-familiar voice drawled mockingly.

May closed her eyes briefly, taking a deep breath before answering; Jude Marshall was positively the last person she had wanted to meet this evening. Well… maybe not the last person, she conceded frowningly, but he came pretty close.

'Mr Marshall,' she greeted wearily, deliberately keeping her expression noncommittal as she looked up at him.

Which wasn't easy when he looked so devastatingly attractive!

She had thought David handsome in his dark suit and blue shirt when they'd met in the foyer of the hotel earlier, but Jude Marshall in a dinner suit was something else; his shoulders were wide, his waist tapered, his legs long and lean, the snowy white of his shirt emphasising the golden tan of his face and hands, those grey eyes appearing almost silver against that tanned skin.

May straightened determinedly. She was not going to sit here like some gauche schoolgirl overwhelmed by a handsome, sophisticated man. Even if that was how she felt…

'Or wearing wellington boots and woollen hats,' she returned dismissively, knowing that she at least looked presentable this evening.

Jude's gaze swept assessingly over her appearance, grey eyes narrowed as he took in her newly washed hair as it swayed silkily over her shoulders, her dark green dress shimmering against her slender curves to reveal the silky length of her legs.

His gaze returned deliberately to her face. 'Obviously not,' he drawled before turning slowly to look at the man who sat with her. 'I don't believe we've been introduced…?' He raised dark brows pointedly.

Other than behaving as rudely to Jude as he had to

him the previous evening, May knew that David had no choice but to stand up and introduce himself.

'David Melton.' He held out his hand politely.

'Jude Marshall,' Jude returned as economically, an edge of mockery to his voice as he looked at the other man assessingly. 'Melton…?' he repeated slowly. 'Now where have I—?'

'I believe our table is ready, David,' May cut in forcefully even as she rose gracefully to her feet, having noticed the waiter hovering around in the background trying to attract their attention. 'If you'll excuse us, Jude…' she added decisively, green gaze challenging on his.

He returned that gaze steadily for several long seconds, and then his gaze slowly dropped down the slender length of her body. By the time his gaze returned to her face, May could feel the heated wings of colour in her cheeks.

As well as a slight trembling of her limbs, and a shortness of breath, as if she had been running…

'You're dining at the hotel?' he prompted sharply.

May suffered a sinking feeling in the pit of her stomach. It had never occurred to her, when David had asked her to join him here for dinner, that, being the best hotel in the area, this was probably the hotel Jude Marshall was staying at. But it occurred to her now.

It also occurred to her, from the way he was dressed, that Jude Marshall was dining here, too. And not alone, if the formality of the dinner suit was anything to go by.

'Obviously.' She eyed him challengingly. 'And you?'

'Obviously,' he returned dryly. 'I'm just waiting for my dining companion,' he confirmed lazily. 'Perhaps the four of us could get together for a drink after we've eaten?' Dark brows rose challengingly over those mocking grey eyes.

And perhaps they couldn't! She was here with David, and it was pretty obvious that Jude's dining companion was going to be a beautiful woman; the last thing she wanted was to sit and have a drink with the pair of them at the end of the evening. It would probably choke her.

'I don't think so—thank you,' she added belatedly. 'Some of us have to get up early in the morning,' she added pointedly.

'Thanks for the offer, anyway,' David cut in cheerfully before the other man could come back with the cutting reply that was obviously hovering on those sculptured lips, David taking a firm hold of May's arm as they turned to follow the waiter into the dining-room.

And May could feel that icy grey gaze following them every step of the way.

Her breath left her in a heavy sigh as she sat down at the table, the first indication that she had of having held it in, her legs feeling slightly shaky, too. But Jude Marshall had that effect on her, she acknowledged heavily; she seemed to want to either hit him or kiss him at any given moment—and just now the former had definitely won out.

'I'm really sorry about that.' She gave David a rueful smile. 'I'm starting to feel as if that man is haunting me!' Both waking and asleep.

Sleep, despite her exhausted state, had been very hard to come by the previous night, thoughts of Jude Marshall, of the way he had kissed her, preventing her from drifting into a relaxed state.

What on earth had prompted him to kiss her at all? Oh, she knew that he was angry with her, a frustrated anger, at her total indomitableness. But she wouldn't have thought that was reason enough for him to have kissed her…?

David shrugged. 'He is rather—forceful.'

That was one way of describing him! All that May really knew at this moment was that her evening was completely ruined, the very fact that Jude was eating in the same room as her enough to put her off her food. Or to relax enough to enjoy David's company.

She sighed. 'He's a nuisance,' she acknowledged heavily.

David gave her a searching glance. 'Would you rather we ate somewhere else?'

She gave him an incredulous look. 'We can't do that!'

'Of course we can,' he assured her mildly.

May shook her head dazedly. 'But—but—we've ordered our food, and—and everything!' Even now she could see the waiter heading towards their table with their first course.

David shrugged. 'So we'll unorder it. The last thing I want, May,' he continued firmly as she would have protested again, 'is for you to feel under some sort of strain. The idea of this evening was for us to have a sociable dinner together, to relax and get to know each other a little better. Something we obviously aren't going to be able to do with Jude Marshall in the room.' He put his napkin down on the table and stood up to talk quietly to the waiter, the latter looking completely nonplussed as he returned to the kitchen still carrying the plates of food. 'I'll be back in two minutes,' David promised before striding over to the *maître d'*.

May watched him dazedly, hardly able to believe that David was willing to go to another restaurant just because he sensed how uncomfortable she was now that she knew Jude Marshall was dining here, too.

But as she saw Jude enter the dining-room at that moment, the beautiful woman who moved so gracefully at his side, she knew that there was no way she could have remained here now even if David had wanted to do so.

The woman was tall and slender, her ebony dark hair cut stylishly short, the glowing beauty of her face dominated by luminous green eyes, her mouth a pouting invitation, the low-necked dress she wore revealing a creamy expanse of shoulders and breasts, her legs long and slender.

There was no doubting that, despite being in her forties, the woman was absolutely stunning, and as she and Jude walked to their table every pair of eyes in the room followed their progress.

Except May's.

After that first glance she had got hastily to her feet, not waiting for David to return but rushing quickly from the room, not stopping until she reached the relative sanctuary of the foyer, her breath coming in short gasps, her pulse racing so fast she could feel the blood pulsing through her veins.

What on earth was *she* doing here?

'Coward!' Jude murmured huskily.

May's shoulders had stiffened as she forked fresh hay into the lambing pens, so he knew she was aware of his presence behind her, but she made no effort to turn and answer his accusation.

Because accusation it most certainly was.

Jude hadn't been able to believe it when, having seen April seated opposite him at the dining table the previous evening, he had turned to glance around the restaurant in search of May and her own dining companion.

Only to find that she hadn't been there!

His mouth tightened. 'May, I said—'

'I heard what you said.' She turned sharply to face him, her features set in cool challenge as she looked at him questioningly.

He raised mocking dark brows. 'Well?'

'Well what?' she returned scathingly.

'Don't let's start that again!' He gave a disgusted shake of his head. 'Why did you leave the hotel so suddenly yesterday evening?'

'Did I?' she returned dismissively, obviously completely ignoring his frustration with the way she answered his questions with one of her own. Deliberately so? Probably, he acknowledged heavily.

Jude scowled. 'You know damn well you did.'

'We left the restaurant, Jude,' she corrected dryly. 'That doesn't mean we left the hotel,' she added pointedly.

Jude's scowl deepened as he easily understood her implication, his narrowed gaze searching on her almost defiant expression. If May were to be believed, then instead of eating she and David Melton had gone upstairs together to one of the hotel bedrooms…

'Besides,' she continued hardly, 'I'm surprised you even noticed our departure considering the identity of your own dining companion.' The last was added scornfully.

It wasn't easy, but Jude forced visions of May in David Melton's arms from his mind—for the present! He would get back to that subject in a moment.

His smile was mocking now. 'Ah, you recognised her,' he murmured with satisfaction.

May gave a derisive laugh. 'Along with everyone else in the room! But then, how could anyone not recognise the beautiful actress, April Robine?'

Jude wasn't sure he liked that scornful edge to May's

voice when she spoke of April. He had known the beautiful actress for several months now, had never found her to be anything other than warm and charming, her patience infinite with the fans who so often intruded upon her privacy. Even yesterday evening as they had been eating their meal, several people had come over to their table to ask for her autograph, and none of them had gone away disappointed, in April or the acquired autograph.

'Your friend David certainly found her charming when he came over to our table to say hello,' he bit out caustically.

May was too startled by the statement to be able to hide the emotion, her cheeks paling slightly, her eyes a deeper green than usual. 'I don't know what you mean.' She shook her head dismissively.

'I mean that April and your friend David apparently know each other,' he bit out abruptly, having been surprised himself when David Melton had come over to their table to be greeted so effusively by April. 'In fact, from the warmth with which they kissed each other yesterday evening, you might say they know each other very well!'

Jude frowned as May seemed to pale even more. Two days ago May had assured him that she wasn't interested in David Melton; in fact she had insisted, despite the other man's obvious entreaties, that David Melton meant nothing to her. And yet her reaction now to the other man's acquaintance with the beautiful April seemed to imply otherwise…

May moistened dry lips before visibly swallowing hard. 'What does that have to do with me?'

He looked at her consideringly. 'Everything, I would have thought—if your implication that you and David spent the night together at the hotel is the correct one!' he rasped.

She drew in a sharp breath. 'For your information, I slept in my own bed last night!'

'Meaning that you and Melton only spent the evening in bed together at the hotel?' Jude scorned.

'Meaning that it's none of *your* damned business where I spent yesterday evening!' she returned forcefully.

He was going to shake her in a minute. Or kiss her again. Neither of which was a good idea.

He had learnt that only too well two days ago, could still feel the softness of her lips as they responded to his, the warmth of her curves as her body moulded against his. The very thought of David Melton enjoying those lips and her desirable softness was enough to make him forget everything else. And he didn't want to feel that way. Not over this woman. Or any other woman.

He drew in a deeply controlling breath. 'May, I actually came here to ask you to have dinner with me this evening.'

She straightened, eyeing him mockingly. 'Really?'

'Really,' he confirmed dryly.

May gave a shake of her head. 'Then you have a very strange way of going about it.'

Because he had been sidetracked by talk of her friendship with David Melton.

But it was time to forget about Melton, and April, and concentrate on what he really wanted from this woman.

'Okay,' he sighed frustratedly. 'Let's start again, shall we? May, will you have dinner with me this evening?'

'No,' she answered without hesitation, her gaze mocking. 'And just why is it that everyone seems to think I need to have dinner bought for me at the moment?' she added frowningly.

'Probably because you look as if a few good meals inside you wouldn't come amiss!' Jude's gaze moved deliberately down her obvious slenderness.

'Thanks,' she snapped. 'But the answer is still no!'

He scowled at her stubbornness. 'David Melton has booked you for this evening, too, hmm?'

'No—that's lunch,' she told him derisively, obviously enjoying his frustration.

Jude eyed her scathingly. 'So who's the lucky man tonight?'

'Do you mean to be insulting, Jude?' She quirked dark brows. 'Or does it just come naturally to you?'

His mouth twisted humourlessly. 'A little of both, I think.'

To his surprise she laughed softly, her eyes glowing deeply green, slight dimples beside the soft curve of her lips. God, she was beautiful, he acknowledged frowningly. Wearing no make-up that he could detect, her hair scraped back in an elastic band, wearing those awful clothes she worked in, and she was still beautiful. Too beautiful!

'Perhaps you wouldn't mind answering my question?' he rasped caustically.

She gave a slight shake of her head. 'I thought I already had. You asked me to have dinner with you, and I said no. Although I'm curious as to why you think you would ever have received any other sort of answer?' She looked at him searchingly.

'Because your mother brought you up to be polite?' he returned dryly—realising, too late, that her mother hadn't brought her up at all, that she had died while the three sisters were still babies.

May's eyes were now as hard as the jewels they re-sembled, her mouth unsmiling. 'Any manners I have cer-tainly weren't taught me by my mother,' she snapped coldly. 'Although, again, I'm curious as to why you should think I would feel the need to be in the least polite to you?' she added with hard derision.

'Because I bought you dinner the other evening?' Jude shrugged, starting to find it decidedly warm in here in the thick Aran sweater and faded blue denims that he was wearing.

May gave him a quizzical look. 'In that case, shouldn't I be the one asking you out to dinner? To return the favour?'

'Not the most gracious invitation I've ever received—but I accept,' Jude told her, eyes gleaming with satis-faction.

She looked stunned by the deliberate trap he had set—and that she had unwittingly walked into. 'Now just a minute—'

'Too late, May,' he told her lightly. 'You asked, I accepted.'

'I did not—'

'You most certainly did,' he assured her mockingly, enjoying being the one to have completely disconcerted her this time.

'But I have an Amateur Dramatics meeting to go to this evening!' she protested frustratedly.

'Then I suggest you cancel it,' he dismissed uncon-cernedly. 'I'll leave you to book the restaurant, shall I? I prefer French cuisine if possible, but if not—'

'If you really expect me to give you dinner then you'll get May cuisine, you'll get it here—and like it!' she interrupted impatiently. 'Although—'

'Sounds great,' Jude accepted. 'About seven-thirty suit you?'

'Yes, but—'

'I'll bring the wine,' he continued happily, enjoying her dazed expression. 'Do you prefer red or white?'

'White. But—'

'Seven-thirty, then, May.' He nodded decisively.

May gave him a look of complete exasperation. 'You are the most arrogant, manipulative man it has ever been my misfortune to meet!' she finally burst out frustratedly.

He grinned. 'Takes one to know one,' he returned lightly.

Her eyes widened indignantly. 'I am not in the least arrogant or manipulative.'

'No?' he mocked. 'Well, perhaps I don't know you well enough yet to give a learned opinion,' he allowed softly.

Her eyes flashed angrily. 'And perhaps you never will know me well enough to give a learned opinion!'

He shrugged. 'We'll have to wait and see, won't we?' he dismissed. 'I'll leave you to get on with your work now, as you appear to have a date for lunch today, too,' he added hardly.

For someone who claimed she wasn't in the least interested in David Melton, May seemed to be seeing rather a lot of the other man. Not that it was any of his business, Jude reminded himself frowningly. It was probably just another example of what he considered to be the woman's contrariness!

'How kind of you,' May snapped back, obviously still angry at having been trapped into giving him dinner.

'I thought so.' Jude nodded, deciding this was probably a good time for him to leave.

After all, he would be seeing May later this evening, when they would hopefully have the time to talk more calmly about the offer he had made on this farm.

'With two good meals inside you today, you might actually start to put some weight on those bones, and so look a little less like a waif and stray,' he added hardly.

May was incredibly beautiful, breathtakingly so, but it was a beauty edged with an air of frailty, a certain look of delicacy that didn't suit the hard work she had to do living on a farm.

Although she didn't look too delicate at this moment, Jude acknowledged ruefully; instead she looked as if she would like to pick up the pitchfork she was still holding and stab him through the chest with it.

'For your information,' she bit out through gritted teeth, 'I am naturally slender! We all are,' she added defensively.

Jude gave her a considering look. 'I obviously can't speak for your sisters, May, never having met them,' he said dryly. 'But there's slender, and then there's gaunt— and I know which category you fit into at this moment!' he assured her dismissively.

'And when I want your opinion, Jude, I'll ask for it!' She turned her back on him and once again began forking the straw over in the empty pens.

Obviously that was the end of this particular conversation!

Jude gave a shrug, quite happy with what he had already achieved today. After all, she had called him Jude just now without any prompting from him. And with the promise of seeing May again this evening, he had every hope of achieving much more.

It was only once he was back in his car, driving down the rutted track that led up to the farm, that he realised

May, with this infuriating habit she had of answering his questions with one of her own, hadn't actually given him a sensible answer as to the reason she had left the restaurant so hastily the evening before…

CHAPTER FOUR

'FEELING better?' David prompted concernedly as the
two of them sat in the bar of a pub not far from the
farm.

'Much, thank you,' May answered huskily, guilty
warmth entering her cheeks as she did so, not quite able
to meet David's gaze, either.

She had been in an agitated state the previous evening
when David had left the restaurant and joined her in the
foyer of the hotel, able to feel it as her cheeks had first
paled and then reddened, her eyes glittering brightly, as
if with a fever, her movements agitated as she'd paced
up and down waiting for him.

In the circumstances, it hadn't been too difficult for
David to believe the lie that she hadn't been feeling well,
that she would rather cancel dinner altogether and just
go home.

And it hadn't been a complete lie, May had consoled
herself; she had felt sick, and there was no way she could
have eaten anything feeling the way that she had.

But she had agreed to have lunch with David today
only as a means of escaping yesterday evening, still felt
too nauseous to contemplate eating anything.

And Jude Marshall's visit to the farm this morning, a
stark reminder of yesterday evening, had done little to
alleviate that feeling!

She moistened dry lips. 'You said yesterday, David,
that there is someone you would like me to meet…?'

'Why, yes.' He looked surprised at the change of subject.

May nodded. 'I believe I know who that someone is. And I have to tell you—'

'May, I simply thought over what we discussed in London a couple of weeks ago—' David sat forward in his seat, looking at her intently '—and I realised that you seemed to change after I had told you who the stars of the film were to be.' He gave her a sympathetic smile. 'I realise that working with big stars like Dan Howard and April Robine must have sounded a little overwhelming. But Dan is a great chap to work with, and as for April—'

'Jude mentioned that you went over to their table and spoke to her at the restaurant yesterday evening,' May put in stiltedly, if only to let him know how she had guessed who his 'someone' was.

David raised surprised brows. 'He did?'

'He did,' she confirmed, not about to get into a discussion about exactly when Jude had told her that; sufficient to say that May now knew exactly who David wanted her to meet while he was still in the area.

She also knew exactly why that meeting would never take place.

'I'm not in the least overwhelmed at the thought of working with April Robine, David,' she told him hardly, her jaw tightly clenched on her emotions. 'And I certainly have no desire to meet her,' she added harshly.

'But—'

'That is the end of the matter as far as I'm concerned,' May cut in decisively. 'You've been very kind.' Her voice softened slightly as she saw how hurt and confused David now looked. He was hurt and confused! 'But my answer is still no.'

David looked troubled. 'If you would just talk to April you would see—'

'No!' May cut in sharply, drawing in a deeply controlling breath as David looked stunned by her vehemence. 'I'm sorry—' she frowned '—but I really don't want this.'

There was no way she could tell him how much she didn't want it! But he at least had to believe how strongly she felt about all this. Without her actually having to spell the situation out in black and white…

Something she had no intention of doing. To anybody.

But David was perfectly correct in his assessment as to when her attitude to appearing in his film had changed. And it had nothing to do with Dan Howard!

David looked decidedly uncomfortable now. 'April really is a very charming woman.'

'I'm sure she is,' May bit out evenly.

'May—'

'David, I do apologize for being late,' interrupted a huskily breathless voice. 'We left in good time, but we had a little difficulty in finding the place.' The woman gave a ruefully dismissive laugh.

May had frozen into immobility at the first sound of that voice, couldn't breathe, couldn't move, certainly couldn't turn and look at the woman who had just joined them.

But she knew who it was, that huskily attractive voice unmistakable.

April Robine…

May had no doubts that David had set her up, had deliberately arranged for the actress to meet them here— in fact, the other woman's words confirmed that he had. No wonder David had looked so stricken seconds ago at May's vehement refusal to meet the famous actress.

May shot David an accusing glare as he looked at her concernedly before standing up to greet the other woman, every muscle in May's body tensed, all the air seeming to have been knocked out of her lungs as she shook badly.

This couldn't be happening!

It just couldn't be happening!

Her worst nightmare—but it was all too real!

May had thought, with her refusal of the part in David's film, that she had avoided this ever happening, that she could put it all from her mind once again. And, instead, she now found herself confronted with a woman she had no desire to meet—ever!

'May,' Jude Marshall greeted mockingly.

Now she did move, turning sharply in her seat to see Jude standing next to April Robine, his expression one of taunting challenge. Answering the 'we' in April Robine's initial statement...

But at least while May was looking at Jude she didn't have to look at the actress who stood at his side.

She was nevertheless completely aware of the other woman, could hear her talking softly to David, could smell the perfume she wore. A perfume that made May's head spin!

'Are you okay, May?' The mockery left Jude's face as he looked down at her concernedly.

'Of course I'm okay,' she replied brittlely as she stood up, willing the dizziness to dissipate; she was not going to faint. She was not! 'I didn't expect to see you here,' she added with husky rebuke.

He could so easily have told her earlier that he knew she wasn't lunching alone with David, that he and April Robine were to join them—giving May the opportunity not to appear!

But, then, maybe Jude had realised that? If not the actual reason for it...

'I didn't want to ruin the surprise for you,' Jude came back mockingly.

May gave a shaky sigh. 'These sort of surprises I can well do without.'

The humour left Jude's eyes as he looked down at her searchingly. 'You really don't look well, you know,' he finally murmured.

Her head went back challengingly. 'Maybe I'm just overwhelmed—' to use David's word! '—at finding myself in such exalted company!' she bit out scathingly.

This was awful. Terrible. Any second now she knew that David was going to introduce her to April Robine. What would the other woman's reaction be to such an introduction? Would she be as horrified as May was? Or something else? Whatever April Robine's reaction to meeting May, May had no doubts that the actress would hide it much better than she could.

Jude gave a slow shake of his head. 'I don't think too much overwhelms you, May,' he murmured frowningly.

He was right, it didn't. She had decided long ago that she was as good as anyone else, that she could do anything she chose to do, that nothing and no one had the power to unnerve her.

With the exception of April Robine...

'May—' David turned to lightly clasp her arm, drawing her to his side '—I would like to introduce you to April Robine. April, this is May Calendar,' he introduced happily.

May looked the other woman full in the face for the first time, the actress's beauty indisputable, her hair a short black cap surrounding flawless features, very slender in a deep green cashmere sweater and fitted black trousers, looking nowhere near middle-aged, which May knew the other woman to be.

There was also no hint of recognition in the other woman's eyes as she calmly returned May's gaze.

Jude watched May concernedly as the introductions were made, her cheeks unnaturally pale, green eyes appearing huge against that paleness. He was convinced, no matter what she might claim to the contrary, that something was seriously wrong with her.

'Miss Robine,' she was greeting now, the words forced through her clenched jaw.

'Oh, please do call me April,' the beautiful actress requested with her usual warmth. 'And may I call you May?'

Jude was still watching May, saw the nerve pulsing in her throat as she swallowed convulsively. What on earth—?

'I would rather you called me Miss Calendar,' she answered the other woman abruptly. 'As I would rather call you Miss Robine,' she added dismissively.

What on earth was wrong with her? Jude finished his earlier thought incredulously in the tense silence that followed May's rude statement.

May had been annoyed with him when they'd first met, had plenty of reason to dislike him, but even so she had never spoken to him in this coldly dismissive voice. From the little he had come to know of her the last few days, he doubted she had ever spoken to anyone quite like this before.

Maybe he should have prewarned her about this meeting, after all; it would certainly have given her time to get used to the idea.

She was probably just nervous, he allowed. After all,

April had been an internationally acclaimed actress since she'd taken Hollywood by storm almost twenty years ago, was recognised wherever she went, was highly respected by her fellow actors and the public alike. This must be a little like meeting an icon, someone you had thought untouchable as well as unreachable.

Yes, that had to be it. As soon as May realised how warm and friendly April was, she would start to relax. She might even start to enjoy herself…

'That's a ridiculous idea, May,' he dismissed lightly as he moved to hold back a chair for April to sit down. 'If we're all going to have lunch together—'

'Oh, but we aren't,' May answered him tautly, her bag clutched between tightly clenched fingers now. 'I'm afraid I've just remembered something else I have to do, so if you'll all excuse me—'

'No, we won't excuse you!' Jude was the one to answer sharply, David Melton looking on in mute shock, April appearing a little less than her normally composed self, too.

As well she might!

It was perfectly natural for May to feel nervous about meeting April; it wasn't acceptable for her to continue to be rude about it!

Jude drew in a deeply controlling breath, aware that the four of them were attracting a certain amount of attention now from the other people in this lounge bar—and not all of it was because they had recognised April. It must be obvious to even the casual observer that there was a definite air of tension between the four of them.

'Look, let's just all sit down and have a drink together,' Jude suggested lightly. 'We can discuss then whether or not we intend eating lunch, hmm?' He looked at May encouragingly.

She returned his gaze unblinkingly, her expression completely unreadable, her eyes cold. 'As I've already told you, I have something else I need to do.' Her cold mask slipped slightly as she turned to look at David Melton. 'I'm really sorry about this, David.' She spoke huskily. 'But I—you should have warned me!' She turned on her heel and almost ran across the room.

As if the devil himself were at her heels.

'May—'

'Leave her, Jude,' April said, reaching up to put a restraining hand on his arm as he would have turned to follow May from the room.

'Like hell I will!' he rasped, easily moving away, one glance at the hurt so visible in April's beautiful eyes enough to propel him into action.

Jude strode purposefully from the room, almost bumping into May as he found her standing just outside, closing the door behind him as he swung her round to face him. 'What the hell do you—?' He broke off his angry tirade, frowning darkly as he saw the tears coursing down her cheeks. 'May…?' He blinked his utter confusion with this whole situation.

'Leave me alone!' she choked, pulling away from him. 'All of you, just leave me alone!' She glared up at him. 'Go back inside to your—your friend!' she added accusingly, frantically searching through her handbag now for her car keys.

Jude looked down at her frustratedly, totally thrown by the tears still falling down her cheeks. He had followed her intending to give her a good shaking, to demand an explanation for her rude behaviour, but he could see by her tears that there was more going on here than he had at first realised.

'Is it because of what I said to you earlier about David

Melton's obvious pleasure at seeing April when he came over to our table at the restaurant yesterday evening?' he probed frowningly. 'Do you think he's involved with April? Is that what's upsetting you?'

'David..,?' May stared up at him uncomprehendingly. 'David?' she repeated impatiently. 'I don't know what you're talking about, Jude.' She shook her head dismissively, having at last found her car keys.

'I'm talking about the fact that you were damned rude in there just now.' He nodded in the direction of the bar.

'Was I rude to you?' May challenged hardly, eyes overbright.

'No, of course—'

'Was I rude to David?' she snapped.

'I wouldn't give a damn if you were rude to him—'

'Then it must have been April Robine I was rude to,' May bit out scornfully.

'You know very well that it was.' Jude was fast losing any patience he might still have had with her.

May eyed him mockingly. 'And that upsets you?'

'Of course it—' He broke off, taking several deeply controlling breaths. He never raised his voice in anger, never became angry if at all possible; anger had a habit of making logical thought impossible, behaviour irrational, and those were two things he didn't allow. 'May, for goodness' sake tell me what's wrong with you?' he prompted evenly.

'Wrong with me?' she repeated tauntingly. 'Why, nothing is *wrong with me*, Jude. I've already told you, I simply have something else I have to do.'

'So important that you have to go and do it right now? So urgent that you can't even sit down and have lunch with us first?' he said disbelievingly.

'Yes,' she answered flatly.

His mouth tightened. 'And the tears? I suppose they're for nothing, too?'

Her eyes flashed angrily. 'Let's leave my tears out of it—'

'No—let's not,' Jude rasped harshly, grasping her shoulders. 'I want to know what's going on, May—and you're going to tell me,' he assured her grimly.

'No-I-am-not!' she bit out between gritted teeth, at the same time trying to pull away from him.

Jude had no idea what all this was about, couldn't even begin to understand what was making her behave in this strange way. And he didn't like feeling in the dark in this way!

He stared down at her impotently, anger fighting with his sheer frustration over the situation. There was only one way he had found to subdue this woman—

'Let me go, Jude!' May ordered coldly, as if she had already guessed what his intention was.

'No.' He shook his head uncompromisingly. 'I— ouch!' He gave an involuntary cry of pain as May turned her head and bit the side of his hand, releasing her abruptly to look disbelievingly at the teethmarks clearly visible on his skin. 'What the hell did you do that for?' He looked at her dumbfoundedly.

She gave an unconcerned shrug. 'I asked you to release me, you refused—'

'And that was reason enough to bite me?' He scowled darkly.

May gave a humourless smile. 'It's okay, Jude, I'm not rabid or anything—'

'Going on the evidence of the last few minutes, I wouldn't be too sure about that!' he muttered disgustedly.

Her mouth tightened, her expression bleak. 'If you

want answers to your questions, Jude, then I suggest you go back in there and ask them of April Robine—although I can't guarantee they will be truthful ones,' she added scornfully.

Jude became suddenly still. April was the problem here, not David Melton, after all...?

Jude hated it when he didn't know what was going on. Hated it even more knowing May had no intention of enlightening him...

'Maybe I'll do that,' he said slowly.

'Fine,' May snapped hardly. 'Would you tell David—?'

'I'm not telling David anything!' Jude cut in scathingly. 'I'm not your messenger-boy, May; if you have something to say to David Melton, then go back in and tell him yourself!'

She drew in a sharp breath, glancing at the pub door, eyes so dark a green now they looked almost as black as the pupil. 'I'll pass, thank you,' she murmured huskily, grimacing slightly. 'I've already kept you from your lunch long enough,' she added dismissively.

Jude continued to stare at her frustratedly for several long seconds before giving a rueful shake of his head. 'I doubt any of us will feel like eating after what just happened!'

She gave a cool inclination of her head. 'That's your prerogative.'

'No, May—that's the situation you have created,' he rebuked harshly.

'I didn't create it—*she* did!' she returned forcefully, giving an impatient shake of her head as she seemed to realise she had said too much. 'I really do have to go, Jude,' she said shakily. 'I—you—you just don't understand!' she cried shakily.

'Then enlighten me!' he pressured frustratedly.

'I—I can't!' She shook her head firmly. 'I'm sorry, Jude. Really sorry,' she choked intensely before turning and hurrying over to unlock her car.

Jude made no move to re-enter the pub, stood in the porchway watching as May drove away, more confused by what had just happened than he would like to admit.

May had spoken just now as if she and April had already met before today, that it was some sort of past conflict between the two women that had caused her behaviour just now. And yet April's own behaviour hadn't implied any such conflict on her part, and she had made no mention on the way here of already being acquainted with May.

But perhaps April hadn't known it was May that David Melton had intended introducing her to today?

No, that didn't make any sense, either, because April had been as graciously charming as always even after the introductions had been made. So maybe the resentment was all on May's side, and for something so obscure April didn't even have knowledge of it?

Jude gave a puzzled shake of his head. It was one explanation for May's behaviour just now, but surely the two women must have met at some time for this situation to have developed, even if April seemed to have forgotten the incident?

Which gave rise to yet another puzzling question: how on earth could two such disparate women as May Calendar and April Robine have possibly met before? And when?

Although English, April had lived in America for almost twenty years, most of her work based there, too.

And as far as Jude was aware, May had rarely been away from her beloved farm, even for holidays.

Ask April for the answers he wanted to his questions, May had told him—but with a seeming certainty that those answers wouldn't be truthful ones...

CHAPTER FIVE

'MAY...'

May swayed slightly in the action of climbing down from the cab of the tractor she had just driven back into the yard.

Having hurried home several hours earlier from that luncheon appointment she had believed was with David alone, she had filled the rest of the afternoon and early evening with the regular but necessary jobs about the farm.

She had been expecting this visit, of course, but, even so, now that it had happened she still felt the shock of recognition moving chillingly down the length of her spine.

'May, I think the two of us need to talk—don't you?' April Robine prompted huskily.

May deliberately kept her back turned to the other woman, fighting to control the array of emotions she knew must be moving swiftly across her expressive face.

There had been no car visible in the yard a few moments ago to tell her of the other woman's presence here, no pre-warning of this confrontation. The only positive thing about it that May could see was that she was alone here on the farm, that neither of her sisters were here to witness this.

'May?'

She stiffened her spine, turning slowly to face the other woman as she continued to step down onto the cobbled yard, at the same time registering the red car

66

parked beside the garage, and so not visible to anyone entering from the lane. As May had done...

She looked up resentfully at the other woman. 'You knew I didn't want you to come here.' It was at once a statement and an accusation.

The actress looked less controlled than she had at lunchtime today, lines of strain beside her eyes, her face pale beneath her impeccable make-up, still dressed in the cashmere sweater and fitted black trousers she had worn earlier.

'In fact,' May continued derisively, 'I'm surprised you could still find your way here!'

April Robine flinched as May's deliberate taunt obviously hit home. 'I remember everything about this place, May—'

'Really?' she cut in scathingly. 'Then you'll remember the way out again, won't you?' She turned away, moving to unfasten the trailer from the back of the tractor, her hands shaking as much with rage as shock.

How dared this woman come here? How dared she!

No—she wouldn't cry. Wouldn't give this woman the satisfaction of knowing how much her mere presence here, of all places, hurt and upset her.

'Still here?' she taunted as she turned to find the actress standing as if frozen.

April Robine looked at her searchingly, her face having lost all colour now. 'I was sorry to hear about your father last year—'

'Were you?' May cut in hardly, her hands clenching at her sides. 'Were you really?' she repeated scornfully.

April's eyes flashed angrily at May's obvious scepticism. 'Yes, I was really,' she snapped. 'I—he was— James and I may have had our differences, but I never wished him any harm—'

'Oh, please,' May muttered disgustedly. 'Spare me the insincere platitudes!'

'They aren't insincere,' the actress sighed. 'Far from it. May, you were very young, you can have no idea—'

'No idea of what?' May glared at the other woman. 'Of my father's unhappiness because his wife had left him?' She gave a disbelieving shake of her head. 'I may have been ''very young'', as you put it, but I wasn't too young to see that my father lost the will to live himself after you left, that it was only because of his three children that he managed to carry on at all!' Her face was flushed, her eyes feverish, her breasts quickly rising and falling beneath her thick black sweater as she breathed agitatedly.

'They were my three children, too!' April cried emotionally, her hands raised appealingly.

May became very still, all anger leaving her as that chill once more settled down her spine.

January. March. May. Yes, they had been this woman's three children. And she had left them as well as their father, had walked out on all of them to follow a star, to become a star herself.

And two weeks ago David Melton had ironically offered May the film role of Stella, with April Robine playing the title role of Stella's mother!

May had been so excited when David, a well-established film director both in England and America, had picked her out of a local pantomime as a possible actress in the film he was shooting this summer, claiming that she was perfect for the part of Stella, the heroine's daughter. But all of that excitement had died the moment David had told her who was to play the part of her mother.

David had claimed May was perfect for the part.

Of course May was perfect for the part!

David couldn't know how perfect...

Because April Robine really *was* her mother!

For years she had denied that fact, by tacit agreement with her father had brought January and March up with the impression that their mother had died while they were still very young. Only to have the woman brought vividly back to life in this intrusive way!

May looked coldly at the other woman. 'Our mother is dead,' she stated flatly.

April gasped, her face paling even more. 'Is that what January and March think, too?' she choked disbelievingly.

'It's what we all think,' May assured her hardly. 'Only I know that my mother was a beautiful, selfish woman, who cared more about fame and fortune than she did for her husband and three young daughters. She died for all of us the moment she made that choice,' she added coldly.

April swallowed hard, her beautiful face pale and haggard as she looked every inch her forty-six years. 'I knew James hated me, but I never thought—'

'He didn't hate you,' May cut in incredulously. 'He loved you. Only you. Until the day he died,' she concluded emotionally, knowing it was the truth, that their father had never looked at another woman in the years after April had left him, that he had continued to love his ex-wife despite what she had done.

April closed her eyes briefly, swaying slightly. 'There didn't have to be a choice,' she breathed shakily. 'Your father—'

'I absolutely refuse to discuss my father with you!' May cut in forcefully, glaring at the other woman. 'I lived with him for over twenty years after you left, I saw what your leaving did to him—so don't presume to come here all these years later and tell me anything about him!' She breathed agitatedly.

The other woman swallowed hard. 'We have to talk, May—'

'Why do we?' she challenged. 'I have nothing to say to you. And, after all these years, I can't believe you have anything to say to me, either!' she added scathingly.

The beautiful face softened with emotion. 'Do you have any idea how I felt when David told me that the young woman he had picked out to play opposite me in his next film was called May Calendar?'

May grimaced scornfully. 'I can imagine!'

'No, you can't,' April contradicted softly.

'If it was anything like the way I felt when I learnt you were the star of the film, then, yes, I can!' May insisted hardly.

She had been so shocked, so stunned by the knowledge, that she had hurried home on the next train back to Yorkshire from her screen test in London, informing her sisters that she had turned down David's offer, and that she didn't wish to discuss the subject any further, knowing only too well David kept insisting why she was perfect to play opposite April Robine in the role of her daughter.

The actress shook her head. 'Somehow I don't think so,' she murmured softly. 'Tell me about January and March. Are they—?'

'They are none of your business!' May assured her hardly, wondering when this nightmare was going to be over.

April's mouth firmed determinedly. 'Jude tells me that they are engaged to marry two of his closest friends—'

'You've told Jude that we're your daughters?' May gasped disbelievingly.

The other woman raised derisive brows. 'What do you think?'

May gave a disgusted snort. 'I think you wouldn't want Jude, of all people, to know you have three daughters aged in their mid to late twenties!'

After all, Jude was around ten years younger than the woman he was obviously intimately involved with—to know that she had three such grown-up daughters, not that much younger than himself, would be a bit of a dampener on the relationship, May would have thought!

April frowned darkly. 'That isn't the reason I haven't told him. May, I don't know what impression you've formed of my being with Jude earlier today, but I can assure you—'

'I don't need or want your assurances, Miss Robine—on anything!' May cut in coldly. 'And neither do January and March—'

'You can't speak for them,' the other woman protested.

'In this case, yes, I can,' May said with certainty. 'They grew up all these years without a mother, they certainly don't need one now that they are about to marry the men they love!'

'Especially one like me, is that it?' April finished flatly.

'That's it.' May nodded firmly, wishing the other woman would just leave, the strain of these last few minutes beginning to tell. She turned away, not sure how much longer she was going to last before she broke down in tears.

This was her mother, for goodness' sake, the mother she had adored for the first five years of her life, the woman she had had to learn to live without after April had walked out on her husband and children to pursue her acting career. Just the smell of April's remembered perfume earlier today had been enough to make her head spin.

'I've given David my answer concerning the film role; I don't think we have anything more to say to each other?' Her expression was deliberately challenging.

'David tells me you're a very good actress,' April prompted huskily.

She shrugged. 'He seems to think so.'

April nodded. 'And exactly where do you think that acting talent came from?'

May's eyes flashed deeply green. 'The same place that January's singing talent and March's artistic one came from, I expect!' she snapped, knowing that none of them had inherited those talents from their staid, unimaginative father.

'January sings and March paints?' April murmured incredulously.

'Yes—but I'm sure we would all willingly give up those talents not to have you as our mother!' May came back insultingly.

April paled even more. 'Are you giving up your chance of stardom because I happen to be in the film, too?' The other woman gave a pained frown.

May gave her a scathing glance. 'Some of us do have our priorities in the proper order!'

April flinched at the deliberate taunt, her chin rising challengingly as she looked at May with narrowed eyes. 'You—' She broke off as both of them became aware of the sound of an approaching vehicle. 'Are you expecting anyone?' April prompted frowningly.

Jude!

It had to be him, a brief glance at her wrist-watch having told May that it was seven-thirty, the time Jude had said this morning that he would arrive for dinner this evening, with a bottle of white wine.

After their conversation at lunchtime she hadn't thought for a moment that Jude would keep their dinner engagement for this evening, but the timing was too much of a coincidence for it not to be him.

Damn!

What was she going to say about April Robine being here? More to the point, what was April Robine going to say about her own presence here?

Jude's foot almost slipped off the accelerator as he drove into the farmyard to see May and April standing there obviously deep in conversation.

What on earth was April doing here? A muddy farm-yard was positively the last place he would ever have expected to find the beautifully elegant actress, he acknowledged with amusement, the contrast between the two women even more extreme now that May was back in her working clothes, that woollen cap once again pulled down over her hair.

Remembering May's deliberate rudeness to the other woman earlier today, her absolute adamance that she had nothing to say to April, he was more than a little puzzled to find the two of them here together this evening…

He parked his car beside April's red one, getting out to slowly walk over to join them. 'Ladies,' he greeted lightly, giving them both a quizzical look.

'Jude!' April was the one to greet lightly. 'I had no idea you were coming here this evening,' she added teasingly.

He gave a slight inclination of his head, still completely in the dark as to exactly what was going on between these two women, and as such reluctant to commit himself either way. 'I had no idea you were coming here, either,' he returned noncommittally.

May gave a disgusted snort. 'Have you ever noticed how Jude answers a question with a question?' she derided.

April gave him a considering look, head tilted enchantingly to one side. 'Now that you mention it—'

'I actually answered a statement with a statement this time,' Jude defended curtly, having the strange feeling, despite these two women's obvious differences, that they were somehow in league at this particular moment.

'Same difference,' May dismissed mockingly. 'The end result, of your giving out very little information, is still the same,' she expanded as he raised questioning brows.

'Perhaps,' he allowed guardedly.

May gave April a knowing look. 'See what I mean!' she derided.

April smiled warmly. 'I do.'

Jude raised dark brows. 'Are you invited for dinner, too, April?'

'No!'

'I don't—'

Both women began talking at once, May emphatically in the negative, April a little more ambiguous.

'I don't think I'm invited,' April finished ruefully.

'Pity,' Jude murmured after a brief glance at May's stubbornly set expression.

It would have been interesting watching the interplay between these two such different women—he might even have learnt some of the reason for the antipathy between them, on May's part, at least. April, he realised, was more unsettled than angry.

'I'll leave you two to your dinner, then,' April dismissed lightly, seeming to take some effort to gather her usual equilibrium, her smile bright and meaningless, certainly not accompanied by the usual warmth of her eyes.

Jude eyed May mockingly. 'I'm not sure May has remembered that she invited me, either!' he drawled derisively, the fact that she was obviously dressed for working on the farm not looking too promising.

No doubt after their fraught conversation at lunchtime May had decided that he wouldn't be coming for dinner this evening after all; it afforded him a certain amount of satisfaction to know that he had disconcerted her by arriving, after all. But not too much—he still had no idea what the tension was between May and April.

'I remembered the invitation,' May assured him dryly. 'The chicken casserole has been in the oven for several hours.'

It might have been, but Jude still doubted that May had ever thought he would be joining her this evening to eat it!

'Enough for three?' he prompted pointedly.

May's expression darkened. 'I—'

'I'm sorry, but I already have a dinner engagement for this evening,' April cut in smoothly. 'In fact—' she glanced at her gold wrist-watch '—I had better be going, or I shall be late.' She turned to May. 'I hope I shall see you again before I leave,' she said huskily.

'How long are you staying in the area?' May looked at her coldly.

April shrugged narrow shoulders. 'I'm not sure yet…'

May nodded abruptly. 'Well, in case I don't see you again, have a safe journey home.'

In other words, Jude easily interpreted, however long you happen to be staying in the area, don't come back here to see me!

This really was a very strange situation, an even stranger conversation—one that Jude, for one, found completely puzzling.

'Thank you,' April accepted heavily, her smile even more strained as she turned to Jude. 'I'll probably see you later.'

He nodded abruptly. 'You can count on it.'

She gave a rueful smile. 'I thought I might! I-it really was lovely to meet you, May,' she added huskily.

A sentiment that May, Jude noted frowningly, had no intention of echoing. In fact, she looked so cold and unapproachable she might have been carved from ice.

What was this?

What possible reason could May have for feeling so antagonistic towards April? An antagonism, he now realised, despite April's apparent calm at lunchtime, that her presence here this evening meant she was equally aware of.

As he watched April walk over to her car, her face deathly pale as she drove out of the farmyard, Jude vowed that he would get an answer to those questions, either from May or April, he didn't really care which.

CHAPTER SIX

MAY eyed Jude surreptitiously as the red car turned out of the farmyard, taking April Robine with it, knowing that Jude must be completely confused at finding the actress here when he arrived after the way the meeting had gone between the two women at lunchtime, that he must be completely puzzled about the whole situation.

Well, she for one had no intention of enlightening him. And, after her brief conversation with April Robine as Jude had arrived, she knew that the other woman wasn't about to do so, either.

April Robine...

Strange that was the only way that May could think of the other woman, but also knowing the reason for that was probably that she refused to recognise her as the mother who had deserted her when she was only a child of five.

What sort of woman did that? Walked out, not only on her husband, but on her three young daughters, aged only five, four, and three? Not one that May wanted to know, or be associated with, that was for sure!

She drew in a harsh breath, her gaze deliberately non-committal as she looked at Jude. 'If you would like to go into the kitchen and get warm, I'll join you in a few minutes,' she dismissed, knowing a few minutes wouldn't be near long enough to her to compose herself after speaking to April Robine, but at the same time recognising that was all the time she had.

'I'm not cold,' Jude dismissed evenly, despite the icy

wind whistling through the farmyard. 'In fact, I think the air in the kitchen might be even more chilly than it is out here!' he added pointedly.

'Really? The Aga keeps it very warm in there, I can assure you.' May was deliberately obtuse.

'I wasn't referring to the heating system, and you know it!' Jude rasped, gaze narrowed to silver slits as he looked down at her probingly.

'Do I?' She shrugged, turning away. 'I just have to check on the— What do you think you're doing?' She gasped as Jude grasped her arm and swung her roughly back to face him.

'Are you going to tell me what's going on, or do I have to find out for myself?' he prompted harshly.

May stared up at him frowningly. This man was probably her mother's lover, had probably been so for some time; if anyone owed him any explanations it certainly wasn't her!

Her mouth firmed determinedly. 'Why don't you ask April Robine?' she snapped. 'Although the two of you seem to have a very—relaxed relationship, considering you're here having dinner with me and she's off to have dinner with someone else!' she added insultingly.

Jude's gaze narrowed even more. 'And what's that supposed to mean?'

May shrugged. 'Whatever you want it to mean.' She sighed, suddenly realising she was too weary to get involved in another situation of conflict. 'It's been a long day already, Jude, and I'm tired and I'm hungry, so do you think we could postpone this—whatever this is— until after we've eaten?'

He looked down at her for several tension-filled minutes, before slowly releasing her arm, a mocking smile curving his lips now. 'You weren't expecting me to turn up for dinner this evening as arranged, were you?' he murmured with amusement.

'In all honesty? No,' she confirmed dryly. 'But then, you're a man that likes to do the unexpected, aren't you?' She shrugged. 'Probably as another means of putting people off their guard,' she guessed shrewdly, knowing by the way his mouth tightened that she was right in her assessment. Well, he needn't have bothered on her account this evening—she had already been well and truly 'put off her guard' before he'd even arrived!

'And you're a woman who likes to analyse too much,' he dismissed. 'I'll go and get the wine from the car.'

May watched him as he strode away, his movements fluid, the icy wind stirring the darkness of his hair, his masculine vitality unmistakable.

What was his relationship to April Robine? Lover? Friend? What? May had no idea, but until she did it would be foolish of her to allow her own attraction to him to go any further than it already had.

Which wasn't all that easy to do when he deliberately set himself out to be charming as they ate their meal together later, telling her several amusing stories about Max, Will and himself when they were at school together, the earlier tension seemingly forgotten. And yet May knew that it wasn't. Not really. By either of them…

'Do you have any other family beside your parents, Jude?' she prompted curiously as they lingered over coffee and an orange-based liqueur she had found at the back of the cupboard, given to them a couple of years ago as a Christmas present and never opened.

He grimaced. 'Siblings, that sort of thing, do you mean?'

'That sort of thing,' she confirmed dryly; since the death of her father the previous year, her sisters were

the two most important people in her life, and not to be
so easily dismissed.

'I'm an only child, I'm afraid.' Jude shrugged. 'Probably just as well, considering the amount of toing and
froing I had to do between America and England during
my childhood.' He grimaced. 'I don't think we ever
lived in the same house for more than a couple of years.'

Which probably also accounted for his seeming lack
of roots now. It would also explain his complete lack of
understanding where her attachment to this family farm
was concerned...

'I know where you're going with this, May.' He sat
back, smiling.

She sighed. 'Do you?'

'I think so.' He nodded. 'But it doesn't change the
fact that this farm is too much for you to manage alone.'

She bristled resentfully, still not completely over April
Robine's visit here earlier. 'No doubt April Robine ech-
oes your sentiments,' she snapped, having no doubts the
other woman was completely mystified concerning
May's stubbornness about selling this farm to Jude;
twenty-two years ago she hadn't been able to get away
fast enough!

'April?' Jude echoed frowningly. 'What on earth does
she have to do with any of this?'

May blinked, realising—too late—that she had allowed her personal resentment towards the other woman
to show once again. And in a way Jude couldn't possibly
understand. 'Well—'

'I don't discuss my business dealings with April, if
that's what you're implying, May,' he assured her
hardly.

Her eyes widened. 'Why don't you?'

'Because I— May, exactly what sort of relationship is it you think I have with April?' he prompted slowly.

She shrugged. 'The two of you obviously arrived here together, are staying at the hotel together—'

'We arrived together because I was coming over on business anyway, and it turned out April had some business of her own to take care of in the area, too,' he said with a pointed look in May's direction. 'And although we're both staying at the same hotel—'

'You really don't owe me any explanations, Jude,' May cut in, standing up abruptly, deciding she really didn't want to know what this man's relationship was to her mother.

Because in spite of everything, his increasingly pressurised efforts to buy the farm by his sheer presence every time she turned around, his friendship with April, she was attracted to him herself.

Jude turned to look at her. 'Don't I, May?' he said softly, standing up himself now.

May looked across at him with widely apprehensive eyes. Too much had already happened today; she simply couldn't cope if Jude were to kiss her again.

Which, it seemed, he had every intention of doing!

She fitted so well against him as he took her in his arms, the curves of her body fitting perfectly into his, her mouth responding to the touch of his like a flower to the sun.

It was all so simple when Jude held her like this, kissed her like this; nothing else mattered. It was only—

She couldn't think any more, could only feel, her arms moving up about his neck as the kissed deepened, became more demanding, Jude's hands moving restlessly up and down her spine, quivers of warmth moving through her wherever he touched.

'You're so beautiful, May,' Jude breathed huskily as his lips travelled the length of her creamy throat, his tongue seeking the hollows he found there, teeth gently biting her earlobe.

May shivered with desire, feeling engulfed by a warmth she had never known before, knowing that she wanted this man, wanted him as she had never wanted any other, that she longed for the hard nakedness of him against her own heated flesh.

How could she feel any other way with Jude kissing her like this, touching her like this, one of his hands moving to cup her breast now, the silk of the blouse she had changed into earlier no barrier to his caress as his thumb moved rhythmically against her hardened nipple?

He drew in a deeply controlling breath, his hands now moving up to frame the warmth of her face, his forehead resting on hers as he looked into her eyes. 'I want to make love with you, May,' he groaned huskily. 'And I think you want to make love with me, too,' he added softly.

She drew in a quivering breath, knowing it was what she wanted, too, wanted more than she had ever wanted anything in her life before, felt as if she might wilt and die if Jude didn't make love to her. Now!

Which was ridiculous when they were in the kitchen, the only place for them to make love on the coldness of the flagstones beneath their feet...

'But I don't want any regrets, May,' Jude continued gently, his thumbs lightly caressing her creamy cheeks, his silver gaze easily holding hers.

May couldn't break that gaze, trapped in the emotions

coursing through her, feeling on fire with need of him. She wanted him—how she wanted him.

'Will it help if I assure you that there is nothing between April and myself?' he prompted at her continued silence.

May stiffened as if he had struck her, suddenly cold as ice in Jude's arms, her eyes wide with shock.

April!

April Robine!

The woman who had once been her mother.

Jude inwardly cursed himself as he saw the change come over May at the mere mention of the other woman, the way her eyes had widened, lost their dreamy arousal to focus sharply, her body suddenly stiff as a board even as she began to push him away from her.

She turned away. 'I think you had better go,' she choked, her face buried in her hands.

'May—'

'No, Jude!' She moved sharply away from his reaching hands, turning fully to face him, green eyes dark with an emotion it was impossible to read. 'I invited you here for dinner, Jude, not to—'

'Don't be any more insulting than you need to be, May,' he cut in raspingly. 'I kissed you. You responded.' He gave an impatient shake of his head. 'Don't try and make it less—or more, than it was.' He looked at her with narrowed eyes.

She gathered herself together with effort, standing tall, straightening her shoulders determinedly. 'Yes, by all means, let's be adult about this, Jude,' she bit out. 'After all, that's what we both are, isn't it?' she dismissed with forced brightness.

He didn't want to be adult about this, wanted to grasp her by the shoulders and give her a thorough shaking.

Which would achieve precisely what? he prompted self-derisively.

Not a hell of a lot, he acknowledged, but it might make him feel a temporary respite from the sheer frustration he felt at this whole situation.

He wanted May, he admitted it. Wanted her pretty badly. But so many things stood between them, it seemed, not least his friendship with April.

Which was something he definitely didn't understand.

And May had no intention of confiding in him...

He gave her a searching look. 'Why didn't you tell me that you're an actress, that the reason David Melton is being so persistent is because he wants you to take a part in one of his films?'

He saw May's eyes widen at the fact that he even knew that much about her. Well, damn it, he had certainly wanted some sort of explanation from David and April for what had happened at lunchtime. Besides, what was wrong with David Melton having told him that much, at least? It had certainly put his own mind at rest concerning the other man's intentions towards May.

He only wondered at May's complete determination that she would never appear in that film...

'Wanting and getting are two different things,' May answered him tautly. 'I'm sure David must also have told you that I've turned down his offer? Several times.'

His mouth twisted. Yes, the other man had been most emphatic concerning his interest in May. 'He told me.' He nodded. 'He was a little hazy as to why, though,' Jude added slowly.

'Was he?' May gave a humourless smile.

Jude looked at her searchingly. 'Is it because of your determination to hang onto this farm?'

Something flickered in those normally candid green eyes, something that was masked before he had time to even begin to analyse it—giving him the distinct impression that whatever May was about to say in answer to his question, it was far from the truth.

He also knew that, until this moment, the one thing May had given him had been honesty—no matter how insulting or rude it might have been!

'Yes, that's it,' she dismissed easily.

Too easily, too smoothly, Jude knew, his frustration with this situation deepening. 'I don't believe you,' he bit out hardly.

Her eyes widened mockingly. 'And is that supposed to bother me?' She gave a rueful shake of her head. 'Jude, I think you have an overinflated opinion of your own importance. Especially where I'm concerned!' Her eyes flashed warningly.

'May...!' he snapped impatiently, knowing she was back to being deliberately insulting.

Her brows rose tauntingly. 'Jude?'

His mouth thinned angrily. She was the most difficult woman it had ever been his misfortune to meet. Seconds ago she had been responsive and pliant in his arms, on the brink, it seemed to him, of the two of them making love together, and now she was back to being that mockingly defensive woman that just made him want to shake her until her teeth rattled.

Which action would get them about as far as her deliberate antagonism.

'May, you—' He broke off as she suddenly looked startled before moving quickly to the kitchen window. 'May, what is it?' He frowned his irritation.

'I'm not sure—oh, no…!' she groaned achingly, her face white as she turned from looking out of the window. 'I—it's—what have you done, Jude?' she groaned accusingly.

He looked startled. 'Me? But—'

'You knew I didn't want— How *could* you—? What am I going to do now?' she wailed emotionally.

'What the hell are you talking about?' Jude demanded impatiently even as he strode purposefully over to look out of the window, easily recognising at least two of the people getting out of the car that was now parked in the yard. And having recognised Max and Will, it wasn't too difficult to work out that the two beautiful dark-haired women with them, their likeness to May apart, had to be their fiancées, January and March.

Or to know, by one glance down at the anxiety on May's face, that her two sisters were the last people she wanted to see right now.

And from the accusing way she had looked at him just now, the way she had spoken, she obviously believed he had something to do with her sisters arriving back here so unexpectedly.

CHAPTER SEVEN

'How *could* you?' May demanded again, tears of frustration brimming in her eyes. 'You *knew* I didn't want them back here—'

'May, whatever you may think of me,' Jude cut in forcefully, 'I did not tell anyone that you were managing here alone, least of all your sisters, or Max and Will.'

She stared at him for several long seconds, not sure whether she believed him or not, but knowing that she didn't have time at this moment to debate the subject.

She turned agitatedly. 'You have to go,' she told Jude forcefully, clasping her hands together so tightly that the knuckles turned white. 'No—you have to stay,' she amended frantically, moving agitatedly about the room now as she tried to decide what she should do for the best, all the time her brain racing.

January and March were the last people she wanted back here, now of all times, May all too conscious of the fact that April Robine was only miles away. And that January and March had no idea, despite the fact that the woman was an internationally acclaimed actress, that she was also their mother.

While they were all growing up it had never occurred to May that either of her sisters need ever know that their mother hadn't really died twenty-two years ago but had deserted them. Even once May had realised that the actress who had become April Robine was their mother, it hadn't seemed necessary to tell her sisters the truth; after all, what were the chances of any of them ever

87

meeting the famous actress, by accident or design? None, May had decided.

Wrongly...

And now both her sisters had returned home unexpectedly, and April Robine was in a hotel only a few miles away.

What was she going to do?

Jude was obviously wondering the same thing—if for totally different reasons—as he dropped the kitchen curtain back into place before turning to look at her, dark brows raised mockingly. 'Make your mind up, May,' he drawled. 'Do I go or do I stay?'

She wanted him to go, of course, as far away from here as it was possible for him to go—and for him to take April Robine with him. But as she knew there was no chance of that happening, especially now that Max and Will had arrived, his presence here might be helpful in trying to explain away some of the agitation she was too disturbed to be able to hide.

'You stay,' she told Jude firmly, grasping his arms to sit him down on one of the kitchen chairs. 'Just don't— try not to—' She drew in a deeply controlling breath, willing herself to calm down, knowing that she mustn't make Jude suspicious of her behaviour, either.

What a mess. What an absolute nightmare. What on earth were January and March doing back here? The last time May had spoken to January, she and Max were having such a good time they were staying on in the Caribbean for another week, and had several days to go yet, and March had been nicely ensconced in London meeting her future in-laws. So, if Jude really hadn't told them she was alone here, what were either of them doing back here?

May straightened, forcing herself to calm down.

'Would you please stay, Jude?' she said evenly. 'But could you not—?' She moistened dry lips. 'Please don't mention either David Melton or April Robine's presence in the area?' She looked at him pleadingly, hoping that mentioning David, too, might put him off the scent of it really being the famous actress she didn't want mentioned.

Jude calmly returned her gaze, obviously completely puzzled by her behaviour—but too much a man who liked to be in control, of any situation, to admit to the feeling.

Well, for the moment that would do. Oh, May had no doubts that Jude would demand a more detailed explanation at a later date, but she would deal with that problem when the time came. For the moment she just needed his cooperation over that one point.

He frowned. 'Don't your sisters know about the film offer?'

'Yes, they know about it,' she snapped impatiently. 'They also know that I've turned it down.'

'But not that David Melton is in the area hotly pursuing the subject?' Jude guessed shrewdly.

'No, not that.' May sighed irritably.

'Or that April is here to help press the point. May, what is your problem with April?' he rasped as May felt herself pale just at the mention of the other woman.

She drew in a deeply controlling breath. If he were to mention April Robine in front of her sisters... 'I really would rather not discuss this any more tonight, Jude.' She looked at him determinedly.

Jude's mouth twisted derisively. 'You do realise my silence is going to cost you?' he drawled mockingly.

'Yes,' she sighed her impatience, able to hear the happy murmur of her sisters' voices outside the door now, willing to promise Jude anything right now to ensure his silence concerning April Robine.

'Dinner tomorrow evening?' he prompted softly, obviously also aware of those approaching voices.

May's eyes widened. 'Just dinner?'

Jude frowned darkly, his expression harsh. 'What else did you think I had in mind?' he grated.

'I have no idea,' she dismissed impatiently. 'But dinner tomorrow sounds fine.'

'You don't know how glad I am to hear that!' Jude rasped disgustedly. 'May, I have no idea what sort of man you think I am, but I do not go around—'

'Shh,' she cut in warningly, moving hastily across the room to pick up the coffee-pot as the door began to open, as if she had been in the act of refilling their cups.

The next few minutes were filled with a babble of happy voices as the three sisters greeted each other, January and March absolutely thrilled that their having arrived home unexpectedly as a surprise for May had so obviously worked.

Surprise? May wondered with inward exasperation—her sisters had nearly given her that heart attack Jude had once referred to.

But there was still Jude to introduce to January and March, Max and Will having already greeted their friend, obviously puzzled by his seemingly easy presence here after all the things May had said about him in the past.

'Jude and I ate dinner together while he continued his campaign of trying to talk me into selling the farm,' May breezily explained his presence here to her two future brother-in-laws, deliberately ignoring Max's searching look and Will's puzzled one; the last time she had spoken to either of these men she had made her feelings concerning the absent Jude Marshall perfectly clear, and now here he was, apparently happily ensconced in her kitchen, after having eaten dinner with her.

'Jude can be very persuasive,' Max acknowledged softly.

'Very,' Will echoed dryly.

May turned determinedly away from their two knowing glances. 'January, March, this is Jude Marshall,' she told her sisters more assuredly.

'Jude,' January greeted, shaking his hand guardedly.

'Did you check the food for slow-acting poison before eating?' March, with her usual outspokenness, suffered from no such niceties as she beamed him a mischievous smile.

Jude had stood up as the introductions were made, standing a couple of inches taller even than Max and Will, his sheer physical presence completely dominating. 'I believe you have to be March,' he murmured appreciatively. 'I've heard a lot about both of you,' he explained dryly at March's questioning look. 'As to the poison, I think May and I have what's called a truce at the moment,' he drawled in answer to March's question, at the same time turning to give May a smile that could only be described as intimately loaded.

May's eyes widened, and then she frowned. What on earth was he up to now? Whatever it was, she didn't like it!

'That's great,' Will said with obvious relief.

March nodded as she stood at his side. 'So much better if the best man and the chief bridesmaid don't have any inclination to stab each other part way through the marriage ceremony!' she agreed happily, hazel grey-green eyes sparkling with the mischief that was never far from the surface where March was concerned.

'Best man—'

'Chief bridesmaid—?' May gasped over the top of Jude's own obvious shock.

'Don't look so surprised, you two.' January laughed, obviously a lot happier now than when she had left for her holiday with Max two and a half weeks ago.

For which May was very grateful. January had been very upset after her recent ordeal with a stalker, hence Max's suggestion of a holiday to help her get over it; it seemed to have worked, January absolutely blooming with happiness now.

'Who else would we want as our two main witnesses?' March took up the conversation, grasping both May's hands in hers. 'We thought a double wedding at Easter would be rather fun,' she added encouragingly.

'Very nice,' May assured weakly, very happy for both her sisters, but not so happy at the thought of sharing such a family occasion with Jude Marshall, of all people.

Although it had always been on the cards that would be the case; Jude was obviously an extremely close friend of both Max and Will, their business differences over the buying of this farm apart.

'We would be honoured, wouldn't we, May?' Jude answered for both of them, once again flashing her that intimate smile.

It was a smile, after his recent blackmail into having dinner with him tomorrow evening, that May completely mistrusted.

He was enjoying himself, Jude easily acknowledged. January and March were everything that Max and Will had claimed them to be: absolutely beautiful, charming, with an underlying spark of self-determination that so echoed the one he recognised in May.

It was also interesting to see his hitherto confirmed-bachelor friends so obviously deeply in love with these two beautiful women.

But most of all he was enjoying the fact that for once May was completely disconcerted, that the unexpected arrival of her two sisters had so obviously shaken her. To his eyes, at least. He didn't think that any of the others were aware of it in the same way that he was…

Although there was still the little problem of May having assumed he was behind this surprise arrival of the engaged couples, he acknowledged with a grim tightening of his mouth.

He might be many things, but, despite his previous teasing, he had known all too well that May didn't want either of her sisters told that she was alone here, and, whether he agreed with that decision or not, he had respected it.

'So what brought the four of you back here so unexpectedly?' he prompted casually.

'You mean, because darling May hadn't seen fit to tell any of us that she was managing alone here?' March said dryly with a reproving look at her eldest sister.

Jude gave the middle Calendar sister a look of appreciative respect; obviously these three women had intelligence as well as beauty. Not that he had really doubted that; it would have taken an exceptional woman to attract either Max or Will. It seemed that all three Calendar sisters were that.

May looked uncomfortable at the accusation. 'There was absolutely no reason to tell any of you—'

'But of course there was,' January was the one to cut in concernedly this time, linking her arm with May's as she smiled at her affectionately. 'You can't possibly do all the work here on your own. And to answer your question, Jude—' she turned to him smilingly '—Will telephoned Max on his mobile to tell us the good news about him and March, only to discover that the two of us were still in the Caribbean…' She trailed off with a rueful shrug.

Jude turned to give May a pointed look, receiving an unconvinced glare back.

She really was the most stubborn—

'So, of course we decided to come back immediately,' January said firmly as May would have spoken. 'We met up with March and Will in London, and—'

'Here we all are,' March announced dryly. 'One big happy family.' She looked at Jude with challenging grey-green eyes.

There was a sharpness to March that Jude completely appreciated, easily returning that challenging gaze; Will was certainly going to have his work cut out being married to the middle Calendar sister.

'And we brought champagne to celebrate,' Will put in lightly, obviously not in the least concerned, holding up the two bottles of the bubbly wine he had brought into the house with him.

'March, would you mind helping me get out the champagne glasses?' May prompted briskly, obviously relieved to have something else to do rather than stand around discussing what they had all been doing the last week or so.

Jude having, as he had told May earlier, no siblings of his own, Max and Will had become the brothers Jude had never had, and he was quite happy to spend the next half an hour or so sitting drinking champagne as the six of them toasted everything and everyone, from the newly engaged couples to the best man and chief bridesmaid.

Although he could see by the expression on May's

face that she found the prospect of the latter highly unattractive.

'Look on the positive side, May,' he teased as he moved to stand next to her, shamelessly taking advantage of the situation by slipping his arm lightly about the slenderness of her waist. 'The best man and chief bridesmaid usually partner each other,' he explained. 'Which will save either of us the trouble of having to find someone else to take to the wedding.'

She shot him a quelling glance as he grinned down at her, at the same time wriggling uncomfortably against that restraining arm. 'I'm sure that isn't usually a problem for you, Jude,' she snapped scathingly.

'I was thinking more of you, actually,' he drawled, continuing to grin down at her.

May's cheeks coloured fiery red, and Jude could see by the angry flare in her eyes that she would like to have told him precisely what he could do with his thought.

In fact, she might have just done that, if January hadn't neatly stepped into the conversation. 'You have to see our engagement rings, May.' She laughed. 'Show her, March.' She held out her slender left hand, at the same time that March obligingly did the same.

The two rings were almost identical, an emerald surrounded by slightly smaller diamonds.

'And neither of us knew what the other had chosen until we met up yesterday.' March smiled ruefully.

'What on earth are you doing here?' Max took the opportunity of this distraction to quietly prompt Jude.

Jude gave a shrug, his attention still fixed on the pleasure of the three Calendar women as they admired the engagement rings. 'You knew I was flying over,' he replied as softly.

'But not actually here,' Will joined in the conversation. 'Tell us, did May take a shotgun to you the first time you appeared on the farm?' he added with obvious amusement.

Jude turned to grin at his friend. 'If she had been awake she may just have done that!' he admitted dryly. 'She's certainly fiery enough,' he acknowledged.

Max raised surprised brows. 'May is?' He sounded doubtful.

'May is,' Jude confirmed frowningly; it seemed to him that he and May had done nothing but argue since the moment they'd first met. Or kiss...

'No, that's March,' Will assured him happily. 'May has always been the most reasonable of the three.'

'I agree with you there.' Max nodded slowly, the more serious of the three friends. 'May has always been the easiest of the three sisters.'

Jude gave a firm shake of his head. 'We can't be talking about the same woman,' he assured them dismissively. 'May has been nothing but a pain in the—' He broke off abruptly, the conversation between the three sisters having suddenly ceased, his own voice the only sound to be heard in the otherwise silent kitchen.

'You were saying...?' March arched dark brows at him mischievously, obviously enjoying his discomfort.

And he was discomfited, Jude inwardly acknowledged. It was one thing to say something in confidence to close friends, something else entirely for the subject of the confidence—and her two sisters—to hear what he had said!

And May—the minx—was obviously enjoying his discomfort as much as her sisters were, her mouth twitching with amusement, eyes glowing deeply green.

'Jude?' she prompted with deliberate innocence.

'May—' he gave an exaggerated nod of acknowledgement '—I'm sure that even you would admit that we haven't always—seen eye to eye, since I arrived here?' he derided.

'That could be a little difficult when you're at least eight inches taller than I am,' she returned noncommittally, evoking the laugh from the others that she had obviously hoped for, and breaking the awkwardness of the moment in the process.

At the same time neatly getting Jude out of the tight corner—he admitted it—he had backed himself into.

'Let's drink another toast,' January put in lightly, holding up her glass. 'To a successful wedding.'

'A successful wedding,' Jude echoed with the others, although it was to May that he mockingly saluted his glass, knowing by the narrow-eyed look she gave him in return that she still wasn't happy with the thought of partnering him to the wedding.

He wondered how she would react if he suggested bringing April instead...

CHAPTER EIGHT

'DON'T let us keep you from anything, Jude,' May prompted firmly a few minutes later, knowing she probably sounded rude, but at the same time wishing him away from here. With Jude gone, there would be no chance of April Robine's name being mentioned... 'I'm sure we all appreciate what a busy man you are, and Max and Will are obviously staying here tonight,' she added lightly.

He returned her gaze challengingly for several long seconds, seemed on the brink of saying something, and then changed his mind as the tension relaxed from his shoulders. 'I do have a couple of things to attend to when I get back to the hotel,' he accepted softly, putting down his empty champagne glass.

She would just bet he did, May acknowledged tautly, talking to April Robine—and probably not just talking, either—being amongst them. 'Then we really mustn't delay you any longer, must we?' she returned with saccharine sweetness.

It was as if there were only the two of them in the room as their gazes met—and clashed—neither of them seeming aware of the other four people present as those gazes continued to war silently.

'Why don't the rest of us go over and see Ginny and the twins while May and Jude say goodnight?' January was the one to suggest brightly, putting down her own empty glass and looking at March and the other two men expectantly.

'"Ginny and the twins"...?' Max echoed doubtfully even as he prepared to follow her by putting down his own glass.

May smiled at him encouragingly, having taken a great liking to this often overly serious man, knowing that January's warm impetuosity was exactly what he needed to brighten his previously rigid lifestyle.

'It's a female thing,' Jude assured his friend wryly. 'I'll see the two of you some time tomorrow,' he told the two men as they followed their fiancées out of the kitchen.

Leaving May alone with him. Which was the last thing she wanted. But at the same time, she recognised that it was probably necessary; she hadn't finished saying to him earlier all that needed saying, before her sisters and their fiancés had arrived.

'I know. I know.' Jude held up defensive hands as she would have spoken. 'Don't mention David Melton, April Robine, or the film role, to either of your sisters. Did I get that right?' he added tauntingly.

May gave the ghost of a smile. 'You know that you did.' She grimaced. 'It's just that—I don't want—' She broke off awkwardly, shaking her head distractedly.

She couldn't even begin to explain, not to this man, or anyone else. All she knew was that the situation, with the arrival home of her two sisters, had suddenly become so much more complicated. So much so that she just wanted to hide herself away until the danger had passed. And that was something she just couldn't do!

Jude stepped forward, standing very close to her now, looking down at her concernedly as he reached up to caress her cheek. 'Have you never heard that it sometimes helps if you share a problem?' he prompted huskily.

May gave a choked sound, somewhere between a laugh and a sob, she realised heavily. 'Not this problem,' she assured him softly, and certainly not with Jude, of all people. 'They're all so happy, aren't they?' She looked wistfully across towards the barn to where her sisters and their fiancés were no doubt admiring their favourite ewe and her new offspring.

Jude's thumbtips moved beneath her jaw, raising her face so that she was looking directly at him, that grey gaze sharply probing. 'But not you,' he said after a few seconds. 'May, I didn't mean it just now about your being a pain in the—'

'Backside?' she finished ruefully.

'I was going to say proverbial,' he corrected dryly, those thumbtips lightly caressing against her jaw now.

'Yes, you did mean it.' May laughed huskily, wishing he would stop touching her in this way, but feeling powerless to stop him. 'And I know that I have been.' She nodded heavily. 'I just—maybe it would just be better for everyone if we were to sell the farm, after all.' She sighed agitatedly, no longer sure what was the right thing to do. For any of them.

Jude's gaze narrowed. 'You don't really think that,' he said slowly, shaking his head.

'Hey, you're the one that wants to buy it, remember?' she reminded him incredulously. The last thing she had expected was an argument from Jude against her selling the farm.

'So I am.' His mouth twisted ruefully. 'I don't know what I was thinking of,' he added self-disgustedly.

May gave him a searching look. He had seemed different this evening, in the company of his two closest friends, not quite so much the cold-blooded businessman that he usually liked to appear.

She smiled. 'You know, Jude, maybe you aren't such a—'

'Careful, May,' he warned dryly.

'I was going to say hard-headed businessman as I thought you were,' she defended reprovingly.

'Don't you believe it,' he warned hardly. 'Tonight was social.'

She raised dark brows. 'Meaning tomorrow evening will be business?' she taunted.

Jude gave a self-derisive shrug. 'I wouldn't go that far.'

Neither would she. They didn't seem to be able to be in the same room for very long without Jude either kissing or touching her—very disturbing when May had been so determined to keep him at arm's length.

He wasn't at arm's length now, either, standing far too close to her for comfort, those caressing thumbs against her jaw as he lightly cupped her face in gentle hands.

She was falling in love with this man, May realised in sudden shock as she stared up at him.

How on earth had that happened?

With everything else that was going on in her life—David, April Robine's presence in the area, the increasing pressure to sell the farm—how on earth had she managed to fall in love with Jude Marshall, of all people?

His gaze sharpened. 'What is it?' he prompted concernedly. 'You suddenly went pale again,' he explained, frowning darkly.

Pale—she was surprised she hadn't collapsed altogether at the discovery she had just made about herself.

Her lips clamped together as she moved sharply away from him, a shutter coming down over her normally candid gaze. 'I'm tired,' she bit out abruptly, deliberately not looking at him, instead watching as his hands fell ineffectually down by his sides. 'It—I really think you should go now,' she added tautly.

Before she completely lost it. If she hadn't already... Falling in love with Jude Marshall, an obvious friend of her estranged mother's, wasn't exactly a sane thing to do, now was it?

And she was becoming slightly hysterical, May realised shakily. Any minute now she was going to start babbling incoherently, or cry, which was probably worse.

'After all—' her mouth twisted scathingly '—I'm sure April must be expecting you back at the hotel some time tonight.'

Jude's gaze narrowed shrewdly as he seemed to guess her remark had been deliberately antagonising.

But what else could she do? The whole fabric of her life seemed poised in the balance now that she knew she was in love with this man.

Oh, like most women she had her dreams of eventual love and marriage, but in those infrequent day-dreams she had always fallen in love with someone who loved her in return, a kind, caring lover who wanted to love and cherish her for the rest of her life, as she would love and cherish him.

Jude Marshall looked as cherishable as the rogue bull her father had purchased a couple of years ago, before he had had to resell it a few weeks later because of its unmanageability; no one had been able to get near it without the risk of being gored.

Jude was just as untouchable.

He was also the close friend of a woman she would always loathe and despise...

* * *

Jude watched May frowningly, the emotions flitting too quickly across her normally candid face to be analysed.

She had also—he knew this without a doubt—just been deliberately rude to him concerning his friendship with April.

April...

If May wouldn't give him the answers he wanted, then perhaps April would. It was worth a try, he decided.

'I'm sure she is,' he lightly answered May's deliberate taunt, determined not to get into yet another argument with her—especially as that seemed to be what she wanted. 'I'll book a table for us somewhere and pick you up about seven-thirty tomorrow evening, okay? May,' he added firmly as she would have spoken, 'when I ask a woman out that's usually exactly what I mean— and that includes calling to collect you in my car,' he added decisively.

She frowned across at him. 'I don't recall there being any asking involved.'

Yes, she was spoiling for yet another fight—and she wasn't going to get one. Not with him, at least.

His mouth thinned determinedly. 'I'll call for you at seven-thirty,' he repeated evenly.

May's derision was obvious as she gave him a scornful smile. 'Effectively ensuring there's no possibility of anyone seeing us out together at your hotel?' she taunted.

Jude drew in a deeply controlling breath before answering her. 'I have no one to hide from, May,' he rasped harshly.

'No?' She raised challenging brows.

He was going to throw caution to the wind in a minute, go back on his earlier decision, and kiss the life out of her—something guaranteed to result in another fight.

'Your father should have smacked your bottom more when you were a child,' he bit out tautly, his hands clenched at his sides as he fought the urge to take her in his arms.

She gave a wistful shake of her head. 'My father didn't believe in physical punishment for any of his children.'

'Making their husband's role all the more difficult!' he dismissed hardly.

May's smile deepened. 'Max and Will don't seem to have any complaints.'

'Yet,' he scorned.

Her smile faded as suddenly as it had appeared. 'Ever,' she snapped with certainty. 'January and March are both lovely young women—'

'Aren't you just the teeniest bit prejudiced?' Jude derided, knowing he had her rattled now with what she saw as criticism of her sisters.

'And isn't your nose just the teeniest bit out of joint because your two closest friends are about to get married and break up the bachelor threesome?' she returned challengingly.

Jude drew in a sharp breath. Not out of anger. Not out of indignation. But because a part of him knew that she was right...

He had been friends with Max and Will for years, the three men often spending huge chunks of time together, playing hard as well as working hard. It was a little unsettling to realise, with Max and Will's recent engagements, the pending marriages, that time was now over.

And he didn't thank May for bringing his attention to the fact.

'Doesn't that idiom, considering your obvious closeness to your two sisters, apply equally well to you?' he taunted, instantly wishing his words unsaid as May paled, telling him that his taunt had hit its mark. 'This is getting us nowhere, May,' he dismissed, moving away impatiently. 'Whatever it is you're trying to do with this conversation, I refuse to play. Okay?' he added hardly, aware of how he had nearly completely lost his temper.

Something that never happened. As May had so acutely guessed from the beginning, he gave little of himself away, either verbally or emotionally, something that anger was guaranteed to do.

Except that May Calendar seemed able to get under that barrier he had deliberately erected about his emotions, seemingly without any effort whatsoever...

'I have no idea what you're talking about,' she dismissed, moving across to the kitchen window. 'They're all coming back now, so—'

'It's time for me to leave,' he finished impatiently. 'May, considering the favour I'm doing you—not mentioning Melton or April,' he explained at her questioning look, 'you could be a little politer to me than you've been the last few minutes.'

Her mouth twisted humourlessly. 'I'm afraid you don't bring out that quality in me,' she drawled. 'Any more than I bring it out in you,' she added pointedly. 'Now, if you wouldn't mind, I have some beds to make up for my unexpected guests...'

Jude's gaze narrowed. 'You—'

'Still here, Jude?' March Calendar mocked as she was the first of the quartet to enter the kitchen. 'We thought you would have left long ago.'

'Then you thought wrong, didn't you?' Jude bit out irritably; another Calendar sister who needed her backside smacked. 'Max, would you mind walking out to my car with me?' he prompted lightly.

'No problem,' his friend dismissed, turning to give January a lingering kiss on the lips before following Jude from the farmhouse.

This was certainly going to take some getting used to, Jude realised ruefully as the two men walked over to his hire car; Max had always been more of the loner of the three men, enjoying relationships but never allowing any female to get too close to him. Obviously that had all changed with his obvious love for January Calendar. No doubt Will was as entranced by March.

'They're quite something, aren't they?' Max drawled ruefully as he seemed to guess at least some of Jude's thoughts.

But not all of them, thank goodness—because Jude had just come to the startling conclusion that, if he weren't very careful, he could end up as bewitched by May Calendar as his two friends were by her sisters.

How the hell had *that* happened?

When had it happened?

More to the point, *why* had it happened? The last thing he needed, the last thing he wanted, was to fall in love with any woman, let alone one as prickly as May was turning out to be.

'Jude?' Max prompted concernedly.

He gave his friend a startled look, realising Max was still waiting for an answer to his casual statement. Casual to Max, that was. That was the last thing it was to Jude.

'Quite something,' he acknowledged hardly. 'Although I didn't really bring you out here to talk about the Calendar sisters,' he added harshly.

'You didn't?' Max leant back against the hire car.

'You and May seemed to be getting along just fine when we all arrived,' he added speculatively.

'Don't start,' Jude warned, eyes glinting silver. Max and Will were probably the only two people who really knew him well, and the last thing he wanted was for either of them to get the idea he was interested in May in anything but a business way. 'I want to buy this farm from her,' he rasped. 'I would hardly be rude to her.'

Max shrugged. 'That's never stopped you being rude to people in the past.'

'You—' Jude couldn't help himself—he laughed. 'You're right.' He nodded, still grinning ruefully. 'But May's been having a hard time of it managing here on her own.' He shrugged. 'I—I felt sorry for her.'

Max's eyes widened at the admission.

As well they might, Jude accepted irritably. Feeling sorry for people he was trying to beat in business had never been part of his make-up, either. But it was better that Max think that than to have the other man guess how confused Jude's emotions had really become where May was concerned. So confused he didn't know what they were himself any more.

'Not that she would thank me for the sentiment,' he continued derisively. 'The woman had more spikes than a hedgehog!'

Max laughed appreciatively. 'So if you didn't want to talk about the Calendar sisters, what did you bring me out here for?'

Jude straightened. 'You remember April, of course?' he prompted guardedly, knowing that the other man did; they had both become friends of April's while in America.

'Of course.' Max nodded. 'How did it go with her after I left the States—?'

'She's here,' Jude cut in decisively. 'At the hotel. Oh, not staying with me,' he added impatiently as Max's expression turned to one of speculation. 'She had some business of her own to do over here, so we travelled over together, that's all— What the hell are you looking at me like that for?' he demanded as Max raised questioning brows.

'Like what?' Max returned innocently.

'Oh, never mind.' Jude felt too irritable, too disquieted altogether, to be able to deal with this right now. 'The thing is that May has taken some sort of instant dislike to her— You're doing it again!' he snapped as Max once again looked speculative.

Max shrugged. 'April is a very beautiful woman—'

'The way April looks has nothing to do with May's dislike of her; as far as I can tell she disliked her before the two of them even met.' He sighed his impatience.

'Interesting,' Max murmured slowly.

'Interesting or not, all I want from you is a promise not to mention April's name in the Calendar home. Don't ask.' He sighed again as Max looked more puzzled than ever. 'I have yet to get to the bottom of that particular story, but when I do I'll let you know, okay?'

'Okay.' Max shrugged, straightening. 'Say hello to April for me,' he added as Jude got into the car.

'Will do.' He nodded before driving away, hoping that Max wouldn't see his hurried departure for what it really was.

Escaping from May and the confusion of emotions that suddenly went with her...

CHAPTER NINE

''I WANT to know exactly what you told Jude last night,' May stated flatly.

'And a good morning to you, too, May,' April Robine returned dryly, perfectly composed as she moved to sit in the chair opposite May's in the hotel lounge, looking as beautiful as ever in a tailored black dress that showed off the perfection of her figure and long, slender legs.

May continued to scowl; she hadn't come here to exchange pleasantries with this woman.

In fact, she wished she didn't have to be here at all, but in the circumstances of her having dinner with Jude this evening she really needed to know what he knew.

'It's raining outside,' she dismissed uninterestedly. 'And I repeat, what did you tell Jude last night?'

'You know, May,' April said consideringly, her head tilted to one side, 'your manners were better at five years old than they are now!'

May felt the warmth of colour enter her cheeks, the barb hitting home in spite of herself. She had been brought up with impeccable manners—they all had; they just seemed to have gone out of the window since the advent of Jude Marshall and April Robine into her life.

'When Reception informed me you were waiting to see me downstairs, I ordered coffee for us both. Thank you.' April turned to smile at the waitress as she arrived with the coffee tray. 'I hope you don't mind?' she prompted May lightly as she sat forward to pour the aromatic brew.

'You go ahead,' May invited stiffly once they were alone again. 'I had a coffee before leaving home.' And she certainly hadn't come here to spend a sociable half-hour with this woman.

'It won't choke you to have coffee with me, you know, May,' April said tautly, eyes flashing deeply green.

May gave a barely perceptible shake of her head as she recognised that angry characteristic in the other woman as one of her own. In fact, apart from the length of their hair, and the obvious difference in their ages, the similarities between the two women were so notice-able, to May at least, that she was surprised no one else—namely David or Jude—had put two and two to-gether and come up with the appropriate answer of four.

But it was only a matter of time...

'That's a matter of opinion,' she snapped dismis-sively. 'I only want to know—'

'What I told Jude last night,' April finished dryly. 'And my answer to that is, why should I have told Jude anything, last night or any other time?'

This wasn't going to be as easy as she had thought it would be, May realised heavily. The last thing she had wanted to do was come here and talk to this woman at all, but she really had felt that she had no choice in the matter; Jude was already far too superior in his manner for her liking—if April were to tell him of their family connection then the whole situation would become un-bearable.

As it was May had found it very difficult to continue to act normally with her two sisters and their fiancés after Jude's departure the previous evening, knowing Jude was intelligent enough to realise that if she wouldn't give him any answers to his questions his only other source of information was April…

She gave an impatient movement of her hand. 'Because Jude knows there's something going on—he just doesn't know what it is. At least, he didn't…' she added pointedly.

April poured coffee into the second cup, adding the cream before placing it on the table in front of May. 'I take it you still don't like sugar in hot drinks?' she prompted huskily.

No, she still didn't like sugar in hot drinks—but it was completely disturbing to realise that this woman remembered her well enough to know that…!

'Miss Robine—'

'April,' the older woman cut in tersely. 'If you can't call me anything else, then call me April,' she added firmly as May looked at her frowningly.

Call her anything else…? What sort of 'anything else' did the other woman have in mind? Surely not 'Mother'.

May nodded abruptly. 'April,' she ground out tersely. 'I don't want any coffee. I don't want to exchange polite pleasantries. I just want—'

'To know what I said to Jude last night,' the other woman repeated heavily. 'But as I haven't seen Jude since we all met at the farm together yesterday evening, I have no idea why you think I have told him anything.'

May's eyes widened. April hadn't seen Jude again last night…? Could Jude possibly be telling the truth when he denied having any sort of intimate relationship with the beautiful actress? It was incredible if that really were the case, but as they both denied that such a relationship existed—

What difference did it make in the huge scheme of

things? Jude's friendship with April alone was enough to make him a danger to the harmony of her family.

Although May couldn't deny the small surge of warmth inside her at the knowledge that the man she loved wasn't involved with the woman who had been her mother. Not that she thought her own feelings for him were going anywhere, either, but it would make those feelings unbearable if she knew he was intimately involved with April.

'Did something happen, May?' April prompted frowningly. 'Have you and Jude argued—?'

'Jude and I have done nothing but argue since the moment we first met. In fact, before we first met.' She grimaced.

'Explain that last remark, please.' April frowned.

May sighed. What difference did it make if April knew about the farm? It was absolutely none of this woman's business, but at the same time it really didn't matter if she knew; April's own interest in the farm—if she had ever had one—had ended long ago.

May shrugged. 'Jude wants to buy the farm.'

April looked surprised. 'What on earth for?'

'The reasons aren't important; the farm isn't for sale.'

'But—'

'It isn't for sale,' May repeated firmly, her own eyes flashing a warning now.

Two pairs of identical green eyes warred for several long seconds before April gave a puzzled sigh. 'Okay, Jude wants to buy the farm, you don't want to sell; are you trying to tell me that's the only involvement between the two of you?'

'Of course that's the only involvement between the two of us,' May assured her impatiently. 'Do I look like the type of woman Jude Marshall would be romantically interested in?' she added disgustedly.

April sat back in her chair, looking at May consideringly now. 'And why shouldn't he be interested in you?' she finally said slowly. 'You're beautiful. Intelligent. A very talented actress, according to David,' she added ruefully. 'So why shouldn't Jude be attracted to you?'

'Never mind,' May dismissed impatiently.

'But—'

'My only interest in Jude is what you may or may not have told him about our own—connection,' May cut in determinedly.

'Nothing,' April snapped. 'Absolutely nothing,' she repeated tightly. 'And I presume you want it to continue that way?' She arched dark brows.

'Most definitely,' May scorned. 'And I don't want you coming to the farm again, either,' she added hardly.

Pain flickered across the beautiful features so well known to film and television viewers alike, the eyes now a dark, unfathomable green. 'You really hate me, don't you?' April choked.

'How I do or don't feel about you really isn't important,' May dismissed impatiently. 'January and March arrived back home unexpectedly last night, and—'

'January and March are here, too?' April breathed huskily, eyes wide, her beautiful face lit with anticipation.

May scowled her displeasure at the other woman's response to this information. 'You're dead, remember,' she stated flatly.

The other woman flinched as if May had physically struck her, all the colour fading from her cheeks, the deep red lipgloss she wore standing out in stark contrast to that paleness.

'You enjoyed saying that.' April winced, putting up a hand to cover the emotional quiver of her lips.

May felt a momentary guilt at April's obvious pain, but it was a guilt she quickly squashed as she remembered this woman's abandonment of her husband and three young daughters. After all, this woman was the one who had left them, not the other way around. And she really couldn't expect that any of them would want to see her again now.

'You're wrong, I'm not enjoying any of this situation,' May assured her emphatically. 'It just happens to be fact.' She shrugged. 'You—'

'How did your father explain the money?' April cut in frowningly. 'What did he tell you all? That there was a rich uncle around somewhere who liked to help out occasionally?'

May looked at the other woman for several long seconds, and then she turned to rummage through her handbag, finding what she was looking for almost immediately. 'I called at the bank before coming here this morning,' she told April woodenly. 'I wanted to be able to give you this.' She held out the piece of paper in her hand.

April's hand visibly trembled as she reached out to take the paper, that trembling increasing as she looked down at the cheque May had given her.

'It's all there,' May told her evenly. 'Including the interest.'

Tears swam in the pained green eyes as April looked up at her. 'He didn't use any of it,' she groaned. 'Not a single penny.'

It had been the shock of May's life when, on the death of her father, she had been informed of the money in his bank accounts, one that was used for the everyday expenses, and predictably contained very little, a second one that contained a few hundred pounds her father had saved for a rainy day, and a third that contained an amount of money that made May's eyes widen incredulously. Until informed by the bank manager that an amount was placed in that account every month, increasingly so, and had been for the last twenty years. It had been the almost twenty years that had given it away; after that it hadn't taken too much intelligence to work out who could have been making those payments...

'No, he didn't,' May confirmed huskily. 'Did you really think that he would?' She gave a pained frown.

April swallowed hard. 'I—I hoped that he would. I—wanted you girls to have things, pretty things—'

'Why?' May laughed humourlessly. 'Did you really think that ''things'' could make it up to us for not having a mother?' She shook her head incredulously. 'I'm glad my father didn't use any of that money, I would have been disappointed in him if he had.'

The amount in the account was an absolute fortune, could have made all of their lives so much easier, but May knew very well why her father had refused to use it, even to ease the lives of his daughters as they grew up. For the same reason May had refused to touch a penny of it since he had died...

'You're so like him.' April spoke huskily now, shaking her head slightly. 'You look like me, but you're so like your father—'

'I'm glad of that,' May said with satisfaction, but nevertheless the barb—if indeed that was what it had been meant as—hit home; this woman believed her to be like the man she hadn't been able to stay married to, to the point that she had left her children in order to escape him.

But her father had been a good man, an honest man. Not always able to show his affection, perhaps, but none of his daughters had ever doubted his love for them. As May had never doubted that he had continued to love the wife who had left him until the day he'd died...

'Believe it or not, so am I,' April choked emotionally. 'Are January and March like him, too? Do they—?'

'I absolutely refuse to discuss them with you,' May cut in coldly, hands clenched angrily in her lap. 'You—'

'Well, hello, ladies,' interrupted a silkily familiar voice. 'Having another one of your cosy little chats?' Jude prompted lightly as he came to stand beside the table they sat at.

Cosy hardly described the chat between the two women, May fumed angrily, wondering how much of their conversation Jude had overheard before interrupting them, turning to glare up at him suspiciously, only to have that angry gaze met with by one of bland indifference. Whatever Jude might or might not have overheard he wasn't about to give any of that away from his expression.

But April, May was at least relieved to see, had had the foresight to push the cheque she had just given her away in her own handbag. Away from curious eyes...

'I telephoned the farm earlier, but neither January nor March had any idea where you were,' Jude informed May as he sat down at the table with them without being invited.

May stared at him impotently, once again having that feeling that this whole situation was rolling away from her...

Jude continued to look at May for several seconds, but could gauge very little from her expression. She was getting as good at this as he was himself.

It had been quite a surprise to see May chatting away with April when he'd stepped out of the lift a few minutes ago, the two of them looking intensely serious about something. He had considered—briefly—not interrupting them, but on second thoughts had decided the opportunity of talking to the two of them together was too good to miss.

'Why were you trying to find me?' May spoke sharply, her voice husky, as if she were finding it difficult to talk at all.

Jude relaxed back in his chair, his expression deliberately inscrutable. 'I wasn't. I actually telephoned to talk to Max, but March seemed to assume it was you I wanted to talk to, and before I could correct her on the matter she had explained that neither she nor your sister had any idea where you were.'

May's mouth firmed at this disclosure. 'I can see I will have to ask my sisters to be a little more—circumspect, in what they tell complete strangers about my movements!'

In spite of himself, Jude felt some of his inscrutability slip at her deliberately insulting tone, knowing it was what she wanted but unable to stop the tightening of his mouth and the narrowing of his eyes. She really was—

'Max?' April repeated lightly, drawing his attention to her and away from May. 'Is Max here, too?' She smiled delightedly.

'He is.' Jude nodded ruefully. 'And he's now engaged to marry one of May's sisters,' he explained dryly, no longer looking at May but nevertheless aware—if puzzled—by the way she had stiffened as April's comment revealed that she obviously knew Max, too.

'How lovely,' April said with genuine delight, her eyes glowing deeply green. 'March or January?' she prompted interestedly.

'January, as it happens,' May was the one to answer curtly. 'Although I can't see what difference it makes to you which one it is,' she added disgruntledly.

April looked flustered. 'Well...no. But—' she gave an impatient shake of her head before turning to smile at Jude '—I'm so pleased for Max,' she told him huskily.

So was Jude, well aware of the reason for Max's previous determination never to fall in love, pleased that someone as beautiful and charming as January Calendar had managed to overcome Max's barriers.

But it was May's reaction to April's acquaintance with Max that intrigued him...

Jude nodded. 'We'll have to arrange for us all to have dinner together one—'

'No!' May gasped protestingly, although she seemed to regret the protest as soon as she had made it, a shutter coming down over her eyes even as her face paled.

Jude gave her a quizzical glance. 'I didn't mean this evening,' he drawled mockingly, having no intention of anyone intruding on his evening with May. As seemed to have happened every other time he had tried to spend time alone with her.

'I didn't think you did,' May snapped dismissively, obviously not in the least concerned with that. 'But I'm sure Miss Robine is far too busy for socialising on that scale,' she added with what looked like a pointed glare in April's direction.

April returned that glare, neither woman seeming aware of Jude's presence as the silent war of wills continued for several long seconds.

Giving Jude time to study them unobserved. They

were both such lovely women, inside as well as out, that it was totally unbelievable to him that the two of them didn't even like each other. Well…no, that wasn't strictly accurate; April seemed to like May well enough, it was May who was so antagonistic.

What could she possibly have against someone as charmingly gracious as April—?

Jude froze in his seat, his gaze suddenly fixed as he looked at the two women, the expressions of determination on their faces absolutely identical. In fact, apart from the twenty or so years' difference in their ages, the two faces bore a striking resemblance to each other…

What?

His gaze narrowed as he studied the two women more closely, noting the ebony hair, the creamy brow, deep green eyes, the generously kissable mouth, pointed determination of the chin, the slender curvaceousness of the body.

My God…!

Apart from the difference in their ages, these two women might have been sisters. But as they couldn't possibly be sisters, that only left—

But it couldn't be!

Could it…?

CHAPTER TEN

'YOU know, don't you?' May said huskily, her gaze not quite meeting Jude's.

She had been dreading seeing him again this evening, ever since this morning at the hotel when she had finally broken her gaze from April Robine's to turn and see Jude looking at the two of them as if he had just been punched between his eyes—or that he couldn't quite believe what his eyes had been undoubtedly telling him. Except, May was sure by the shutter that had suddenly come down over those silver-grey pools, that he had believed it...

But after that first shocked reaction, he had continued to chat quite amiably with the two women, obviously had had no intention of going anywhere, leaving it to May to have been the one to make her departure, knowing there had been nothing further she could do there that morning. In fact, if what she suspected concerning Jude was true, she had probably made things worse.

And so she had left the hotel, totally distracted as she'd carried out the work on the farm for the rest of the day, picking up the telephone in the hallway at least half a dozen times with the intention of cancelling their dinner engagement for this evening, only to have put it down again as she'd accepted that she would only have been delaying the inevitable. Besides, there was always the possibility—more than a possibility—that Jude had questioned April once May had left the hotel...

His expression had been unreadable when he'd arrived

at the farm to pick May up at exactly seven-thirty, look-ing extremely handsome in a dark business suit, grey shirt, and neatly knotted tie, receiving raised-brow looks from both Max and Will as they'd helped January and March prepare their own dinner, although neither man had actually made any comment about the fact that Jude and May had obviously been going out to dinner to-gether.

May had chosen her own clothes carefully for this evening, not wanting to give the impression she'd thought she was actually going out on a date with Jude—which she most certainly wasn't—but at the same time needing to look a bit more glamorous than she usually did. If only to give her more confidence than she'd ac-tually felt. The fitted dark green above-knee-length dress, teamed with a contrasting black jacket, had seemed about right to her.

Although she hadn't been quite so sure of that when they'd arrived at the French restaurant where Jude had booked them a table for the evening, having heard of its exclusivity, of course, but never having even contem-plated coming here herself; a farmer's income didn't stretch to frequenting places like this.

Jude had been chattily polite on the drive here, very solicitous as they'd been seated at their table, consulting her on her preference to wine before ordering. But to May that had all been just delaying the inevitable, and now that they had ordered their food, the wine had been opened and poured, she knew she couldn't delay any longer.

'Jude?' she prompted softly when he didn't answer her earlier comment. 'Did you—did you talk to April once I left this morning?' She couldn't exactly blame him if he had; from the look of stunned disbelief she had seen on his face this morning he had a lot of questions he needed answers to.

'Well, of course I talked to April once you had left this morning; it would have been rude not to,' he drawled dismissively, sipping his wine. 'What do you think of this?' He held up his glass. 'Is it dry enough for you—?'

'It's fine,' May dismissed impatiently, not having even tasted it, but sure that it was going to be as perfect as everything else about this tastefully decorated and efficiently run restaurant. 'Would you stop avoiding the issue, Jude, and just—?' She broke off, drawing in a deep breath, closing her eyes briefly before looking across at him. 'You do know, don't you, Jude.' It was a statement this time rather than a question.

He grimaced, leaning forward to put down his wineglass before answering. 'I—damn it, May, how can it be possible?' He frowned darkly. 'You're—April is—' He made an impatient movement with his hand.

'Yes?' May prompted softly, almost feeling sorry for him as she sensed his confusion, his disbelief.

He gave an abrupt shake of his head. 'Even if you hadn't told me so yourself, Max and Will have both informed me, on separate occasions, that both your parents are dead,' he said exasperatedly.

'They are,' she confirmed abruptly.

Jude gave a decisive shake of his head now. 'We both know that isn't true,' he rasped. 'May, my eyes weren't deceiving me this morning—'

'I never implied for a moment that there is anything wrong with your eyesight,' May assured him dryly.

'Then we both know that April is your mo—'

'She gave up the right to that title twenty-two years

ago when she walked out on her husband and three small daughters,' May cut in harshly.

'So it is true,' Jude breathed softly, looking totally stunned now, as if, despite what he had already said, he hadn't quite been able to believe his own suspicions until that moment of confirmation.

May picked up her glass and took a sip of her wine, giving Jude the time he needed to collect his thoughts, but at the same time giving herself some Dutch courage; this was turning out to be more traumatic than she had even imagined.

'You didn't ask April?' May couldn't keep the surprise out of her voice; the pair seemed to be such friends, it had seemed logical to her that he would have talked to the other woman about his suspicions.

'Of course I didn't ask April!' Jude rasped impatiently, sitting forward to once again pick up his wine-glass and take a much-needed swallow of the white wine. 'I told you, we don't have the sort of close friendship that would allow me to intrude on her private life in that way.'

'But you think we have?' she derided with a disbelieving smile.

His eyes glittered silver. 'I didn't bring the subject up, May—you did,' he reminded hardly.

She gave a shrug. 'We could hardly have spent the whole evening together and totally ignored the subject.'

'Not with any comfort, no,' he accepted heavily. 'But if you had chosen not to mention it, I doubt that I would have, either. I'm totally at a loss to understand any of it, May,' he continued agitatedly as she would have spoken. 'And, as I'm sure you're totally aware, that isn't something I admit to lightly,' he added self-derisively.

'No.' May gave a rueful smile.

'Do January and March know their mother is still alive?' he prompted softly.

May's smile faded. 'No,' she said hardly. 'And I don't want them to know, either.' And for that to happen, she now had to ask for this man's cooperation. Something she wasn't sure he would give... 'How do you think they would both feel if they were to be told the truth now? How would you feel?' she reasoned impatiently.

'But it isn't me, May,' he came back explosively. 'It isn't you, either, not really—'

'Of course it is—'

'No.' He gave a slow shake of his head at her angry outburst. 'If my guess is correct, and from what I've observed the last few days, then you've always known your mother was still alive, it's January and March who have lived in ignorance of the fact. And maybe that was the right thing to do at the time, I don't know.' He gave a baffled grimace. 'But do you really think, now that April is here, in England, only ten miles or so away, that you have the right to keep that information from your sisters any longer?'

May bit back her own angry retort as their first courses were delivered to the table, still silent once they had been left alone once again.

Because the truth of the matter was, she wasn't sure herself any more that she had that right.

Oh, she had never doubted the rightness of what she'd been doing as they'd all been growing up, had known that it was easier for everyone—but especially their father—if questions about the mother the two younger sisters barely remembered were kept to a minimum. Which they wouldn't have been if either January or March had realised their mother was still alive, was now a successful actress living in America.

But these last few weeks, since May had been offered the role in a film playing the part of April Robine's daughter, had been something of a strain, made even more so because of David Melton's persistence in trying to get her to accept the part.

And she didn't welcome Jude putting into words the question that had been plaguing her the last few weeks, but especially so since April Robine had arrived on the scene.

With Jude, of all people…

Jude watched the emotions flitting across May's expressive face, knew that he had hit a raw nerve with his last question.

But what else could he do? Now that May had actually confirmed what he had only suspected this morning, he felt he had no choice but to play the devil's advocate. Which was guaranteed to make May hate him all the more.

If that were possible…

'She's the reason you turned down the offer of the film role, isn't she?' Jude realised shrewdly. 'You were trying to avoid something like this happening.'

'Can you blame me?' May's eyes flashed angrily.

She was hurting, he could see she was hurting, and he wanted nothing more at that moment than to take her in his arms, assure her that everything was going to be okay, that it would all work itself out.

But the former he didn't think she would accept at all, and he wasn't sure the latter were true.

How did you set about telling two grown women of twenty-six and twenty-five that the mother you had told them was dead was actually very much alive and staying in a hotel ten miles away?

Worse, how was May going to stop April telling January and March the truth, if that was what she chose to do? If they needed any telling after meeting the actress face to face, that was.

He now knew that it was April that May had reminded him of the first day he'd come to the farm. Despite the fact that the women were such a contrast to each other, April always chicly elegant, May dressed in overbig clothes that day, an unattractive woollen hat pulled over her hair, there had still been enough of a likeness between the two women for Jude to have felt a jolt of something. He just hadn't known what that something was until this morning…

'I'm not the one you have to worry about blaming you for anything, May,' he told her gently. 'It's January and March you have to convince of that.'

He wished the words unsaid almost as soon as he had said them, May's face paling dramatically, her eyes huge green pools of pain in that paleness.

He put out a comforting hand, the sudden anger that flared in her eyes stopping him from actually touching her; she was so tense now she looked as if the merest touch might shatter her.

'I might have known this would be your attitude,' she snapped scornfully, her hands tightly gripping the napkin spread on her lap. 'It must be so easy to sit in judgement, in the total security of being an only child of obviously caring parents. But you can have no idea of what it was like when—when April left us the way she did. No idea.' She was fighting back the tears now, obviously determined to remain in control.

That was May's problem, Jude realised achingly; she had always been the eldest sister—by one year, for goodness' sake—the one who took all the problems of the family on board and sorted them out for all of them. But who sorted out May's problems…?

He shook his head. 'It's too big a burden for you to carry alone any more, May—'

'And who's going to help me?' she cut in tauntingly. 'You? Somehow I don't think so.' She looked at him scornfully.

Jude schooled himself not to react to that scorn, knowing that May was hurting very badly at this moment, that, no matter what she might say to the contrary, she must be filled with doubts as to the rightness of her own actions in keeping the truth from her two sisters. Or else she wasn't the warmly caring woman he thought she was…

He shrugged. 'I would help, if I could, and if you would let me—which you obviously won't,' he accepted dryly before she could speak. 'But I was thinking more along the lines of April—'

'Oh, please!' she cut in scathingly. 'April is the last person I want help from!'

Once again Jude held back his initial response to this scornful remark; losing his own temper wasn't going to help this situation at all. Besides, May was agitated enough for both of them.

There was also the factor that they were sitting in a crowded restaurant, the tables not particularly close together, but close enough that several people had already glanced their way when their voices had become slightly louder than was normal; this really wasn't the place for this conversation to take place.

'Let's eat, hmm,' he suggested softly, picking up his own knife and fork in preparation of eating the gravid lax he had ordered. 'Most things look better on a full

stomach,' he added as May made no move to do likewise
with her garlic prawns.

She continued to look mutinous for several long seconds, but a glance around the restaurant, where several
people still seemed to be casting them curious looks, was
enough to convince her of the rightness of the action.

Not that there was much chance of May achieving a
full stomach on the amount of food she ate, merely picking at the prawns, and pushing uninterestedly about the
plate the chicken she had ordered to follow. As for conversation, that was almost nonexistent, Jude wary of introducing any subject that was going to tip May over
the edge of the tight control she had over herself, and
May herself not in the least conversational.

Not the most successful of evenings, Jude acknowledged as May refused dessert but ordered a cup of strong
black coffee to finish off their meal.

'May—'

'I don't wish to discuss this with you any more, Jude,'
she snapped warningly, eyes flashing deeply green.

So like April's, Jude realised with that dazed feeling
that was becoming so familiar to him.

Why hadn't he seen the likeness between the two
women sooner?

What difference did it make when he discovered the
likeness? he instantly chided himself. He had realised it
now. That was the real problem, wasn't it…?

What would May have done if he had never seen the
similarity between the two women? Would she simply
have persuaded April to go away quietly? Or something
else? Because he had a feeling, whether May liked it or
not, that April's days of 'going away quietly' were over.

He had seen the look of excited anticipation on April's
face this morning just at the mention of January and

March, could easily see that, having now met May, April would want to meet her other two daughters, too.

Something May was totally against.

He drew in a deep breath. 'Whether you like it or not, May, you're going to have to discuss this situation with someone.'

'Why am I?' she challenged hardly.

The uneasy truce they had come to during their meal was obviously at an end, Jude accepted ruefully. 'Because you are,' he reasoned softly. 'May, April isn't going to disappear just because it's what you want her to do—'

'Why isn't she?' May put in sharply.

He gave a weary shake of his head. 'You're doing it again, May. Answering a question with a question,' he explained at her enquiring look. 'No matter how much you might want to do so, May, you can't keep running away from this situation—'

'I'm not running away from anything!' she defended heatedly.

He grimaced. 'It certainly looks that way from where I'm sitting.'

'Does it really?' she bit out scornfully. 'Well, you're totally wrong about that. Just as you're totally wrong about what I can or can't do,' she assured him with hard dismissal, throwing her napkin down on the table-top before standing up. 'And what I want to do right now is walk out of here and go home—'

'I drove you here,' he protested impatiently.

'Then I'll get a taxi,' she told him uncaringly, picking up her bag and walking out of the restaurant, glancing neither left nor right as she went, intent only on leaving.

Jude stared after her frustratedly, at the same time aware that several other people in the restaurant had watched May's obviously stormy departure with interest, watching curiously now to see if he would follow her.

Not that he was in the least interested in what other people thought, about him, or anyone he was with, for that matter. It was May that concerned him now.

And, damn it, he didn't want to be concerned about her. Didn't want to be concerned about any woman to the extent that May Calendar had got under his skin.

Because he could no longer deny that she had done that, completely, and, he was very much afraid, irretrievably.

Which left him precisely where?

Following May out of the restaurant, that was where that left him, he acknowledged begrudgingly even as he stood up to pay the bill and hurry outside in pursuit of her.

CHAPTER ELEVEN

WHY was there never, ever, a taxi around when you wanted one? May wondered emotionally as she stood on the pavement looking up and down the road, tears of frustration blurring her vision.

She should have known Jude wouldn't help her, should have known that he would take April's part in all this. She didn't know what she had been thinking of even considering appealing to his caring instinct—Jude Marshall didn't have a caring instinct in the whole of his body, had only invited her out this evening at all because he still intended to buy the farm. He—

'Get in the car, May,' Jude instructed through the open window of the car he had just parked on the road in front of her.

'I would rather walk the whole way home than get in a car, or anything else, with you!' she assured him emotionally, hurriedly wiping away the tell-tale tears with the knuckles of her hands as she turned away with the intention of doing just that.

Jude swung out of the driver's side of the car, slamming the door behind him before walking round to where May faced him so defiantly. 'Do all three of you have some sort of death wish?' Jude rasped angrily even as he grasped her arm and swung her round to face him. 'First January is involved with some sort of stalker,' he enlarged at her outraged expression. 'And now you're contemplating walking the ten miles home, at eleven o'clock at night, along roads that are so dark an attacker could be hiding behind every bush.' He gave a disgusted shake of his head.

May stared up at him in the light from the street-lamp overhead. 'An attacker behind every bush'? What sort of area did he think this was? This wasn't London. Or one of the other crowded cities. This was a quiet little backwater in the north of England—

And only weeks ago there had been a stalker in the area, someone who had taken pleasure in beating up women.

But he had been caught, May instantly derided her own thoughts; what were the chances of there being a second person like that in an area this uninhabited?

She shook her head. 'I'll find a taxi along the way,' she assured him dismissively.

Jude's mouth thinned. 'Get in the car, May.' There was no menace in his voice, just flat fury, his eyes glittering silver in the lamplight as he opened the passenger door for her to get in.

She looked up at him frustratedly. 'You're overreacting, Jude—'

'*I'm* overreacting?' he repeated explosively. 'You just walked out on me in the middle of our meal in a crowded restaurant—'

'The coffee stage is hardly the middle of a meal, Jude,' May cut in impatiently.

His hand tightened painfully on her arm. 'May, so far this has been far from the most enjoyable evening of my life, I am not going to add returning to the hotel, only to worry about your safety for the next couple of hours, to the list of things that went wrong with this evening.'

She glared up at him frustratedly, knowing him well enough to realise that if she did start to walk home, he was quite capable of following slowly along beside her in his car all the way back to the farm. Put like that, she might as well be warm and comfortable inside the car...

'All right,' she conceded forcefully. 'But I do not want to discuss April Robine any more tonight.'

He arched dark brows. 'May, do you really think you're in any position at this point to attach conditions?' he muttered impatiently.

The passenger door to the car stood open; Jude was obviously much bigger and stronger than she was, perfectly capable of pushing her inside the vehicle whether she wanted to go or not, in fact. And yet she somehow didn't think he would do that...

Her mouth set stubbornly. 'You agree not to discuss April Robine, or I don't get in the car.'

He gave a frustrated sigh. 'All right,' he snapped harshly. 'Just get in, will you?' he added wearily.

May gave him a long considering look before turning to get inside the passenger side of car, determined not to talk to him at all unless she absolutely had to—they had both said too much already this evening.

Luckily, Jude seemed disinclined to talk, either, driving in stony silence, the journey seeming to take twice as long to May because of the obvious tension between the two of them.

But what else could Jude have expected? He was treading on ground he had no business trespassing on.

Even if he had realised April Robine's connection to her family, a little voice taunted her.

Yes, even then. Because it was family business, concerned the four women involved, and no one else. No matter what Jude might think to the contrary.

'Thank you,' she told him stiltedly once he had parked the car in the farmyard some time later.

Jude turned off the engine before turning in his seat

to look at her. 'Very politely said, May,' he said dryly. 'But which part of the evening are you thanking me for—the meal, or the company? Because, to my knowledge, you didn't enjoy either one!' he added hardly.

'Nevertheless, thank you,' May insisted distantly before turning to open the door and get out of the car without a second glance.

But instead of going straight into the farmhouse she walked over to barn where the last of the newly delivered ewes and lambs were being kept for the moment, switching on the low light over the door as she went in. She had already noted the lights on in the farmhouse when they'd arrived, knew that her two sisters and their fiancés were probably still up, and unwilling for the moment to go inside and face them all. Especially as they would probably all be filled with curiosity concerning her evening out with Jude.

An evening that had been a disaster from start to finish, she readily acknowledged as she dropped down onto one of the bales of hay, burying her face in her hands in total despair.

What was she going to do?

What could she do, when, despite May's request for her not to do so, at any moment April Robine herself could come to the farm and reveal her identity to January and March? And if the other woman did that, what were January and March going to make of May's duplicity all these years?

'May…?'

She looked up defensively at the sound of Jude's voice in the semi-darkness, the first indication she had had that he'd followed her into the barn rather than driving straight off after she'd got out of the car.

'What do you want?' she demanded, hastily wiping the tears from her cheeks as he advanced into the barn.

Jude drew in a harsh breath. 'Why haven't you gone into the farmhouse?'

She gave a humourless smile. 'Why do you think?'

He moved forward, coming to sit beside her on the bale of hay. 'I meant what I said earlier. About it being time someone was there for you for a change,' he explained abruptly at her questioning look. 'I'll be there for you. If you'll let me.'

May gave him a quizzical look. Exactly what did he mean by that remark?

Whatever he meant, she knew she couldn't accept his offer, had to deal with this alone. As she had since her father had died.

'Maybe there is a way in which you can help me, Jude,' she said slowly.

He tilted his head to one side. 'Yes?'

She straightened determinedly. 'Buy the farm. Immediately.'

He sat back as if she had struck him. 'Buy the farm…? But—'

'Immediately,' she repeated as the idea began to grow and take shape in her mind. 'January and March can be married in London; both Will and Max are based there anyway. And—'

'And what about you?' Jude cut in harshly. 'What are you going to do? Accept David Melton's offer, after all?'

'Of course not,' she dismissed impatiently. 'That would defeat the whole object—'

'Because getting away from April, as quickly and as far as possible, is the object,' Jude finished disgustedly, turning to grasp the tops of May's arms. 'May, didn't you listen to anything I said to you earlier? Can't you see that my buying the farm under these conditions, with the sole intention of taking your sisters and yourself away from here, isn't going to solve a thing?' He shook her slightly. 'April is here now. She's real. And nothing you can do or say is going to change that.'

May shook her head determinedly. 'Once she realises that I meant what I said earlier, she'll go away again. Back to America—'

'And what did you say to her that would make her do that?' Jude frowned.

Her chin rose defiantly. 'The truth, that January and March believe she's dead—'

'I saw the look on April's face earlier today, May,' Jude cut in insistently. 'April is longing to see January and March. Wants, as she already has with you, to see the women they have become—'

'She has no right!' May cried agitatedly, standing up abruptly, uncaring as she hurt her arms wrenching out of Jude's grasp.

He grimaced. 'Obviously April believes she does. Look, May, I can't even begin to understand what happened here over twenty years ago, but—'

'She left us, walked out on the three of us when we were only babies; I, for one, don't need to know any more than that,' May assured him scathingly.

'She walked out on your father, too, May,' Jude said quietly.

'And it almost killed him,' she acknowledged harshly. 'I know, because I watched what her desertion did to him. He never married again, you know—'

'Neither has April,' he pointed out softly.

She shook her head. 'I'm not interested in what *she* has or hasn't done. Don't you see? This is all your fault, Jude,' she turned on him accusingly. 'None of this would have happened if you had never come here and brought her with you—' Her words were cut off abruptly as Jude stood up to pull her forcefully against him, his mouth coming fiercely down on hers.

It was a kiss that May, after the first few seconds of struggle, returned just as fiercely as emotions quickly spiralled out of control.

Here, now, nothing else mattered but the fiery passion that blazed so strongly between them, May returning kiss for kiss, caress for caress, her hands against the naked warmth of his chest as she shed first his jacket and then his shirt.

Jude's mouth was warm against the arched column of her neck, teeth gently biting her earlobes before his tongue moved moistly to the dark hollows that shadowed the base of her throat, discarding her jacket to pull the zip to her dress slowly down the length of her spine.

The hay was warm and soft beneath them as they lay down upon it, Jude half lying across her as his lips returned to possess hers.

May gasped her pleasure as Jude's hand moved to cup her breast, feeling his touch through the silky material of her bra, the nipple already pert and aroused, Jude's tongue searching the heated moisture of her mouth.

She wanted him, how she wanted him. All of him.

Her back arched instinctively as Jude's lips moved to the naked pertness of her breasts, paying homage to each as he kissed their arousal, tongue laving the rosy tips as pleasure rippled uncontrollably through every particle of May's being, his hand moving softly across the flat planes of her stomach to the lace panties beneath.

Her fingers convulsed fiercely in the darkness of his hair as she held him to her, wanting him never to stop, wanting this pleasure never to end.

Heat began in the centre of her body, deep inside her, rising quickly as it pervaded all of her body, on fire now as the hitherto unknown sensations caused her body to arch and then fall down, down, down...

'It's all right, May.' Jude suddenly cradled her fiercely into the hardness of his body. 'It's all right,' he soothed as the spasms continued to rack her fevered body.

Reality came back with the force of a blow as May realised exactly what had just happened between them, what she had allowed to happen.

It wasn't 'all right'.

How could it be, when she was so deeply in love with this man...?

Jude felt May moving emotionally and mentally away from him even as he continued to hold her physically close to him.

He hadn't meant for this to happen, hadn't intended—

Of course he hadn't intended for any of this to happen, but he could already feel the way May was putting her barriers back in place, even higher now that she knew he was capable of breaching them even beyond her imagining.

But it was beyond his own imagining, too. How could he ever have known? He had never thought...

May's response to him, his to her, was a complete revelation to him, too, completely beyond any other experience he had ever known. Even now, when he could feel her drawing away from him, he wanted her. And not just physically...

'Let me go, Jude,' she rasped coldly.

He drew in a ragged breath, making no move to comply. 'May—'

'I said let me go.' Her voice was like ice now, although she made no move to push him away from her, acquiescent but removed as she lay lifeless in his arms.

There was no need for her to push him away, Jude knowing her withdrawal from him was already complete, no matter how close in proximity they might still be physically.

And they were close, their near-naked bodies still entwined, Jude able to feel the slender length of her against him from shoulder to thigh, the dark silkiness of her hair against his face.

But in reality she might as well have been a million miles away.

And it shouldn't be like this. What they had just shared, their completely uninhibited response to each other, was something to explore further, not deny.

As May was denying it, even now sitting up to straighten her dress, her face deliberately turned away from his in the dim light given off by the low bulb overhead.

'May, I'm not going to leave this here,' he assured her determinedly even as he pulled on his shirt and buttoned it with slightly unsteady fingers.

'Leave what here, Jude?' She seemed to have recovered slightly, her voice scathing now. 'We've had a little romp in the hay, that's all—'

'No, it is not all, damn it!' he rasped furiously, eyes glittering with the emotion as he turned to look at her. 'Just now—what happened between us—' He drew in a deep breath, choosing his words carefully. 'That isn't usual, May.'

'Sexual desire isn't usual?' she returned mockingly, standing up to move away from him. 'You have straw in your hair,' she added derisively.

'So do you,' he dismissed impatiently, moving to stand beside her. 'May, that wasn't just sexual desire—'

'Of course it was,' she insisted waspishly. 'Admittedly, it went a little too far, but that's probably because emotions were running high anyway—'

'Stop it, May!' he rasped harshly, his hands once again grasping her arms as he held her immobile in front of him. 'I can't say I'm any happier about this revelation than you appear to be, but—'

'Revelation?' she repeated scathingly, green eyes hard as she looked up at him unflinchingly. 'As far as I'm concerned, the only revelation that took place here tonight was that I'm not as immune to physical attraction as I thought I was.' She gave a shrug. 'I'll know better another time,' she added hardly.

Jude looked down at her with narrowed eyes, his gaze searching on the shadows of her face, finding nothing but cold dismissal in her expression, green eyes deliberately unreadable.

His hands dropped away from her arms. 'That's all this was to you—physical attraction?'

'What else?' she scorned dryly. 'We seem to have been sending sparks off each other, in one way or another, since we first met. Tonight, what just happened, was just a natural outlet for those sparks.' She shook her head, her smile self-derisive. 'It was better than hitting each other, I suppose!'

Jude looked at her frustratedly now. Did she really believe what she was saying? Or was she just as disturbed by their reaction to each other as he was, but chose to belittle its importance rather than confront it? Because he couldn't believe, from what he knew of May, from what he had come to know of her whole family, that she had ever behaved in this abandoned way with any man before him.

Or was it just that he wanted to believe that she hadn't…?

Why the hell would he want to believe that?

He had been involved with quite a lot of women during his thirty-seven years, and he had never expected any of them to be untouched, a virgin, so why should he imagine that May was? Why should he want her to be?

Because he did.

That was the only answer he could give himself for the moment. The only answer he could accept for the moment. Because, loath as he was to admit it, he was more disturbed by his response to May, by her response to him, than she appeared to be.

He needed to get away from here—far away from May—to try and work out for himself exactly what all this meant.

His mouth thinned. 'Perhaps you should go inside now,' he rasped dismissively, bending down to retrieve his jacket, shaking the straw from it before putting it back on. 'No doubt your sisters have seen the car outside and are wondering what's happened to us both,' he added ruefully, having been completely aware of the interest shown earlier by Will, Max and the two younger Calendar sisters in the two of them spending the evening together. But, like May, he had chosen not to satisfy that curiosity. How much longer he would be able to continue doing that, he had no idea.

May nodded abruptly. 'I—would rather you didn't come in with me,' she told him huskily, her face now slightly pale in the semi-darkness.

He gave a humourless smile. 'I hadn't imagined that

I would,' he conceded dryly, that smile turning to a scowl as he lifted a hand and May instantly flinched away from him. 'I was only going to remove the straw from your hair,' he rasped harshly.

'Oh.' Colour heightened her cheeks now. 'Sorry,' she muttered, no longer meeting his gaze.

Jude frowned grimly as he concentrated on removing the straw from the darkness of her hair, his movements deliberately businesslike, all the time knowing that one movement of encouragement on May's part, even the slightest relenting in her stony expression, and he would sweep her back into his arms. And this time he wouldn't be able to let her go.

But it was as if she sensed that, stepping sharply away from him as soon as all of the hay had been removed from her hair, turning away from him as she picked up her own discarded jacket.

He couldn't let her go like this.

But what choice did he have? He still had no idea himself what was going on between himself and May. Only that something was. And it was a 'something' he didn't want in his life.

Which left them precisely where?

Nowhere, he realised heavily.

But he didn't want to be 'nowhere' with May, wanted— What did he want? Until he knew that, until he completely understood his own feelings of wanting her but at the same time needing to push her away from him, he had no choice but to let May go.

Even if that meant that her barriers against him would be so much higher the next time the two of them met?

Even then, he told himself firmly. Maybe it would even be better, for both of them, if her barriers were so high he didn't stand a chance of crossing them. Ever.

'I'll walk you back to your car,' she told him stiltedly as she walked towards the door.

His mouth twisted grimly. 'Making sure I've left the premises this time?'

May shrugged. 'I doubt anyone could make you do anything you didn't want to do!'

This woman could, Jude realised with shocking clarity. Even now he wanted to draw her back into his arms, to kiss her until they were both senseless.

Again…

'No, they couldn't,' he confirmed abruptly at the same time as he inwardly acknowledged his reluctance to go, to leave this woman.

Which was exactly the reason he had to go. Now!

'Would you tell Max that I'll call him tomorrow?' he said abruptly.

May nodded distantly. 'I'll tell him.'

'Thanks,' he accepted tersely before getting back inside the car to start the engine, raise a hand in brief farewell and drive away.

Don't look back, Jude, he told himself firmly. This woman meant trouble for him. With a capital T.

Don't look back!

His glance moved to the driving mirror as if drawn by a magnet, May still standing in the farmyard exactly where he had left her, moonlight showing her in stark relief, her face white against the darkness of her hair.

His Nemesis…?

All his adult life he had gone where he wanted, done what he wanted, enjoying brief, meaningless relationships with women if they happened to present themselves.

Now the thought of not being with May, the possibility of not seeing her again, had shattered into a million pieces all his carefully constructed life of no ties, no commitments.

The question was: what was he going to do about it? If anything…

CHAPTER TWELVE

'THAT was Jude,' Max informed May as he strolled back into the barn where she was placing eggs in trays.

'Oh?' May kept her voice deliberately light, at the same time as her heart began to beat more rapidly in her chest.

May had assumed, when March had called over to Max as he'd helped her with the egg-collecting that he had a telephone call, that it might be Jude; it was still too early in the day for anyone but a close friend to have rung.

It had been quite bemusing watching the fastidious Max as he'd moved around the far-from-clean henhouse collecting the eggs for her, after declaring that he had every intention of being a help rather than a nuisance while he was staying here.

But all thought of amusement had faded when March had called him into the farmhouse to take the telephone call, May wondering exactly what Jude was calling the other man about, as taut as wire by the time Max rejoined her.

She glanced up at him now, noting the slight frown between his eyes. 'Everything all right?' Once again she kept her tone deliberately light.

'Fine,' he confirmed ruefully. 'Jude has to go away for a few days, that's all,' he added dismissively.

Had to? Or had Jude simply decided to do so?

May's heart had skipped a beat at the news, although she wasn't sure whether it was from relief or despair.

After last night, half of her wished she never had to see Jude ever again, and the other half longed to do so. Because she loved him with all her being!

She curled up inside every time she thought of being in Jude's arms the previous evening, of the intimacies they had shared; how could they possibly face each other again without remembering that intimacy?

They couldn't, was the obvious answer, and maybe these few days' reprieve were exactly what she needed to face that moment if—when—it came. The fact that Jude had removed himself from the area pointed to the fact that he wasn't too eager for the confrontation, either!

But, unfortunately, it also meant there was no possibility of him taking up her offer of selling the farm to him immediately...

Which, the awkwardness with Jude apart, left her with the same problem as yesterday: how did she avoid April Robine coming here and introducing herself to January and March?

'Er—' she gave Max a bright, meaningless smile '—is Jude going away on his own, or is Miss Robine accompanying him?' If April were going, too, then that would solve that problem for a day or so, too.

Max gave her a searching look, May returning that look—she hoped—with smiling indifference.

May had come to know Max quite well over the last few weeks, knew he was a man of deep reserve, that aloofness no shield for his undoubted intelligence.

Although, January had confided in her yesterday, Max seemed to be making some effort to actually contact his own estranged mother, with a view to at least removing the strained relationship that had existed between them since his mother's desertion of her husband and son when Max was still only a child.

May hadn't known whether to laugh or cry yesterday when January had sat and told her all this as the two of them had enjoyed a cup of coffee together, the situation so like the one that May now found herself in with their own mother.

Although, for obvious reasons, she hadn't been able to tell January any of that...

'I didn't ask,' Max finally answered her. 'Is it important?' he added softly.

'Of course not,' May dismissed briskly—a little too brisk, she realised as Max gave a troubled frown. 'January wasn't breaking any confidences, but she mentioned to me yesterday that you are trying to contact your mother, that you may be inviting her to the wedding?' She deliberately made an abrupt change of subject.

Max's brow instantly cleared. 'I'm thinking of it,' he confirmed dryly. 'Meeting January, falling in love with her, being loved in return, has changed my outlook on things somewhat,' he acknowledged ruefully.

'I would think it might.' May smiled warmly.

He nodded. 'I've come to realise that not everything is as black and white as I always liked to think it was, that what happened over thirty years ago, seen through the eyes of a young child, didn't necessarily happen the way I remember it,' he added self-derisively.

May gave him a frustrated look; nothing Max had said so far, about his own mother's desertion, was helping with the situation she now found herself in with April. Was it really that easy? she wondered. Was it possible to forgive, if not forget, the childhood abandonment by one's parent?

'What is it, May?' Max prompted concernedly. 'You've been very—preoccupied, since we all came back,' he explained at her questioning look. 'Not your normal self at all.'

May gave him an inquisitive look. 'And just what is my "normal" self?' she said ruefully.

He shrugged. 'Calm. Decisive. Level-headed. Able to see a situation clearly where others sometimes can't,' he added, obviously referring to his own inability a few weeks ago to recognise his true feelings for January.

And, like Max, May knew she was no longer any of the things he had described her as being.

Because of Jude. Because of April Robine. Just because of this whole awful, complicated situation.

'Jude mentioned to me that you have offered to sell the farm to him, after all,' Max continued evenly.

May could feel the guilty colour heighten in her cheeks. Of course there was no reason why Jude shouldn't have mentioned the offer to Max; he was still the other man's lawyer, after all. It was just… 'Then he shouldn't have done,' she snapped. 'I haven't had chance to discuss it with January and March yet—'

'It doesn't matter.' Max shook his head dismissively. 'May, Jude isn't going to accept the offer.'

She became very still, her expression puzzled now. 'He isn't?'

'No,' Max confirmed wryly.

'Why isn't he?' she demanded frustratedly. 'It was what he wanted. What he came here for. What on earth—?'

'The reason he telephoned me just now was to ask me while he's away to submit Will's second set of plans, the ones excluding this farm, to the local planning committee,' Max informed her quietly.

May was well aware of the fact that Will, as Jude's architect, had drawn up two sets of plans for the proposed health and country club he intended building on the neighbouring Hanworth Estate, also knew that one of those sets of plans included this farm, and that the other one didn't. The question was, why was Jude choosing to submit the latter?

She shook her head. 'I don't understand.'

'Actually—' Max gave a rueful smile '—neither do I.'

May burst out laughing at this blunt admission from a man who, as a lawyer, was often carefully ambiguous in his own statements. 'Well, that's honest, I suppose,' she conceded. 'Although it doesn't help me, does it?' she added frowningly.

'Not if you're really serious about selling, no.' Max grimaced. 'You can be sure that January and March will agree to anything you decide to do about the farm,' he assured lightly. 'After all, it's you it affects the most.'

Yes, it was, and in the circumstances she had decided the best thing to do was sell. The problem with that appeared to be that Jude no longer wanted to buy.

She frowned darkly, quickly coming to a decision. 'Max, has Jude already gone? Or is he still at the hotel?'

Max looked momentarily stunned by the question, and then he gave a rueful shrug. 'I don't think he was calling from his mobile, so I presume he must still be at the hotel— May, where are you going?' he called as she spun on her heel and walked quickly towards the door of the shed where they had been working.

She glanced back at him briefly. 'To the hotel, of course.'

'But—'

'Max—' she turned back impatiently '—did Jude tell you when he would be coming back?'

'No,' Max answered slowly.

She nodded. 'Then there's no telling when that will be, is there? In which case, I intend talking to him before he leaves.' Jude might have time to waste, but she certainly didn't.

'Do you want me to come with you?' Max offered softly.

May became very still. She would like nothing better than the moral support, at least, of the company of this self-assured man who was in love with her youngest sister. But at the same time she appreciated that each time she and Jude had spoken together the last couple of days their conversation had always returned to the subject of her connection to April Robine—and that was something May did not intend discussing in front of Max.

She gave him a grateful smile. 'It's good of you to offer, but no, thanks. I'm sure I'll be fine on my own,' she assured with a lot more confidence than she actually felt.

Max didn't look in the least reassured by her words, either, frowning darkly. 'Are you sure? Jude sounded— a little terse, this morning,' he warned ruefully.

At the moment, sensitive as May was to her own love for him, a terse Jude Marshall would be preferable to the seductive one of last night. 'I'm sure.' She nodded confidently. 'If you wouldn't mind continuing to collect the eggs for me…?' she added teasingly.

'Not at all.' Max returned her smile. 'This last couple of days have been a complete leveller for me; I had no idea how hard farmers have to work.' He grimaced.

May gave an appreciative laugh as she let herself out of the shed, although her smile faded to a look of grim determination as she made her way quickly to her car.

If she gave herself too much time to think then the mountain might just change its mind about going to Mohammed!

Jude came to an abrupt halt as he stepped out of the lift, completely unprepared for the sight of May, having spotted him alighting from the lift, striding confidently towards him across the reception area of the hotel.

Despite the earliness of the hour, several other heads turned to look in her direction as she walked towards him, including that of the wide-eyed receptionist. Not surprising, really—May looked as if she had come here straight from the farmyard, her coat old and mud-stained, with disreputable jeans tucked into muddy wellington boots, and the latter were making a terrible mess of the pristine whiteness of the hotel floor tiles.

The situation might have been funny at any other time, but, still raw from their encounter the previous evening, Jude wasn't in the least pleased to see May here, muddy boots or not.

He hadn't slept at all the previous night, had paced the hotel suite for hours as he'd tried to come to some sort of inner acceptance of what had happened between himself and May, to clarify and then dismiss it as just a situation that had got completely out of hand. He had tried to do that...

By the time daylight had appeared through the windows Jude had known he was no further towards doing that than he had been the previous evening, deciding that he had to follow his initial reaction—and that was to get himself away from May, from this situation, and hope that he would be able to make sense of it then.

Seeing May again before he left had not been part of his plans.

He scowled down at her as she came to an abrupt halt

in front of him, eyes deeply green against the whiteness of her face. Eyes the same deep green as April's...

His mouth tightened as he remembered May's complete implacability over that situation. 'What do you want?' he rasped unwelcomingly, gaze narrowing ominously as she seemed to flinch at his words. 'You're making a hell of a mess of the floor,' he added disgustedly.

May blinked, instantly looking down, eyes widening self-consciously as she seemed to realise for the first time that she was wearing muddy boots. 'Never mind.' Her chin rose challengingly as she looked back at him. 'I'm sure they'll add the cost of cleaning it to your bill.'

Despite himself, Jude felt his mouth twitch with amusement; not too much bothered this woman, did it? 'I'm sure they will,' he acknowledged dryly. 'So, what can I do for you, May?' he prompted wearily.

'Max told me you've asked him to submit the final architect plans that don't include the farm,' she told him bluntly.

Jude drew in a sharp breath. Damn Max for doing that. Jude had thought he would be long gone by the time May discovered what he had done. But at least now he knew the reason that May had turned up here so suddenly...

Not that he had thought for one moment that it was a change of heart on her part—

Hadn't he?

Hadn't some part of him begun to hope that perhaps she felt more towards him than physical attraction? And even if she did, what then? Jude deliberately shied away from that thought. She hadn't realised anything like that. Her only interest in him was still the farm.

His mouth thinned. 'Then he had no right to tell you—'

'You told him first of my offer to sell the farm,' May defended heatedly.

They could go on like this all morning, Jude realised heavily; to his knowledge, May had never backed down from an argument yet.

'So?' He was deliberately obstructive; this woman had caused him nothing but grief since he had first met her, and his previous night of no sleep hadn't helped his mood one little bit.

Her cheeks flushed angrily. 'So I had told you I would sell it to you,' she reminded tautly.

'Immediately.' He nodded uninterestedly.

'Well?' May demanded impatiently.

'I seem to remember that I told you I am no longer interested in buying it,' Jude replied calmly.

Her eyes sparked deeply green. 'You're just being bloody-minded now.'

He raised dark brows. 'I am?'

'Yes, you are,' she snapped. 'I don't—'

'May, could we go and sit down somewhere?' he interrupted dryly. 'We're attracting a certain amount of attention standing here,' he explained as she frowned her irritation with the suggestion. Not that it particularly bothered him who was watching them, but he had a feeling, with hindsight, that May just might.

She glanced around them impatiently, affording the receptionist a less than friendly scowl as the other woman ogled them unashamedly, obviously fascinated by the stark contrast they made, Jude dressed in a business suit, shirt and tie, May looking more like a tramp who had walked in off the street in the hope of being given a warming cup of coffee by some charitable guest.

May turned back to him impatiently. 'I really don't give a damn what they think—'

'But I do.' Jude clasped her arm, turning her firmly in the direction of the deserted lounge just to the left of where they stood. 'Sit,' he instructed as she made no effort to do so.

'I'll make the seats all dirty, too,' she answered dismissively. 'Jude, you're just being difficult because I—'

'No doubt they will put that on my bill, too,' he rasped. 'I said sit, May,' he bit out through gritted teeth as she stood facing him. 'And think very carefully before you continue that previous statement,' he added grimly as she sank reluctantly into one of the armchairs.

'Because I refuse to listen to you concerning April...' she finished with obvious puzzlement for his grim attitude.

Ah, April...

Jude gave an inner wince for the mistake he had almost made. Of course May hadn't been going to refer to her dismissal last night of the intimacies they had shared...

'I think you're being unreasonable about that, yes.' He nodded confirmation as he sat down opposite her. 'But it in no way affects my decision concerning the farm,' he added hardly as she would have spoken. 'I don't work that way, May.'

'No?' she came back challengingly. 'It seems to me that you do.' She didn't wait for him to answer. 'Your sole purpose in coming here was to purchase the farm, and now that it's been offered to you you say you don't want it!' She shook her head. 'That doesn't make any sense to me. Unless—'

'I said I don't work that way, May,' he bit out grimly.

'But you wanted the farm so badly a month ago,' she reminded exasperatedly.

So badly he had sent Max here for the sole purpose of purchasing it, no matter what the cost. And instead of acquiring the farm for him Max had ended up falling in love with the youngest Calendar sister. And then Will had arrived to draw up the plans for the proposed health and country club, only to fall in love with the middle Calendar sister. And so he had finally come here himself to see what on earth was going on. Only to—

'And now I don't,' he rasped, knowing that in future he wanted as little to do with May Calendar as possible. 'Look, May—what the hell—?' Jude broke off his involuntary exclamation to stare dazedly across the reception area.

As if his thinking of them had conjured them into being, he could now see Max and Will, January and March entering the hotel, all of them looking as disreputable as May in the clothes they had obviously been wearing this morning to work on the farm.

'Is this some sort of delegation?' Jude turned to challenge May impatiently even as he stood up slowly.

But one look at May's face, the colour slowly draining from it, was enough to show him that the arrival at the hotel of her two sisters, at least, was the very last thing she wanted.

And Jude knew exactly why that was...

CHAPTER THIRTEEN

WHAT on earth were they *doing* here?

The next question, following on quickly from the first, was what was she going to do? April Robine was still somewhere in this hotel, could come into the reception area at any moment…

May turned frantically to Jude, appreciating that after last night he was probably the last person she could ask for help, but also knowing that perhaps he was also the only one who could help her at this moment.

'Do something,' she hissed breathlessly, the other four not having spotted them sitting in the lounge yet, talking to the receptionist at this moment, probably asking her where Jude could be found.

Jude looked down at her, dark brows raised. 'Like what?'

'I don't know,' May returned exasperatedly. 'They're your friends; get rid of them.'

He shrugged. 'They're your sisters, and their fiancés, you get rid of them.'

'Thanks for nothing!' May snapped disgustedly, feeling her panic rise as, having been told exactly where Jude could be located, four pairs of eyes now turned in their direction. 'Jude…!' she pleaded, desperately clutching his arm now.

He looked down at her frowningly for several long seconds before his gaze shifted to her hand tightly grasping his arm. 'Okay,' he agreed briskly, seeming to have

156

come to some sort of decision. 'But whatever I say, back me up, hmm?'

Now it was May's turn to frown; she didn't like the sound of this one little bit.

But what choice did she have but to trust him? None, came the resounding answer.

'Fine,' she acknowledged hastily before turning smilingly to greet her sisters, Max and Will. 'What are you all doing here?' she prompted lightly, receiving a slightly apologetic grimace from Max, who had obviously been badgered into telling her sisters where she had gone.

'Looking for you,' the outspoken March answered bluntly. 'What are you doing here?' Her eyes were narrowed with suspicion.

May drew in a deep breath, wondering when Jude was going to start saying something. 'I—'

'She was getting herself engaged to me,' Jude announced lightly.

May's head snapped up as she stared at him in total astonishment. He called that saying something. Well, it was certainly that, but how on earth was she supposed to back him up in a claim like that…?

It didn't help that he now looked slightly dazed at his own comment, as if unaware himself of what he had been going to say until after he had said it…

'Congratulations!' Will was the first of the four newcomers to find his voice, moving forward to kiss May lightly on the cheek before shaking Jude warmly by the hand. 'Looks like the Calendar charm worked its magic again,' he added with a grin.

May was still staring at Jude, totally transfixed. Why on earth had he said something so stupid? Worse, how did he think they were ever going to be able to extricate themselves from such an announcement?

More to the point, what good had announcing their engagement done towards encouraging her sisters and their fiancés to leave the hotel?

'Welcome to the family, Jude.' January moved on tiptoe to kiss him lightly on the cheek before turning to hug May.

'Welcome, Jude.' March nodded, a little more reserved in her congratulations towards him, although she gave May a rib-crushing hug seconds later.

Only Max, it seemed, with his added astuteness from his conversation with May earlier this morning, sensed that something wasn't quite right about this situation, his brows raised questioningly at May over March's shoulder.

She gave a barely perceptible shake of her head; she had no idea what was going on, so how could she possibly even begin to explain it to Max?

Jude, the instigator of this situation, still seemed totally nonplussed by his own behaviour, although the dazed look was starting to leave his face now as his expression became more unreadable by the second.

'It's a little early, but I think champagne is in order, don't you?' Will announced happily.

May glared at Jude, still willing him to say something, do something, to get them all to leave. Although, going on his last effort, perhaps he had better not bother.

She turned back to the others. 'We're hardly dressed for it, are we?' she dismissed lightly with a pointed grimace at their disreputable clothing; Jude was the only smartly dressed one amongst them. 'I thought we would all go back to the farm—'

'And break up the party?' Jude smiled, finally seemed

to have found his voice, moving closer to May now as his arm moved lightly about her waist. 'Champagne sounds like a wonderful idea.'

'I'll go and ask the receptionist to bring us some.' Max spoke quietly. 'Would you like to come with me, May?' he prompted softly.

May gave him a grateful smile; even a few moments' respite from what was turning into a complete farce would be welcome.

'It doesn't take two of you to order champagne, Max,' Jude was the one to answer him before May even had a chance to do so, his arm tightening about her waist. 'Besides, the road to love has been rather a rocky one, and I'm loath to have May away from me for even a few seconds,' he added huskily. 'She may just change her mind between here and the reception desk,' he added with a challenging look in her direction.

Change her mind! Making her mind up in the first place would have been rather nice.

Not that she thought for a moment that this engagement was meant to be a real one. She wouldn't be feeling so desperately unhappy if it were.

She had known after last night how deeply in love she was with Jude. Completely. Utterly. There was no way she would have responded to him in the way she had if she weren't. Which was why his announcement just now, made for appearances' sake only, gave her such an aching pain in the region of her heart...

'May and I will go and order the champagne,' Jude assured the other man. 'You all make yourselves comfortable. We won't be long.'

Long enough, May hoped, for her to tell him exactly what she thought of his effort to help the situation—it was now ten times worse.

* * *

'*Wait,*' Jude instructed as May turned to him as soon as they had left the lounge.

'You—'

'I *said* wait, May,' he repeated tautly, having been expecting this verbal reprimand as soon as they were alone, but nevertheless choosing to delay it for a few more minutes. 'In fact, wait here while I order the champagne.' He grasped her shoulders to halt her several feet short of the reception desk, walking on alone.

Not that he didn't think May had a perfect right to be furious with him for having announced their engagement in that unexpected way; he had been more than a little stunned by it himself.

But having once made the announcement, he had begun to realise that he actually liked the sound of it, that the thought of being engaged to May wasn't an unpleasant prospect at all. In fact, the more the idea sank in, he realised it was exactly what he wanted.

He had been fighting his feelings for her for days now, choosing to put many different labels on his behaviour rather than face up to the real reason he felt so protective towards her. He had even thought, by leaving this morning, that once May was out of sight she would also be out of mind. What an idiot!

He was in love with May Calendar…

The thought of not seeing her, not being with her, even not arguing with her, was a completely unpalatable one.

If she hadn't arrived at the hotel in the way that she had, how far would he have got? To the motorway? All the way to London? Or would he have got as far as the borders of Yorkshire and realised that in leaving May he had left the most important part of himself behind?

The latter, he now believed…

But he hadn't known, really hadn't realised—or just refused to accept…?—the way he felt about her, until he'd heard himself announce their engagement. And then it had all become amazingly clear, so utterly right that he knew he was fighting a losing battle in trying to leave her. Separation wouldn't change the way he felt about her, it would only make that separation harder to bear.

How to convince May of that—that was the question.

How ironic. The self-assured, self-contained Jude Marshall, brought to his emotional knees for love of a woman who claimed to feel nothing but physical attraction towards him. It would be funny if it weren't so heart-wrenchingly painful.

'Champagne's on its way,' he told her lightly as he returned to her side. 'Cheer up, May,' he added mockingly, not at all reassured by the paleness of her face. 'It's only an engagement, not an actual wedding.' Persuading May into marrying him was going to be much more difficult.

She shook her head. 'It isn't that,' she breathed huskily, looking past him now, her eyes having taken on a haunted look. 'April Robine just came down in the lift…!' she added weakly.

Jude turned sharply, just in time to see April stepping out of the lift, turning to laugh huskily at the person who accompanied her.

Jude's eyes widened as he saw David Melton follow April into the reception area, knowing by the way that May stiffened at his side that she had also seen the other man, added two and two together, with the earliness of the hour, and probably come up with the same conclusion that Jude had—David Melton had spent the night at the hotel.

Great. In all the time Jude had been friends with April, which was getting on for six months now, he had never known her to be involved with anyone, romantically or otherwise. And now, when May already had such prejudice against her, April was obviously involved with the film director.

A man Jude still wasn't a hundred per cent certain that May didn't have feelings for herself...

Jude turned back to her decisively. 'It may not be what it looks, May,' he attempted to reassure her, at once struck by the irony of his protective feelings towards May actually stretching to the point where he didn't want anyone to hurt her, including another man.

A month ago, a week ago, he wouldn't have cared one way or the other about anyone else's actions, would have considered it their own business and no one else's, but with his newly realised feelings for May he knew that anyone, anyone at all, attempting to hurt her would bring his wrath down upon their head.

Her mouth twisted derisively, a pained look in her eyes. 'Of course it's what it appears,' she snapped dismissively. 'So tell me, Jude—' she looked up at him challengingly '—what do we do now?'

Good question.

But as he had no idea in which direction he was coming from—to keep April away from the two daughters who had lived in ignorance of her existence for over twenty years, or to punch David Melton on the nose for trifling with May's affections while so obviously involved with April, a move definitely guaranteed to draw attention to the other couple—Jude really had no idea.

Which was probably another first for him, he acknowledged.

No wonder he had chosen never to fall in love before; at the moment he didn't know whether he was on his head or his heels, and as for any feelings of positive action...

Chosen to fall in love.

Who was he kidding? There had been no choice involved in loving May; he simply did.

He gave a rueful grimace. 'We could always invite the two of them to join us for a glass of champagne?'

May glared up at him. 'Very funny. Now come up with an answer I would find acceptable.'

He didn't have one. He really didn't. But very soon the situation was going to be taken out of his hands anyway, April and David moving away from the lift now, which meant that at any moment they were going to see May and Jude standing a short distance away.

And then all hell was going to break loose.

CHAPTER FOURTEEN

MAY didn't have time to wonder what April was doing in the company of David Melton this early in the morning; the fact that April was standing only feet away was what held her immobile.

January and March were sitting in the lounge just across the reception area, and at any moment April might turn that beautiful head and see them there. There was absolutely no chance, once she had seen them, that the actress wouldn't recognise January and March for exactly who they were; the likeness between the three sisters was as unmistakable as their likeness to April herself.

She looked at April and David, turning slightly to look at her two sisters chatting away happily in the lounge, before turning back to April and David.

May couldn't breathe. Her head felt light! She was going to—

'You can't faint here,' Jude told her firmly as he took a grip of her arm.

Why couldn't she? If she were to faint, then—

'It's too late for that, anyway,' Jude murmured at her side.

It was too late, but it was David Melton who had spotted them rather than April, the film director leaning towards the beautiful actress to murmur something in her ear, April turning slowly towards them, her eyes deeply green in a face gone suddenly white.

And she hadn't even seen January and March yet.

May groaned inwardly, knowing the reason for the older woman's obvious distress was the memory of the last meeting between the two of them.

But what else could she have done but tell April to stay away from them, and in such a way that the other woman would have no doubts about how strongly May felt?

'I told you I would be here for you, May,' Jude reminded huskily, his grip tightening on her arm as the other couple began to walk in their direction.

Yes, he had told her that. But not that it would be as her so-called fiancé.

Could this situation get any worse than it was? May wondered dazedly.

'How fortuitous that we should see the two of you this morning,' David was the one to greet brightly. 'Just in time to celebrate the engagement.'

May turned to glare accusingly at Jude; she had thought his announcement just now had been completely spontaneous—the surprised look on his own face had seemed to imply that it was—but if the other couple were aware of it, too...

'David...' April murmured protestingly, the colour coming back into her cheeks as she gave May an embarrassed glance. 'I thought we were going to keep that to ourselves for a while?' she added awkwardly.

May looked from April to David, frowning as it dawned on her that David hadn't been referring to her own supposed engagement to Jude at all, but to his own. To April...

'We were,' David acknowledged apologetically, reaching out to squeeze April's hand reassuringly. 'But I thought, as May and Jude are actually here now...' He turned to raise questioning brows at May.

He knew. The knowledge was there, in his eyes, a mixture of compassion for her, and pleading on behalf of the woman he had just asked to marry him.

May's gaze shifted abruptly to April, easily able to read the uncertainty in her expression as she returned May's gaze, that same pleading in those deep green eyes.

What did they want from her? Pleasure? Forgiveness? Heartfelt congratulations? What?

Jude gave her arm a brief squeeze before stepping forward to kiss April lightly on one cheek. 'I'm very happy for you,' he told her huskily. 'David.' He held his hand out to the other man.

'Thanks.' David gave a boyish grin as he took the proffered hand.

Which left them all waiting for May's response...

She blinked, looking across at the woman who had been her mother, for the first time wondering—

Max had told her that not everything was as black and white as when seen through a child's eyes, that he had made mistakes about his own mother's actions; could there possibly, just possibly, be a way for her to be wrong about April, too? After all, as Jude had already pointed out to her, despite the fact that April was a beautiful and desirable woman, she hadn't remarried while their father was still alive...

May didn't know any more, had no idea how any of them were going to wipe out the past, all she did know was that she could no longer even try to control what was going to happen in the next few minutes.

'Congratulations, David,' she said warmly before turning to April. 'I'm very pleased for you, April,' she told the older woman huskily, moving forward to kiss her lightly on the cheek.

There were tears in April's eyes as she looked at her. 'Thank you,' she returned gratefully.

May looked at her wordlessly for several moments, her own vision blurring slightly as she felt close to tears herself.

This wouldn't do, she told herself firmly; the two of them couldn't just stand here blubbing.

She breathed deeply, knowing the moment of truth had arrived—whether she was ready for it or not. 'April, there are some people over here I would like you to meet,' she said evenly, moving to link her arm with April's as she turned her in the direction of the hotel lounge.

She heard April draw in a sharp breath beside her, turning to see April staring across to where March and January were sitting with Max and Will, also knowing that there could be no mistaking exactly who the two young women were.

'May...?' April choked at her side.

May gave an encouraging squeeze of her arm. 'It will be all right,' she told the other woman with more confidence than she actually felt; she really had no idea what was going to happen when April was introduced to March and January.

Did either of her sisters still remember their mother? Would they recognise the beautiful April Robine as being that woman?

None of them had ever discussed their mother as they were growing up, May because of the necessity of not distressing their father, her sisters just hadn't mentioned her after the first few months of asking where she had gone.

In truth, May really had no idea whether either of them would make the connection between the interna-

tionally acclaimed actress, April Robine, and the woman
who had been their mother.

April swallowed hard, still staring across into the
lounge, her voice huskily emotional when she spoke.
'They're both so beautiful. You all are,' she added shakily.

May gave a rueful smile. 'We all look like you.'

'They're all as kind and charming as you, too,' Jude
cut in softly.

May turned to give him teasing smile. 'I'm not sure
you've always thought that in my case.'

He gave an unapologetic shrug. 'I don't mind admitting when I'm wrong.'

Meaning that perhaps she shouldn't, either?

If she *was* wrong...

'Ah, the champagne has arrived,' Jude said with satisfaction as he saw the waitress crossing Reception with
the laden tray, glad of something mundane to relieve the
tension that was slowly building, his pride in May at
that moment making him feel choked with emotion himself. 'I'm afraid we'll need two more glasses, and probably another bottle of champagne,' he told the middle-
aged woman smilingly.

'Champagne?' David Melton raised puzzled blond
brows as they began to follow the waitress into the
lounge.

'We'll explain later,' Jude told the other man dismissively. 'Let's go and drink a toast to your and April's
future happiness,' he encouraged briskly, his narrowed
gaze fixed on May as she walked ahead of him beside
April.

This couldn't be easy for her, he knew, and he wished
there were something he could do to help her, at the

same time knowing that all he could do was to be there for her, as he had promised he would. The question of their own engagement would, no doubt, come under discussion later.

When he would do everything within his power to persuade May into making it fact...

'Is it going to be all right, do you think?' David prompted frowningly at his side, his worried gaze also concentrated on April and May.

All right for whom? For April and her three daughters? Jude had no idea how January and March were going to react to meeting April, or if they were going to react at all. As for May, he still wasn't sure she didn't have feelings for this man at his side, and if she did, then her mother's engagement to David certainly wasn't going to help any possible future relationship she might have with April.

'We'll have to wait and see, won't we?' he returned unhelpfully, his newly found charitable feelings, because of his love for May, certainly not extending as far as the man at his side.

The four seated around the table stood up as they all entered the lounge, Jude quickly taking in their individual reactions to April's presence. Will looked admiring, as most men did when they first met April. Max looked pleased to renew their acquaintance. January and March were a little harder to read; after an initial brief glance at each other, their equally guarded gazes turned to May.

A May who was completely flustered as she tried to make the introductions.

'See to the champagne, hmm,' Jude instructed David Melton abruptly before stepping smoothly forward to stand at May's side, taking her hand into his to squeeze reassuringly. 'April and Max already know each other,' he lightly took over when May gave his hand a grateful squeeze back. 'Will Davenport,' he told April as she shook the other man's hand. 'My architect, on occasion, and also March's fiancé. And these two lovely ladies are May's sisters, March and January.' He smiled at the two of them.

His heart ached for April as she hesitated about what to do next, whether to shake the two sisters' hands, or just smile warmly. But as her hands were obviously shaking badly, and the smile was more than a little rocky, too, as she looked on the verge of tears, Jude had a feeling that April wasn't going to be able to achieve either with any degree of aplomb.

'And this is April's fiancé, David Melton.' May was the one to step into the breach as the film director began to hand around the full champagne glasses.

January took the glass he held out to her. 'Aren't you the film director who offered May a role in your film?' She frowned at him quizzically.

'I am,' he confirmed with a smile.

'April is to play the starring role in the film.' Once again it was May who spoke. 'David asked me to play the role of Stella, her daughter,' she added huskily.

Complete silence met this announcement, but Jude, deliberately watching March's and January's reactions this time, once again saw that look pass between the two younger sisters.

What did it mean?

Because there was definitely something in that look, something he couldn't read, but which the two sisters obviously could.

May was looking at her sisters anxiously now, obviously wondering if she had gone too far, her hand trembling slightly in his.

'Typecast, hmm.' The more outspoken March was the one to finally speak, grey-green hazel eyes gleaming with rueful laughter.

'What—?'

'You—'

Both May and April began to speak at once, both stopping abruptly to turn and look at each other before turning sharply back to look at January as she spoke.

'We know April is our mother, May,' she said reassuringly. 'We've always known,' she added with a shy glance in April's direction.

'Well, since we were old enough to watch one of your films on the television or go to the cinema,' March put in dryly.

Jude wasn't sure whether it was May or April who looked the more stunned by this last statement.

CHAPTER FIFTEEN

'I SIMPLY can't believe that the two of you have always known the truth.' May looked at March and January exasperatedly.

The eight of them had adjourned to the impartiality of Jude's hotel suite after the bluntness of January and March's admission, the four men having gravitated to the other end of this vast sitting-room, chatting away quite amiably as they sat and enjoyed the champagne, at the same time leaving the four women to the privacy they so desperately needed—even from the menfolk in their lives.

Although May wasn't too sure about the so-called 'man in her life', had no idea what she and Jude were going to do about their 'engagement' when all of this was over...

March gave a shrug. 'You and Dad always seemed so sensitive about the subject, so we just never mentioned it.' She turned to April. 'But we both knew the first time we saw one of your films. You don't forget your own mother,' she added huskily.

'Certainly not,' January confirmed forcefully. 'We've been so quietly proud of you,' she told April shyly.

May had to blink back the tears—again—at this further admission of her sisters' pact of silence concerning their mother, and she could see that April was visibly moved, too. Don't hurt them again, she silently willed the other woman. Please!

April swallowed hard, her face pale. 'I—'

'A little angry, too, of course,' March put in sharply. 'After all, we may have been proud of you, but we would much rather have had you at home. With us,' she added gruffly, her usually abrupt manner shaken for a moment.

April closed her eyes briefly, the tears escaping down the paleness of her cheeks, clinging to her lashes as she looked at them all once again. 'Believe it or not, I would much rather have been at home with you all, too—'

'But—'

'With you *all*,' April repeated firmly over the top of May's protest, holding her gaze steadily as she continued to speak. 'I loved the three of you, but I loved your father very much, too.'

Now May was completely thrown, had never thought— But Jude had pointed out to her only last night that April had never remarried; maybe she had never done so because she still loved their father...?

April gave a heavy sigh. 'I can see I shall have to try and explain it all to you—except I don't really understand it all myself.' Her hands twisted together in her lap. 'I was eighteen when I married your father, nineteen when May was born, and March and January obviously came along shortly after that, too,' she added affectionately. 'We were such a happy family.' She frowned. 'Everything was perfect. And then—I belonged to the local amateur dramatic society, was spotted by an agent, and offered a role in a play then touring the country, but ultimately arriving in London for a six-week run.'

So like her with the film role David had offered, May realised, also acknowledging the lure she had felt to accept the offer despite the upheaval it would have created on the farm. Had her mother felt that same pull, despite having a husband and children?

April grimaced. 'James wasn't happy about the situation, naturally. And for weeks I accepted that, knew that it wasn't really practical, that I had responsibilities.'

As May had realised she had responsibilities to March and January...

But she had acted on those responsibilities—their mother so obviously hadn't.

She gave Jude a less than confident smile as he looked across at her with frowning concern; it was still too early in this conversation to know where it was going exactly...

'I so wanted to do it, you see,' April acknowledged huskily. 'I was only twenty-four, and the chance to act, to go to London—it was like a fairy tale come true.' She gave a sigh. 'So I spoke to James about it again, explained that I could travel home on Sundays, that we could get someone in to look after you all with the money I would earn, that it would only be for a matter of weeks, that once I had done this thing it would be out of my system.'

May knew the aching need April was talking about, had felt it herself these last few weeks, a mixture of excitement at the prospect of succeeding, with disappointment that, because of the circumstances, she would never know the answer to that.

April shrugged. 'I pleaded with James to just let me have this one chance. He—he gave me an ultimatum, said that if I went out the door with the idea of acting in the play, that I would never come back in it.' She gave a shake of her head, her face white now. 'I didn't think he meant it.'

'But he did,' March said heavily.

April swallowed hard. 'Yes, he did. I couldn't believe it at first.' She shook her head. 'The company had toured as far as Manchester when I received a letter from a solicitor, accusing me of unreasonable behaviour for deserting my husband, and three children all under the age of five. I telephoned James immediately, of course, but he refused to speak to me, said that any communications between the two of us in future would be made through his lawyer.'

This was all news to May, but, despite her own anger towards April and her deep love for her father, she could actually believe that he was capable of doing what April said he had; May's love for him hadn't made her blind to the fact that James Calendar had been a hard, uncompromising man.

April's hands were gripped together so tightly now that her knuckles showed white. 'Your father received full custody of the three of you at the divorce, by claiming I was an unfit mother who had deserted her children in favour of an acting career, bringing in the fact that I was now of no particular fixed abode, with a career that was at best nefarious. I was given limited access, to be agreed with your father.' The tears began to fall again. 'He never agreed. We went back to court several times, but your father always had so many reasons why it wasn't practical for me to have the three of you to even stay with me, one of you had a cold and he wouldn't allow the other two to come without you, or the four of you had something else planned for the day I suggested. None of it was helped by the fact that I couldn't find any more work after the play had finished its run, that I was having to stay in a run-down boarding house. By the time I was in a position to have you with me, three years had passed. James assured me that none of you even remembered me,' she added achingly.

Oh, they had remembered their mother all right. All of them had, May now realised dazedly.

Max was right, nothing was ever completely black or white; there were always several shades of grey in between…

'I never stopped loving James,' their mother told them huskily. 'A part of me always continued to hope—but it wasn't to be.' She sighed softly. 'The whole situation went too far. There was no common ground on which we could agree, let alone come to terms over, least of all our children.' She grimaced. 'So I left England. Went to America to start again. And the rest, as they say, is history.' She looked down at her hands.

'Not quite.' May spoke up at last, more moved than she would ever have believed possible by what she had just heard. She wasn't sure she would have survived as composed and charming as April undoubtedly was if she had found herself in the same position. 'You didn't just move to America and forget about all of us—'

'Of course not.' April looked deeply shocked at the suggestion. 'Never a day went by when I didn't think about you, wonder what you looked like now, long to be there to share in your laughter, to dry your tears whenever you were hurt or upset. But it was all too difficult, because of the situation between your father and me, and so I—'

'You sent him money to help bring us up,' May put in softly, nodding confirmation of this fact to January and March as they gave her a surprised look; they didn't remember any luxurious influxes of money during their childhood, either. 'Dad never touched a penny of it,' she told them. 'I discovered it all sitting in a bank account after he died.'

'But—'

'How could he—?'

'Please don't blame your father,' April cut in on January's and March's protests. 'He—he did what he thought was for the best.'

May looked at her. 'You can still say that, after what he did to you, as well as to us?'

'I told you, I loved him. Always,' April added emotionally. 'I didn't know he had died until after—after the funeral, must have cried for a week once I learnt of his death. You don't have to be with someone in order to continue loving them,' she added simply.

'But afterwards.' March frowned. 'Why didn't you come to see us then?'

April gave the ghost of a smile. 'I thought I had.'

It all suddenly became crystal-clear to May; April's obvious friendship with David, his offer to her of a part in his film, the fact that April was to be the star of that film...

She looked at April with tear-wet eyes now. 'Did David know that it was your own daughter that you had asked him to come and watch act?'

April gave May a tearful smile at her astuteness. 'Not until I told him last night, no,' she acknowledged. 'He was as dumbfounded as everyone else has been!'

'But you *were* the one who sent him to Yorkshire to watch me in the pantomime, weren't you?' May realised emotionally.

It all made such sense now, David 'happening' to be in the audience that night, the fact that he had sought her out to offer the film role, his persistence since then, April's own appearance for added pressure.

'David's sister lives in the area—'

'I know that,' May dismissed impatiently. 'But it was

still you who asked him to come and watch me act, wasn't it?'

April gave her a concerned look. 'He wouldn't have offered you the part if he hadn't thought you were good enough—'

'I know that,' May assured her gently, her smile encouraging now. 'How did you know about my acting in the amateur dramatic society?'

April swallowed hard. 'I made a few enquiries about you all after your father died. I came to watch you one evening before talking to David. I—don't be cross, May,' she added pleadingly at May's start of surprise. 'Don't you understand, I had to finally see at least one of you?'

'Even if we didn't see you?' May frowned.

'Even then.' April nodded sadly.

May shook her head, standing up. 'I'm not in the least cross,' she assured huskily, moving to stand close to where April sat. 'I can't even begin to imagine what it must have been like for you all these years…!' she murmured emotionally. 'To know, and yet never to feel you had the right to—oh, Mum,' she choked tearfully as she bent down to hug the woman who was still her mother.

Jude had been watching the four women concernedly even while he gave the appearance of joining in the conversation with the other three men, an emotional lump in his throat as he saw May stand up and move forward to hug April, tears falling softly down the cheeks of both women.

It was going to be all right, he realised as January and March stood up to do the same thing, May standing to one side of them now, sobbing uncontrollably.

He stood up compulsively. 'If you gentlemen will ex-

cuse me?' he bit out abruptly, not even sparing them a
second glance as he crossed the room to May's side.
'Come with me,' he told her softly even as he took a
firm hold of her arm and took her through to the adjoin-
ing bedroom, closing the door firmly behind him before
taking her into his arms, gently stroking her hair as she
continued to cry against his shoulder.

'I'm so proud of you, May,' he told her gruffly. 'So
proud!'

He loved this woman—how he loved her—and seeing
her cry like this was like a physical pain.

'This is stupid,' May finally surfaced to murmur, wiping impatiently at her tear-wet cheeks. 'I have no idea
why I'm still crying,' she added disgustedly.

Jude moved to the bedside table and gave her a tissue
from the box there, giving her a few more seconds to
mop up the tears. The result, if she did but know it,
wasn't exactly flattering, her eyes puffy and bloodshot,
her cheeks blotched with red. But she still looked utterly
beautiful to Jude, so much so that he desperately wanted
to take her back in his arms and kiss her—something he
was sure she wouldn't welcome from him at the moment.

'It's been an emotional time for you all,' he murmured
noncommittally.

'Yes,' she acknowledged gruffly. 'I—we'll work it
out, Jude,' she assured him determinedly. 'Love, I've
just realised, makes people behave in strange ways.'

'Yes,' Jude confirmed flatly, thinking of his own reaction now to having fallen in love with May; he hadn't
exactly been gracious about it, had he?

Was it too late for them? Would May ever be able to

forgive him for some of the things he had said and done this last week? He certainly hoped so, because the thought of his life without her in it was a very bleak prospect, indeed...

CHAPTER SIXTEEN

MAY looked up at Jude, feeling almost shy with him now in the intimacy of his hotel bedroom. 'You were going away,' she reminded him.

'Yes,' he confirmed heavily. 'But I was coming back.' He indicated he obviously still had possession of the hotel suite, several of his personal belongings in the room, a couple of books on the bedside table, several suits hanging in the wardrobe.

'Oh.' She nodded, moistening dry lips. 'Are you still going?'

He drew in a ragged breath. 'Not if I can persuade you into making our engagement a reality, no…'

May looked up at him sharply, her gaze searching, looking for signs of mockery in his face. There weren't any, only the gleaming silver eyes showing any expression, and it wasn't mockery… 'Jude…?' she murmured uncertainly.

His hands clenched into fists at his sides. 'May, I've been a fool, an arrogant, pigheaded—' He broke off as she began to laugh. 'It isn't funny,' he said exasperatedly. 'Here I am trying to apologize, and you're laughing at me!'

'I'm not laughing at you, Jude.' She shook her head, her laughter stopping as quickly as it had started. 'I'm laughing at this whole stupid, painful situation.' She drew in a determined breath. 'Jude, I love you. Do you love me?' That breath lodged in her throat as she waited for his answer; if she had misunderstood what he had said a few minutes ago about their 'engagement' she was going to feel so stupid—

'How could I not love you?' Jude groaned emotionally. 'You're good, and kind, and honest—'

'Too much so on occasion,' she put in, a warm glow starting to build inside her, a warmth that was becoming stronger by the minute.

'Never that.' Jude gave a firm shake of his head. 'You're beautiful, desirable, everything that I could ever want in the woman I love—'

'You're making me blush now,' she murmured self-consciously as the warmth reached her cheeks. 'Jude...' She took a tentative step forward, still looking up at him uncertainly.

His hands moved up to cup either side of her face, his gaze intent on hers. 'Do you care for David Melton?'

'David...?' she echoed frowningly. 'Certainly not. What on earth—?'

'I love you, May Calendar,' Jude told her fiercely. 'I love you, I want to marry you and spend the rest of my life loving you. Will you have me?' he added less certainly.

Would she have him? The thought of Jude walking out of her life had been tearing her apart for days. Would she have him!

'Oh, yes,' she told him forcefully. 'But on one condition...' She held back slightly.

'Anything,' he promised without hesitation.

He really did love her. Not that May had had any doubts after what he had just said, but this complete capitulation confirmed it; there would be no half measures in their marriage. Ever.

'Buy the farm,' she told him huskily.

'But—'

'We all grew up there, and, despite everything, it was a happy childhood,' May continued determinedly. 'But it's time for us all to move on now. I will always love my father,' she told him huskily. 'But I think the future belongs to my mother.' Getting to know her, having her get to know all of them; it could take the rest of their lives. But, however long it took, May now accepted that April deserved to know her daughters.

'And us,' Jude prompted softly.

'Oh, definitely to us,' May assured him, her eyes glowing with her own love for him as she looked up at him confidently. 'I love you so much, Jude. So very much…!'

'You said it was only physical attraction,' he reminded her painfully.

'Self-protection,' she admitted huskily.

The next few minutes were taken up with Jude kissing her, thoroughly, purposefully, *deliciously*.

'We could make it a triple wedding,' he suggested some time later.

'So we could,' she immediately agreed. 'With April as the maid of honour, and David as best man—now that the original chief bridesmaid and best man have decided to get married themselves.'

It really was a wedding with a difference, Jude thought wryly as he stood at the church altar waiting for May to arrive at the church, Max and Will standing beside him as they waited for January and March.

Not only was the stepfather of all the brides acting as best man to all the bridegrooms, but the mother of the brides, having only recently been reconciled with her three daughters, was now about to give them all away to their future husbands.

It had been suggested by the three sisters, at a family get-together to discuss the wedding, that this role was much more suited to April than maid of honour, April obviously deeply touched by this honour from her three daughters.

April had married her David in a quiet ceremony the previous month—well, as quiet as it could have been when one of the newly married couple was an international film star, and the other an international film director, Jude recalled wryly.

But they had all been there, May acting as April's witness, Jude as David's, the eight of them disappearing off to a restaurant for a quiet meal to celebrate before the happy couple went off on a two-week honeymoon.

If anything, Jude's love and admiration for May had deepened during the last eight weeks, April's transition from film star into 'Mum' made all the easier for all the sisters because of May's obvious complete acceptance of her as such. The press, he had no doubts, would have a field day early next year once they realised that mother and daughter were appearing in a film together...

His heart began to beat faster as the playing of the church organ announced the arrival of the brides, a nerve pulsing in his jaw as he clenched his teeth together in anticipation.

'I've just seen May, Jude, so she hasn't changed her mind,' Max turned to softly tease him.

'They're *all* there, thank goodness,' Will added huskily after a brief nervous glance towards the back of the church.

Jude grinned at the two men. Strange, he had always

thought of these two men as close as brothers, and now they were about to become that in fact...

But all other thoughts fled his mind as he turned and saw May as she led the way down the aisle, a proud April at her side, the love shining in May's eyes echoed by the love in his own.

His own...

As he was May's.

Always.

Celebrate 100 years of pure reading pleasure with Mills & Boon®

To mark our centenary, each month we're publishing a special 100th Birthday Edition. These celebratory editions are packed with extra features and include a FREE bonus story.

Plus, you have the chance to enter a fabulous monthly prize draw. See 100th Birthday Edition books for details.

Now that's worth celebrating!

July 2008

**The Man Who Had Everything
by Christine Rimmer**
Includes FREE bonus story *Marrying Molly*

August 2008

Their Miracle Baby by Caroline Anderson
Includes FREE bonus story *Making Memories*

September 2008

Crazy About Her Spanish Boss by Rebecca Winters
Includes FREE bonus story
Rafael's Convenient Proposal

Look for Mills & Boon® 100th Birthday Editions at your favourite bookseller or visit
www.millsandboon.co.uk